*For Stella Elstob, a true friend,
with all my love and thanks*

Chapter One

'Oh no! This is like a dream coming true,' Lisa Martin declared in a panic. 'What am I going to do when I wake up and find out none of it's real?' Her jade-coloured eyes were showing equal amounts of laughter and misgiving as she looked around the house that was soon to be hers. Though she didn't normally consider herself a pessimist, when life was treating her this well she couldn't help feeling a tad concerned.

'Yeah, like that's really going to happen,' her niece, Roxanne, retorted with a roll of her eyes. 'No, don't say any more or you'll really start getting on my nerves. This is perfect, Lisa, and if you can't accept perfect then you might as well give up now. Right?' The question was directed at her mother, Amy, who appeared to be enjoying the moment between her sister and daughter.

'Right,' Amy agreed.

'You don't always have to side with her,' Lisa complained.

Amy's eyebrows rose. 'Would you rather I said it's all bound to end in disaster?' she challenged.

Lisa looked faint.

'It's fantastic!' Roxy insisted. 'We've never even

set foot in a house like this before, any of us, and now to think it's going to be ours . . .'

'*Ours?*' Lisa cried, staging a revival.

'Well, yours,' Roxy conceded, 'and David's. Better not forget him, since he's paying for it all.'

Relenting with a smile, while melting like a teenager, Lisa said, 'And yours whenever you want to come.'

'Oh good,' Roxy piped up happily, 'because we've already chosen our bedrooms.'

Lisa looked startled. 'You have? Where was I when that happened?'

'Hello? On the phone,' Roxy reminded her. '"Oh darling, it's so wonderful. I'm loving it more every time I see it, and the girls adore it too."'

'Too right we do,' Amy confirmed, walking towards the sliding glass doors that vanished into the walls when opened, but were currently spattered with rain and the sticky residue of installation pads.

Lisa heaved a little sigh of ecstasy.

They were in the magnificent, week-old Boffi kitchen of the spectacular Queen Anne manor that she and David would soon call home, admiring the brushed-granite work surfaces and chic, streamlined cabinets which occupied most of the east wing's ground floor. Across the way, thinly veiled by a sweep of rain right now, the west wing with its long wall of beautifully arched French windows on the lower level, and fancy filigree railings that enclosed a long balcony on the upper, sat facing them with all the elegance of a courtesan showing off her superior assets. Inside this wing was the Romanesque swimming pool, with two luxurious en suite bedrooms above.

The main body of the house, which linked the two wings in a sedate sort of embrace, as though lending some of its older grandeur to the newer constructions, was mostly sitting room on the ground floor, plus a library for David, a spacious study for Lisa, and a large hexagonal entrance hall where a marble staircase rose to the landings above. Apart from the hall, cloakroom and David's library, each of the downstairs rooms opened on to a deep pale stone terrace which descended in wide, low steps to a sunken courtyard below, where the landscapers were still at work.

Beyond the courtyard, and all around the house, the newly laid lawns were currently soaking up a downpour, while the short drive at the front of the manor which connected a set of black iron gates to the pale limestone facade was glistening in the wet between a pair of towering beech trees. Though the renovation was still some way off completion, it was already an exquisite home, made all the more so by its uninterrupted views down over the hillside to the glimmer and sweep of a lake that, today, misted by rain, was like an apparition coming and going across the valley floor.

As Roxy, who was a very busy eighteen-year-old, flipped out her mobile to take a call, Lisa wandered over to the kitchen window to link Amy's arm.

'It's Granny,' Roxy told them, 'but I'll take it out in the hall. The reception's not very good in here.'

Barely registering her departure to go and speak to their mother, Lisa and Amy continued to gaze out at the view, each quietly pursuing her own thoughts, undisturbed by the hammer and drill of work going on around them. The day was so dreary that they could see their reflections in the glass almost as clearly as the scene beyond, and in spite of the trepidation in her heart, Lisa couldn't help noticing her own smile.

'Is it really happening?' she whispered. 'Can you pinch me please so I can make sure I'm not dreaming?'

Amy gave her a nip, then hugged her arm. 'This is all yours,' she told her softly, 'and what's more, it's only the beginning.'

As Lisa's heart caught on the thrill of it, her eyes returned to her reflection. She was tall and shapely with mesmerising green eyes, a wide, full-lipped mouth and a mane of ash-blonde hair that she invariably braided into a single French plait. At thirty-nine she was, according to David, even more sensuous now than she'd been when they'd first known one another almost twenty years ago. Whether or not that was true wasn't for her to say, but she certainly hoped she had more sophistication and self-awareness than the gauche young thing she'd been back then.

'To think you've waited this long,' Amy sighed dreamily. 'It has to feel worth it. I know it would to me.' Though she was like Lisa in height and colouring, and many of their mannerisms were strikingly similar, she'd always lacked the aura that seemed to surround her sister. This used to be a problem when they were younger, but never

4

was now, mainly because their lives had taken such different turns over the years – Amy's to enduring marital bliss and domesticity, Lisa's through a successful career and the kind of heartbreak she'd never want to experience again following a turbulent relationship that she was over now, so rarely discussed.

Out in the hall Roxy was saying to her grandmother, 'No, David's not here, but apparently he's back at the weekend. Honest to God, Granny, I can so see why Lisa's gone head over heels for him. He's absolutely to die for. I mean, he might be quite a bit older than her, but you'd never know it from the way he looks and acts.'

'He's only fifty-three,' Matilida retorted. 'In my world that makes him a mere youngster.' She gave a sigh. 'To be honest, I am a bit worried about Lisa marrying an older man. It's fine while you're still young, you don't think about getting old then, but later on . . . Anyway, we mustn't look on the black side, must we, because I'm sure she knows what she's doing, and the important thing for now is that you like David, because that's what'll mean the most to her.'

'Absolutely no way could you not like him,' Roxy insisted. 'And she really deserves to be happy. I mean, I know she always goes on that she doesn't mind being on her own, but it's not right, is it, someone like her not having a man? She's so gorgeous, and all my friends think she's sex on legs.'

'Mm,' Matilda grunted disapprovingly, 'I don't know about that, but I can tell you this, it's good to see the smile back on her face after all she went through with Tony, but don't tell her I said that, because we mustn't mention him, must we? So now, you just make sure you don't go causing us any scandals when you're up at Oxford, because as a politician's wife Lisa's going to have the spotlight on her from all sides, and I know you and your shenanigans, young lady, so don't think I don't.'

In the kitchen, Amy was saying teasingly, 'So tell me, how many properties did he have to sell to buy this one?'

Lisa's tone was mild as she said, 'Only two. The flat in London and the house . . . well, *the* house.'

Amy cast her a sidelong glance. *The* house meant the family home that David's now deceased wife had created over many years.

'He signed the lion's share of the business over to the darling daughter last week,' Lisa added.

At that Amy's eyes glinted. 'Well, isn't she a lucky girl,' she commented tartly.

'Indeed, since this now makes her the proud owner of an apartment block in the centre of Bristol, three town houses that she rents out on the floating harbour, and however many projects the company has in development.'

'Plus her own personal pile right here on the lake. Have you found out yet where it is? Can you see it from here?'

'No, apparently it's too far over, and slanted more to the next lake than this one.'

Easily able to imagine what a desirable home it would be, Amy was shaking her head in quiet amazement, and, if the truth be told, no little envy. 'I only wish we had a dad who was half as generous,' she said ruefully. 'Actually, it would be a start if he was half as rich.'

'Not to mention alive,' Lisa commented wryly. 'Anyway, none of David's properties – correction, *Rosalind's* properties – is worth what they used to be, thanks to the economic downturn. Not that she's going to suffer, I'm sure.'

'And I'm presuming David has enough to get by without all these assets?'

Lisa's eyes twinkled. 'Apparently,' she replied, 'but we don't get into big discussions about what he's worth.'

'Well, whatever it is, it's obviously a lot less now than it was a month ago, thanks to his daddy generosity.'

'Indeed,' Lisa murmured. Being able to downplay David's personal wealth, even to Amy, seemed important right now, when the country's economy was still staggering towards a shaky recovery. In David's position, as the honourable member for the West Country constituency of Northavon Valley, to be seen to be surviving too high on the hog was never going to play well with the electorate, especially while everyone was still extremely sensitive over the MPs' expenses scandal. Fortunately, David had come out of that scurrilous affair relatively unscathed. However, he'd lately been treated to some unwelcome publicity over his haste in planning to marry again, and over this house, which, one of the local tabloids had gleefully reported, was costing somewhere north of two million pounds. David's only comment, delivered by Miles, his head of staff, was to remind the reporter who'd run the story that Mr Kirby's business affairs were a matter of public record, and that his property portfolio had been built up long before he'd been elected to office. No mention had been made of Lisa, since it wasn't an issue he was prepared to start defending himself over when his personal decisions were his own business and nobody else's.

'So, do you know if Rosalind's seen this house yet?' Amy asked, as Roxy came to join them at the window.

'Oh God, we're not talking about her, are we?' Roxy protested. 'I'm sorry, I know her mother died and everything, and it must be really hard for her, but hey, it happened eight months ago, so isn't it time for her to start getting over it? And anyway, it's not as if you were having an affair with her dad while her mother was still alive, is it, so I don't get what her problem is.'

Lisa and Amy avoided exchanging glances, since these days nothing got past the vigilant Roxy. However, it was true David and Lisa had only started seeing one another after Catrina's death, but they did have a past which neither Lisa nor Amy had yet got round to telling Roxy about. The fact that Rosalind knew at least something about it, however, had become abundantly clear when her father had informed her, less than a month ago, that he was intending to marry again. The shock of discovering he'd been in a secret relationship almost since her sainted mother had passed away had been bad enough, but on learning that his choice of bride was to be no less than the woman her dying mother had feared he was having an affair with ... Well, Lisa hadn't been there to witness the explosion, but she'd seen for herself how badly shaken it had left David, doting father that he was, so she wasn't holding out too much hope of her and Rosalind becoming bosom pals any time soon.

'You know, what really gets me,' David had said on his return from breaking the news, 'is that she's a grown woman with a family of her own, yet she still seems to think she's running my life.'

'Girls are always very possessive of their dads,' Lisa reminded him, remembering how she and Amy had always been with theirs until he'd died suddenly when she was twelve and Amy was fifteen.

'That may be so,' David responded, 'but the sooner Rosalind understands that I'm entitled to a life of my own, the better it'll be for everyone.'

'Of course it will, she just needs time to get used to things.'

'I understand that, but I'm afraid I don't appreciate how rigidly she's set herself against you when she's never even met you. It's not as though anything's going to change in my relationship with her. I shall continue to be as good and attentive a father as I hope I've always been, and . . . Well, I'm sure, or I shall remain hopeful, that once she realises you're not going to do anything to try and disrupt that, she'll come to accept you as warmly as she should.'

Lisa was definitely not holding her breath for that, any more than she had for Rosalind to accept her father's invitation a couple of weeks ago for her to join the select party to celebrate his engagement. In fact, Lisa would have been perfectly happy to wait at least another year before going public with their relationship, but David was having none of it. He might still be in the prime of his life, but time wasn't exactly on his side. Moreover, he wasn't prepared to go on playing ignominious ducking and diving games with the press, trying to keep Lisa a secret when he couldn't have felt prouder to have her in his life. He loved her, wanted to be married to her, and though he understood Rosalind's feelings and was deeply sorry to be hurting them, he simply wasn't prepared to wait.

So, for the time being at least Lisa was in no doubt that the conflict between Rosalind's loyalty to her mother and her fierce attachment to her father was going to be something of a feature in their lives. And boy, was she seeing signs of the attachment being fierce. The woman hardly did a thing without consulting her father first, then reporting back to him after, and as time went on Lisa was starting to wonder if David might actually be a more significant part of his daughter's life than her own husband.

'I know,' Roxy said, linking arms with both Lisa and her mother as they wandered back towards the entrance hall, 'why don't we take one more look around? It's so fantastic, I don't want to leave yet.'

Lisa glanced at Amy, who shrugged as if to say why not.

'OK,' Lisa said, happy to stay as long as they liked, 'why don't you show me which rooms you've chosen for yourselves, so I can be sure not to allocate them to anyone else.'

Roxy's laugh was infectious, and as they stepped

around the builder's debris to start climbing the stairs, she said, 'I was thinking, Lis, that the pool would be a great place for parties. You know, a bit of skinny-dipping after a few vodka shots ... Group sex. You probably wouldn't even hear us, you're so far away up there in the bedrooms.'

Lisa laughed as Amy rolled her eyes.

'Why doesn't anything ever shock you?' Roxy complained, giving her mother a push.

'Because we've already been there and done it,' Amy informed her. 'Now, I'm on the lookout for a space that I can use as a studio, because I think it's high time I released my inner artist ...'

'Ugh, no, please don't,' Lisa shuddered. 'I've seen the kind of stuff you come up with, and you're already starting to scare me with all this talk of moving in.'

Amy twinkled. 'Don't rule it out,' she advised, 'because I'm sure Theo would be every bit as happy to live here as he is at our house. And just think of how lonely you could be with David away in London most of the week – and if you go with him, well, someone should be here to take care of the place, wouldn't you agree?'

Giving it some mock consideration, Lisa said, 'Well, I'm not sure what David will have to say about it ...'

'Are you kidding, he'll jump at the idea,' Roxy assured her. 'You know how mad he is about us. In fact, if you'd turned him down, I reckon he'd have married us, don't you, Mum?'

'Without a doubt,' Amy agreed.

'And Dad wouldn't mind, because he'd be glad to get rid of us.'

11

Amy's eyebrows shot up. 'Speak for yourself,' she retorted. 'It's you who drives him nuts with all your backchat and boyfriend issues.'

'Which reminds me,' Lisa cut in, 'are you still seeing Alistair?' By now they were on their way into the master bedroom, where a carpenter was at work fitting out the walk-in closets.

'Oh *puhlease*,' Roxy grimaced, popping a finger into her mouth to suggest something gross. Then, pushing open the bathroom door to give the limestone emporium another drooling inspection, 'I'm back with Rory now, do you remember him? The one with the Orlando Bloom eyes and David Beckham physique.'

Amy looked at her askance. 'You wish,' she muttered.

Roxy produced a long-suffering sigh. 'I can see it, even if you can't,' she informed her. 'Now, listen up, please, in five minutes' time I think we should go and take a look at my room again.'

Lisa was puzzled. 'Why five minutes?'

Roxy looked at her in amazement. 'Duh! Because that's how long it takes to do a lap of this room.'

Flipping her as she laughed, Lisa strolled across to the windows where she stood gazing down at the lake for a while, thinking about David and how happy they were going to be here. It really was a dream coming true, and though she was concerned about Rosalind, and surprised in some ways by how changed David was from the man she used to know, she was finding the joy of getting to know him again every bit as thrilling and romantic as she had the first time around.

'It's amazing,' Amy was saying, as she examined

the alabaster pillars that would soon form the posts of a super-king bed, 'the way a room this big can still manage to seem cosy, and there's not even any furniture in it yet.'

Lisa's eyes glimmered softly. 'I love this room,' she murmured, looking up at the high, corniced ceilings as she kicked off a shoe to sweep a foot over the silky pile of the carpet. When she was alone at night, which wasn't often these days, she'd often picture herself and David here, just the two of them, either reading, or watching TV, or making love with all the passion and tenderness they'd known before, and with the expertise and knowledge of their own bodies they'd gleaned over the years. Could it really be happening? Were Lisa Martin and David Kirby actually going to be married in less than two months?

'Yes, yes and yes again,' he'd murmur whenever she asked him, and she'd laugh as he scooped her up in his arms, swinging her round like the young slip of a thing she'd been when she first knew him. If anyone had told her then that she'd be close to forty before they were finally together she'd never have believed it, she might even have done away with herself right there and then. *Forty!* How could she be that old when she still felt so young?

'That's how it goes,' her mother told her. 'Look at me, I'm almost seventy but in my head I'm still thirty. Well, maybe thirty-five. Anyway, the important thing is, you're still young enough to have children . . .'

'No, no, don't go there,' Lisa protested. 'I'm definitely too old for that, and anyway, we know it's pretty certain I can't have them.'

'You've never been tested.'

'But Tony and I hardly ever used anything.'

'So the problem could be his.'

It wasn't, because two years into their relationship he'd had a one-night stand with an old girlfriend and managed to get her pregnant. That was when Lisa should have walked away and never gone back, but she'd been so besotted with him that once the trauma of it was over and the pregnancy had been terminated she'd stupidly, blindly, ended up forgiving him.

'Hello!' Roxy sang, waving a hand in front of Lisa's face. 'Earth to Lisa, Earth to Lisa, time to go and look at my room now,' and grasping her aunt's hand she dragged her back out to the landing and over to the east wing. Here two more bedrooms and bathrooms opened off a builder-cluttered corridor, which was colourfully lit from one end by a towering stained-glass window.

As they entered the room Roxy had chosen and Roxy started to gush over the sunken lounge and letterbox fireplace, Amy drifted on over to the windows, rubbing a circle into the steamy pane, so she could look down over the front drive. Spotting a car at the gates, she watched it for a while, expecting it to come in. When it didn't she said, 'Someone's outside. Is the bell connected yet?'

Looking round, Lisa said, 'I don't expect so,' and going to join her she peered through the makeshift porthole to check what, or who, was out there. 'I can't see anyone,' she said. 'Where are you looking?'

'They've gone again now,' Amy answered, 'but it was a black car.'

Lisa almost laughed. 'Well that narrows it

down,' she said, taking out her iPhone as it bleeped with a text.

'It's back,' Amy said, peering out again. 'Oh, hang on, looks like they're turning round.'

'Maybe they're lost,' Roxy suggested.

'But this is a private road,' Amy reminded her. 'No one's supposed to drive down unless they're visiting someone who lives here. It's what all the CCTV cameras are about, to keep out the undesirables.'

'Actually, I think I know who it was,' Lisa said quietly.

Roxy and Amy turned round and saw, to their surprise, that her face had paled.

'Read this,' Lisa said, and passing the iPhone to Amy she watched her sister's expression change as she too registered the text.

When Amy looked up again she and Lisa didn't have to communicate with words. Such a message could only have come from one person.

Rosalind Sewell was a petite, pretty woman with the kind of inky black curls and stunning blue eyes that not only portrayed her Irish ancestry beautifully, but had always made her father's heart sing with pride. Her complexion, just like her mother's and grandmother's, was as pale as a winter sky, while her lips were as red as the roses that grew around her rambling nineteenth-century mill house.

Right now she was standing at the window of the cluttered and homely farmhouse kitchen watching her nine-year-old son, Lawrence, climbing through the drizzling rain up to the tree house that his father, and hers, had constructed for him a little over a year ago. No one had been entirely sure whether or not Lawrence had wanted one, but it had seemed like a good idea, and since it had been there he'd gone to it most days – even in the depths of winter, when there were no birds or squirrels to keep him company, or leaves to protect him like a nest and help fend off the wind.

While there he often just sat, sometimes rocking, or humming, or, when the martins and sparrows were around, holding out his fingers for them to come and perch. They never did, but nor did he ever seem to give up hope that they might. Occasionally he'd invite a friend to join him, but he didn't have many friends, and all too often when Rosalind called around to try and find him some company the local children had other things to do.

He'd been diagnosed with Asperger's several years ago now, so she'd had time to try and get used to it, and to prepare herself for how their lives were going to be as he grew up. Intelligent and handsome though he might be, a real head-turner whenever she took him into town, with his unruly mop of dark curls and brilliant blue eyes – exactly like hers – he was never going to acquire the same social skills as other boys. This wasn't to say he didn't engage with those around him, because he did, from time to time, he even seemed to enjoy having company occasionally, in so far as she could tell if he really enjoyed anything.

He didn't get bullied as much these days. The teachers kept a close eye on him, and she was always there at three thirty on the dot to take him home, in spite of them living less than half a mile away from the school. Once he'd been beaten up quite badly in the lane that ran from their house down to the village, so she wasn't prepared to let him do the walk alone again.

Why were children so cruel? Why couldn't they understand that being different didn't mean someone had no feelings? Wouldn't it make more sense to behave protectively towards a child who was injured, even if they couldn't see the injuries? It didn't work like that though, as she knew only too well, and how many times had she asked herself these questions? As many times as she'd asked God why this had to happen to her little boy. There were no answers, only tears, and misunderstandings, and Lawrence, always seeming so alone and gentle in his confusion, at least to her. To others she knew he often appeared aggressive or withdrawn, or just plain weird because of the faces he pulled or odd things he said.

Spotting him hovering at the window of the tree house, she gave him a wave. It pleased her a lot when he waved back, even though there was no smile, just a small movement of his hand that anyone else might not have noticed. Knowing better than to expect any more she turned away, and was just trying to remember what she'd decided on for tea when her mobile bleeped with a text.

Her heart immediately jarred with unease. She wasn't really expecting Lisa Martin to respond to the message she'd sent – the question she'd posed was rhetorical, so didn't require a reply. *Would you be so quick to jump into my mother's grave?* But maybe Ms Martin felt she had something to say.

The text turned out to be from her solicitor confirming an appointment for the following day, and she wasn't sure if she was angry, or relieved. Probably both, and so much more besides.

Putting her hands to her head she massaged the ache in her temples, and tried to block out the images of that enormous house on the hill where her father was going to live with the woman his devoted wife of thirty years had so feared. Such a flagrant betrayal of her mother, such a callous dismissal of his own, and her, devastating bereavement, was haunting her night and day. It was so unlike him to be cruel that she could hardly make herself believe it was happening. He'd always been kind and open and honest, someone she trusted with all her heart and knew she could depend on no matter what. And this wasn't the only contradiction she'd detected in him lately, because for the last year, perhaps even longer, there had been occasions when he'd seemed almost furtive, even duplicitous, and distracted in a way that had sometimes driven her insane. However, she supposed she hadn't really been herself either. How could they carry on normally when they were struggling with the fear of losing the person they loved most in the world? This was what she'd always believed to be the reason for her father's uncharacteristic behaviour, but since he'd told her about Lisa Martin she'd been bitterly tormented by the same suspicion that had plagued her mother's final days, that he was having an affair with the girl he'd almost ended his marriage for twenty years ago.

Rosalind knew that if she turned out to be right

about that, then as deeply as she'd always loved her father, she wasn't sure she'd ever be able to forgive him. Nor would she ever, *ever* be able to accept Lisa Martin into their lives.

Dropping her head in her hands, she took a deep shuddering breath. She hadn't really expected her text to achieve anything, but during the moments she'd composed and sent it it had made her feel better. Now, though, she felt as though her entire world was falling apart.

Chapter Two

David Kirby was striding through the underground walkway between Westminster Palace and Portcullis House, looking as pleased with himself as any man might who was soon to be married. The fact that there were a few other stories going on behind the face he was showing to the world was none of the world's business – indeed he wasn't much inclined to think about them himself at the moment, because so far today was turning out to be a good one.

Following dutifully in his wake as they rode the escalator into Portcullis House were his handsome and fiercely ambitious head of staff, Miles Farraday, and two very able-bodied but slightly less dazzling researchers. For his own part, David rarely considered his looks, which were actually, with his shock of grey hair, intense dark eyes and excellent six-foot physique, nothing less than striking.

He was returning to his office from the chamber where he'd spent the past half an hour sitting on the back benches listening to Prime Minister's Questions. Not a particularly edifying experience, considering how badly the PM had performed – David wasn't someone to enjoy watching another man squirm – and in truth, there weren't many who could have done better while under such pressure to resign.

David hadn't tabled any questions himself; instead he'd left the ferocious attack on the Cabinet's handling of a security breach to the Leader of the Opposition, who'd practically licked his lips before getting stuck in. However, maintaining a discreet silence hadn't stopped the BBC coverage switching to him more than once. Their interest in him was undoubtedly due to recent rumours that he was to be reinstated as Foreign Minister at the next reshuffle, this being the position he'd held before standing down to spend more time with his ailing wife. Since he and the Foreign Secretary were known to be close friends, the odds on him succeeding were very much in his favour. However, it was widely believed that the present incumbent, for whom few but the PM had a particularly high regard, was unlikely to go without a fight.

David had realised long ago that politics at every level wasn't just an endless round of dirty business, it was pure Hobbesian theatre with more skulduggery and Machiavellian connivings lurking the corridors of power than headless ghosts. From the start he'd thrived on it, throwing himself into the Westminster machine as lustily and ambitiously as any man would with an eye on high office. His first ministerial post had come quickly, and two others had followed before he'd been appointed Foreign Minister. It was then that he and Colin Larch, the Secretary of State, had struck up their friendship, and he, himself, had gained a reputation for what became known as Kirby's Whisky Evenings – rowdy cross-party gatherings that he generally hosted at his spacious Pimlico apartment. These get-togethers used to be one of the hottest tickets in town, and now that a respectful time had passed since the loss of his wife, several colleagues, and journalists, had made it known how eager they were for him to reinstate them. He didn't have any plans to do this, life had moved on since then, and things, he, had changed during the time he'd restricted himself to playing no greater a role than that of a local MP.

Now, as he and his team walked alongside the famously controversial trees in the limestone lobby of Portcullis House, heading towards the coffee bars and eateries at the far end, Miles was briefing him on the rest of the day's schedule. Though David was taking it in, at the same time he was recalling how uncomfortable he'd felt while the camera was on him. He never used to be publicity-shy, quite the reverse in fact – if he had a cause to fight he'd instruct his media people to marshal as many cameras, microphones and notebooks as the city could offer. And he couldn't say he was exactly leery of the limelight now – or was he? Certainly he no longer got the same buzz from it, if anything it seemed to make him edgy and even irritable that the press were paying more attention to him than to those he felt to be more worthy.

After offering some words of support to a fellow MP from the north who'd recently been accused by the *News of the World* of engaging in three-way sex in his Westminster office, David assured him he believed it was a set-up, and stepped into the lift Miles was holding open for him.

'Do you really believe him?' Miles asked as he pressed to go up.

David eyed him levelly. 'About what?' he asked.

Miles looked surprised. 'The sex thing.'

David shook his head impatiently, making it clear it was a subject he didn't want to discuss. 'Excuse me,' he said as his iPhone bleeped with a text. With any luck it would be from Edith at the Foreign Office, letting him know what time the Secretary was due back tonight. However, it was Lisa's name that came up, and experiencing the rush of pleasure he often felt when remembering she was back in his life, tinged with an unwelcome and unnecessary residue of guilt, he decided to save the message until he was alone.

As they walked into his compact suite of offices where Karen, his PA, was at her desk and piles of dossiers, letters and reference books were stacked around all available surfaces including the floor, Miles was once again relaying information from the clipboard he was carrying. '. . . and Tom Walker wants to know if you'll consider taking over from Bill Wainwright when he steps down at the end of this term,' he was saying as David hung up his jacket and went to sink into his large swivel chair.

'Remind me what that is?' David said, loosening his tie.

'Communities and Local Government.'

David appeared thoughtful.

Miles allowed a minute or so to pass, then said, 'Shall we get back to him on it?'

David's eyes came to his. 'Yes, let's do that,' he replied.

Miles made a note. 'Remember, you're also considering heading up two other select committees. European Scrutiny and Home Affairs.'

David arched an ironic eyebrow. Miles didn't really think he'd forgotten, did he? No, it was just Miles's way of spelling out how in demand his boss was. It made the highly ambitious lad feel good to know his fortunes were yoked to someone deemed to be on his way up again, and no doubt it was supposed to inflate David's sense of importance too.

'David,' Karen called out from the next room, 'I've got someone on the line from the Beeb. They want to know if you can be in the line-up for *Question Time* the week after next when they're in Bristol.'

'Can I fit it in?' he called back.

'I can make it work, if you're up for it.'

David's eyes went to Miles again. How would he react if he said he wasn't? Badly, was the answer, so David said, 'Then give them a yes. And make sure,' he added to Miles, 'that we're up to speed on everything before I go on.'

'It'll be there,' Miles assured him. 'Actually, that brings me to the feature you're doing for *The Times* next week? They're asking if your er . . . lady friend would be willing to take part too.'

'Her name is Lisa, as you well know,' David retorted crisply. 'I'll talk to her. Now if that's all, close the door on your way out.'

It wasn't often he was brusque with his staff, particularly Miles, of whom he was extremely fond, but in this instance Miles had deserved it. David's daughter taking exception to Lisa was one thing, for Miles to do the same was wholly unacceptable. However, for the time being he was willing to believe that Miles was far too sensible, not to mention caught up in the machinations of Westminster, to allow his concerns about the haste of his boss's new relationship to continue being an issue for long. If his attitude persisted, Miles would be likely to find himself out of a job.

Knowing how much it would hurt him to let Miles go, he gave a troubled sigh and swivelled his chair to stare out at the spectacular view of New Palace Yard with its grand carriage entrance (out of bounds to the public), soaring tower of Big Ben and Jubilee Fountain. There was a time when this reminder of how privileged he was to be sitting at the heart of the nation's powerbase had given him such a high that Number 10 had seemed almost as attainable as his own front door. Today, he could feel the tension of a headache starting to bite, along with the uneasy restlessness that overcame him more often than he'd care to admit these days.

He was baffled by it, and anxious about how he seemed to be losing touch with his usual ebullient self. Obviously Catrina's illness had had a profound effect on him: watching the life drifting slowly and painfully from someone he loved and had been so close to for so long was the most arduous and heart-rending of ordeals. And it wasn't as though he was expecting to be over it yet, of course he wasn't, but having Lisa back in his life should, surely, be making him more upbeat and positive about the future than he seemed to be. He kept wondering if it would make a difference to the way she felt about him if he were to confess that he might no longer have it in him to get to the top. Since she was something of a high-flyer herself, she was presumably expecting the same from him.

Closing his eyes, he let his head fall back against the chair and took several deep breaths. These moments of self-doubt didn't usually last long, so he should try to ignore them because experience had taught him that within a few minutes, half an hour at the most, he'd be back on form and just about ready to fly Lisa to the moon if it was where she wanted to go. He wondered what Rosalind, his fellow astronaut until now, would make of that, and almost groaned aloud.

The last thing he needed, or wanted, was a rift in his family. He loved his daughter more than his own life and wasn't willing to tolerate even the thought of becoming estranged from her, but how on earth was he going to persuade her to accept Lisa when she'd got it into her head that he'd been cheating on her mother while Catrina was ill? However, he had to admit that contacting Lisa again so soon after Catrina had gone probably hadn't been the wisest decision he'd ever made. It was too late to go back on it now though, and even if he could he knew he wouldn't, because Lisa already meant as much to him, if not more, than she had when they'd first been together almost twenty years ago.

They'd been at Bristol University then, he as a switched-on young lecturer – or so he'd liked to consider himself with his anarchic views on the Establishment, passion for rock music and MPhil/PhD in Government – and Lisa as a second-year student, not one of his because she'd been reading French and Spanish while he was tutoring Politics. They'd met during a Fairport Convention concert at the Colston Hall where one of the university rock bands had managed to get themselves a gig as a support act – no small achievement considering Fairport's line-up, and one that had to be recognised as such by students and staff alike.

He couldn't remember now who'd introduced him to Lisa, he only remembered the crush of the crowd and the throb of the music and the overpowering intensity of the attraction that had leapt up between them like an electric charge. It had been so unexpected and consuming that he'd been unable to get her magnificent eyes, or lips, or the tantalising creaminess of her skin out of his mind for days afterwards. Had he not been married, and a father, he knew he'd have gone out of his way to find her again, but as flirtatious as he could often be back then, his wife and daughter had always meant everything to him. So even if he'd been willing to risk his career for Lisa, he certainly wasn't going to risk losing them.

This admirable resolve might never have faltered had Catrina not descended into one of her depressions around that time and taken herself and Rosalind off to Ireland to stay with her parents. It wasn't the first time she'd abandoned him while in the grip of a black despair, and on both previous occasions he'd allowed no more

27

than a few days, possibly a week, to pass before flying out to Dublin to persuade her to come back. This time, angered by her continued refusal to seek professional help, or to recognise that eight-year-old Rosalind wasn't just his daughter too, but the very essence of what gave his life purpose and meaning, he'd told her to stay where she was until she'd damned well sorted herself out.

It was hard to know now, so long after the event, whether his uncharacteristic cruelty had been a shameful and ludicrous attempt to clear a path – and his conscience – for an affair with Lisa, but looking back from this level of maturity and honesty he had to confess that it probably wasn't wholly unconnected. He'd become almost obsessed with Lisa by then, was constantly going out of his way to catch glimpses of her, and spent endless hours fantasising about how it would be to make love to her. Weeks, possibly even months went by after Catrina left – or what had felt like weeks and months – before he persuaded Lisa to meet him, in secret, but even then they'd kept everything on what, in retrospect, seemed a farcical intellectual level, their discussions ranging from the merits of modern film techniques to the justification of violence in the ongoing miners' dispute, to the barriers of language between cultures. It was only when Catrina completely blindsided him by instructing a lawyer to start divorce proceedings, shocking him into a stupor and Lisa into – as it turned out – a false sense of security, that Lisa had finally agreed to sleep with him.

Recalling that magical night now, he could almost feel himself floating in the sublime sensuality of it all over again. She'd been so young and beautiful, almost ethereal, yet so alive with passion and a need to learn that even from the distance of all those years, it still seemed as though she'd cast some kind of a spell over him. At the time it had felt as if nothing else mattered any more. He belonged to her, and she to him. They would never be able to get enough of one another, even if they spent an entire lifetime trying.

He hadn't realised that he'd lost all sense of how he felt about Catrina, because apart from Lisa all he was really aware of was how desperately he missed his darling little bossyboots and Bo Peep of a daughter. Even so, being with Lisa had felt so right and so necessary that it just didn't seem to make any sense to fight to save his marriage.

Since there was no way he could continue at the university while conducting a relationship with a student that he wasn't prepared to give up, he'd resigned his post at the end of the following term without any regrets at all. Or none that he could recall now, but why would he have had any when he'd gone straight into the property-development side of Catrina's faltering interior-design business? Everything had been laid out on a plate for him there, and to his surprise he'd found the intensely competitive world of commerce and high finance a far greater challenge and stimulus than he'd ever expected.

When Catrina had found out that he was rescuing her company she'd immediately offered to sign everything over to him, since she had no intention of coming back, she claimed. For reasons he'd never been able to explain then, nor could he now, he hadn't accepted. He supposed it just hadn't felt right for her to give everything up so easily – or maybe, in spite of feeling certain he wanted to marry Lisa as soon as he was able, he'd been uncertain about her committing at such a young age. Then again, he simply hadn't wanted to let go of Catrina and Rosalind. Speaking to his daughter on the phone most days and spending only brief weekends with her, when he flew over to Dublin to find her mother in a slump and her looking lonely, was breaking his heart. He still felt wholly responsible for them and wanted, more than anything, to be able to see Rosalind every day so he could get involved with what had happened to her at school, and take her out for treats and read her stories at night the way he always had. Though he did his best to hide this longing from Lisa, he clearly hadn't been successful, because he still recalled the night she'd whispered to him, her voice full of tears, 'One day we'll have children of our own, and if it's all too much for Catrina by then, coping with a child and her depression, perhaps Rosalind can live with us too.'

By then he and Lisa had been together for more than a year, and were still as besotted with one another as they'd been at the start, possibly even more so. It never even crossed their minds that anything would ever come between them, because in spite of the difference in their ages and ambitions, nothing mattered more to them than the time they were together.

Then one day Catrina called, out of the blue, asking if he'd go over to Dublin. 'We need to talk,' she'd said, 'and I think it should be face to face.'

Though there had been no more lawyers' letters trying to bring their marriage to a conclusion, he'd flown out there feeling so certain that she wanted to make their separation official that when she'd told him she wanted to try again, it had come as such a shock that he simply hadn't known what to say.

'Rosalind misses you,' she'd told him, her anxious blue eyes glittering with tears, 'and so do I.'

He could only look at her, unable to respond.

'I haven't told you this before,' she went on, 'because I didn't want to get your hopes up, or mine either, but I've been receiving treatment for my depressions and I think . . . Well, the doctor says the drugs are working well and that I ought to start living a normal life again now. And I feel ready to, David, I really do. It's as though a huge weight has been lifted off me, and even my parents are saying that I'm like my old self at last.'

How had he replied? What words had he used to try and express how pleased he was for her, while at the same time letting her know that it was too late? Whatever he'd said, he guessed it hadn't been forceful enough, or perhaps he'd said nothing at all, because the next thing he knew she was chattering on happily about Rosalind and how important it was for her, for them all, to be a family again.

'But Catrina,' he'd finally managed, 'you know I've met someone else.'

Though her lovely face had paled, she'd tried to cover her unease with a shrug and a laugh as she'd said, 'But it's not serious, is it? She's very young, and I'm sure she's not expecting anything to come of it.'

'I don't think you understand . . .'

'She's just someone who's been keeping you company while I've been sorting myself out,' she went on. 'I understand that. I mean, I'm madly jealous, of course, but I know it's my own fault that you've been unfaithful so I promise I won't ever hold it against you. We can start again, David, but this time it'll be better. We can build the business together, watch Rosalind grow – and it's time, don't you think, that she had a brother or a sister?'

'Catrina,' he said wretchedly, 'I don't know how to say this without hurting you, but Lisa isn't just someone I've been seeing to fill in the time. I love her. I want . . . We've talked about . . .' The look of devastation that came into Catrina's eyes turned his words to dust. How could he crush her now when she'd struggled so hard to get back on top?

'Are you saying you don't love me any more?' she whispered shakily.

Feeling his heart tearing in two, he heard himself saying, 'Yes, of course I love you. I mean . . . Oh God, I don't know what I mean. I thought, when you asked me to come here, I was expecting you to . . .' Realising he was about to mention divorce, he let the words fade into oblivion.

'I'm sorry,' she said, seeming to crumble before his eyes. 'I've obviously got everything wrong and now I'm making your life difficult all over again and it's not what I meant to do. I swear it. If you love her, then maybe it's best you forget about me.'

'No, I can't do that, and nor do I want to. You're still my wife . . .'

'But if you don't love me . . .'

'That's not what I'm saying. I do love you, and

32

you're right, we have to think about Rosalind, it's just that I can't simply walk out on Lisa. We've built a life together, we have plans and . . .'

'But the company is *ours*, remember, and it was you who insisted it stay that way. I thought it was because you were still hoping we'd run it together one day.' She swallowed nervously. 'I'm sorry if I got it wrong,' she added quietly.

He'd been unable to recall then why he'd insisted the company remain in both their names. All he could think about was Lisa and how she was going to take it when he told her that in spite of loving her to within an inch of his life, he loved his wife and daughter too, and he was very sorry but their relationship couldn't continue.

What happened over the following days and weeks was as blurred by time now as it was by the terrible guilt he'd tried for so long to suppress. He guessed that various snatches of memory would probably never be lost to him, or his conscience, such as Lisa's quiet, yet somehow explosive, acceptance of his decision, followed by the sheer awfulness of her moving out of their flat. Then had come the news delivered by one of her friends that she'd dropped out of uni before achieving her degree. Realising straight away that this was because she couldn't face staying in the same city as him and Catrina where she could run into them at any time, he'd considered moving the business and his family to London, or Plymouth or even Dublin – anywhere, just as long as he managed to give Lisa back something that was hers. However, the company was already established in Bristol, and Lisa, wherever she was,

was refusing to take his calls or answer his letters. All he ever received was a curt note from her sister, Amy, telling him to honour his decision and think only about his wife and child from now on and let Lisa go. 'She needs to get on with her life, and so do you,' she'd finished.

It had taken a long time for him and Catrina to regain the closeness they'd lost, probably longer than he remembered now, but eventually he'd found that provided he didn't torment himself with thoughts of Lisa and what she might be doing, he could immerse himself in the joy and relief of having his daughter back in his life. It was, in the end, what mattered most, because whatever mistakes her parents might have made, it would be the worst thing in the world to make her suffer for them. As adults, he kept reminding himself, they would get over the damage they'd caused one another, but an innocent child wasn't equipped to deal with the harsh realities of life. She needed the security of her parents' love to nourish her through her tender years, so that she'd be prepared to deal with the world when the time finally came for her to fly the nest.

It was true to say that neither he nor Catrina had ever dreamt of making the kind of money they eventually did. It was literally as though everything they touched turned to gold, whether it was renovating old properties and selling them on, or constructing entire new developments of flats and affordable housing. During their fourth year of official partnership, when Rosalind was twelve and they were celebrating thirteen years of marriage, they moved out of their three-storey house in Hotwells to a stunning Georgian mansion overlooking the Chew Valley lakes. With her by now locally famous flair for interior design, Catrina set about turning the grand old property into what became known as her masterpiece. Every room and niche, each stairwell and landing, window, attic, cellar and outbuilding, was lovingly and exquisitely restored to its original splendour. It was her pride and joy, and over the years its interior, and its gardens, came to feature in several glossy magazines, both national and international.

All that was missing in their lives by then was the longed-for second child. Though there had been several pregnancies since their reunion, each had ended in a miscarriage which had proved so devastating for Catrina, both mentally and physically, that in the end David had insisted that their beautiful healthy daughter was family enough for him. This was when Catrina had finally stopped subjecting herself to the need for a second child as a way to hang on to her husband, and had given up her womb to the hysterectomy the doctors were urging.

David's decision to go into politics had come about one evening when he and Catrina were hosting one of their by now legendary dinners for several local dignitaries who included their MP, Jack Fielding, an eccentric old friend who was about to retire. Only later did David learn that Catrina had put them all up to persuading him to run for office, but that was typical of her, standing aside while other people took the credit for something that was her idea.

He stood at the next election and won the seat

with a decent majority. Within a relatively short space of time he'd been appointed Parliamentary Private Secretary to the Minister for Sport. A year later he was made Parliamentary Undersecretary at DEFRA, followed by a short spell in Work and Pensions, before achieving his promotion to the Foreign Office. Since Catrina was closely involved in each step of his career, this post was as big a cause for celebration for her as it was for him. They were on their way to the top, and with Colin Larch, the Foreign Secretary, being tipped as the next leader it was all in sight.

Then came the devastating news that Catrina had stage four breast cancer.

Though she fought the disease, and seemed to overcome it, in less than a year she was fighting it again, this time in the liver. The struggle was terrible. She was terrified of dying, and David couldn't bear to think of losing her. It was during this time, when she was weak from the treatment and spaced out by drugs, that she started to talk about Lisa, whose name had never been mentioned since the day Catrina had returned to Bristol.

David was unable to understand why, with no evidence at all, Catrina seemed so convinced that he was either seeing Lisa while he was in London, or meeting up with her while he was travelling abroad. In the end, it was largely because of this false conviction and how much it was upsetting her that he'd resigned from his ministerial post in order to spend more time with her.

Though he'd never have admitted it, mainly because there was no reason to, the truth was Lisa had been on his mind a lot since he'd moved into the public eye. He'd found himself interested to know what she was doing now, and where she might be. Was she married? Did she have children? Was she even still in England? He dared to hope if she saw him on the news, or read about him in the papers, that she might get in touch, simply to say hello, but she never did.

It was always while he was away from home that the memory of her, and thoughts of what might have been, had seemed to draw so sharply into focus. Consequently when he did actually see her, quite unexpectedly, at an embassy party in Paris, he'd thought for a moment he must be dreaming.

It was an extraordinary moment, when everything around him seemed to fade, and even his mind felt blurred. The only clarity seemed to be her. She was talking to someone, but she must have known he was there, because she had glanced over and raised her eyebrows in greeting with no surprise at all. If anything, those mesmerising green sloe eyes that he remembered so well and that had hardly changed at all had looked slightly teasing.

From that moment on his struggle to stay focused on the politicians and dignitaries present was all but lost. Knowing she was in the room, and unable to control the way he was responding, was overwhelming him with a force he could never have foreseen. Behind the friendliness of his smile was a chaos of emotion, beneath each word he spoke were a thousand more he wanted to say to her. It surprised, yet excited him to realise how connected he felt to her. It was as though they were communicating on a level that was neither visible, nor audible – as though the ghosts of their younger selves were already merging and dispensing with all the intervening years.

If he'd thought she was beautiful when she was twenty, seeing her then, in her mid-thirties, so poised and elegant, and yet somehow, impossibly, more sensuous than ever, was completely blowing his mind. He knew he had to talk to her, to find out who she was now, why she was at this party, what she had been doing with her life since he'd last seen her. Was there a chance they could meet? Would she be willing? What would happen if they did?

Hearing his iPhone bleep again, David turned away from the past and felt the present closing in on him in a way that was oddly disorienting, which probably wasn't surprising given how far he'd wandered down memory lane.

Retrieving the mobile from his pocket, he only remembered there was a text from Lisa when he saw it there on the screen, and experiencing an uplifting sense of pleasure and relief simply to see her name he opened the message. Then, realising how disloyal his feelings were to Catrina, he felt his conscience absorbing his joy into a darkness that only deepened when he read Lisa's message.

You might want to see this, she'd written, and without having to go any further he guessed right away that she was forwarding a text from Rosalind.

He was right.

Would you be so quick to jump into my mother's grave?

With a groan of anger that tailed off to exasperation and despair, he closed down the message and debated whether or not to call his daughter straight away. Her behaviour was outrageous and could not be tolerated, but her misunderstanding of the truth wasn't going to be easily corrected, and an angry phone call now certainly wouldn't do it. In fact, the way things were going he was half afraid nothing would.

Deciding to tackle her face to face when he was in Bristol at the weekend, he pressed in Lisa's number and reached her on the second ring.

'Hi,' she said, in the kind of tone that never failed to reach his pulse.

'Hi,' he replied. 'What are you doing?'

'I'm at Amy's going over the wedding plans. I take it you got the text.'

'I did,' he confirmed, and swivelled his chair to look out of the window again. 'I'm sorry. Are you upset? Of course you are.'

'Only for you.'

'Do you have any idea what prompted it?'

'I think she came to the house while we were there. Someone was outside in a black car at the same time as the message turned up. I didn't want to forward it, but Amy was with me, so I knew if I didn't tell you she would.'

'You have to keep me in the picture,' he reminded her. 'If you don't I won't be able to do anything about it.'

'You've got enough on your mind.'

His frown deepened for a moment. She was right, he had, more than she realised, but he certainly wasn't going to worry her with anything else. 'What did Amy think of the house?' he asked.

'She loved it. Roxy was with us too. I think they're planning to move in.'

He laughed. 'Did it make you happy to be there?' he asked. 'It's definitely what you want?'

With an incredulous cry, she said, 'How could it not be, as long as you're in it too?'

'Is the right answer,' he told her. 'Did you see the builder? Actually, I spoke to him earlier, or was it yesterday? He's still assuring me we'll be in long before the wedding.'

'It was yesterday,' she replied, 'and I told him just now that we'd better be, because with the ceremony happening there, and so many people flying in specially, such as the celebrant and the musicians . . . Why am I telling you this when you already know? I guess I'm just afraid that the whole thing will start to evaporate if I don't keep pinning it down with words.'

Loving the way she could make light of her insecurity, maybe because it helped him to do the same with his own, he said, 'You can tell me as many times as you like, I'm always happy to hear you sounding so happy. Now, what are the chances of you getting to Bristol tonight? I miss you, and I don't feel like waiting till the weekend to see you.'

'If you mean what are the chances of me getting to London, given that I'm already in Bristol, or near Bath, to be exact, then actually, pretty good. I had a call from . . .'

'Hang on,' he interrupted as the door opened. 'What is it?' he asked Miles.

'Colin's back,' Miles told him, referring to the

Foreign Secretary. 'He wants to know if you can go over there.'

'Tell him I'm on my way,' David answered. Then going back to Lisa, 'Sorry, I have to go,' and he rang off.

It wasn't until he was on his way out of the door that he realised how abrupt he must have sounded, so taking out his iPhone he quickly called her again, saying, 'I could have done that better.'

'You could,' she confirmed. 'But it's OK, I'll see you at the apartment tonight, unless something else comes up and you can't make it.'

'Don't worry, I won't let it,' he assured her.

Chapter Three

Lisa was gazing out of the carriage window, watching the countryside passing in a blur as the high-speed train whisked her from the West Country to Paddington. A newspaper was open in front of her, but she'd stopped reading a while ago, her mind being too full of the house and the wedding and the huge turnaround her life was taking for her to focus on much else for long.

To think that after all these years of flying solo, as Amy liked to put it, she was actually trampling over all her doubts about true love and commitment and throwing herself headlong back through time straight into the arms of the man she had no good reason to trust. She smiled warmly to herself. That was then, and this was now, and actually she wasn't afraid. After all that had happened to her down the years, she doubted she was capable of being that hurt again. Besides, it wasn't as if anything could go wrong this time around, or at least not in the way it had before.

And if that wasn't tempting fate . . .

She'd always known that dropping out of uni had been her only choice back then. She simply couldn't have stood to run into David with his wife, to have to pretend not to know him, or to watch him pretend not to know her. She'd been so devastated by their break-up that the only place to go, it seemed, was home. Her mother had done her best to comfort her, but Matilda, still in her forties at the time, had been working as a legal secretary back then and was, Lisa learned later, involved in a difficult relationship of her own. Since this meant that she hadn't had much time available for a heartbroken younger daughter who'd thrown herself into an affair Matilda had always been dubious about anyway, it was left to Amy, who'd already graduated from Exeter and didn't yet have a permanent job, to decide that the only cure for a broken heart was adventure. So, in her inimitably capable way, Amy had whisked Lisa off to Paris where their aunt, who officially resided in Monaco, kept an apartment in the Seventh arrondissement. During the first weeks they were there Lisa had remained inconsolable, and had so longed for David to get in touch that she could only wonder now how Amy had managed to put up with her.

They'd ended up staying in Paris for the next two years, working in bars and department stores and anywhere else that would have them, before moving on to Madrid, where they'd spent eighteen months experiencing great success either as tour guides, or teaching English as a second language. It was only a matter of weeks after they'd arrived at their next stop, Rome, that Amy had met Theo and fallen head over heels in love. He was there on secondment from a firm of British lawyers who were running an exchange programme with their

Italian counterparts. Since he was due to return to London at the end of the month, and Amy couldn't bear to be parted from him, Lisa had bidden her sister a tearful farewell and gone off to seek more adventure alone.

Having a natural gift for languages, she'd eventually fallen into a job working as an interpreter for an agency based in Geneva. More often than not she was flying all over the world translating for businessmen, politicians, lawyers, journalists, and on one memorable occasion a pair of Australian cannabis smugglers.

After three wonderfully exotic and exciting years circumnavigating the globe in private jets and first-class cabins, or being helicoptered on to the decks of luxury yachts, one of her regular clients made her an offer she couldn't refuse. As the owner of a TV station in Hong Kong he was inviting her to present a new travel show they had in development. Since the idea appealed, she met the producers, was given a camera test and by the end of that same year her programme was airing all over the Far East and Australia. It was during this time that she'd met and fallen madly in love with Tony Sommerville, a fellow Englishman who was in Hong Kong for all sorts of reasons, one of which was to make fortunes out of other people's money – in other words, he was an investment banker. To say he had charm was like saying a bank had cash – the supplies were endless and it bought him everything he ever wanted. Or, as she'd once told him, it was like saying a snake had venom, because he used his charm the same way, to stun his victim and rob them of everything. He'd laughed so hard at that that she'd slapped him.

Their relationship was tempestuous from the start, but it was also tender and loving, and so full of wild and wonderful surprises that in spite of never really trusting him, she could never bring herself to give him up. She was crazy about him, and knew that in his own way he felt the same about her, but as for marrying him and settling down to have the family they both wanted, she knew she'd be insane even to consider it. He simply didn't have it in him to live a normal life back in England, which was where she wanted to end up, close to her sister and most of all to her niece, Roxy, whom she absolutely adored.

Three years had now gone by since she'd returned to London to join the team of a new Sunday lifestyle magazine. Tony hadn't come after her, as she'd expected when their relationship had broken up, nor had he tried to persuade her to change her mind. In fact he'd hardly been in touch at all, which should have made it easier for her to get on with her life, but discovering that she hadn't meant as much to him as she'd thought had made it even harder to get over him. It wasn't until she'd met David again that she'd realised how foolish she was being to hold on to a dream that could never possibly come true. In spite of everything he said, Tony really wasn't the marrying kind, and as fantastic as he might be with Roxy, and probably every other child he met, the very thought of him as a father could only fill her with relief these days that she'd never fallen pregnant while they were together.

She had no idea where he was now, nor did she wish to know.

While she was out there gallivanting around the globe Amy and Theo had moved to Somerset, where Theo had become a senior partner with a law firm in Bath and Amy had landed a job as the events manager for a local country house hotel. Roxy had gone to school locally, and Amy and Lisa's mother, five years after retiring, had taken up residence in a nearby warden-assisted community where they were able to help her cope with her sometimes crippling bouts of arthritis.

Though David was Amy's local MP, Lisa had never run into him during her frequent visits, nor, apart from once after he'd been made Junior Minister, did she ever try to get in touch. She hadn't heard back then, so she'd simply reminded herself that what had happened between them was a long time in the past. He'd probably forgotten all about her by now, she'd tell herself, though she still thought about him often, particularly when feeling lonely and despairing of ever meeting the right man.

By the time she finally ran into him at an embassy party in Paris, she'd been with the lifestyle magazine in London for almost six months, and was still a long way from getting over Tony. She'd been with Jean-Luc that night, a French diplomat who was a dear old friend and whose partner, Simon, had been unable to make the occasion. So, being in town she'd agreed to step in at the last minute, and since Jean-Luc was one of the few people she'd ever told about David, when they'd once exchanged stories about their early years,

46

he'd understood perfectly when she'd informed him he'd be going home alone that night. It wasn't that she'd intended to leave with David, far from it, it was simply that the shock of seeing him had affected her far more profoundly than she'd ever have expected. Fortunately she was self-composed enough not to let it show, and had even managed to look flirtatious, she thought, when she'd glanced at him, as though the last time they'd seen one another was no more than a month ago. In reality, finding herself in the same room as him had thrown her into such unexpected disarray that she'd ended up leaving the party without even saying goodbye to the host. Later, she'd regretted fleeing like a frightened Miss Bennet – after all, she was thirty-six years old by then, so she should have been able to handle herself with far more style. Unfortunately, though, age didn't seem to be any sort of defence, or even ally, when it came to being confronted by the man she'd suddenly found herself every bit as attracted to then as she'd been back in her teens.

When he called the following day she should have been surprised, but actually she wasn't. Somehow, she'd known he would find her, and in spite of telling herself she must not, under any circumstances, agree to see him, when he'd asked her to meet him at a cafe in the Sixteenth, she hadn't even hesitated.

It was already six o'clock by the time Lisa's train pulled into Paddington, leaving her less than an hour to get to the flat and make it ready for when David came home. *Ready for when David came home.*

What a thrill she got from that! She could still hardly believe they were together at last, and not only together, but just weeks away from their wedding.

She was going to be Mrs Kirby!

The teenage romanticism of that made her want to laugh out loud. Of course she'd always be Lisa Martin, she was too established in her career to be known as anything else, but to her and David she'd definitely be Mrs Kirby.

Though she was still a travel writer with the same lifestyle magazine she'd joined three years ago, she'd started a sabbatical two months ago and wasn't due to return until the middle of next year. This meant that apart from being able to organise her own wedding, a task that was becoming more consuming and thrilling by the day, she could also, once they were back from honeymoon, make a start on the novel she'd long wanted to write.

How had life suddenly become so perfect?

It was curious, indeed amazing, how seamlessly, even eagerly, she seemed to be slipping into her role as one half of a partnership. She'd never imagined she'd find it so easy to be with someone all the time when she certainly hadn't before – though it had to be said living with Tony was often like being on her own, since he'd been away such a lot. Was it simply because she loved David so much that she'd been able to shrug off her jealously guarded freedom and independence as effortlessly as an old shawl, with hardly a backward glance? Or had she in fact, as Amy insisted, been far lonelier since her break-up with Tony than she'd ever want to admit, even to herself?

'It's time to stop running,' Amy had told her. 'You're ready to make a commitment at last, and you couldn't have chosen a more wonderful man.'

Amy was certainly right about that, because the way Lisa felt about David was showing her how empty, and in a way pointless, or at least aimless, her life had been since they'd been forced to let go, or maybe since she'd broken up with Tony. She'd had no real structure to her days for what seemed too long now, nothing to make them feel worthwhile, and no one who made her look forward to going home. Now she was always impatient to see David, and knowing he felt the same was, without a doubt, the best feeling in the world.

Her apartment, which had been her London base for the last fifteen years, was on the second floor of a spruce white Regency house, just off Old Bond Street, with a blue plaque over the front door letting the passing world know that a lawyer and philanthropist no one ever seemed to have heard of had once been the occupant of this sumptuous dwelling. She guessed it had probably been a single residence at the time, whereas now it comprised four spacious flats and three studios, one in the attic and two in the basement.

After collecting her mail from a box in the hallway, she dug out her keys as she climbed the stairs, chatting on her mobile as she went, letting her editor's secretary know that yes, she was back in town, and yes, even though she was on sabbatical she was free to come in for a meeting tomorrow afternoon.

'He's going to be out all morning,' the secretary told her, 'or he'd see you . . .'

'It's OK, you don't have to explain,' Lisa interrupted. 'Three o'clock's fine. I can find plenty to do in the morning.' Like catching up with the interior designer who was helping to turn her and David's new house into a dream home; visiting the hairdresser for a practice run, dropping in to find out how her favourite designer was coming along with her wedding dress. The list was endless, but Brendan's secretary didn't need to know all that, she simply required reassurance that Lisa, like the dutiful columnist she often was not, would be in Brendan's office at the appointed hour the following day.

Letting herself into the apartment, she dropped the mail next to the flashing answerphone, and hoisted the two bags of groceries she'd brought in with her off to the kitchen. Like most rooms in the building, it was large with a high ceiling and tall sash windows. She'd started to grow herbs in the decorative boxes on the outside sills. Since David had made this his home too, all kinds of fancy appliances and cookware had begun to appear amongst the tired old melamine units and chipped, but now trendy, butler's sink. Having someone to cook for meant she needed all this stuff, she'd decided, however she still wasn't even close to matching David when it came to culinary skills. Left alone with four ingredients and a microwave oven, as he had been at the beginning, he'd still managed to turn out a scrumptious pasta dish, which they'd eaten gazing into one another's eyes like the new lovers they were, almost afraid to glance away in case the dream vanished while they weren't looking.

After piling everything into the fridge Lisa poured herself a glass of chilled white wine, kicked off her shoes and padded through the double French doors that opened into the sitting room. With its original ornately carved marble fireplace, swag drop cornices and towering Regency windows hugged by a pair of black lacy balconies, it still bore all the hallmarks of a grand old salon. The eclectic collection of furniture, most of which she'd shipped from far-flung corners of the globe, ranged from a magnificent Thai chest to a matching pair of hand-sewn Moroccan sofas, a vibrant Mexican tapestry à la Frida Kahlo, and a very snazzy Italian desk that had set her back almost five thousand euros. At the centre of the room, amidst a colourful assortment of Indian silk pillows a faux bearskin rug lay in submission beneath her focal-point coffee table. If the vendor of this highly unusual piece was to be believed, it had started out life in the nineteenth century as the secret door to a Zanzibar harem. True or not, she had fallen in love with it during a few memorable days with Tony on the island, so now it was nestling in a bespoke walnut frame, and where there had once been a magnificent black iron handle, a sculpted ceramic pot with a flowering cactus had been sunk into the space, while the rest of the surface was protected by glass.

Finding the room as stuffy as she'd expected, she went to draw down both windows to let in some air, along with the hum of traffic, then took herself off to the bedroom, which was much quieter and cooler, to prepare herself, and it, for the evening ahead.

As soon as David let himself in the front door he could tell Lisa was already at home. The mere scent of the place, a kind of citrusy musk mingled with an essence that was pure her, was all it took to assure him of this, and to smooth out the frown in his brow along with some of the troubles in his mind. Would he admit that he was later than he'd expected because he'd managed to go all the way to his old flat in Pimlico before remembering it wasn't where he lived now? Perhaps not. She'd only think he was hankering after his old life, or missing Catrina, or losing the plot, and while the first two held elements of truth, and the latter probably shouldn't be ignored, this was exactly where he wanted to be now. With Lisa, who was changed in so many ways, and as far as he was concerned all for the better, though once he'd never have considered it possible. He knew that she found him changed too, but to his surprise she insisted that the absent-mindedness and moments of introspection that had occasionally driven Catrina nuts – certainly towards the end when she'd been in too much pain for patience – were wonderfully endearing. He wished he could think of them the same way, but more often than not they frustrated him as much as they had Catrina. It was worrying him too, a great deal more than he wanted to admit. He'd started to wonder if he might be falling into a depression, but was unable to imagine how that could be when he was happier than he'd been in years.

This wasn't meant to be disrespectful to Catrina, because of course they'd been happy together, but a relationship that had been motoring along the same lines for thirty years was unlikely to supply the same charge as one that was setting out on a brand-new journey.

Hearing Lisa moving around in the bathroom he called out to let her know he was back, and went to the kitchen to pour himself a drink. He was feeling much more relaxed now than he had a few minutes ago, the tension was ebbing and his spirits were emerging from the shadows of worry. He loved how at home he felt in this apartment, it was as though he'd been coming here for years, so what on earth had directed him to Pimlico this evening? Old habits, he supposed, and too much going on in his mind. Whatever, it didn't matter. He was here now, and knowing that she was going to join him at any moment was enough to melt away all the concerns and complications that had weighted his day.

Carrying his drink into the sitting room, he sank down on one of the sofas and let his head fall comfortably into the cushions. Sometimes it felt as though he'd kept a part of himself locked away inside, just waiting for this, and now it was happening perhaps his real life was finally starting to unfold.

His thoughts drifted back to the moment they'd met, after the embassy party, in a Parisian cafe, when she'd waited only until their coffees had been delivered to a discreet corner table to say, 'This is a mistake.'

He'd smiled at her and she'd regarded him

curiously. 'I was thinking the same thing,' he explained, 'but now I'm here I know it's one I'd make again.' He'd wanted to reach for her hands, but had held himself back. It was too soon, they didn't know each other any more, so why did it feel as though they still did? 'I couldn't not see you,' he told her.

She lowered her eyes.

As he sat watching her, absorbing everything about her, from the creamy softness of her skin to the exotic slant of her eyes and the elegance of her hands, he'd never felt such a sense of being in the right place, even though it could hardly have been more wrong.

'How did you manage to get away?' she finally asked. 'Don't you have security people following you?'

He laughed. 'I'm not important enough for that.'

She appeared amused. 'But you will be, soon enough, I imagine.'

Her voice, so husky and soft, seemed so familiar that he could almost feel himself falling back through the years. 'Let's not rule it out,' he replied, arching an eyebrow with irony.

She allowed her gaze to meet his for a few brief seconds. 'I sent a card when you were made Foreign Minister,' she told him. 'I know I probably shouldn't have, but I thought, if it went to your office . . .' He was looking surprised. 'You didn't get it?'

He shook his head. 'One of the secretaries probably forwarded it to my home,' and that was when he'd understood what must have prompted Catrina's suspicions towards the end. 'But don't let's talk about me,' he said. 'I want to know about you, who you are now, what's been happening to you . . . Are you married?'

Though he was surprised to find out she wasn't, it had thrilled him, which was neither noble, nor right. Then she told him about her column and he'd realised, finally, why the *Lifestyle* section of the Sunday paper always seemed to disappear before he could get round to it. Poor Catrina, he'd thought sadly, still so worried after so many years.

'How's your wife?' she asked.

He hadn't told her then about the cancer. It was in remission and they were still hopeful it wouldn't make a return. 'She's doing well,' he replied.

'And are you happy?'

Her bluntness threw him. He didn't want to lie, but now the question was before him, he couldn't be sure what the real truth was. 'I guess it depends how you're measuring it,' he said in the end. 'We've been lucky, our business took off in a way neither of us expected, and we have a wonderful daughter.'

She smiled. 'Tell me about her. How old is she now? I guess twenty-six?'

'Twenty-seven.'

'Is she like you? Does she have your eyes, your smile? I love your hair, by the way. It suits you, silver. Makes you look very distinguished.'

'And I love yours,' he murmured, allowing his gaze to run over the ash-blonde silkiness of hers, and wishing his eyes could be his fingers. 'I'm glad you kept it long. The plait is . . . very you.'

She looked down at her cup, but when she

picked it up she didn't drink, only sat staring at the table, seeming to want to speak, but perhaps like him, she couldn't find the right words when there were too many wrong ones trying to be spoken.

In the end her eyes came to his and even before she spoke he felt as though the world was falling apart. 'I ought to leave,' she said.

'Can we stay in touch?'

'I don't think we should.'

'I can't just let you go.'

Whatever she said next was lost in the mists of time, all he remembered was her slipping away, leaving him sitting there, and though he'd wanted nothing more than to go after her, he hadn't. It was a decision he'd regretted for a while, but only until he'd discovered how sick Catrina really was. Nothing in the world, not even Lisa, could have persuaded him to cheat on his wife then. He wasn't even sure he'd have been able to, anyway.

Lisa was lying in David's arms, savouring the descent from a release that had exploded like a starburst inside her, and wondering if he really was the best lover she'd ever had. Or was she telling herself that because she'd rather he was in that role than Tony? Annoyed that Tony should even enter her mind at such a time, she abruptly shut him out again and let herself drift in the pleasure of knowing that her and David's bodies were still as in tune as their minds, and that their hunger for one another was as insatiable as the need to catch up on so much lost time. She knew they'd make love again tonight, and she smiled secretly to herself as she watched her fingers, pale and slender, trailing over the muscular darkness of his thigh.

'Are you OK?' David murmured, turning to look at her. 'Hungry?'

'Mm, starving,' she replied. 'I brought some steaks in from M&S, or we can go out if you prefer.'

He sighed and stretched, then wrapped her tightly in his arms. 'I'd like you to remain exactly as you are, so I guess we'd better stay here,' he decided.

She gave a moan of pleasure as he kissed each of her nipples before getting up from the bed. 'Am I allowed to put on anything at all?' she asked, her eyes performing a bashful coquetry as she gazed up at him.

He shook his head.

'Not even a napkin when I eat?'

He continued to shake his head. 'If you drop anything, I'll sort it out.'

After using the bathroom she followed him out to the kitchen and laughed to find him wearing nothing but an apron as he tenderised the steaks before putting them on the grill. 'If your constituents could see you now,' she teased, slapping his bottom on her way to the fridge. 'Or any of your Right Honourable colleagues ... Which reminds me, how did your meeting go with Colin Larch today? Don't tell me, you're about to be reinstated as Minister?'

David's eyebrows arched in their adorably ironic way. 'That can only happen when there's a reshuffle,' he reminded her, 'and there won't be one of those during this parliamentary term.'

'But he wants you back?' she prompted.

'Yes, he does, but actually that wasn't what we discussed.'

When he didn't elaborate she turned around, bringing the wine bottle with her. 'So?' she said. 'Can you tell me, or is it *classified*?'

He was smiling as he said, 'Yes, to both.'

Her eyes sparkled mischievously. 'Which can only mean it was about his bid for the leadership?'

He nodded, and held out his glass for her to refill it. 'Again, nothing's going to happen this side of the summer recess, and we'll have to see what's going on in the world, never mind the country and the polls, before we put anything into motion later in the year. That said, Colin's a very strong candidate, popular with the people and within the Party, so as much as anything it's going to be a question of getting the timing right.'

Lisa was smiling wickedly. 'Do you think he'll appoint you as Foreign Secretary if he does get the leadership?' she asked, clinking her glass against his.

'One step at a time,' he cautioned. Then, capitulating, 'But I guess, provided I want it, it's not beyond the bounds of possibility.'

Her eyebrows went up. 'Do you think you might not want it?' she asked.

His eyes stayed on hers. 'Would it bother you if I didn't?' he countered.

Startled, and vaguely confused, she started to shake her head. 'I don't suppose so,' she replied,

'I just thought, presumed, it was something you'd set your heart on.'

He took a sip of his drink. 'Yes, it is, or was,' he said, 'but now, well, I . . . Is that your phone or mine?'

With a roll of her eyes she said, 'One of us really has to change our ringtone,' and going out to the hall she listened, trying to track down where the ringing was coming from. Realising it was his jacket, she scooped it up and took it to him.

As he dug out the phone she draped the jacket round her shoulders and returned to her wine.

'Colin,' he said, tucking the mobile into the crook of his neck so he could talk to the Foreign Secretary as he continued to cook. 'What can I do for you?'

'I might ask you the same question,' came the reply.

Puzzled, David said, 'I don't follow.'

'Where are you?'

'At home, with Lisa. Why?'

'Did you get my message? Dinner, seven o'clock, usual place.'

David stopped what he was doing. 'I checked my voicemail about an hour ago,' he said, 'there was nothing.' Then, 'Listen, I'm sorry. Something's obviously got screwed up somewhere. Have you ordered yet? We could come and join you. Or you could come here?'

A chuckle tumbled down the line. 'Now you're talking, because no way am I going to deprive myself of an evening with the lovely Lisa, so if you can bear to share her for a couple of hours, I'll come there.'

David was looking at Lisa as he said, 'We'll have a drink waiting for when you arrive.' He was frowning as he rang off, and quickly going through to his voicemail he checked again to see if there were any messages. Nothing. However, there was an email from Miles reminding him that *The Times* wanted an answer on whether Lisa was willing to take part in the interview next week.

'What do you think?' he asked, when he finished telling her about it.

'Well, first up,' she said, 'I think I'd better get dressed if Colin's on his way over, if only to go out and get another steak. And about the interview . . .' She pulled a face. 'I'm not sure. If we only had ourselves to consider I'd say yes right away, but I can't help worrying about how it will go down with Rosalind, seeing us together like that.'

'Mm, yes,' he said, his tone conveying the guilt he felt at not thinking of Rosalind himself. 'I'm sorry. She's having a tough time right now, what with everything . . .'

'I know, it's OK, you don't have to explain. Incidentally, have you spoken to her about the text she sent me this morning?'

'No, I've decided to leave it till I see her at the weekend. I don't want to be preparing her for an article that's bound to feature our upcoming nuptials at the same time. That really won't help matters at all.'

'So no to *The Times*?'

'I'm afraid so.'

Picking up her wine Lisa went up on tiptoe to kiss him. 'You're a good father,' she told him.

He smiled and kissed her again. 'I don't think she'd agree with that right now,' he said quietly. 'In fact, I know she wouldn't, but all things considered, I suppose I can't really blame her for that.'

Chapter Four

Ever since Rosalind and her husband Jerry had moved into this house with its sweeping views of the lake, and the meandering swell of the Mendips beyond, her parents had come for lunch on Saturdays. Dee, her aunt, who lived in the next village and helped to run the constituency office, generally fitted them into her busy schedule too, and more often than not Rosalind's close friend Sally came to join them. In fact, all their friends were invited whenever they wanted to come, they simply had to let Rosalind know a day in advance and a place would be set for them.

Today, since Sally was in bed with a bout of summer flu and Dee was helping out at a car boot sale, while Jerry, who was a pilot with BA, was away until Tuesday, the large farmhouse table that she often laid for as many as eight, or even ten for this weekly ritual, was set only for three.

After popping the lasagne – one of Lawrence's favourites – into the oven, she remembered to prime the timer, and resisting the urge to start on the wine before her father arrived, she ran upstairs to close the windows before the storm that seemed to be threatening had a chance to break. Since the old mill had originally been converted and extended for a Bristol sea merchant and his large family, it was a rambling place with five bedrooms and three bathrooms, all of which had been more recently renovated, furnished and decorated by Rosalind and her mother. This meant that almost everywhere Rosalind turned there was a memory of Catrina waiting to spill its joy and grief all over her. The loss was still so raw in her heart that sometimes it felt as though it was deepening instead of lessening, and during moments of utter despair all she wanted was to be able to go and join her mother wherever she might be, leaving this complicated and cruel world behind her.

On the way out of her and Jerry's bedroom where the wrought-iron bedstead was raised on a dais that enabled them to lie back against the pillows and enjoy the views, she caught her reflection in the antique cheval mirror that had once been her mother's, but was now hers. Seeing how gaunt and dishevelled she looked, she darted into the bathroom to pull a brush through her curls, another gift from her mother, and apply some colour to her cheeks. She didn't want her father thinking she wasn't coping, because she was, quite well as a matter of fact, no thanks to him. Her eyes closed, and taking a deep breath she blew it out slowly before opening them again. The woman in the mirror was watching her with caution, seeming unsure whether to keep her there to continue brightening herself up, or simply to let her go. She looked tired and anxious, which was hardly surprising when she'd been up in the night listening and worrying as Lawrence padded about the house, switching lights on and off, flushing toilets, pulling curtains open and closed, tidying chairs into place, turning on taps, and doing whatever else made him feel certain that the house was functioning normally, before going back to bed.

She was glad Jerry hadn't been there to hear it. He had less patience with their son than she did. On the other hand, he was the one with the early morning call, and pilots, above practically everybody else, needed to get the right amount of sleep. She sometimes wondered what he really thought of Lawrence. She was sure he loved him, and would do anything in the world to make him happy, in so far as anyone could make Lawrence happy, but it had to be hard for Jerry never being able to hold his son, or share the same things with him that other fathers shared with their nine-year-old boys. As his mother there was nothing in the world she wouldn't give to be able to pull Lawrence into her arms and envelop him in one of the giant bear hugs her father used to give her when she was small. Or to smooth a hand through his silky curls, or to hear him laugh uncontrollably the way children should, so it had to be the same for Jerry.

Poor Jerry. Poor Lawrence. Poor her.

'Hello? Are you in here?'

'Oh Dad, yes,' she gasped. 'You made me jump.'

'Didn't you hear me calling?' he asked, as she came out of the bathroom.

'Sorry,' she said, 'I was miles away. How are you?' and walking into his arms she squeezed him tight and felt herself longing to sink even deeper into the comforting circle of his embrace. 'Have you seen Lawrence?' she asked. 'He's in the tree house.'

'Not any more. He's at the table now, piecing together a new jigsaw. Are you OK? You look tired.'

'He was up to his usual tricks during the night,' she confessed, and gazing into his wonderfully tender eyes she felt her own starting to well with tears. 'Come on, lunch will be ready soon,' she said, quickly linking his arm. She didn't want him to see her crying, because she didn't want him to know how fragile she was really feeling. Nor did she want to start his visit off by confessing how afraid she was that they were drifting apart. She knew he'd insist it wasn't the case, that it was all in her head, and he loved her every bit as much now as he always had. Actually, she didn't doubt that, but she'd never dreamt he'd behave the way he had since her mother had died.

She couldn't think about her mother now or she really would lose it.

'So, you brought him a new jigsaw,' she said chirpily, as they started down the stairs. 'I hope he didn't snatch it.'

'As a matter of fact, he even said thank you.'

Her heart swelled with pride. Of them all her father had always been the one Lawrence responded to most, he even seemed to get some of his terrible jokes, and for the past year or so he'd taken an interest in what was happening in Parliament, asking which policies her father was supporting, or what he was doing to help someone in the constituency. For a boy of nine he had an extraordinary understanding of current affairs, but like his occasionally oddly formal vocabulary and reluctance to make eye contact, it was all a part of the syndrome that made him not quite like everyone else.

Not wanting to appear too eager for a drink, she stood over Lawrence watching him sorting the pieces of his jigsaw, while her father uncorked a bottle of Spanish wine. It was a Belondrade y Lurton which they'd first discovered while on a family holiday at La Residencia in Deià, Mallorca. They'd visited this hotel most summers for a week or ten days, in addition to a week or two spent somewhere else in the Med such as a Greek island, or the French Riviera. At the end of December they'd fly off somewhere hot – Barbados, Mauritius, Thailand – to escape the post-Christmas gloom. They hadn't been able to go anywhere these last two years because of her mother's treatments, and Rosalind was still trying to come to terms with the fact that they probably wouldn't ever go anywhere as a family again.

'Is Dee joining us?' David asked, as he passed her a glass.

'Thanks,' she said. 'She sent a text earlier saying she'd pop in for coffee after the car boot sale.' She clinked her glass to his and took a large, restorative sip. 'So how are you?' she asked, going to check the lasagne.

It was a moment or two before she realised he hadn't answered, and when she turned round she found him staring curiously out of the window.

'Is someone there?' she asked.

Seeming not to have heard, he said, 'So how are you?'

'I'm fine,' she replied, watching him turn back. Obviously his mind had been on *her* and now he was no doubt wishing he hadn't bothered to come here. 'What about you?' she said, fighting back more tears of resentment. 'When does the summer recess start?'

'I believe it's the twentieth,' he said. 'Anyway, about a month from now.'

She tensed in case he mentioned the wedding that was due to take place two weeks later, but he didn't, even though she knew it must be uppermost in his mind.

'David,' Lawrence said, which was what he always called her father, 'Noah's Ark can't have been real, because it isn't possible to fit all those animals on board, and he was 600 years old when God told him to build it and people don't live that long. Plus, the geological column shows various anomalies that disprove it.'

David smiled, and went to sit next to him. 'What do you know about the geological column?' he asked, watching Lawrence's nimble fingers sorting through two thousand pieces to create an intricately detailed picture of Noah and his Ark.

'I know that beneath the surface there is topsoil, then coal, then dried-up river bed with desiccation cracks in the mud.' He looked at David's iPhone as it started to ring.

'It's Miles,' David told him, and Rosalind guessed the reason he'd announced the caller was to let her know that it wasn't his girlfriend on the line. 'Yes, Miles, what can I do for you?' he said, getting up from the table to go and fetch some peanuts from a cupboard. 'Don't tell me you're at the office. You are allowed to take weekends off, you know.' He laughed at Miles's response, then said, 'No, Dee's not here at the moment. Can't you get her on the mobile? She's probably switched it off. Anything I can do?' He munched as he listened, then said, 'No problem, you'll be arriving around six tomorrow night, instead of just after lunch. The surgery's in Keynsham on Monday morning, I believe. Yep, I'll be coming up to London with you straight after. OK, good. See you then,' and ringing off, he tipped a generous supply of nuts into a bowl and carried them to the table.

'So where's Jerry this weekend?' he asked, going back to the fridge.

Rosalind glanced at the clock. 'Right now, on his way to Cape Town. Thanks,' she added, as David topped up her glass. Would he register the significance of Cape Town and make some comment? She wasn't sure whether she wanted him to or not, but when he didn't she felt angry and let down. He never used to be so dismissive or neglectful of her feelings, and he obviously knew how difficult it was for her every time Jerry flew back to the place where he'd had an affair, so why didn't he say something? Because all he could think about was *her*, that was why. 'There are some accounts I need to go through with you after lunch, if you have time,' she said, feeling suddenly unbearably lonely as she emptied a packet of salad leaves into a bowl.

'I have,' he confirmed.

'David, are you going to be Prime Minister?' Lawrence asked, keeping his eyes on his jigsaw.

'Not this week,' David told him.

'There have been fifty-two prime ministers of Great Britain,' Lawrence informed him, 'starting with Sir Robert Walpole in 1721 right through to the man who's there now. These animals are called walruses.'

David glanced over and pulled a face. 'They could be mammoths,' he said, 'or hairy cows with horns, hard to tell.'

Lawrence looked at him, blinked slowly, then returned to his task.

Rosalind exchanged a smile with her father. He was one of the few people who could get away with contradicting Lawrence.

Out of nowhere, she began asking herself how they were going to manage at Christmas and birthdays from now on? They always celebrated their special occasions as a family, Lawrence looked forward to it, but how could they get together if that woman was going to be around? She probably wouldn't even invite them into her home, but even if she did, Rosalind would rather cut off her feet than allow them to cross the threshold of the woman who'd probably dance on her mother's grave, given half a chance.

'Darling, what are you doing to that salad dressing?' her father asked. 'If you shake it any harder it'll turn into soup.'

'Sorry,' she said, trying to give a laugh. 'I guess I'm a bit on edge today. Jerry and I had words last night – nothing serious – but then I hardly slept, and there are some issues going on with one of the properties on Clifton Vale . . .'

'Anything I can help with?'

'No, no, it'll be fine. I'm going over there on

Monday to talk to the tenants. Nothing for you to worry about. Ah, the lasagne's ready,' she declared as the timer beeped. 'Can you take it out, please? Lawrence, go and wash your hands, there's a good boy.'

'I have to finish this first,' he reminded her.

Knowing that to throw him off track would either trigger one of his tantrums or silence him for days, she didn't argue, simply took three plates from the warmer and set them on the table.

By the time the meal was over Lawrence had regaled them with a chronological list of prime ministers, an alphabetical list of animal species, every football team in the premier league and every player. This last surprised, and touched her, because he'd never shown any interest in his father's favourite sport before, so maybe he'd memorised all those names to try and impress him. Who knew?

'Feel like going fishing tomorrow?' David said, as they cleared the table.

'Yes, that would be very enjoyable,' Lawrence replied. 'I'm going on the computer now,' and after wiping his face with the paper towel his mother was offering, he folded it neatly, handed it back and left.

'It's such a lovely day, we should have eaten outside,' Rosalind commented, as she began filling the kettle.

'We can always have our coffee out there,' David suggested. Closing up the dishwasher and reaching for her hand, he said, 'Now, we can go on avoiding the real issue between us if you like, but unless we discuss it, it's never going to be resolved.'

Rosalind's face was already tightening. 'I don't see what there is to discuss,' she responded shortly. 'Your mind seems to be made up, so obviously what I think doesn't count.'

'Come and sit down,' he said, trying to lead her to the table.

'I'm making the coffee,' she reminded him, and pulling herself free she turned her back.

Stifling a sigh, he watched her take down the cafetière and start to ladle in three scoops of fresh grounds. 'I saw the text you sent to Lisa on Thursday,' he told her. 'Can't you see you're only hurting yourself, behaving like this?'

'Well, that's OK,' she snapped, 'because anything that hurts me is obviously fine by you, or you'd stop seeing her.'

'Rosalind, I'm going to marry her . . .'

'I don't want to discuss this.'

'We have to. The wedding isn't far off now and I'd like you to be there.'

'I'm sorry, but it's not going to happen.'

'Please listen to me . . .'

'No, you listen to me,' she cried, spinning round furiously. 'I don't want that woman in our family. She's nothing to me, *nothing*, do you hear me?'

'But . . .'

'She's a gold-digging whore, Dad, and for you to try and foist her on us when Mum's only been dead for a matter of months just goes to show how much our feelings mean to you.'

The troubled look that came into his eyes told her how deeply she'd hurt him, but she didn't care. He needed to understand how much he was hurting her too.

'Please don't ever call Lisa that again,' he said roughly. 'You don't even know her, so to be . . .'

'I know all I need to know, thank you very much. She almost broke up your marriage once, and she even tried to see you when Mum was ill. For all I know Mum was right, you did see her then.'

'She never contacted me once when your mother was ill.'

'That's not true! I saw the card she sent . . .'

'Your mother was . . .'

'And look how fast she managed to get her claws into you once Mum had gone, and you, fool that you are, aren't doing anything to try and stop her. She's no good for you, Dad. She's a hanger-on, a nobody . . .'

'Rosalind . . .'

'. . . she jets around the world with the rich and famous thinking she's something special, when all she is is a lame excuse of a writer who contributes absolutely nothing of any value to the world, and who's never been able to hang on to a man because, apart from you, they've been able to see straight through her.'

'When you've quite finished . . .'

'I've hardly even started . . .'

'Rosalind, I'm not going to stand here allowing you to say these things when you don't even know what you're talking about. I know your mother had some difficulty towards the end believing that I wasn't seeing Lisa . . .'

'Because she knew you were.'

'How could she, when I wasn't?'

'I don't care what you say, she knew that woman had got to you again. She tracked you down in

72

Paris, and from then on you kept wishing Mum would hurry up and die so you could get on with your sordid little love affair without any interruptions.'

David's face was ashen. 'Darling, that is not true,' he told her forcefully. 'I did everything I could for your mother while she was ill.'

'Except love her, and that's all she ever wanted from you, to know that you really loved her.'

'Of course I loved her.'

'So much that her body hardly had time to turn cold before you were . . .'

'Stop this,' he interrupted shakily. 'Whatever you're telling yourself, or your mother told you . . .'

'Do you miss her?' she shouted.

David blinked.

'You were married to her for thirty years, so do you miss her now?'

'Yes. Very much, in fact.'

'You're lying!'

He said nothing. He couldn't. His words were like startled birds in flight.

'Why aren't you defending yourself?' she cried angrily. 'It's your conscience, isn't it? You know you've behaved badly, that what you're doing is wrong . . .'

'I can . . .'

'Why did you sell Mum's house? You know how much it meant to her, and to me . . . It's where I grew up, for God's sake. It was our family home. All our memories are there, and you just upped and sold it like it was any other property on our books. How could you do that? It was *our* house, and signing everything else over to me doesn't make up for it, so don't try telling yourself it does.'

'I can't win, Rosalind. You're not listening . . .'

'Tell me why you sold it.'

He started to speak, but his words had gone again.

'Answer me!' she cried. 'What's the matter with you? I want to know why you sold it.'

'Darling, ask yourself, would you . . .' He swallowed and tried again. 'Would you really want Lisa living there, feeling the way you do about her? Of course not. And she wouldn't want to live there either. Your mother and I . . . We were very happy in that house, but our time had come to an end. Surely you must see that. I couldn't go on rattling about there on my own . . .'

'All I see are strangers tearing up her flower beds, knocking down walls, treating the place as though it's some kind of ruin instead of one of the most beautiful houses for miles around.'

'Look, I know it must be hard, every time you drive by, seeing how they're changing it, but we have to move on.'

'I don't want to move on,' she shouted, tears suddenly streaming down her cheeks. 'I want her back. She shouldn't have died. She was too young . . . Oh God, Dad, it's horrible without her. I miss her so much . . .'

As she fell sobbing into his arms, David held her tightly, keeping his eyes closed to hold back his own tears as the depth of her loss overwhelmed him. 'There, there,' he soothed, pressing a kiss to her hair. 'I know how much she meant to you, and . . .'

'Why did you have to go to that woman when you did?' she spluttered angrily. 'Couldn't you have waited a bit longer? It was so quick, and Mum didn't deserve to be kicked aside like that.'

'That's not what I did,' he assured her. 'Your mother meant the world to me . . .'

'Oh dear,' a voice said from the open kitchen door. 'Is this a bad time? Would you like me to go away again?'

'No, no, come in, Dee,' Rosalind said to her aunt. 'We're not discussing anything you don't already know about.'

Dee Lorimer's usually lively round face was creased with concern as she watched her niece break away from her father's embrace, dabbing her eyes and trying to suppress a bout of sobs. Dee's eyes went quickly to David, as though seeking enlightenment, but he merely shook his head.

'If you don't mind, I'd like you to go now, Dad,' Rosalind said. 'I don't want to seem rude or to hurt your feelings. At least, not any more than I already have . . .' Her smile was weak. 'We can meet for dinner, if you like? Unless you have other plans, that is.'

He swallowed and glanced awkwardly at Dee. 'I'm afraid I do,' he admitted.

Rosalind nodded resignedly. 'She's here, in Bristol?'

'She'll probably be on her way by now.'

'Where are you staying?'

He started to answer, then stopped.

'Don't worry, I'm not planning to drop in, or

do anything to break up your cosy little love nest, wherever it is.'

David looked at Dee again, but she was keeping her eyes down, clearly not wanting to get caught in the middle.

'We're staying with her sister, over near Bath,' he said.

Rosalind's eyes turned glassy. He was being sucked into another family, they were going to lose him, and she didn't know how to stop it. 'Perhaps you'll call if you have time,' she said, failing to keep a shrill note from her voice.

'Of course I will,' he promised, coming to kiss her.

She tried to smile, and decided not to remind him of how often he'd made the same promise lately, and had ended up letting her down. The father she'd always known and loved would never have done that, so what more proof did she need that Lisa Martin was stealing him away?

Lisa could see, even feel, David watching her as she strode towards him through the sunshine, the diaphanous flow of her dress swishing softly around her calves, and the gentle breeze blowing along the platform lifting the brim of her straw hat. He was standing just inside the gates to the car park at Bath Spa station, leaning against the railings with his arms folded and eyes darkened with pleasure as he waited for her to reach him. Though she knew people were watching, and she was smiling like an adolescent, she couldn't help it, and nor did she really care. All that mattered to her was that he was there, and looking every bit as smitten with her as she was with him.

'Do you think kissing in public is allowed when you might be recognised?' she murmured, holding her hat as he swept her into his arms.

'Who cares?' he replied, and planted his mouth firmly on hers.

She was flushed and laughing happily as he released her, and tucking an arm through his she let him take her weekend bag as they walked to the car.

'How was the shopping?' he asked, as he opened the passenger door for her to get in.

'I'm glad you asked,' she replied, throwing her hat on to the back seat. 'Sofas are ordered, so are the guest beds, and our bed will be just as soon as we decide on the mattress. However, they can definitely make it to fit the existing posts.'

'Mm, sounds like we're making progress.' Going round to the driver's side, he slipped in next to her and pulled her into another embrace. 'You look stunning,' he told her. 'I love this dress. It has a very saucy way of showing off what's underneath.'

She bubbled with laughter. 'I hope not,' she whispered, 'because there isn't anything underneath, except me.'

He gave a lustful groan. 'If we weren't in a public place . . .' he said.

'What would you do?' she challenged.

Leaning over he murmured in her ear, and her smile was lost in a wave of desire.

'I called into Amy's on the way to collect you,' he told her as he reversed out of the parking space.

'Your mother's already there, and they're planning a barbecue for this evening with the weather being so good.'

'Great. So, it'll be just the five of us?'

'I believe Roxy was threatening to join us, but then someone rang and we were royally dumped.'

Lisa smiled, remembering only too well how lively and dismissive of grown-ups she and Amy had been at Roxy's age.

'So did you find out why Brendan had to back out of your meeting yesterday?' David asked, as they joined the dual carriageway heading out of town.

'Apparently his gran had a fall so he had to rush up to Lincoln. Luckily, she's OK. He emailed this morning to apologise for the last-minute cancellation, and we've rescheduled for Tuesday.'

'Did he say what he wants to see you about?'

'No, but knowing him he wants a bit of a gossip. Now, tell me about you. How was your lunch with Rosalind today?'

Her heart sank as, keeping his eyes on the road, he reached over for her hand.

'I see, that bad,' she said, gazing down at the dazzling three-carat diamond he'd bought her for their engagement.

'It'll change,' he said.

Hoping he was right, but doubting it, she said, 'In time for the wedding?'

At that he sighed, and after merging into the single-lane traffic he said, 'It's possible. Anything can happen between now and then.'

Like a miracle, she was thinking. 'Did you happen to mention the text?'

He didn't answer straight away, and she was about to let the subject drop when he said, 'Mm, but she's in a bad place at the moment so . . .'

She turned to look at him. 'So?' she prompted.

He shook his head.

Not quite understanding, but not wanting to push too hard either, she said, 'Was Jerry there today?'

'No. I'm not sure where he is, but he's not usually away for much more than a week.'

'Does she still think he's playing around?'

'I don't know. The subject didn't come up, but I'm sure it's all sorted out now.'

With a sigh, Lisa turned to stare out of the window. 'I can't help feeling sorry for her,' she said. 'It must seem as though her world is falling apart . . . Do you think it might help if I talked to her, tried to get her to see that we could actually be friends if she'd allow it?'

Bringing her hand to his lips, he said, 'It's a lovely thought, but I don't think now is the right time. She's still . . .' He gave a shake of his head, as though not really wanting to go on.

'Grieving?'

'Yes, she . . .' He stopped again, then after a moment he said, 'Tell me, did you hear from Brendan?'

'I just told you . . .'

'Yes, sorry, I meant Belinda. Is that her name, who's making your dress?'

'Isabelle,' she corrected, 'and I spent most of yesterday morning with her. It's fabulous, or it will be when it's finished.'

He smiled playfully. 'I can hardly wait to see

it. You'll look sensational, I have no doubts about that. By the way, have you made up your mind yet where you'd like to go on honeymoon?'

'Actually, I think I have . . . Oh, hang on, who's this?' and reaching into her bag she pulled out her iPhone. 'It's a Hong Kong number,' she said, thinking first of Tony, then of who she was hoping it would be. 'Please let it be Sheelagh or Baz. Hi, this is Lisa,' she cried down the line.

'Darling, it's Sheelagh,' came the reply. 'Sorry it's taken me so long to get back to you. We flew into Hong Kong yesterday – did our agent tell you?'

'Yes, he did. You're there for a week?'

'Yes, then it's Singapore, Sydney, oh heavens I've forgotten the schedule, but that's not important, what is, is that we'd absolutely love to sing at your wedding. We're honoured you'd ask, and don't you mention another word about paying us, do you hear me?'

'But I know how . . .'

'Enough! We're due back in Jamaica mid-July, so we'll have a couple of weeks at home before we fly over to join you.'

'Oh Sheelagh, this is fantastic news. You at least have to let us pay for your flights.'

'Forget it. Now, tell me, have you heard from Royston yet?'

'Yes, he emailed a couple of days ago and more fantastic news, he and the band can make it too, all the way from New Orleans. Oh my God, we're so international,' she laughed, turning to David and finding him laughing too.

'When were you ever not?' Sheelagh teased.

'Now, it's gone midnight here, and we're horribly jet-lagged so we're off to bed. Baz sends his love, and we'll call again in the next couple of days to discuss details.'

As she rang off Lisa closed her eyes and gave a groan of pure joy. 'This is going to be the most beautiful wedding,' she murmured.

Reaching for her hand again, David said, 'Are you still sure about limiting the guest list to fifty? We can always go higher.'

'No, I think fifty's a perfect number. If we start going over that we'll never know where to stop.'

'So it's only the musicians and the celebrant who are coming from overseas?'

'Correct, and I think it's amazing the way they're all managing to fit us into their schedules. If you knew how popular Royston's jazz band is, and everyone who's anyone wants Heather Shannon to bless their wedding. She lives in Arizona, I'm sure I told you, but she's flying in from Mumbai when she comes to us. I've known her for years. You're going to love her. Oh, and the flowers are coming from abroad too, at least some of them are. Apparently it's not the right time of year for lily of the valley, so the florist is arranging to import them from Holland. And my aunt Judith is coming from Paris – we couldn't leave her out, just because she doesn't live in this country.'

'Of course not.'

'Which reminds me, I really must try to see the caterer while I'm here. He's French, in case you'd forgotten. He's coming up with some great suggestions, but Amy and I need to go for a tasting. Actually, you can come too, if you have time.'

With a laugh he said, 'I probably won't, but it's kind of you to offer.'

Casting him a look, she continued listing everything that still had to be ordered, booked, agreed, decorated, or transported, making both their heads spin until finally they were pulling into the gravelled courtyard in front of Amy and Theo's quaint farmhouse cottage. It was picture-book with its roses and clematis struggling for supremacy over the old grey walls, and a very excited golden retriever leaping up from her vigil outside the front door.

'Lucy!' Lisa cried, jumping out of the car to hug her beloved dog, who was actually more Amy's since she lived here. However, it was Lisa who'd saved her from being sent to the dogs' home when her previous owners decided to up sticks and decamp to Down Under.

'Hello, old girl,' David laughed as Lucy bumped against him, demanding a fussing from him too, though he barely managed more than a pat before she was looping around Lisa again, whipping them both with her wildly enthusiastic tail.

'I've just had a thought,' David said, as they started round the side of the house. 'I'm taking Lawrence fishing in the morning, so why don't I drag Lucy along too? I think he'd like to meet a dog.'

'That's a lovely idea,' Lisa agreed, linking his arm. 'You'd love that, wouldn't you Luce,' she called after the dog who was keenly leading the way, 'because you're great with kids, aren't you, my angel.'

'Ah, you're here,' Theo said, coming out of the

conservatory as they appeared on the terrace. 'I thought I heard the car pull up. Lisa, looking gorgeous as ever,' he told her, pulling her into a bruising, brotherly embrace, while shaking David's hand. Though he was easily as tall as David, and his hair almost as silver, he was a far rangier build, making his limbs appear longer and looser and his gait somehow springier. He was also, like David, a good-looking man, but in an earthy, unkempt sort of way, which didn't immediately cast him as the successful solicitor he was.

'The girls are under the pergola,' he informed them. 'They've already started on the margaritas so you have some catching up to do.'

'Here already,' Matilda said, shading her eyes as Lisa came to give her a hug. 'We were just talking about you.'

'Now why doesn't that surprise me,' Lisa commented, sinking down next to her mother while blowing a kiss to Amy, who was filling two more glasses with cocktails. Matilda Martin's serene beauty had faded now, but it was plain to see where her daughters, Lisa in particular, got their looks from. 'How's life in the fast lane?' Lisa asked her.

'Hectic,' Matilda sighed. 'I have such a busy social life these days I've had to buy a diary. Do you play bridge?' she asked David.

With a wry smile he said, 'Not yet, but I'll be sure to let you know when I do.'

Apparently pleased with the answer, Matilda gave a small chuckle and picked up her glass.

'I hope you've got the wedding in your diary,' Lisa remarked, helping herself to an olive.

'Oh, I shan't forget that,' her mother assured her. 'Actually, yours isn't the only one that week. Cyril and Florence, you met them at the Easter do, they're tying the knot two days before, would you believe, and wait for this, we girls are having a bit of a hen night next Tuesday.'

Lisa's eyes rounded as she glanced at Amy. 'Please tell me what this hen night entails,' she implored.

With a mischievous gleam, Matilda said, 'We're going to live it up at the Cinema de Lux with a cup of tea after. I don't think we've agreed on which film we're going to see yet. Florence is keen for something a bit risqué, a couple of the others want a horror and the rest of us would rather have a romantic comedy. I suppose it'll depend what's on in the end. Are you planning a hen night, darling? If you are, I'd like to be invited.'

'You'd be top of the list if I was having one, but I probably won't.'

'What about you, David?' Matilda asked. 'Are you having a stag night?'

His eyebrows arched. 'Do you know, I haven't even thought about it,' he confessed, 'so I suppose the answer is no.'

Matilda nodded mildly and picked up her glass again. 'I'm starting to feel a bit squiffy,' she warned Theo.

'Don't worry, I'll be ready to catch you,' he assured her.

Laughing, she sipped her drink and smiled tenderly as she watched Lisa reaching for David's hand. 'So am I allowed to ask about the dress?' she enquired.

'Not in front of David,' Lisa replied, 'but I can promise you it's not a Scarlett O'Hara number, nor will there be a veil.' Experiencing a rush of euphoria as she pictured what it was actually like, she looked at David and wanted to hug him madly for making her so happy.

'What about the honeymoon?' Amy asked. 'Any decisions on that yet?'

'Good question,' David replied. 'You were about to tell me,' he reminded Lisa.

'You mean you aren't surprising her?' Matilda protested.

'I would if I could decide where to take someone who's been everywhere. It's best that she chooses, preferably somewhere she's always wanted to go but hasn't got round to yet.'

Matilda was clearly pleased with the answer. 'There you are, my girl, the world's your oyster, so where will it be?'

'Actually,' Lisa said, 'I'm probably going to surprise you all, because I've been giving it a lot of thought, and it occurred to me that while I've been jetting all over the globe for years, I've never really seen anything of England. So, where I'd like to go for my honeymoon is a place everyone always says is stunning and that I really ought to visit before I die.'

'Which is?' David prompted.

Her eyes were sparkling. 'The Lake District,' she announced.

David blinked, while the others murmured bemused approval, mixed with a suspicion that it might be a joke.

Theo was the first to say, 'It's a great choice.

We've been there several times, and we love it, don't we?'

'Absolutely,' Amy confirmed.

'Have you ever been?' Lisa asked David.

He shook his head. 'Actually, no, I haven't.'

Her smile was dazzling. 'Then we can discover it together, and if it's OK with you I'd rather not have all the fancy five-star Michelin nonsense, because that's how I always travel. I know, I know, I shouldn't complain, and I'm not, but I'd love to go to a place that's just a charming, bijou hotel with sumptuous beds, gorgeous views of a lake and a real sense of . . . of . . . What's the word I'm looking for?'

They all looked at one another and seemed to go blank.

'Intimacy?' Matilda suggested.

'That's it!' and everyone laughed. 'Intimacy,' Lisa repeated softly, looking at David.

His eyes were shining. 'Then the Lake District it shall be,' he said, saluting her with his glass. 'Shall we choose together where we stay, or will you leave it to me?'

She gave it some thought, then leaning forward to kiss him, she said, 'I'm happy to put myself in your hands. I know you won't let me down.'

'No pressure there then,' Theo commented under his breath, and once again everyone laughed.

Chapter Five

It was usual for Miles to stay with Dee when he
came to the constituency, mainly so they could
prepare ahead of time for David's surgeries or
town hall meetings, or whatever other business
was at hand. Tonight, Rosalind had decided to
join them, bringing Lawrence with her, who was
in the next room on Dee's computer. She wasn't
entirely sure what she was hoping to gain from
coming here, apart from a reassurance from Miles,
perhaps, that he too considered Lisa Martin an
extremely bad influence on her father.

So far, though, Miles had hardly committed
himself on anything, which wasn't untypical, but
at least Sally, Rosalind's closest friend, who'd come
along too, loaded up with Lemsips and Kleenex,
hadn't been backward in steering the subject
round to where Rosalind wanted it to be.

'It seems to me,' Sally was saying, her naturally
ruddy cheeks flushed an even deeper colour than
usual, thanks to her lingering flu and the wine,
'that he's so besotted with the woman at the
moment that he's hardly thinking about anything
else.'

'Which would be why he forgot to tell Dee that

Miles was coming at six this evening,' Rosalind pointed out, 'and not at midday, as previously arranged, leaving Dee sitting there at the station wondering what on earth had happened.'

'It was lucky you had your phone turned on,' Dee informed Miles, 'or I'd have been very worried when you didn't get off that train.'

Miles was looking fairly worried himself, but he still didn't comment.

'There's obviously just no getting through to him,' Sally declared, blowing her nose.

'Is anyone trying, that's what I want to know?' Rosalind demanded, fixing her eyes on Miles. 'I'm doing my best, but he's either not listening, or he changes the subject, or he comes out with something threatening and macho, like, "I don't ever want to hear you say that again." He's behaving like an adolescent, going round in a bubble of infatuation and blinding himself to what she's really like, and I'm sorry, but he needs to be told.'

'I have to agree,' Dee said solemnly. 'I've known your father many years now, and he's definitely not himself. And quite frankly, it beggars belief that he'd do something like this to your mother's memory when he's always been such a loyal and sensitive man.'

'All Mum ever wanted was for him to be happy,' Rosalind ran on, 'she even kept telling him that he must get married again, but I know how afraid she was that it would be to *her*. I can't bear to think of how upset she used to get about it. Dad saw it too, and I'm not saying he wasn't sympathetic, or didn't do his best to reassure her, because he did, but then what does he do as soon as Mum dies?'

'I just hope all this strange behaviour isn't going to end up having a detrimental effect on his career,' Dee mumbled.

Speaking at last, Miles said, 'Actually, I think it's already happening.'

Rosalind's eyes sharpened with alarm.

Sweeping back the loose strands of hair that had tumbled over his forehead, he went on, 'Dee's right, there's definitely been a change in him over the last few months. It's becoming quite noticeable now . . . He doesn't seem to be focusing on what you're saying, or he's lost interest in it, or . . . I don't know, it's hard to put into words. It's like he's just not *there* at times. And I'm not the only one who's noticed, because I had a call from no less than the Foreign Secretary on Friday morning, to ask me if David was all right.'

Rosalind's eyes dilated with yet more alarm. 'What made him ask that?'

'Apparently they had dinner together on Thursday night, and Colin thought David seemed a bit, vague was how he put it, about how he wants to go forward during the next parliament. Obviously, I assured him David is more than ready to support him, and to retake his position as Minister, but I don't mind telling you, getting a call like that took me aback a bit.'

'You see,' Rosalind cried, 'she's going to destroy all his chances of making a comeback, and before we know it he'll be lucky to hold on to his seat, never mind joining the front benches. Just thank God I managed to get him to sign the business over to me before she had a chance to get her grasping hands on it, or he could end up with nothing at all.'

'Listen, I know he's well off,' Sally chipped in, 'but it can't have escaped everyone's notice that he's a pretty attractive man, so it's not as if having money and status are his only attributes. I know you won't want to hear this, Ros, but I could easily fancy him myself.'

'You've had too much to drink,' Rosalind snapped at her.

'Actually, I had another call on Friday,' Miles continued gravely. 'I can't say who it was from, but apparently the Foreign Minister who's likely to lose his position in David's favour has been digging up some information about her.'

The atmosphere sparked as this promise of gossip fell into the room like an electric charge. All eyes were on him as he said, 'I'm sorry, I can't reveal anything at this stage, but I can tell you this, if it gets out it's likely to upset the Party, which in turn could do a lot of damage to David's chances of going forward.'

Rosalind sat back in her chair, torn between triumph and worry. 'Does Dad know about this?' she asked.

'Not yet. I have to choose my moment, and I'd appreciate it if you don't mention anything when you speak to him. It's very sensitive and has to be handled in the right way.'

Though they were clearly itching to be told what it was, they all knew better than to press the issue, since Miles's loyalty to David came above everything.

'Just tell me this,' Rosalind said, 'does *she* have any idea Dad's enemies are gunning for her?'

'I can't see how she would,' Miles replied.

'So what's likely to happen next?' Dee asked.

'I don't know, but I'm seeing my source on Tuesday to get an update from that end, and the following morning I've got a meeting scheduled with a couple of David's closest supporters. They have to be told what's going on so we can brainstorm the possible uses the information could be put to. That way we'll be better placed to start working on damage control should it turn out to be necessary.'

There were several moments of silence before it was broken by Lawrence, standing in the doorway. 'Mum, it's eight thirty in the evening, so I have to go to bed.'

Seeing his dear little face so serious and purposeful, Rosalind's expression immediately softened. 'Of course, darling,' she said, getting up to go to him. 'Would you like to stay in your room here, tonight?'

The struggle of having to deal with the unexpected was clear on his face. 'It's eight thirty,' he repeated. 'I have to go to bed.'

'And you have a bed here, at Aunt Dee's, which you know you can use whenever you like.'

His eyes came angrily to hers.

She smiled down at him, but was careful not to touch him.

'How was your fishing with David today?' Dee asked. 'Did you catch anything?'

'No,' he replied flatly, 'but David brought a dog

with him, called Lucy. She was very efficient at fetching sticks.'

Dee smiled. 'How lovely,' she said, glancing at Rosalind to see if she knew who owned the dog.

'Her,' Rosalind whispered. 'OK, darling, off you go. I'll come and check on you in about half an hour. You know where Aunt Dee keeps your spare pyjamas.'

After he'd pounded up the stairs they sat quietly listening to his footsteps clomping above, as their thoughts returned to what had been said before the interruption. In the end Miles's mobile broke the silence.

'I have to take this,' he said, and getting up from the table he walked out on to the patio in order to speak in private.

'One of his many girlfriends?' Sally ventured.

Rosalind shrugged. 'Possibly. Probably.' Though she might share her father's respect and affection for Miles, right now she couldn't be less interested in who he was speaking to, unless it was connected to this new information that had come to light about Lisa Martin. 'What do you think this secret could be?' she said, looking at Dee.

Dee shook her head. 'I guess we won't find out until Miles wants us to,' she replied.

'Well, whatever it is, let's hope it manages to bring Dad to his senses before that damned wedding, because I'm certainly not having any success on that score and God knows I'm trying.'

Lisa was laughing as she and David drove through the early morning sunshine dappling the northern swathe of his constituency. They were on a high after leaving the house, where Brazilian slate slabs were now covering the entrance hall, and a team of painters were already at work in the kitchen and bedrooms. The plumbers were there too, finishing off the heating system for the pool, while the gardeners were a good way through creating the water features that were to cascade down each side of the steps to the courtyard, where they'd tumble over the edges into specially constructed troughs that fed into ponds each side of the garden.

'It really does look as though it's going to be ready in time, doesn't it?' Lisa sighed joyfully. 'Even if it isn't, we'll have to make them sort out something for the day.'

'Of course,' David agreed, 'but you heard what Stanley said, and I've employed that man too many years to start doubting his predictions now.'

Lisa's eyebrows rose. 'Then he's unique as a builder,' she commented, 'because from everything I've heard and experienced they never finish on time. Or on budget.'

'Well, he hasn't let me down yet, and I'm confident he won't over this. He knows how important it is. OK, there might be some finishing touches to do after we've moved in, but you wait and see, every room will be . . .' He broke off and checked his rear-view mirror, even though they were on a straight road with no other traffic around.

'Every room will be . . .' Lisa prompted.

He glanced at her, rapidly trying to pick up what he'd been saying. 'Uh . . . yes, functional by the time August 4th comes round . . .'

'What!' she shrieked. 'Please tell me you're joking.'

He seemed perplexed.

'You're definitely joking,' she decided, 'because I know that *you* know we're getting married on the third. Well, legally it's happening on the second, but the big do, as you well know, is on the third.'

He started to grin. 'I was thinking about the honeymoon,' he told her. 'We're leaving on the fourth, yes?'

'Indeed. Are we driving there?'

'Of course. Now, am I dropping you back at Amy's, or will you come with me?'

With a guilty groan she said, 'Darling, I give you my word, once we're married I'll get involved in constituency business, but for now, not only do I not fancy being faced with your sister-in-law dragging a chilly smile from the depths of her frilly white blouse . . .'

'You've never met her.'

'It's how I imagine her. Is she like Catrina?'

'Actually, hardly at all. She's much more . . . countrified, I think you could call it. Or horsey, maybe, and . . . how do I put this delicately? Not particularly into men. She left her husband for another woman fifteen or more years ago, but the woman ended up running off with another man a couple of years later, and now dear old Dee fills her time with the WI and all sorts of good causes, and her son, Wills, of course, who I'm sure I've already told you about.'

'He's the nephew in Brussels working on his PhD?'

'That's right, and I still have to call him about the wedding. The last time I spoke to him he assured me he and his girlfriend would be coming, but I want to be sure that he doesn't mind about me asking Lawrence to be my best man.'

Lisa broke into a smile. 'I think it's lovely that you've chosen Lawrence,' she told him. 'I still can't quite believe that Rosalind's allowing it.'

He grimaced. 'She hasn't mentioned it since I brought it up,' he confessed, 'but I put it to her while Jerry was there, because I knew she probably wouldn't argue then. And now I'm going to remain hopeful that because it's something special for her son, she'll find it in her to come too.' He checked the offside mirror and began merging into a fast-flowing stream of traffic. 'So, if you're not going to join me for the surgery this morning, what are you going to do?' he asked.

'Amy and I have a tasting to go to at midday,' she reminded him.

'Of course. Which I suppose means you won't be meeting me for lunch?'

Surprised, she said, 'I thought you were going back to London when the surgery's over.'

'I was, but I've decided to stay on another day, because I'd like to spend a little time with Rosalind. I'm worried about her, and I think it would be a good idea to see her again before next weekend.'

Lisa looked at him and smiled. Reaching over to brush the backs of her fingers over his cheek, she decided to let the subject of Rosalind drop.

'Do you mind going back on your own this afternoon?' he asked.

'No, of course not,' she assured him. In fact, having some time to herself this evening would allow her to catch up with a few friends on the phone, and, if possible, to try winkling out of her editor exactly why he wanted to see her tomorrow.

It was past one o'clock by the time David and Miles left the Baptist church in Keynsham where they'd been using the front entrance lobby and one of the vestries for the morning's surgery. Though the room had little ecclesiastical about it, more an air of modern indifference, David still couldn't help feeling at times that he was in a confessional. It was amazing the things some people told him, from marital problems to medical intrigues, criminal plots, and spiritual epiphanies. One dear old man once asked him if it was possible for his wife to continue to vote, even though she was dead, because she was definitely still around, haunting him. Then there was the woman who'd turned up one morning with drawings and mathematical calculations to demonstrate why sleeping policemen strategically placed on the M4 would slow down the speed freaks and reduce accidents.

Most, however, came to seek his support in matters in which they weren't being well served, or to air their views and grievances, or in recent months to offer their condolences, which he had found very touching. No one had turned up yet to congratulate him on his forthcoming nuptials, though he had received a few letters and emails expressing some surprise, and in one case, disgust, at such unseemly haste in rushing back to the altar when his poor dead wife was still so fresh in everyone's minds. Though she was in his too, he had no intention of using this truth as some sort of defence.

This morning's visitors had included an agitated upper-crust woman wanting to vent her frustration with a system that dished out endless benefits to single mothers, so was it any wonder the number of teenage pregnancies was soaring? Another bossy, finger-wagging female expressed outrage at the local council who'd planted the wrong trees on a new housing estate so the roots were now starting to turf out the drains, and was anyone doing anything about it? No, they jolly well were not, so as the local MP it was incumbent on David to sort the matter out, pronto, before they were up to their necks in each other's sewage. The last visitor of the morning had turned out to be a plucky, likeable young chap who'd dropped in to let him know that he was intending to read Government at LSE, as David had, and to suggest that if there was any chance of some work experience he, David, could do a lot worse.

Naturally David had taken a note of the boy's details, which he'd passed on to Dee at the end of the session, along with all his other notes and instructions on how to proceed with each of the cases.

Dee was still at the church now, making sure the place was empty before locking up, but she'd be following on any minute to join them for a bite to eat at the Globe at Newton St Loe.

'How are you getting to the station after lunch?' David was asking Miles as they crossed the main road and started down the alley next to the Old Bank pub.

'Dee's offered,' Miles replied, fishing out his mobile as it started to ring. 'Ah, Tristan,' he declared, referring to one of the researchers. 'About time too.'

As he took the call David strode on into the car park to find his Mercedes standing out like royalty at a jumble sale amongst all the old Fords and Vauxhalls belonging to the pub's patrons. It was a stark reminder of why he generally let Dee drive him to constituency events in her old Volvo, because flaunting his wealth in the face of voters was a singularly insensitive and unpleasant way to behave.

After removing his jacket, he was just thinking about calling Lisa when he realised that the key he was using to open the car was refusing to go in the lock. He checked to make sure it was the right one and tried again, but it still wouldn't fit.

Starting to get annoyed, he attempted to force it in but there was simply no way it would go.

Gritting his teeth he tried a different key, but that wasn't any good either. Unable to believe it, he stood back to get a good look at the car. There was no doubt it was his, *The Times* was on the back seat where he'd dropped it earlier, and so was the pile of catalogues Lisa had given him to take back to London.

Feeling more frustration starting to boil up inside him he tried the keys again, and when they still wouldn't work he completely lost it. 'What the hell is going on?' he raged as Miles came up behind him. 'I can't open the damned car.'

Miles blinked in surprise as he looked at the keys. 'Where's the remote?' he asked cautiously.

David's face was rigid as he turned to him. 'The keys won't fit,' he seethed furiously, as though somehow it was Miles's fault.

'But you don't usually . . .' Miles began. Then, 'Shall I give them a go?'

Slapping them into Miles's hand David stood aside, so angry now that he was tempted to drive a fist into the bloody car – or Miles, if he somehow succeeded where he had ridiculously failed.

Miles glanced at the keys, then at David. 'These aren't for the car,' he said, almost apologetically.

David glared at him.

Swallowing drily, Miles asked, 'Do you have the ones with the remote control?'

Feeling his temper surging back to fever pitch, David thrust his jacket at Miles and began patting his shirt and trouser pockets so hard it hurt.

'They're not here,' Miles said, after checking the jacket. 'You must have left them at the church. I'll go and see.'

As Miles ran back across the car park David dropped his head in his hands, the ferocity of his temper abating now almost as quickly as it had flared. Why the heck had he flown off the handle like that? They were just keys for God's sake, and so he'd made a mistake. It happened. He had a lot on his mind, and for some bizarre reason he'd momentarily forgotten that he had a remote control to open the car doors. Yet how could he have forgotten when it was something he did every day without even thinking? And he never used to get angry over trivial things, or worked up about issues that could easily be resolved, so what the hell was going on with his tolerance level? He had to get a grip on himself, because outbursts like that just weren't acceptable, or indeed rational. And when he added them to the feelings of anxiety he'd been suffering over all sorts of things lately, such as how far he wanted to take his career, and whether Lisa would still want him if he chose to remain a backbench MP, or even if he was actually ready to get married again, he could really start to think he was losing the plot. Where on earth was it all coming from? It wasn't as if he doubted his feelings for her, or hers for him. At least, he was sure of them most of the time, but he couldn't deny there were moments, like now, when for no logical reason he found himself in an odd place of disorientation and even insecurity, as though he'd somehow fallen out of kilter with himself, never mind his own life.

None of it was making any sense. He was losing a grip on what he was thinking, and even feeling, and whenever he asked himself why it could be, his mind immediately began charging off past all common sense and reason to plunge headlong over the horizon into a nightmare of imagined possibilities.

Taking a deep breath, he lifted his head and stared across the car park to where Dee and Miles were hurrying towards him. Seeing how worried they looked, he quickly pulled himself together, assuming the kind of self-mocking smile they knew well as he held out a hand to take the keys Miles was dangling ready to drop into it.

'Dee found them on the desk,' Miles told him. 'They must have been under some paperwork or something, and you didn't notice when you picked it up.'

Assuming an even greater irony, David said, 'Well, hopefully they'll get me into the flat when I return to London.'

Miles's laugh rang awkwardly as he glanced at Dee, who was still looking perplexed.

'Come on then,' David said cheerily, 'let's go and eat, shall we? I don't know about you two, but I'm starving,' and using the remote to flip up the locks he got into the car, ready to drive away.

'Are you all right?' Amy asked, bringing the car to a stop outside Bristol Parkway station. 'You've been very quiet since we left the caterer's. Are you having second thoughts about him?'

Lisa smiled as she looked at her. 'No, I loved what he gave us today, didn't you? And his testimonials are very impressive.'

'So you're definitely going with him?'

'Absolutely. I told him so before we left. Didn't you hear me?'

'I was on the phone, remember?' Amy glanced at the time. 'It's another twenty minutes before the next train, and I'm not in a rush, so come on, what's really going on with you? You're hiding something from me, and I want to know what it is.'

Lisa sighed and let her head fall back. 'It's nothing really,' she said. 'I just . . . I don't know.'

'Lisa,' Amy said in a tone Lisa knew well.

Turning to her, Lisa said, 'OK, tell me this, does David seem all right to you?'

Amy's eyebrows rose in surprise. 'What on earth do you mean?'

'I'm not sure. Well, I suppose I keep wondering if the stress of everything is starting to get to him a bit. I told him a month ago, when he decided we should get married in August, that it was all too soon, but he wouldn't listen. He wants to do it then, and that's that.'

'Are you saying that you don't?'

'No, not at all. Most of the time I can hardly wait, but actually there's no particular reason to rush, and if we were to postpone everything by a year maybe that would be enough time for Rosalind to come around, and if she did . . .'

'Hang on, hang on. You can't let her rule your lives,' Amy protested. 'You want this wedding as much as David does.'

'I know, but think how we'd have felt if Mum had raced off up the aisle with someone else less than a year after Dad went. We wouldn't have liked it very much, would we?'

'Probably not, but if it was what she wanted, and he was a good man, we'd have found a way to live with it.'

'That's just it. I definitely don't think Rosalind sees me as "good".'

Turning in her seat, Amy said, 'Listen, David will find a way of dealing with his daughter, and in the meantime all you have to do is focus on the wedding, because it's going to be an absolutely wonderful day. You'll be the most beautiful bride. He'll be the proudest man alive. All your closest friends and family will be there cheering you on. The musicians and the minister are flying in from all over to make it special for you, and as far as I'm concerned, you couldn't deserve it more. So promise me you're not going to let anything, or anyone, spoil it for you, particularly not her.'

Lisa smiled and squeezed Amy's hand. 'OK, I promise,' she whispered, in spite of knowing that she was no more able to control Rosalind than Amy was.

Rosalind was sitting at the kitchen table with the contents of her father's briefcase laid out in front of her. There had been such a fuss before he'd left this morning, trying to find his car keys, which had finally turned up in Lawrence's room, that after dumping his holdall and some files on the back seat of the car, he'd promptly managed to go off without his briefcase. This, coming hot on the heels of the peculiar incident yesterday that Dee had told her about, when he'd tried to use his front-door keys to open the Mercedes, was yet further proof, to her mind, of the state of agitation Lisa Martin had worked him into over weddings and new houses and God only knew what other kinds of demands she was making, when what he should really be doing was dealing with his grief.

He did feel it, didn't he? Surely he must.

Naturally, she'd called him the minute she'd found the briefcase on the drive, but by then he was already halfway up the M4, so she was now waiting for a courier to come and collect it.

She'd enjoyed having him to stay last night. For once they'd managed to spend some time together without it descending into bitterness or tears, but that was only because they'd made a pact on the phone before he turned up that they wouldn't discuss his girlfriend, or the wedding. She'd told him she didn't want him to come if it was only to talk about her, but he'd assured her that all he wanted was to make sure they were friends before he returned to London – and to be certain that she knew he'd never allow anything to come between them.

Quite how he was going to manage that when he seemed so determined to marry the Martin woman, Rosalind had no idea. However, since Miles had revealed the fact that some new information had come to light which could change things quite radically, she'd been feeling a little more hopeful that her father was going to be brought to his senses long before the fateful day dawned.

Then, only moments ago, her confidence had faltered badly and was now draining away as she gazed down at everything shc'd taken out of his briefcase. She knew she shouldn't have gone looking, but she hadn't been able to stop herself, and the card she'd found that he'd written, but not yet sent, was so romantic that she knew, had it been meant for her, from Jerry, it would have made her the happiest woman alive.

On the front in an uneven red foil script were four lines, one above the other: *I love you for ever; je t'aime; my one and only; love of my life.* Inside, in his own hand, was, *You make me so happy, my darling. I wonder by my troth, what thou and I did till we loved.*

Rosalind had no idea which poet he was quoting, but it hardly mattered. Simply to think of her mother, and how little she seemed to mean to him now, filled her heart with so much sadness she could hardly bear it. It was as though his marriage had faded into a distant background, leaving no more than a vague imprint on his memory that he barely even looked at now. All he could see was *her.* More than thirty years of

marriage, bringing up a child, building a business, sharing dreams, seeing one another through
the bad times, and being there for each other in
ways that made two people one, were rendered
nothing by this card.

It wasn't hard for her to imagine how her
mother would feel were she able to see it, because
Rosalind knew what it was like to feel insecure
in a husband's love. That her dear, kind, wonderful
mother who'd absolutely adored her father should
have suffered those terrible feelings too was even
worse than having gone through it herself.

'Your father's a good man,' her mother had said
weakly during the days before she'd finally let go.
'He stood by me, and you . . . He's always been
there for us, always, and I know he'll never let
you down, because he loves you very much. You
mean everything to him, Rosalind, far more than
I ever did.'

But she had meant something to him, Rosalind
was sure of it, and more than just something,
because he'd loved her too. *He did, Mum, he really
did, and he's lost without you, I just know it.*

As more tears trickled down her cheeks, Rosalind
screwed up the card and let it drop to the floor
where she squashed it underfoot. He might wonder
what had happened to it, but she didn't care. Let
him think he'd lost it, the way he had his keys this
morning . . . The pretence of what had happened
then twisted the grief inside her to a point that
made her sob out loud. He'd blamed himself for
being careless, saying he must have put them down
when he'd gone to say goodnight to Lawrence, but
they'd both known that it was much more likely

that Lawrence had hidden them, because he didn't want him to leave. To think of Lawrence feeling deeply enough to do something like that was tearing at her in a way that almost nothing else ever could. He showed so little emotion, gave almost nothing of himself, yet something in him had connected with her father, and because of that, and because she loved them both so much, she must pray to God that she was never forced to deliver an ultimatum to her father. If she did, and he chose *her*, what on earth would she and Lawrence do?

Chapter Six

'What the hell are you doing here?' Lisa cried in shock.

There was only one person in the world she'd ever have greeted like that and she really didn't want to believe he was sitting there now, grinning up at her in the way he'd always considered devilish, as though he had every right to be at this table in Gordon Ramsay's Claridge's, when as far as she was concerned it was Brendan who should be there, and if not Brendan then anyone, *anyone* but the man she was glaring at.

Tony Sommerville rose to his feet and before she could stop him he'd swept her into a crushing embrace. 'It's wonderful to see you too,' he told her, giving a wink to the waiter. 'God, I've missed you.'

'Let me go,' she said through her teeth.

'Did you say champagne?' he asked, tilting his tousled dark head to one side. 'Great idea. Should have thought of it before, cos this is certainly cause for celebration. Make that a bottle of the best,' he told the waiter. 'Pink,' he added, 'the lady has always had a preference for it, and I don't imagine that's changed.' Then before the waiter could beat him to it, he pulled out a chair for her to sit down.

Since her legs had gone weak with shock she hit the seat with an unladylike thud. 'Where is Brendan?' she demanded, as Tony returned to his own chair, his familiar style of waistcoat and collarless shirt over jeans stirring memories that instantly annoyed her for the way they were trying to evoke a fondness that had no more business at this table than he did. Then, getting a picture of what had happened, how he'd come to be here, she said, 'No, don't bother answering that. This is obviously a set-up. You talked him into it ... I'd forgotten how far back you two go. What a *fool*. Why didn't I see this coming?'

Tony's chin was resting on one hand as he grinned at her lovingly.

'Don't look at me like that,' she hissed, glancing round to see if anyone might be watching.

Slapping his own face for misbehaving, he straightened his expression while completely failing to douse the merriment in his eyes. Tall and dark he certainly was, but hardly classically handsome, since his lazy blue eyes were too narrow, his beaky nose was boxed crooked, and his smile ... Well, she had to admit it had a tendency to come good there, because it was as dazzling and captivating as ever, damn it to hell.

Angered by how flustered she was, she said, too fiercely, 'I'll ask again, what are you doing here?'

'You know,' he replied, seeming puzzled, 'before you came, I was trying to work out how long it's been since we last saw each other. Can it really be three years since you walked out without as much as a goodbye?'

Her eyes widened with amazement. That certainly wasn't how she remembered it. However, it wasn't a subject she cared to get into, so rather than grace his question with an answer she merely stared at him hard, waiting for him to explain the reason for this subterfuge. Her heart had only performed the ungainly somersault it had when she'd first seen him out of habit, or shock, she assured herself. Probably both.

'I'm here,' he said, 'to save you from yourself.'

She started. 'What?'

Perfectly mildly, he said, 'When I heard you were getting married . . . Well, you and I both know that you're not cut out for it, Lisa. You're looking stunning, by the way, and how old will you be next birthday?'

Torn between wanting to slap him and getting up and walking out, she heard herself saying, 'Forty, the same as you, but clearly only one of us is wearing well.'

Apparently enjoying her riposte, he sat back as the waiter turned up with the champagne, and nodded approval when he was shown the label.

Though sorely tempted to refuse a glass, if only to take that smug look off his face, she wasn't going to leave before finding out what this was really about – or before making it abundantly clear that she did not appreciate him waltzing back into her life unannounced like this. In fact, the day had finally dawned when she didn't want him back in her life at all, so if he had any thoughts in his head about staying he could banish them right now.

When their glasses were full and the waiter had gone, Tony lifted his, and touching it to hers he smiled into her eyes as he said, 'Here's to us.'

The gall of him! Feeling her hand itching again, she said, sweetly, 'To old friends and moving on.'

He seemed to find that amusing, and kept his gaze on hers as he took a sip of his drink. 'So, I'm an old friend, am I?' he said. 'Is that what you've told David about me?'

Bristling, as though he had no right even to mention David's name, she said, 'What makes you think I've told him about you at all?'

He cocked a curious eyebrow. 'Have you?'

Not wanting to get into his banter, she said briskly, 'As a matter of fact, I have. He knows you and I were together, on and off – more off than on – for about ten years, and that we're no longer in touch.'

His frown was baffled. 'I remember it as more on than off,' he told her, 'but hey, that's me. I was always the more romantic one, whereas you ... Well, let's just say the words commitment-phobe and manic independence spring first to mind.'

'That was with you, Tony. David's ... Well, David's ...' She was struggling desperately to come up with something that wouldn't sound corny.

'Different?' he suggested helpfully.

'He's certainly different to you.'

He nodded agreeably. 'Your first true love.'

'Indeed he was. How do you know that?'

He seemed surprised. 'Because you told me. Several times, as I recall.'

Flushing slightly, she said, 'Well, I'm sorry if I

110

repeated myself, but it's true. David is the big love of my life.'

He shook his head. 'No, no. First love, I'll accept, or current, or even last if I have to, but we both know that the real big love of your life was – *is*, as we're both still motoring around the mortal coil – yours truly.'

Her jaw dropped as outrage almost rendered her speechless. 'Well, you really do flatter yourself,' she said bitingly. If only she could come up with something to really cut him down to size. She probably would – long after this was over.

'As you, my darling,' he drawled, 'are very definitely the big love of mine.'

Having seen that coming, she affected a bored roll of her eyes as she said, 'Of course, and this would be why you uttered not a single word of protest when I told you it was over between us.'

He looked at her in amazement. 'What was there left to say?' he cried helplessly. 'You wouldn't marry me, or even live full-time under the same roof as me, and God knows I asked you enough times. I wanted to have children with you, dogs and cats, fairies on the Christmas tree . . . I wanted everything you did, but you'd never believe me, until in the end I had to let you go, if only for the sake of my own sanity. Do you know how crazy you drive a bloke?'

'Stop talking like Crocodile Dundee,' she snapped. 'And if you were being completely honest you'd admit that the real reason you didn't try to make me stay was because you were too ashamed to after very cleverly getting yourself locked up for money-laundering.'

He grimaced awkwardly. 'But it was all a mistake,' he reminded her. 'They never even pressed charges.'

'No doubt because someone bought off the Filipino police.'

'Not true. The money in question had all been legitimately acquired, which my lawyer was able to prove. Surely you must remember that.'

Though she did, she still wasn't convinced the affair had been as above board as either he or his very dubious lawyer had managed to make out. Still, what mattered was that he had regained his freedom, and though the incident had proved the final straw for her, she had to admit she still couldn't be entirely certain she'd have ended up leaving if he'd begged her not to.

'So what are you doing now?' she asked, deciding to steer them off those particular rocks. 'Who's the unlucky woman these days? I know there's sure to be one. Actually, the last I heard you were living with a stripper in Singapore.'

He laughed delightedly. 'Actually, she was an ex-dancer from the Moulin Rouge in Paris,' he corrected, 'and we were living in Senegal, but I understand how these things can get mixed up in translation.'

Her expression remained sceptical. 'So where is she now?'

'As far as I know, still there. We don't keep in touch. I always feel that once something's over, it's over, don't you?'

Knowing how much he'd love her to rise to that, she simply ignored it, and turned to the waiter who'd come to take their order.

'Actually, we haven't looked yet,' Tony told him, 'but I'm sure it won't take a moment,' and after making a quick scan of the set-lunch options he ordered for them both and handed the menu back.

'Did it happen to occur to you that I might have liked to choose for myself?' she asked as the waiter disappeared.

'It did, but then I remembered how you used to love it when I was masterful, so I thought, hey, Tone, why not impress her and show her you can still pull it off.'

Drowning a laugh by taking another sip of her drink, she said, 'So where are you living these days?'

Appearing pleased she'd asked, he said, 'The Cotswolds.'

She almost choked.

'And very pleasant it is too,' he added.

She was shaking her head. 'No, I'm sorry . . .'

'It's true,' he insisted. 'I'm now a very respectable bloke – chap – fellow – whatever you want to call me. Got myself a tidy little pile, I have, not too far from Stroud, and a regular upstanding member of the community I am too.' His hand went up like a stop sign. 'Before you say anything smutty, let me remind you you've never appreciated coarse jokes, so please don't be disappointing or embarrassing yourself now over my upstanding member.'

Trying very hard not to laugh, she said, 'And how exactly did you come by this pile? Actually, don't tell me, you won it in Vegas.'

He squinted. 'Not quite. Monte Carlo.'

She regarded him knowingly. 'And how long, I wonder, before you lose it the same way?'

'Not going to happen. Like I said, reformed character, pillar of the parish. I've even got myself a thriving little business.'

Her eyebrows rose. 'Doing what, precisely?'

He glowed with pride. 'You are looking, my sweetheart, at a gen-u-ine dealer of antiquities complete with shop, stock and toffs on tap.'

She blinked. 'But you don't know the first thing about antiques.'

'You know, it's odd,' he said, frowning, 'but I really haven't found that to be too much of a problem.'

Laughing, in spite of herself, she watched a waiter refill their glasses, and waited until they were alone again to say, 'Did you really win the "pile" – if it exists – in Vegas?'

'It exists, and it was Monte Carlo.'

She waited for him to answer the question.

'All right, I'll come clean, I inherited it from my old granny.'

With a sigh she said, 'You know, I might find that easier to believe if you had an old granny.'

His expression was solemn. 'Well, of course I don't any more,' he said. 'She passed on a couple of years ago, and it turns out her favourite grandson – namely *moi* – was sole beneficiary.'

She still wasn't buying it. 'How come I never knew about this granny?' she challenged.

'Even as you ask, I'm trying to puzzle it out,' he confessed, 'and my only answer is that a bloke, chap, dude, whatever you want to call me, has to have some secrets, or next thing you know he'll have lost his mystery. And as we know a chap etc. without mystery is like a chap without *cojones*. No good to anyone, least of all himself.' He treated her to one of his more dazzling smiles, then in a way only he could, he moved the subject on by saying, 'Now, tell me, how's the lovely Waltzing Matilda? I always adored that woman. Still do, as a matter of fact.'

Her eyes narrowed. 'For some peculiar reason the feeling was mutual, but happily my mother is over you now.'

He grinned. 'Which is, hopefully, more than we can say for you.'

Deciding to ignore him again, she smiled pleasantly at the waiter as he delivered their first course – spring onion and broad bean risotto with pea shoot salad.

'So,' Tony said, after approving the first mouthful, 'you're going to be a politician's wife.'

She didn't bother to answer, since it was neither a question nor any of his business.

'Is he very much older than you?'

'Not really, and anyway, it's none of your business.'

'My sources tell me,' he continued, unstoppable as ever, 'that he's set for great things. So who knows, we could be seeing you on the doorstep of Number 10 one of these days. What a lucky fellow he'd be, all that power, wealth, fame, the whole nine thousand yards and you. You really would be at the top then, my girl.'

Feeling suddenly angry, and oddly protective

of David, she said, 'As a matter of fact it makes not the slightest bit of difference to me what he does, it's him I want to be with, not his job.'

Tony appeared surprised. 'You know, I actually think you mean it.'

As darkly as she could, she said, 'Of course I do.'

'So if he wasn't who he is . . .'

'If he gave up politics tomorrow and decided to become a farmer, or a postman, or a . . . *an antiques dealer* that would be fine by me.'

'Just as long as he has shedloads of cash?'

She sat back, furious and offended. 'Since when did you acquire such a cynical opinion of me?' she demanded. 'You know very well that I've never been a gold-digger, or a power freak.'

'This is true. Just a heartbreaker.'

She took a breath, and let her anger out slowly. 'I won't bother reminding you,' she said deliberately, 'that it actually happened the other way round, and more than once.'

He was shaking his head. 'Not true, because I have never been anything less than mad about you, Lisa, and unluckily for me, by the sound of it, I don't think that's ever going to change. In fact, do you know what my big regret is?'

'No, and nor do I want to.'

'It's that we never had kids, because if we had I swear we'd still be together.'

'No, what we'd be is constantly fighting over custody rights or maintenance or, more likely, how the hell I managed to let you talk me into it when I should have known that I'd be the one left at home taking care of everything, while you carried on gallivanting around the globe.'

His voice was tender as he said, 'You always wanted them.'

Swallowing hard on the disappointment that it had never happened, while reminding herself that if it had she probably wouldn't be with David now, she said, 'You know, I really don't want to have this conversation. What happened between us is in the past, and the fact that we seem to have very different views of it now really doesn't matter. I've moved on, and so, I hope, have you.'

He looked chastened. 'I see. So what you're saying is, you don't have any feelings for me at all now?'

'None whatsoever,' she confirmed. 'In fact, I never even think about you.'

He looked crushed.

'Ever,' she added.

He put down his fork. 'So really I might just as well save my breath and leave?'

She waved a hand towards the door. 'Be my guest – which is not me offering to pay the bill, and if you leave me with it I swear I'll find your antiques shop and burn it to the ground.'

His eyes came alive again. 'It might almost be worth it,' he declared.

Since he wasn't showing any signs of leaving, she continued to eat, knowing he was watching her, but deliberately not engaging either with him or with the feelings he was triggering inside her, because she knew from long experience how false they could be.

Finally, a waiter came to clear their plates, and by the time their glasses had been topped up the next course was being presented – sautéed fillets of Rye Bay plaice, razor clams, pickled baby carrots and coriander velouté.

'Delish,' he commented.

'Good choice,' she agreed after tasting it.

After taking another mouthful, he said, 'Do you know what I'm doing right now?'

In spite of knowing she should not be going along with this, she said, 'You mean apart from eating?'

'I'm trying to say I'm happy for you,' he told her, 'but I confess, I'm not finding it easy.'

'Your happiness is not a requirement,' she assured him, as smoothly as if she meant it, which she did, to a point.

Instead of laughing, as she'd expected, he appeared to consider the comment for a while, then finally nodded.

Rather than allow his contemplation of her life to go any further, she said, 'Why don't you try telling me the real reason you've tricked me into coming here?'

'But I already have,' he reminded her. 'I don't believe you're cut out for marriage – that is, to anyone but me.'

Feeling her temper rising, she said, 'And you have chosen to acquaint me with your ludicrous delusions now because?'

'It's still not too late for you to change your mind.'

At that her fork hit the plate. 'Listen to me,' she said hotly, while trying to keep her voice down, 'I have absolutely no intention of changing my mind either now, or at any time in the future. This is what I want, it's what David wants too, and in less than six weeks I will be his wife.'

His own fork clinked more gently against his plate. 'You know, I have a horrible feeling you mean it.'

'Believe it.'

He nodded for quite a while. 'So,' he said in the end, 'is there any chance of being invited to this wedding?'

Amazed that he'd even want to be, and deeply suspicious of his motives, she said, 'About as much chance as you winning another pile in Vegas.'

'Monte Carlo.'

'Wherever.' Then because she still, probably insanely, had a fondness for him, and quite possibly always would, she swallowed her anger and used a gentler tone as she said, 'Please don't try to spoil this for me. David's a wonderful man and what we have together is very special . . . It's something you and I never managed to find and no matter how long we stayed together we probably never would.'

He spent a moment trying to puzzle it out, but in the end he had to ask.

'Trust,' she told him. 'I don't think I realised how much it mattered until I finally found it. We never trusted each other, Tony, or I never trusted you. I had no idea where you were half the time, or who you were with, or what ludicrous or borderline scam you might come up with next.'

'Project,' he corrected. 'I'm not keen on the word scam.'

For some reason that made her laugh, and resisting the urge to put her hand on his she said, 'OK, project – and by the way . . .'

His eyes came to hers.

'I lied just now. I do think of you sometimes.'

Though he smiled, it didn't last long. 'I'm finding this hard,' he told her, 'but I don't expect you to believe that.'

'If it's true, it'll be because you know you can't have me any more. No, listen,' she said, as he made to protest. 'If I walked away from David now to become Mrs Antique Dealer of the Cotswolds, you know very well that within a matter of weeks you'd be shipping out to Sydney or Sierra Leone or some other hot spot with bizarre-adventure potential.'

He cocked an eyebrow. 'Try me.'

'No. Apart from anything else, I'd never do it to David.'

'That doesn't sound a good enough reason.'

'There are others.'

'So you really do love him?'

She nodded. 'Really, I do, and be honest with yourself, if you hadn't found out about him now another three years or more would have gone by before you came looking for me again, and I'm not even sure you would then.'

He sighed and sat back in his chair. 'Well, you're wrong about that,' he told her, 'because the whole Cotswolds/antique thing was a *project* to show you that I really can settle down and live a normal life – if it's what you want, and I'm still not entirely convinced it is. But OK, let's not go there. It took me a while to get it all up and running, and now,' he sighed again, 'seems I'm too damned late.'

Wishing he wasn't able to pull on her heart-strings quite so effectively, she said, 'You'll find someone else. You always do.'

His eyes came to hers, and after a beat, because he was starting to get to her, she had to look away.

More long moments ticked by until at last she said, 'I think I should probably go now.'

When he didn't object she replaced her napkin on the table and picked up her bag. 'I'll be having words with Brendan about this,' she said, trying to lighten the moment with an attempt at humour.

'Don't be too hard on him,' he responded, standing up with her. 'He's a good guy.'

Coming round the table, he pulled her into a far more tender embrace than he had at the start. 'If anything should go . . . Well, if you ever find yourself . . .'

She knew what he was trying to say and wished he wouldn't.

'I have a card these days,' he finally managed. 'That's a first, wouldn't you say?'

Smiling as he put one in her hand, she said, 'It was lovely to see you. You know I wish you well, don't you?'

He nodded, and she couldn't be sure, but he seemed to swallow a lump in his throat. 'Listen, I'm sorry about your job,' he said, 'but hey, I guess you don't really need it now anyway.'

She frowned. 'I'm on a sabbatical,' she told him.

His eyes stayed on hers for a moment, then seeming to realise he'd put his foot in it, he gave a groan of despair. 'Brendan said . . . Oh hell, I don't know what he said, but I felt sure he'd told you . . .'

'Tony, what do you know that I don't?'

Clearly feeling worse by the second, he said, 'Apparently, the magazine's folding at the end of

October. With all the Internet stuff and everything now, they can't afford to keep it going any longer than that.'

'I see,' she said, feeling a rush of blood pounding in her head. That it was happening at all was bad enough, that she should be finding out like this . . . 'I obviously need to speak to Brendan,' she said, and quickly assuming a smile to try and cover how shaken she was, she planted a brief kiss on his cheek, and left.

By the time she returned to the flat she'd managed to get Brendan on the phone, but evidently not before Tony had, because it was clear from the outset that Brendan was ready for her call.

'Sweetie, I'm sorry, I'm sorry. I blame myself for you finding out that way,' he groaned apologetically. 'I should have made it clearer to Tony that I hadn't had a chance to talk to you yet. He's feeling terrible now, so am I. What can we do to make it up to you?'

'Nothing,' she'd said brutally, and because she was in the street and unwilling to vent her anger in public, she'd taken great pleasure in cutting him off.

To say this unexpected development in her career had thrown her a curve was an understatement greater than any she'd yet come across. That she'd learned about it from Tony Sommerville, who'd had the insufferable nerve to sweep in out of the blue like some B-movie hero in order to 'rescue her from herself' – *goddamn him* – was so mind-blowing that she was finding it very hard to make herself think straight.

She started to pace the room, stopped and started again. She had to find another job, she'd get on to it right away: the fact that her income flow had just been tourniqueted was already starting to feel like a physical amputation. It didn't matter that David was well off, and would no doubt tell her not to worry because he'd take care of everything. What mattered was that for as long as she could remember she'd always earned enough to take care of herself. 'Manically independent' Tony had called her and for once in his life he was right, because her liberty, self-determination, freedom to choose, be, exist, or even breathe, come to that, had always been in her own hands. In fact, her independence was as fundamental a part of her as her personality, so without it she simply wouldn't be herself any more.

She was standing in the middle of the sitting room now, staring at her reflection in the mirror over the mantel. She looked harassed, dishevelled and *lost*, she thought with a chill. 'I'm scared,' she admitted to herself.

'I *have* to be able to take care of myself financially,' she told Amy when she got her on the line, 'if I can't I'll . . . Well, I don't know what I'll do, because I'm not the type to be a full-time housewife. I don't do jams and flower-arranging and jumble sales . . .'

'For God's sake, he's an MP, not a vicar,' Amy laughed when she managed to get a word in.

'But that's what it'll be like,' Lisa insisted. 'I'll have to immerse myself in the local community, organising all their fun runs and pony shows and barn dances, and I honestly don't think I'm

123

equipped for it. I mean, I know it's all worthy stuff and everything, but it's going to turn me into one of those do-gooders who gets on everyone's nerves, or – oh my God, a *Brown Owl!*'

Amy was still laughing. 'You don't think you might be overreacting, by any chance?' she suggested drily.

Lisa wasn't entirely sure. 'All I know,' she said, less hysterically now, 'is that everything's suddenly looking very different to the way it was a couple of hours ago. I'm not even sure who I am without my job, but I do know I need to be my own person. I can't exist in someone else's shadow, not even David's. I'm sorry if that sounds egotistical, but it's how I feel.'

'Have you told David about this yet?' Amy asked.

'I can't. He's doing an interview with *The Times* at the moment and then he's got wall-to-wall meet-ings all day before going to give a talk at some dinner tonight. I'm not expecting to see him until much before midnight.' She took a gulp of air and braced herself for Amy's reaction to what was coming next. 'Actually, there's something else I haven't told you,' she confessed. 'I saw Tony earlier. We had lunch together . . .'

'Lisa, please tell me you don't mean Tony Sommerville.'

Lisa grimaced. 'I wish I could.'

There was a silence, during which she could only imagine her sister doing her Zen centring thing, because Amy's tone was more controlled than angry when she eventually said, 'OK. So how did it come about? And if you tell me you contacted that man now that everything's going so well for you, I swear . . .'

'Let me answer, will you?' Lisa cried.

'Right. I'm listening.'

Lisa attempted her own Zen thing, but couldn't take long with Amy waiting. 'I saw him,' she said deliberately, 'because he worked on Brendan to make it happen. It had nothing to do with me. I had no idea he was going to be there when I went for lunch. Anyway, the point is, he said some things that I think . . . Well, I'm starting to wonder if there's a chance he might be right. Maybe I'm not cut out to be someone's wife . . .'

'Oh for God's sake, I'm not listening to this,' Amy snapped. 'I thought you'd finally reached a point in your life where that man's influence had died with all the promises he never kept.'

'I have. It has. But it doesn't change the fact that . . . Oh hell, I don't know what it doesn't change. I'm all over the place here.'

'Then let me tell you what it doesn't change. It doesn't change the fact that David is a wonderful, generous, honourable and trustworthy man who you're extremely lucky to have back in your life, and who you love more now than you ever did, and who you're going to marry in less than six weeks.'

Lisa felt bludgeoned. 'Am I?'

'You are.'

Lisa took a breath. 'Amy, I know you won't want to hear this, but I'm starting to wonder if I really want to go through with it all. I swear, it has nothing to do with Tony. It's just that I need to *work* . . .'

'No, what you need,' Amy interrupted, 'is to get over the shock of today, and then discuss what's happened with David. You never know, he might have some great ideas about where you can go, professionally I mean, from here.'

'I can't work for him,' Lisa cried, as though it were already on offer.

'So what are you going to do? Throw it all away and run off with Tony Sommerville again?'

'No. I'd never do that. David's definitely the one I want. It's just . . . It's kind of . . . Oh, hell, I don't know what it is.'

'I'd suggest, out of perspective now you've seen Tony.'

'Probably, but Amy, I have to be honest . . . I don't even want to admit this to myself, especially not today of all days, with Tony suddenly back on the scene, but David's . . . It's hard to put it into words, but he's not really like I thought he was going to be. I mean, you're right, he's gorgeous and kind and all the things you said and that I remember about him, but . . .'

'Lisa, stop this. You're trying to talk yourself out of something that we both know you want more than anything.'

'You're right, I do, but you have to agree with me, Amy, David's not as . . . Well, I suppose as exciting or dynamic as I'd expected him to be. He always used to be, but he's changed in ways . . .'

'He's *older*, Lisa. We all are, and over the years most of us have grown up, including David. It's only people like Tony Sommerville who stay the same, and do you really need me to remind you what an emotional basket case you were practically the whole time you were with him?'

'No, of course not, and I swear there's no way I want to go back there again. This really isn't about him. More than anything it's about my job . . .'

'Which you weren't even due to restart until next May, so you have all the time in the world to find another. You're Lisa Martin, remember? You have a well-respected name in travel and journalism, so it's hardly going to be difficult. Anyway, I thought you were going to write a book.'

'I am. At least I was until today, but I'll have to get my employment situation sorted out before I can even think about it now.'

With a sigh Amy said, 'Listen, I get how much your independence means to you – how can it not when you've always had it? Losing it would be like losing your sight, or your hearing . . . Well, maybe not as bad as that, but I do understand, honestly, and so will David. There's no way in the world he's going to try and get you to join the WI, or sit at home all day thinking up new recipes for Christmas cake.'

At last Lisa felt herself starting to smile. 'No, I guess not,' she conceded, 'but I . . .'

'No more buts. Give yourself a break and stop trying to paint yourself into a future that is never going to exist. OK?'

'OK.'

'Good. Now, before you go, tell me how you've left it with Tony? Please let the answer be, I'm never seeing him again.'

With a brief feeling of regret, but only for old

times' sake, Lisa said, 'I certainly have no plans to. We ended on a friendly note, well, sort of, but I made it perfectly clear that there's no going back for us and I'm pretty sure he got the message.'

'Mm,' Amy grunted sceptically, 'from what I know of that man, he only gets what he wants to get. Did you find out what he's doing these days?'

Wincing at the improbability of it, Lisa said, 'He's an antique dealer, apparently.'

Amy gave a cry of laughter. 'Yeah right, and I'm a jockey. Do you know where he's living?'

Deciding it was probably best not to mention the Cotswolds, with them being in the next county, Lisa said, 'He says he's staying in some relative's house somewhere. I didn't really get into it.'

'Well, as we know, wherever he is this week, he'll more than likely be gone by next. Thank goodness. Now comes the all-important question, do you think you still have feelings for him?'

Aware of her heart contracting a little as she turned to meet her eyes in the mirror, Lisa said truthfully, 'I'll probably always have some, but thankfully, they're nothing like they used to be.'

'I'm relieved to hear it. So all this nonsense about not being sure about David has nothing to do with wanting to go back to Tony?'

'Absolutely not.' She was quite certain about that. 'You're right, I was overreacting to everything just now.'

'Which was really only to be expected when you'd just been dealt a double whammy, Tony Sommerville and redundancy, plus we mustn't forget that you're in the throes of organising your own wedding, always a stressful time, particularly for someone who's been single for so long. In fact, frankly, if you didn't have the odd panic attack here and there, or go a bit loopy from time to time, you really wouldn't be normal.'

Smiling, Lisa said, 'Do you reckon David has them too? I sometimes wonder when I catch him staring into space. You know, it worries me, what he might be thinking about.'

'Whatever it is, try to remember this is a challenging time for him too, what with his daughter being the way she is and the demands of his job . . .'

'Not forgetting losing his wife.'

'That too, actually, especially that too, but we know he's in no doubt about taking another, because he's the one who doesn't want to wait.'

'But if I end up coming between him and Rosalind . . .'

'I told you before, he'll sort that out.'

Lisa felt herself melting again. 'It's crazy, isn't it,' she said, 'the madness we put ourselves through when there's actually no need?'

'True, but like I said, you wouldn't be normal if you didn't. Now, if you can promise me you're not about to do anything rash or get yourself worked up over nothing again, I'll have to love you and leave you, I'm afraid. I've got a mountain of work to get through here before I take Mum into Bath to try and find her a hat.'

'I promise,' Lisa replied dutifully.

'Good. Talk to David when you can, and I'll call you tomorrow.'

After ringing off Lisa carried on standing where she was for a moment, not entirely sure what to do next. Unusually she had nothing scheduled for that afternoon, which wasn't good after the lunch she'd just had. However, rather than allow Tony Sommerville to take root in her thoughts, she decided to spend the next couple of hours contacting all the editors she knew to see if they might have something to offer.

Once that was done she set about replying to the string of emails that had poured in lately from friends all over the world. Almost everyone wanted to know how her wedding plans were going, or to congratulate her if they'd only just heard, or to offer their villa or apartment, or even a yacht in one case, if she and David were in need of somewhere to spend their honeymoon. The generosity was overwhelming, and it made her feel quite emotional to realise there were so many people prepared to welcome David into their lives just because of their affection for her.

It was funny, and in a way sad, she reflected, when she finally closed her laptop much later in the day, how no one had mentioned Tony in their messages. They all knew him, at least most did, and as far as she was aware they were as fond of him as they were of her. However, she guessed it would hardly have been tactful to ask if she was still in touch with him, or to pass on any news they might have of him, while congratulating her on 'finally finding the right one', as a few had put it. She hadn't realised they'd never considered Tony to be that. Or maybe they had at the time. It was certainly a delusion she herself had laboured under for long enough, when she'd been so mad about him that she'd actually considered ending it all during the weeks after she'd left and he hadn't contacted her. It hardly seemed credible now that she could have got herself into such a state, but at the time there hadn't felt any point to going on when she couldn't imagine anyone ever being as exciting or challenging or just plain romantic as he was. Even his unpredictability – which she'd detested as much as she'd loved – had set him apart from everyone else, along with his outlandish 'projects' and gestures, and totally irresistible charisma. He could make her feel like the most beautiful and desirable woman alive one minute, and the most neglected and ill used the next.

She found herself wondering if David would ever whisk her off to Zurich – from Hong Kong – on the spur of the moment, simply because she'd expressed a fancy for kalbsbratwurst. Or helicopter her in to some remote part of the Australian outback where he was prospecting for opals, because he was missing her. Or shower her with rose petals from a small plane he'd just won at the tables while she, as the Bikini Babe, was on a beach in the Bahamas doing a piece to camera. Actually, it didn't matter at all if David wouldn't do any of those things – she wouldn't even want him to – but there was no doubt Tony's flair for the unusual and extravagant had been a huge part of her life, and his appeal, back then.

There had also been his unfailing and enraging talent for letting her down, of course – like the time he called from Mexico to make his excuses when she was expecting him for an important function in Turkey – and he was the one who spoke the language. Or the outrageous way he'd left her stranded on an island in the South China Sea to be rescued a day later by an Indian navy ship. He'd forgotten her birthday on a regular basis, almost never called when he said he would, and he was forever investing her money and losing it. (However, it had to be said that more often than not he'd suddenly repay it with twice, even four or five times the amount she'd given him.) As far as she knew he'd never had a proper job, unless playing the financial markets, blackjack and all systems of roulette could be called proper. In fact, she'd met him in Vegas, back when she was young and impressionable and quite possibly, for the first time since David, ready to fall in love. As it turned out, she'd also come extremely close to marrying Tony in Vegas, but by then they'd been together for six or seven years.

He'd had a massive win that day, and they'd both had way too much to drink, so it had seemed like the most natural and fabulous idea in the world to round off the night by getting hitched. They'd even made it as far as the town hall for the licence before fate had decided to stage one of its more peculiar rescues from the jaws of disaster by shoving her under the wheels of a stretch Hummer.

Fortunately, her injuries hadn't been life-threatening; however, they were serious enough to keep her hospitalised for over a week. During this time Tony's apparently unlimited supply of sympathy had got on her nerves to such an extent that finally, in a rage of self-pity and frustration, she'd told him to get lost and just leave her there, and to her amazement he had.

She'd ended up forgiving him, of course, because she always had – eventually – mainly because he had a way of making it impossible not to. It might be something as simple as a dinner he'd cooked himself, or a romantic note wrapped around her toothbrush, or, on one memorable occasion, remembering to call her mother after Matilda had worried herself silly about going to the optician's. Whatever it was, he'd always had a way of winning her over again, and no matter how happy she was to be with David she'd never deny how special her time with Tony had been too.

And now, if he was to be believed, he'd turned himself into a countrified gentleman of Gloucestershire with respectability, property and even a gilt-edged business card. Wondering where she'd put it she dug around in her bag, eventually locating it in the back pocket of her jeans. She couldn't help smiling as she read it, since it looked genuine enough, but it was still extremely hard to get her head around: first, how he'd come by this business, and second, the idea of him living what for him would be a very pedestrian sort of existence. However, knowing him as she did, the whole thing, house, shop and upstanding persona, was far more likely to be a front for something shady or top secret, as he'd no doubt rather put it, than it was to be a bona fide attempt to settle down and impress her – at least she hoped it was, because she truly didn't want to hurt him.

Though a part of her would have liked to tear the card up and throw it away, her younger, naively romantic self decided to hang on to it for now. It wasn't that she had any intention of being in touch, it was simply that discarding it would be like discarding him and though she knew he had no role to play in her future, he'd been a vital and important part of her past. So, for the sake of the many wonderful and colourful memories he'd given her, she decided to tuck his card into the back of her wallet, where it would no doubt fade and disintegrate over time, much like the photograph of Catrina David kept hidden away at the back of his own wallet.

By the time David came home, just before midnight, looking tired and dishevelled, Lisa was the best way through a bottle of wine and, thanks to a long chat with Brendan who was losing his job too, feeling extremely emotional over her future career prospects. Coming to the end of an era would have excited her once, but now she was fast approaching forty with a whole circus of bright new talent less than half her age dancing, strutting, somersaulting and doing heaven only knew what in the wings these days, it was hard to imagine anyone wanting her.

Though she tried to turn the subject round to his evening, it wasn't long before he was handing her tissues as he listened to all her fears about being washed up and put out to grass, which soon ran on to her misgivings about getting married and being an MP's wife and not being able to live up to what he must surely be expecting of her. She decided not to mention Tony because there really was no point – he was simply someone from her past, just as Catrina was from David's.

In the end, instead of looking worried, or even hurt, as she'd expected him to, he seemed to be amused. 'Darling,' he said, taking her hands and holding them between his own. 'You can't really believe I don't understand how important your own identity and independence are to you, and as far as I can see there's no reason for anything to change.'

It took her a moment to digest that, and another for a sneaky suspicion to start raising its head. 'I'm sorry,' she said, 'but if you're going to offer me a job, or some kind of allowance . . .'

'Would I dare?' he broke in laughingly. 'No, all I'm going to offer you is the reminder of how excited you were a few months ago about writing a book. You were full of the publishers you knew and agents, and where you were going to travel for the research. It all sounded very challenging and inspiring to me. So, as I see it, you still have the opportunity to achieve that, with your redundancy money to help fund the trips – and the possibility of your identity being held intact for posterity on the jacket of a number one bestselling book.'

She blinked, opened her mouth to speak and then closed it again. In the end she said, 'I'm not sure if the idea's actually any good.'

'You know it is,' he corrected. 'All it needs is your time and commitment and . . .'

'A miracle?' she interrupted, starting to smile.

He laughed. 'I was going to say and the right place to work, but a miracle could come in handy too.' His eyes were softening as he brushed his fingers over her cheek. 'I'm not coming into your life to try and take it over,' he told her gently, 'I'm here to try and make it feel as complete and worth living as you make mine.'

'Oh God,' she wailed, clasping her hands to both his cheeks, 'how could I ever have thought I didn't want to marry you? You're the most wonderful man in the world, and I couldn't care less about anything else, just as long as we're together.'

His eyebrows arched ironically. 'A tad rash,' he told her, 'but I'll remind you of that the next time you tell yourself you're getting cold feet about me.'

'It's not going to happen,' she assured him confidently. 'Just don't you go doing it about me, OK? Promise?'

'Promise,' he said, pressing a kiss to her mouth, but instead of gathering her up in his arms, the way he usually did, he pulled gently away and went to run himself a bath.

After the evening he'd just had, he didn't have it in him to make love tonight.

Chapter Seven

Jerry was standing in the hall reading the paper when Rosalind came in through the door carrying several Harvey Nichols bags, which she dumped at the bottom of the stairs ready to go up the next time she did. Once she'd have whisked everything out and treated him to a saucy fashion show after the kind of spree she'd just been on, but things had changed between them now, so she generally kept her purchases to herself.

'Hi, everything OK?' she asked, going to give him a peck on the cheek.

'Everything's cool,' he assured her, keeping his eyes on the page in front of him, while scratching a hand over his recently shaved chin. He wasn't wearing his pilot's uniform, so he'd obviously been home for a while, and knowing that he hadn't bothered calling to find out where she was, or simply to let her know he was back, grazed painfully over the rawness inside her.

He was a good-looking, fresh-faced man of medium height and build, with wavy fair hair and a rash of moles over his skin that she always used to tease him were beauty spots. These days they were never mentioned at all.

'I have to hand it to your father,' he commented, 'he's a class act when it comes to avoiding an issue. Have you read this yet?'

After glancing at the article, she said a short 'Yes,' and continued on to the kitchen.

'So we still don't know whether Colin Larch is going to make a bid for the leadership,' he said, coming after her, 'which was what they were really hoping to get out of him, obviously, and they didn't manage to land his girlfriend either.'

'There's a picture of her,' Rosalind pointed out as she filled the kettle. 'And he wasn't backward in saying how much he's looking forward to the big day.'

Stifling a sigh at her tone, Jerry dropped the paper on the table and went to take a beer from the fridge.

Standing with her back to him, staring at the kettle, Rosalind knew she should ask, out of politeness if nothing else, how his recent trip had gone, but even though the words were right there, on the tip of her tongue, she couldn't make them come any further. Maybe if he'd flown somewhere other than Cape Town she wouldn't be having such a problem, but knowing who was there, and fearing what the woman might still mean to him, she was too afraid of his answer to risk asking the question.

'So did you see him at the weekend?' he asked, going to lean against a worktop as he drank from the can.

Realising they were still talking about her father, she said, 'Yes, he came on Saturday, as usual, and again on Monday night.'

'Was it OK?'

'Mostly. Saturday was a bit difficult, I suppose, but everything was fine by the time he left on Tuesday.' She took a mug from a hook and held on to it as she added, 'He left his briefcase behind, so I had to courier it up to London.'

Since there wasn't much he could say to that, he took another sip of his beer and watched her drop a tea bag into the mug, before starting to unload the dishwasher.

'I found a card,' she went on, feeling so tense she might snap. Why was she telling him this when she already knew what his reaction would be? 'It was obviously meant for *her*. Apparently, she's the love of his life.' She swallowed as the meaning of it dug deeply into her heart.

'How come you saw it?' he asked mildly.

She threw him a quick glance, then carried on putting some bowls away. 'That's hardly the point, is it?' she retorted. 'The point is, if *she's* the love of his life, what does that make my mother?'

As his head fell forward a wave of anger swept through her. She wanted to scream, or cry, or smash the dishes against the wall, anything to try and make him understand what this was like for her.

'People say these things when they're in love,' he said. 'It's not meant to minimise what went before, it's simply about what's happening now.'

'And you know that because you've been there, I suppose?'

'Rosalind . . .'

'Don't! I shouldn't have brought it up. It's always a mistake trying to discuss anything with you.'

Though his expression was taut he made an effort to sound consoling as he said, 'You have to let it go, Ros. It's . . .'

'What are we talking about now?' she interrupted. 'My mother? Or the fact that you don't really want to be here?'

His eyes darkened. 'If I didn't, I'd have left eighteen months ago,' he told her curtly.

'And now you regret missing your chance. Has she found someone else, is that the problem?'

'I have no idea what she's doing now. I never see her, we have no contact . . .'

'But you haven't stopped thinking about her, wishing you were with her.'

He flung out his hands. 'Why are you putting words in my mouth?' he cried. 'That's you speaking, not me, and I don't know how much longer you're going to go on throwing this at me, but I do know that I can't take much more.'

Her eyes were flashing with fury in spite of the anguish inside her. 'At which point you'll be able to blame me for our marriage breaking down,' she shot back scathingly. She wanted to stop. She knew she shouldn't be attacking him like this, but as though they had a will of their own, the words just kept coming. 'It won't have anything to do with *you* and the fact that *you* had an affair that lasted *three years* before I realised it was going on.'

'And it's over now,' he insisted, 'at least for me. I just wish it was for you, because we can't go on like this, Rosalind. It's getting so that I'm starting to dread coming home.'

'Don't say that,' she begged, clasping her hands to her ears. 'I want you to come home, I don't want this to be happening, but I'm afraid to trust you, can't you see that?'

'And I don't know what to do to make you,' he replied helplessly.

Her eyes stayed on his, staring at him as though trying to see past all the lies and betrayal, back to a time when they'd been so close that they often knew what the other was thinking. In the end she seemed almost to crumple in defeat as she said, 'No, nor do I.'

Going to her, he started to pull her into his arms, but before she could stop herself she turned away. 'Seeing that card,' she said, returning to the kettle. She took a breath. 'It was like seeing . . .' She tried again. 'It brought it all back, only this time it wasn't only me who meant nothing, it was Mum too, and now I can't get it out of my mind.'

'Ros,' he said gently, 'you really need to talk to someone . . .'

'Please don't suggest I go for counselling,' she broke in heatedly, 'because it's not counselling I need, it's the certainty that you're not seeing her when you go to South Africa; that you're not thinking about her every time you look at me, wishing I was her; that you're not asking yourself all the time if today's the day you should go.'

His despair was complete. 'Why are you doing this to yourself?' he demanded. 'I'm here, aren't I? I stayed because I wanted to, because I love you and I want to try and get back what we once had, but no matter what I say, or do, it never seems to get through to you.'

Her head was in her hands. She was struggling to accept his words, to allow them to be true, but it was so hard. 'Swear to me you're not still seeing her,' she cried desperately.

'I swear,' he said, his voice rising with sincerity.

'On Lawrence's life?'

He seemed to baulk at that, but then in a tone that remained sincere, he said, 'OK, I swear on Lawrence's life that I'm not still seeing her.'

Though Rosalind held his eyes, trying to feel the truth taking root inside her like a drug dispersing a disease, in the end she found herself turning away, so pent up with pain now that she could barely breathe. Did swearing on Lawrence's life have the same meaning for him as it would for her? The words wouldn't change anything, nothing was going to strike Lawrence down as a result of them, so what was the harm in uttering them? Merely to think he might care so little half killed her with wretchedness. However, to be so cavalier, or cold-hearted, wasn't the Jerry she knew, but then nor was the man who'd carried on a relationship with another woman for three whole years before she'd found a hair slide in the pocket of his uniform that she'd known right away wasn't hers. She'd long wondered if the woman – Olivia – had put it there herself in an effort to bring things to a head. Olivia wanted Jerry to commit to her, and this could have been a way of forcing his hand. Rosalind's mother had been certain of it, and so had she at the time, but what did it matter now, because even if it had been the woman's intention, it had ended up backfiring on her. Jerry hadn't left his wife, he'd left his mistress instead. So when it came right down to it she and Lawrence had meant more, unless it was guilt and pity that had kept him here.

A painful silence filled the kitchen as she poured herself a cup of tea, and he made a pretence of returning to the paper. It was like this between them most of the time now: a certain amount would be said, until the fear of going any further shut them down like a sudden break in power. There was too much energy, too many emotions, needs, frustrations and despair overloading the currents between them. So, as usual, they gave themselves some time to back away, to let things cool down a little before attempting to connect again.

In the end Jerry was the first to speak, taking them, to her surprise, down another route that was likely to end in an explosion. 'Did you talk to your father about the wedding?' he asked, making an attempt to keep it mild by appearing distracted by the paper.

'No,' she replied stiffly.

He turned over a page as he said, 'Have you changed your mind about going?'

Once again she said, 'No.'

When eventually he looked up his expression was so despairing that she immediately felt her temper rise. 'I'm not the only one who thinks he's in denial over his grief,' she cried defensively. 'Miles and Dee happen to agree with me, and what's more certain things are starting to come to light about *her* that are causing Miles even greater concern.'

Jerry's expression took on an astonished, then cynical edge. 'What on earth's that supposed to mean?' he demanded.

Her face was turning sour. 'He's not in a position to divulge any details yet, but apparently he's not the only one who's worried. There are . . .'

'Hang on, hang on,' he said, putting up a hand to stop her. 'Are you telling me that Miles has been digging around for dirt on Lisa?'

'What I'm saying is that Dad has political enemies who'll do anything to try to discredit him, and if he weren't so screwed up in his head over Mum dying and thinking he's in love with someone he barely even knows, he'd have checked her out himself before committing to a relationship that's very likely going to end up ruining his career, and everything else for all we know.'

Jerry was staring at her aghast. 'Your father's not a fool,' he stated angrily. 'As far as I can see he knows exactly what he's doing . . .'

'Well, you would think that when we all know that if I were to die tomorrow you'd do exactly what he did, and call up your mistress before the bed had time to turn cold.' The words were out before she could stop them, and all she could do now was watch in shame and horror as he shot to his feet.

'I don't know why I waste my time trying to talk to you,' he growled. 'You're so obsessed with everything that's gone before that nothing about today seems to matter to you. I'm sorry that your mother's dead, Rosalind, I really am because I loved her too, and that's what's at the heart of this. No, don't try pretending it isn't and blaming everything on your dad. You're the one who needs help handling your grief, not him, and there's nothing wrong with that. Catrina was a lovely woman, we all miss her, a lot, but life has to go on, so instead of trying to destroy what he has with Lisa, why don't you try being happy for him that . . . No, don't turn away,' he cried, grabbing her back.

'I'll never be happy for him as long as he's with her,' she spat.

'For God's sake, listen to yourself . . .'

'No, you listen. I know in my heart that my mother will never rest easy until I get him away from that woman. So I owe it to her, and to him, to do everything I can to put a stop to this wedding – and if you cared about me at all, and how I feel, you'd be refusing to go too.'

'My decision about going has nothing to do with the way I feel about you,' he shouted, 'because believe it or not, not everything is about you. On this occasion it happens to be about Lawrence and his role as your father's best man, so how the hell can you not go?'

'Asking Lawrence to stand up for him was a trick on Dad's part to get me there.'

'Didn't you hear what I just said?' he cut in furiously. 'It's not about *you*. It's about the special relationship our son has with your father, so why don't we feel thankful that he has one with someone, because it sure as hell hasn't happened with either of us. Your father's doing something extremely important for him, making him feel valued and trustworthy and responsible, which, in my book, is a wonderful gesture, and nothing at all to do with trickery or persuasion the way you seem to think.'

'You can tell yourself what you like, I know

how my father works, so I know the truth. Now, if you don't mind, I have some calls to make,' and picking up her tea she started out of the kitchen.

'I'm going to the wedding,' he told her, before she could leave. 'I'm going to be there for our son, and your father, even if you won't.'

Though she'd stiffened, she didn't turn back, simply kept on going until she was in her study with the door closed and the key turned in the lock so he couldn't come after her. She didn't want to argue any more; her head was throbbing and every word she uttered either came out the wrong way or somehow seemed to escape his understanding. Why couldn't he see how difficult and painful all this was for her, and how hard she was trying to do the right thing? She loved her father with all her heart, and the last thing she wanted was to hurt him, but sometimes it was what had to happen if it was the only way of saving someone from themselves.

David was standing at the window of his office, hands stuffed loosely in his pockets as he stared down at the raggle-taggle sprawl of a protest group on Parliament Square. They were imprisoned on the central island by steel barricades, a sweating, shouting mass of humanity wielding angry placards and flags, with traffic swirling around them like urgent pinballs firing from an unstoppable machine. Each week brought another demonstration – rising unemployment, the victimisation of Muslims, Middle East policy, mothers against drunk drivers, fathers' custody rights, the environment, petrol prices – there was no end to the issues people could protest about, and no easy solution to any of them.

There was a time when he'd felt he could help them; that he was in a position to make a difference. These days he worried more about how well, or not, he was coping, with his own job, and with his family, particularly Rosalind. It didn't seem so very long ago that he'd been able to kiss everything better for her and make all the demons go away; now it was as though he was the demon, and to think of her hurting the way she was over something he was doing was tearing him apart.

Sighing quietly to himself, he watched a group of his colleagues in their grey suits and jazzy ties crossing the road towards Whitehall. He'd returned from the House a few minutes ago, where he'd spent the morning listening to a select committee hearing on . . . actually, he couldn't recall for the moment what it had been about. He simply knew that he'd been glad to get back to his office where he'd closed the door to signal that he didn't want to be disturbed. Later he was taking a train to Bristol, where he was due to appear on *Question Time* tonight. He'd hoped Lisa would be able to come with him, but she had an early appointment for another practice run with the hairdresser in the morning, so he was going alone. Rosalind and Dee wouldn't be there either – it was too late for Lawrence, so they were going to watch from home.

Catrina would have been there, if she could, but there was no point thinking about that. Instead he allowed his thoughts to fill with Lisa and the night, just over a week ago, that he'd come home to find her in a crisis of doubt. As far as he could tell she seemed to be over it now, and he only wished he could say the same for himself, because that very same evening he'd been experiencing his own particular crisis – and the fear of it happening again seemed to be deepening instead of disappearing. During his speech at a dinner for a group of economists and businessmen his mind had gone blank, and though he'd had his notes in front of him he'd found it impossible to pick up again. Of course, everyone lost their thread once in a while, occasionally it was even amusing, but to have lost it the way he had that night, and for it not to come back, certainly couldn't be passed off as a joke.

He didn't understand how his thoughts could be so clear and present one minute, so full of purpose and meaning, only then to evaporate at the moment they started to become words. It was like biting thin air when expecting an apple, or drowning when he knew he could swim. He'd looked at the faces around him and none had registered. All he'd been aware of was the emptiness of the space he was in, and the strange, echoey sound of the silence. He wasn't sure how much time ticked by before he'd excused himself. A trickle of baffled applause accompanied his departure, and someone had come to ask if he was all right. He wondered now what he'd said. He hoped he was polite.

Though his eyes continued to move over the crowds below, tourists, politicians, policemen in pairs with their fluorescent jackets standing out like bright players in an otherwise dull circus, he was barely seeing them now. He was sunk in the fear of what was happening to him. Though it had been with him for a while, all through Catrina's illness and after, following him like a shadow often too small to be seen, lately it had been looming too large to be ignored. He was afraid to face it, but even so he'd made himself check his symptoms online, knowing already what he was likely to find. There had turned out to be several explanations for his memory lapses and increasing anxiety, but he couldn't stop himself thinking about the one he feared most of all. It couldn't be that – dear God, it just couldn't.

Since he didn't know for certain, he must keep reminding himself that he could be wrong, that there really was a chance the stress and grief that seemed to be gripping him more tightly by the day was taking its toll. The months, weeks, days leading up to Catrina's passing were the hardest he'd ever been through. Even now, thinking of her in so much pain, and knowing how afraid she was of dying, not only because of what might come next, but because of being unable to bear the thought of leaving him, could rack his conscience as cruelly as his heart. The last thing he'd wanted was to see her suffer, but during her final days she'd tormented herself in a way he'd been powerless to stop.

'Listen,' she'd rasped, gazing up at him with her puffy, yellowed eyes, 'I know you've thought about her over the years, and wanted her, and probably rued the day a thousand times over when you decided to stand by me, but I want you to know, David, that nothing's ever meant more to me than making you happy. You've given me a wonderful life, and for that I thank you with all my heart, but if you go to her, it'll be like saying that my life had no real purpose other than to be an obstacle between you and her.'

He'd have loved to be able to say that at the very end she'd gone peacefully with no more fear in her heart, but it hadn't happened that way. He'd waited, hour after hour, for the gentle and unselfish wife he'd always known to return, but she never had, at least not to him. 'She won't make you happy, David,' she'd whispered close to the end. 'She can't, because she's someone else now. Too much time has gone by.'

At the time he'd refused to let her words get through to him, knowing that they were a form of emotional blackmail that was as ugly and destructive as the disease that was eating her. So he'd told himself, when she'd gone, that he mustn't allow all her ramblings and delirium to have any bearing on the rest of his life. The Catrina he'd known and loved for over thirty years was the Catrina who'd always wanted him to be happy, not the woman whose disease had managed to turn her into a stranger.

As the fear of what could be wrong with him rose up like a divine punishment in his mind again, he felt his throat turning dry and his heart blackening with dread. He was longing for Catrina now in a way he never had before. They'd been each other's best friends as well as husband and wife, and not having her to confide in when he needed to so desperately was making her loss even harder to bear. It scarcely even occurred to him to turn to Lisa – they didn't know one another well enough for him to burden her with this. Or perhaps the real reason he was holding back was because he couldn't bear to crush her dreams, or even to think about the possibility of losing her.

Hearing a knock on the door, he resisted the urge to tell whoever it was to go away, and returned to his desk as he called for them to come in.

Miles put his head round the door. 'Yvonne's going to ride in the taxi with you to the station,' he told him.

'Yvonne?'

Miles's eyebrows rose. 'Your media . . .'

'Yes, of course,' David interrupted irritably. 'Sorry, I was thinking of something else. Do you have all the information I'm likely to need so I can look through it on the train?'

'Absolutely.' Coming into the room, Miles closed the door behind him. 'If you have a minute,' he said, looking unusually hesitant for him, 'I was hoping now might be a good time to mention something that's come up.'

David looked at him sharply.

'It might easily turn into nothing,' Miles continued, his discomfort seeming to deepen, 'but I thought I should at least warn you about it.'

'Where's this going, Miles?' David said impatiently.

Steeling himself, Miles said, 'I'm afraid it's going to Lisa and some information that I'm told a certain Foreign Minister and his team have managed to dig up about her.'

David's eyes narrowed. 'And what information would that be?' he demanded.

151

Pushing the words out, Miles said, 'Apparently they've discovered some evidence connecting her, or more accurately someone she was close to, with money-laundering.'

David's expression turned glacial.

'Please don't shoot the messenger,' Miles cried, holding up his hands. 'I just thought you should know . . . As far as I'm aware no charges were pressed, but it seems the man she was involved with was a bit of a dubious character . . .'

David's fury suddenly exploded. 'There's nothing about Lisa's past that I don't already know, Miles,' he shouted, 'so if you, or some . . . some . . . You . . . will not encourage . . .' He put a hand to his head and Miles immediately started forward.

'Are you OK?' he asked.

'Yes, I'm fine,' David snapped, and without meeting Miles's eyes, or uttering another word in Lisa's defence, he grabbed his briefcase and jacket and swept out of the room.

Chapter Eight

'Amy! It's me,' Lisa announced into her mobile. 'I've been trying to get hold of you all day.'

'I know, I know, I'm sorry. I've been in meetings and I've only just got home. Is everything OK?'

'Yes, yes,' Lisa assured her, stepping out of her robe to begin applying her favourite Vera Wang body cream. 'Apart from spending the entire day talking to florists, caterers, dress designers, shippers, landscape gardeners, the list is endless – oh and getting ready for the whirlwind called Roxy to descend on me tomorrow – everything's fine. Do you have any idea yet which train she's catching?'

'Not a clue, but I'll get her to text you. Has David left London yet? It is tonight he's on, isn't it?'

'Yep, ten thirty-five, so don't fall asleep. I know what people your age are like.'

'Speak for yourself,' Amy laughed. 'Where are you going to watch it?'

'Here, at home. I've got a few friends coming over, so we're popping corks and eating in.' Deciding it was too warm to put any clothes on yet, she walked as she was into the kitchen, to open the first bottle. 'Did I happen to tell you,' she said, reaching for a glass, 'that I'm getting married to David Kirby in just over four weeks, which makes me so happy I could burst, or fly, or dance around the moon. Added to which – these miracles are coming thick and fast, so hold on to your hat – his head of staff, Miles Farraday, has only invited me for lunch tomorrow. Can you believe it? Westminster's answer to David Beckham with a rocket-science brain called this afternoon to ask if he could buy me lunch.'

'No way!' Amy cried. 'Any idea what prompted it?'

'Nope, but the really intriguing part is that he's asked me not to mention anything to David *yet*. I've no idea what the "yet" means, but I guess I'll find out tomorrow.'

'OMG,' Amy burbled, sounding exactly like Roxy, 'he's going to declare a passion and beg you not to throw yourself away on a fifty-three-year-old with dazzling prospects when you can have the same package in a twenty-five-year-old.'

'Actually, I think he's closer to thirty, and my take on the secrecy is that he's being cautious in case we don't get along, which is highly unlikely considering how wonderfully easy-going I am.'

'Whoever told you that was lying. Now, I'm hoping you're going to tell me next that you've still heard no more from Tony Sommerville.'

'Not a peep,' Lisa assured her, experiencing a flutter inside at the mention of his name.

'And you're not disappointed about that?'

'Not at all,' she lied, but it was only her ego feeling let down, not her heart.

'Good. And have you called Mum to remind her about the programme? We'll never hear the end of it if she wakes up tomorrow and realises she's forgotten.'

'Already done, but I'll probably send a text as backup. Right, I suppose I'd better put some clothes on before my guests arrive. Is it a gorgeous evening down there? We're having a heatwave here.'

'It's stifling, but I think there're thunderstorms forecast for tomorrow. We want the weather to turn though, so it has a chance to turn back again in time for the wedding. Anyway, I'm gone, talk to you after the programme.'

As she put the phone down Lisa took a sip of the perfectly chilled Viognier she'd taken from the fridge, and was just savouring its flavours when it came to her, like a dandelion drifting in from thin air, where she'd been the first time she'd tasted it. It was at a vineyard in the Napa Valley, with Tony, who'd flown in to join her while she was shooting a programme with a full crew and at least half a dozen oenologists. It was a memorable experience for many reasons, though fortunately the wine experts had not been guests at the private hospitality chateau of a major vineyard, because she dreaded to think how they'd have reacted to Tony and the crew marinating fillet steaks in one-hundred-dollar bottles of Cabernet Sauvignon and then proceeding to drink themselves sense-less on the very best California had to offer right through till dawn. She had to admit she'd been right there with them, and either because they were still young back then, or the wine was so good, amazingly not one of them suffered the next day.

Wanting to dismiss the memory before it led to any more, she picked up the phone to call David, and as soon as she heard his voice she felt herself glowing at how wonderful her life was now.

'Hi, it's me,' she murmured, even though he already knew. 'Where are you?'

'On the train,' he replied quietly. 'Where are you?'

'At home – and guess what I'm wearing?' She used to do this with Tony, but she wasn't thinking about him now.

'Mm, let me see,' David said. 'In my mind's eye it's . . . Well, it's nothing.'

She smiled. 'You're right, and I'm wishing very much that you were here.'

'So am I now. Why don't you tell me what we'd be doing if I were?'

As frissons of desire snaked through her, she began whispering her fantasies, creating a picture of them together that aroused her so much she went to lie on the bed, where she pretended her hands were his. Being where he was, there was little he could say in response, but simply knowing he was listening and imagining, and feeling every bit as turned on, was enough to bring her to a quietly shuddering release.

'You're sensational,' he murmured. 'Did I ever tell you that?'

Her eyes were still closed. 'Once or twice,' she smiled, and moaning softly as a lingering spasm uncoiled inside her, she rolled on to her front and pouted like a teenager as she said, 'Four whole nights without you. I don't know how I'll survive.'

'Somehow we'll manage.'

'I'm sure, but I wish we didn't have to. Are you going to the house tomorrow?'

When there was no reply she wondered if they'd lost the connection. 'Are you still there?' she asked.

'Yes, I'm here, and uh . . . I'll be in Bristol tomorrow.'

'I know, that's why I'm asking if you'll be going to the . . . Oh, of course, I don't mean the House of Commons, I mean our house.'

'Ah yes . . . I'm sure I will.'

'Are you OK?' she asked, frowning. 'You sound a bit . . . I don't know, low?'

'I'm fine,' he assured her, 'but on a train and in a condition that no self-respecting male should be in while alone in public.'

Laughing and loving to think of him aroused, she turned on to her back and was about to start making things less personal when it suddenly occurred to her that while she was talking herself to a climax she might have been imagining Tony at the other end, instead of David. Her heart turned over. That surely wasn't the truth. No, it couldn't be. Tony had only just flitted into her mind that instant, and now he was gone again. Keeping her tone light, she said, 'So are you all prepared for the programme?'

There was a crackling sound before he answered, 'Sorry, what did you say?'

'I asked if you were ready for the programme.'

'Oh, for heaven's sake,' he snapped irritably as

157

the line broke up again. 'I don't know what you're saying. Can you . . .'

'Listen,' she said calmly, 'we'll talk again later. Call as soon as you can when you come off air, OK?'

Receiving no reply she realised the connection had failed, and as someone was pressing her door-bell she quickly pulled on a cream lace teddy and covered it with a sleeveless apricot kaftan that was light and floaty and perfect for such a warm summer evening.

Polly and Umeko were the first to arrive, both of whom she'd known since her interpreting days. Though they were close to forty too, unlike Lisa they hadn't remained single and childless, because both were mothers of two now and the wives of successful businessmen – or Polly had been until her divorce a year ago.

No sooner had they finished hugging and congratulating each other on how well they all looked, amidst grimaces of weight gain and the need for more Botox and why the hell hadn't anyone invented a cure for cellulite yet, than the bell rang again, announcing the arrival of Nerine and Hayley. Nerine, with her clouds of raven-black hair and vibrant make-up, was flamboyantly Greek, steadfastly single and fashion editor of a Sunday tabloid. Hayley, the youngest of them all at thirty-five, was a petite English-rose type in looks, with a dramatic Latin temper passed on from her father, and a fierce passion for art that she shared with her mother. Already married and divorced twice, she now ran an oriental art gallery close to Burlington Arcade which was

158

where she and Lisa had first met, some six or seven years ago. Lisa and Tony had attended an opening there and made three extremely expensive purchases, two of which were now hanging in the sitting room of this flat, and the third Lisa presumed Tony still owned, or, more likely, had sold on by now.

Why did everything keep coming back to him, she wondered irritably to herself. It had only been happening since he'd tricked her into having lunch with him, and now he was hanging around like the aftermath of a dream, and she couldn't seem to get rid of him.

Since Umeko, the natural expert on Japanese food, had volunteered to bring the sushi, she placed herself in charge of setting it out on serving plates, while Hayley and Lisa sorted out chopsticks, plates, tiny porcelain bowls for the soya sauce, and four of the exquisite sake glasses Umeko had given Lisa for her thirtieth birthday. Meanwhile Nerine and Polly got stuck into the wine.

After the wasabi and fresh ginger had been popped into dishes too, and everything had been transported on to the coffee table in the sitting room, they all sank into giant floor pillows to start tucking into the feast.

Never being short of news or gossip, the hours sped by so fast that they almost missed the start of the programme.

'Oh my God!' Lisa cried, leaping up as she spotted the time. 'Please don't let it have started – I want to see him introduced.'

Mimicking David Dimbleby, Polly said, 'And to my left we have the Honourable David Kirby MP,

159

ex-Foreign Minister and soon to be first husband of the gorgeous Lisa Martin. Which reminds me, I have something to tell you after. Don't let me forget.'

'Ssh,' Hayley commanded, as Lisa's heart tripped over the suspicion Polly's news was about Tony. 'It's starting.'

As Umeko passed her a drink, Lisa sank cross-legged on to her cushion, eyes glued to the screen as David Dimbleby announced where they were transmitting from and then the title music rolled. This was followed by a group shot of the panel, so brief Lisa barely had a chance to glimpse who was there before they were showing close-ups. First came a Home Office Minister, followed by a leading light of the Lib Dems, then a nationally recognised Bristolian entrepreneur, a popular columnist from one of the dailies, and 'stepping in at the last minute, Harry Jenks, MP for Bristol North'.

Lisa blinked, unable to grasp what was happening. 'I don't understand,' she said. 'Where is he?'

'They said the other guy was stepping in last minute,' Nerine repeated unnecessarily.

'We were talking about it on the phone just before you came in,' Lisa told them, more bemused for the moment than worried. 'He was on his way there.'

'So he's obviously backed out for some reason,' Hayley said.

'But if he had he'd have let me know,' Lisa insisted. 'Where's the phone? I have to call him.'

As she went to fetch it from the kitchen, Polly lowered the volume and sat quietly with the others, listening to Lisa trying to get through.

'David! Where are you?' she said urgently. 'Why aren't you answering? What's happened? Please call me.'

'I'm sure it's not serious,' Umeko muttered to the others as Lisa disappeared into the bedroom to retrieve her mobile.

'No messages, nothing,' she said, bringing it back into the room. Her face was an ashen replica of the flushed bride-to-be of a few minutes ago.

'I expect he's broken down somewhere,' Nerine suggested.

'He was on the train.'

'Which could have broken down, or got held up for some reason.'

'So why doesn't he call?' She was remembering how uptight and distant he'd sounded earlier, particularly at the end of the call, so maybe he was having second thoughts . . . Except that was hardly going to prevent him appearing on TV. She started to turn cold. 'Maybe there's been an accident,' she said. Then, suddenly panicked, 'Where's the remote? Put on the news.'

In a flash Polly had switched to BBC 24. To everyone's relief there was no live coverage from a crash scene, and none on the Sky channel either.

'So what's happened to him?' Lisa demanded in frustration. 'Why didn't he call as soon as he knew he wouldn't be on? I don't understand.'

'Is there anyone else you can ring?' Hayley asked. 'Maybe one of his family has taken ill.'

Lisa's eyes went to her, then she jumped as the telephone rang. Grabbing it and clicking on, she said, 'David, is that you?'

'No, it's me,' Amy told her. 'Where is he?'

'I don't know! I've tried calling but his phone's off.' She turned round as Nerine said, 'If there'd been an accident, they'd surely have mentioned it on the programme.'

'Not if the family hasn't been notified yet,' Polly reminded her, and immediately wished she hadn't when she saw Lisa's face.

'Did Miles give you a number when he called today?' Amy asked.

'No,' Lisa answered, 'but he rang my mobile . . .' and grabbing her iPhone she quickly scrolled through the incoming calls. 'Damn, he was calling from the office.'

'Try it anyway,' Amy advised. 'You never know, someone might be there.'

After making the connection Lisa listened to the ringtone until the answerphone picked up. Not bothering to leave a message, she was about to speak to Amy again when she heard a beep on the landline. 'Someone's trying to get through, I'll ring you back,' she told her sister, and switching to the other call she said, 'David?'

'Matilda,' her mother corrected. 'I thought you said . . .'

'I did, and I don't know what's happened, Mum. As far as I knew he was appearing tonight.'

'We've all stayed up specially to watch,' Matilda grumbled. 'I was looking forward to it.'

'I'm sorry. As soon as I know why he's not there I'll tell you, but for now I have to try and find out where he is.'

'I hope he hasn't had an accident.'

'Mum! I don't need to hear that, thank you very much. Now go to bed, I'll call you in the morning.'

After ringing off Lisa looked at the others, at a loss what to do next.

Taking out her mobile, Nerine said, 'I'll call the BBC, see if I can get through to someone on the programme. They must have some idea of why he's not there.'

Hayley said, 'Do you know how to get in touch with his daughter?'

Lisa shook her head. 'Unless her number's in the book.'

'What's the surname?' Umeko demanded. 'I'll try and find out.'

'Sewell,' Lisa told her. 'Her husband's name is Jerry – I'm not sure whether that's with a J or a G. Their address must be Chew Magna, I think, or Chew Stoke.' She looked at the phone in her hand, willing it to ring. 'Where are you?' she murmured desperately. 'Why don't you call?'

Rosalind was shouting at everyone to be quiet as she waited for Miles to come back on the line. They were at Dee's house, where she and a dozen or more friends had gathered to watch the transmission, while Lawrence slept upstairs in the room Dee had made his. Since they'd already tried her father's number to no avail, they were now relying on Miles to find out from the programme's producers why her father wasn't on air.

'Rosalind, can you hear me?' Miles shouted, coming back on the line.

'Yes. What's happening? Did you speak to someone?'

'Yes. Apparently they don't know where he is either. When he hadn't turned up, or been in

163

contact half an hour before the show, they dragged Harry Jenks out of the audience to take his place.'

Using anger to smother the worst of her fears, she said, 'He's with *her*. He's forgotten what he's supposed to be doing, because he's so besotted with her he can't think about anything else.'

'That's not him,' Miles told her. 'Besides, I spoke to him while he was on the train, so he was definitely on his way there.'

'Then where is he?' Rosalind cried, aware of the way everyone was watching her. This was so unlike her father that they were all as baffled and worried as she was.

'I don't know where he is,' Miles answered, 'but I'm staying on it.'

It was almost midnight by now. Lisa was curled into a corner of the sofa, both phones on the arm beside her as she waited for news. Before leaving, Umcko had tried Rosalind's number, but had received an answerphone so had rung off without leaving a message. Since then, all manner of scenarios had been running through Lisa's mind, of Lawrence or Rosalind being rushed off to hospital; of David being hit by a car and in a coma with his next of kin by his side who wouldn't bother to call her; of a terrorist gang grabbing him off the street and holding him hostage . . . So many fears, so much to torment herself with, and still nothing to tell her what had gone wrong. She'd even, in some insane corner of her mind, wondered if Tony had something to do with it, but that was just plain absurd. More likely was that another passenger had noticed his state of arousal after their intimate phone conversation and called the police, who had boarded the train at the next station and were now holding him in a cell overnight.

Afraid of where her unhelpful imagination might take her next, she glanced at the clock, wondering if it was too late to call Amy. They'd spoken again after Amy's initial call, but with nothing else to report they hadn't stayed on the line long. She desperately needed to do something, but to go out and look for him at this time of night, when she had no idea even where to begin, was hardly an option, nor was contacting the police, at least not at this stage. So all she could do was remain where she was, putting herself through seven kinds of hell and feeling so distanced from the woman who'd spoken to David a few hours ago that she could have been transported to another planet.

She began running the conversation over in her mind again, not the sensual, sexual part of it, but the moments when she'd asked him if he was feeling low. She wasn't entirely sure why she'd asked that when he hadn't really sounded that way, it was simply that she'd been unable to come up with another word. Nor could she now, unless she listened to her inner demons who were wide awake and raring to party with their best mate, paranoia. If she started giving in to all that she'd be a jabbering wreck in less than an hour, because she knew very well, without consulting her fears and insecurities, just how fragile happiness could be, and how life had some novel and pretty horrific ways of proving it.

'I know,' life would say, 'let's bring David and Lisa back together, and just when Lisa thinks everything's going to work out perfectly we'll punish her for being so full of herself by killing him.'

'Or at least by making it that he changes his mind and doesn't want her any more,' fate would suggest. 'He just thought she was the right one because they had all that unfinished business way back when.'

'You can return her to me, if you like,' destiny would offer. 'I'll make it so she can carry on more or less as before, but with no job this time, so it won't be as easy to keep running away. She'll have to find somewhere to settle, and by the time she's ready to commit to Tony, which is where she really belongs, and she knows it, he'll have married somebody else.'

'Why don't I take her?' death would weigh in. 'If she loses David and Tony she won't want to go on without them, so instead of letting you guys use and abuse her, why don't I do the decent thing and put her out of her misery now?'

Snapping out of the grisly little pantomime, she stood up and went to make a coffee. As she waited for the kettle to boil she began slipping from the firmer ground of common sense again, this time into tormenting herself with what would happen to the house, the furniture and everything else that was already crafted or being shipped from around the world, if David had decided he didn't want her any more. She knew it was crazy thinking this way, that he loved her and wasn't about to give her up, but it was better than being dragged into the terrifying prospect of something awful happening to him. But what if it had? No, no, she couldn't allow herself to go there, it would only make everything seem ten times worse and God knew it was bad enough already.

The landline rang and she almost spilled her coffee trying to get to it. 'Hello?' she said, trying not to sound panicked.

'Hi, it's me,' Amy told her. 'Any news?'

Though the disappointment was crushing, she was so relieved to have someone to talk to that she gave a gulp of laughter. 'No. Nothing,' she said, a surge of useless tears flooding her eyes. 'Nerine finally got through to someone on the programme who told her they had no idea why he hadn't turned up, and Rosalind's not at home.'

'Maybe something's happened to her, or Lawrence.'

'If it had he'd have called by now to let me know. And he'd never let the BBC down like that, so I'm at a complete loss here.'

'And driving yourself nuts, no doubt, which is why I rang. I couldn't sleep either, so I thought we might as well be awake together. What are you doing now?'

'Drinking coffee, waiting. Is Theo asleep?'

'I don't think so, but he's got an early meeting in the morning so he's trying to go off. I'm downstairs in the kitchen with Roxy. She says hi.'

'Hi,' Lisa mumbled, her heart turning over as she remembered that her niece was due to arrive tomorrow for a second fitting of her bridesmaid's dress.

'It'll be all right, Lis,' Roxy said, coming on the line. 'I know it will.'

Lisa forced herself to say, 'Thank you.' How easy it was at eighteen to believe everything would turn out just fine – how difficult it was now.

'Do you still want me to come tomorrow?' Roxy asked.

'Yes, yes, of course.' Then, feeling less certain, 'Actually, let's talk in the morning.'

'OK. I'll put Mum back on.'

'I was thinking,' Amy said, 'maybe we should call the hospitals. If he has been involved in an accident they . . .'

'Hang on,' Lisa interrupted, her heart starting to pound, 'someone's trying to get through. I'll call you back,' and knowing if it was her mother she really would scream this time, she clicked over to the other line.

'Darling, it's me.'

'David! Oh my God!' she cried, clasping a hand to her mouth as the relief sent her reeling. 'Where are you? What's happened? I've been so worried. Is everything OK?'

'It is now,' he replied, managing to sound both tired and amused. 'What an evening I've had, though. You're not going to believe what happened.'

Not caring, as long as he was all right, she said, 'Where are you?'

'I'll get to that. First off, the damned train broke down and where did we happen to be? In the Box tunnel, of course. You know the one that goes on for ever between Chippenham and Bath? They kept putting out announcements saying they hoped to get things sorted in the next few minutes, and when those minutes were up we just got

168

another announcement apologising and repeating the same thing. I couldn't use my phone because we were in the tunnel, and anyway, after I spoke to you Miles called and by the time I'd finished with him my battery was out.'

'But . . .' she interrupted.

He kept on going. 'Which wouldn't have been a problem,' he said, 'had I not finally got to my car at Temple Meads to discover that I'd left the keys in London, so I couldn't get in.'

'Oh no,' she groaned, looking around to see if she could spot them.

'By then the programme was already going out,' he ran on, 'so there was no point taking a taxi there. I took one to Rosalind's instead, only to find she wasn't at home. I finally tracked her down at Dee's which is where I am now, exhausted, ravenous and ready to sue First Great Western to within an inch of its existence.'

As she laughed drily at the craziness of his evening, she could only wish she was with him to try and soothe away the awful frustration he must have suffered. 'What a nightmare,' she sympathised. 'And to think I was so worried . . . When the programme started and you weren't there . . . You can't imagine what's been going through my mind. All that matters though is that you're all right.'

'I am,' he confirmed, sounding more exhausted than ever, 'and sorry I put you through all that stress. I'll tell you one good thing to come out of it though,' he continued in a quieter voice, 'when I was sitting there in the car not knowing what the hell was going on . . .'

'Do you mean carriage?'

Taking a moment to pick up, he said, 'Of course. Having all that time on my hands gave me the opportunity to think about you and how very much you mean to me.'

'Oh, darling,' she said, melting. 'And you do to me. When I thought something had happened to you . . . It was just awful. I couldn't bear it, because my life is complete now in a way it's never been before. I'm not even worried about growing old now – or not very – because I'm going to be doing it with you.'

There was a smile in his voice as he said, 'I'll remind you of that the next time you yelp at a grey hair or get worked up over an imaginary wrinkle.'

'You know, that's one of the things I love most about you, the way you manage to blind yourself to all my little imperfections.'

'You'll always be beautiful to me, no matter how old you are, and you can remind me of that when you're ninety, because if I'm still around I know I'll still feel the same.'

'If I am, then you'd better be too, or there'll be trouble. Now, I should let you go so we can both get some sleep. Call me when you wake up, won't you?'

'Of course. And I'm sorry again about tonight.'

Rosalind was in Dee's kitchen preparing a sandwich for her father while he made his call in the dining room. Though he'd closed the door behind him, she'd still been able to hear, because he didn't seem to have noticed that it had come ajar again.

Now, as he returned the phone to its base, and tucked his notebook away, she put a panini and a cup of tea in front of him and kissed his cheek, feeling not only relieved he was safe, but profoundly intrigued by what she'd just overheard. Why, she'd very much like to know, had he just told Lisa that he'd arrived here in a taxi, when his car was sitting right outside? And, unless she was gravely mistaken, he'd been reading at least some of what he'd told her from his notebook, which was almost equally as odd.

Chapter Nine

Miles was rushing to meet Lisa, a week later than originally planned, since David's extraordinary no-show on *Question Time* had left him and Yvonne with a lot of ruffled feathers to smooth the following day. Fortunately matters hadn't got too out of hand, mainly thanks to Harry Jenks stepping in at the last minute, but he too had been on the phone the next morning wanting to know what the heck had happened to David.

Once the situation had been explained to those he'd let down, or put on the spot, they were all relief and sympathy, knowing only too well how unreliable the trains could be. The biggest relief to Miles, however, was that no one had bothered to check the story, because if they had the lie would almost certainly have leaked out to the press by now. As it was, Miles felt fairly confident that only he and Rosalind knew that all trains from Paddington to Temple Meads had arrived bang on schedule that night. Where David had gone from there remained as big a mystery as why he'd lied to Lisa about taking a taxi to Dee's. Being reluctant to admit to eavesdropping Rosalind still hadn't challenged him on it, and since Miles hadn't overheard the phone call himself he didn't feel able to confront David either.

As the Jubilee line disgorged some passengers at Green Park station, and sucked in a few more, Miles, in his pale grey Armani suit and collarless white shirt, strode up the escalators, too busy checking his BlackBerry as he went to notice the several female heads that turned. Half a dozen new emails had come in during the short time he'd been underground, but none that couldn't wait, so using his Oyster card to exit the station he pressed through the barriers and on out to the street. The part of this peculiar business that was troubling him the most wasn't only the elaborate tale David had concocted about the train and forgetting his car keys, but his reluctance the next morning to call the producers himself to apologise for letting them down. It was completely out of character for him to baulk at doing the right thing – he was usually such a stickler for it that it kept them all on their toes making sure they lived up to his standards. However, on this occasion, he'd left the explaining to his staff while he, according to Rosalind, had driven off in his car without telling anyone where he was going, and when he'd returned a couple of hours later he'd shut himself up in Rosalind's study with his laptop and hadn't come out again until it was time to go and fetch Lawrence from school.

'He seems absolutely fine in himself,' Rosalind had said on the phone over the weekend.

'But he still hasn't mentioned anything about where he went after the train?' Miles had wanted to know.

'Not a word, and I don't want to ask him about it, because it'll be like telling him I know he's lying, and I can't imagine him taking very kindly to the fact that we checked up on him.'

'Nor can I,' Miles agreed, 'but something's obviously going on and I – or we – need to know what it is.'

'Actually, I've been wondering if he's having second thoughts about *her* and is trying to find a way to break it off.'

Since he didn't feel convinced about that, Miles hadn't responded.

'You know how sensitive he is to other people's feelings,' she went on, 'except mine and Mum's, it would seem, but what I'm saying is, if he wants out of that relationship, then being the kind of man he is, he'll be finding it extremely difficult to find a way of letting her down. I reckon the whole thing is probably stressing him half out of his mind, and that's why he disappeared on us, so he could be alone to think.'

Knowing how much Rosalind would like that to be true, Miles hadn't argued, or even expressed an opinion, but if David had missed a scheduled TV appearance simply to work out how to break up with his girlfriend, then as far as Miles was concerned his boss had managed to pull off an overnight morph into someone he didn't know.

It was baffling, and worrying, but now that David had gone off to Bristol to meet Dee for an afternoon surgery in Radstock, the coast was clear for Miles to find out if Lisa was able to throw some light on all this.

*   *   *

174

Lisa was already at the table when Miles arrived seeming harassed about being late and faintly embarrassed, judging by the flush of colour in his cheeks. Suspecting this had more to do with the fool he'd made of himself when he'd tried flirting with her when they first met than it did with his tardiness, she tactfully pretended not to notice.

'I'm sorry, I got caught up,' he apologised, sitting into the chair the maitre d' was holding out for him.

'It's not a problem,' she assured him kindly. 'It's nice to see you. This is a lovely choice of restaurant.'

His smile was polite, possibly even stiff. 'I'm glad you like it,' he replied, turning off his BlackBerry and setting it down next to his plate with his office keys. 'Have you ordered a drink?'

'No, I thought I'd wait and join you in whatever you're having.'

'I have to drive later, I'm afraid, so no vino for me, but please don't let that stop you.'

With a playful grimace she said, 'Actually, it would be good for me to abstain too. I don't want to start putting on weight this close to the wedding, so Evian or similar would be great.'

'I'm sure you'll look stunning on the day,' he said gallantly, and then probably wished he hadn't given the speedy return of heat to his cheeks.

'Just three weeks to go,' she said happily. 'It's coming round so fast I can hardly keep up, there's so much to do.' She smiled up at the waiter as he handed her a menu. 'It's OK, Joe,' she said, 'I don't need to look. I'll have the crayfish risotto.'

After making a quick selection of bangers and

mash, Miles ordered a large bottle of Evian to go with it, then apparently making an attempt to be chatty, he said, 'So what are you planning to do with your sabbatical? I mean, once the honeymoon's over.'

'Well,' she said drily, 'I'm afraid for sabbatical read unemployed because things have changed recently, but that's fine, because I'm thinking about venturing into something new. However, if you don't mind, I'd rather not say what it is just yet, because I'll feel a fool if it doesn't work out.'

'Well, whatever it is, I wish you luck with it.'

'Thank you,' and after the waiter had filled their glasses with water, she raised hers and clinked it to his. 'And what about you?' she asked. 'Do you have anything arranged for the summer?'

'Not yet,' he confessed, sipping his drink. Then, 'I'm sorry, I don't mean to be rude, but I don't have as long as I'd have liked for lunch, a few things have cropped up at the office, so I'd better come to the point of why I'm here.'

Allowing her fascination to show, she propped her chin on her hands and fixed her eyes on his in a way that, unfortunately, sailed the colour straight back to his cheeks.

'When I first invited you to lunch,' he began, his eyes dropping for a moment, 'it was to discuss something other than the matter I'm going to mention now, but we'll come on to it. For the moment, I'd like to ask you if you think something might be bothering David.'

As her light-heartedness faded, she put her hands back on the table, saying, 'I'm not sure what you mean.' Then, deciding this was no time for artifice, 'Actually, yes, sometimes I do.'

He swallowed and glanced down at his glass. 'Has he talked to you at all about what happened last Thursday, when he got stuck on the train?' he asked.

She shook her head. 'Not really, other than on the night it happened. It hasn't been mentioned again since, I suppose because I didn't want to make too big a deal of it, but I don't mind telling you I was worried out of my mind when I didn't know where he was.'

'We all were,' he assured her. His eyes came awkwardly to hers, then moved away again. 'I've checked with First Great Western,' he told her, 'and no trains got stuck in the Box tunnel that night. They all arrived at Temple Meads on time.'

As she registered his words she felt a disorienting confusion coming over her. 'But why would he lie?' she asked, searching his eyes as though he must have the answer somewhere.

'I don't know.'

'Then where was he?' she asked nervously.

'Again I don't know. Rosalind overheard him telling you that he turned up at Dec's in a taxi, but I'm afraid that wasn't true either. He was in his own car.'

Lisa sat back, almost as though he'd struck her. 'Are you sure?' she said. 'I mean, you're not saying this to . . . Well, I don't know why you'd make it up. Have you told him you checked the trains?'

Miles shook his head. 'He's not someone who normally lies, so it's not easy to confront him, but we have to presume that he has a very good reason for it, and I was hoping you might have some idea . . .'

His voice trailed off as a waiter arrived with the food. There were so many thoughts crowding into her head, but not one of them was making much sense. 'I don't understand why he would lie like that,' she said, when they were alone again.

Taking a breath, as though bracing himself, he said, 'Being pretty au fait with what's going on in his professional life, I'm more inclined to think he's worrying about something, or someone, in his personal life.'

'You mean like Lawrence, or Rosalind?' she said, knowing already that he didn't. 'I think you could be right.'

'Or you?' he said bravely.

Forcing herself not to go on the defensive, she said, 'But why do you think he'd be worried about me?'

His eyes dropped again. 'I need to tell you the reason why I first invited you to lunch,' he said, 'because I'm guessing from our conversation so far that David hasn't mentioned it himself.'

Feeling herself growing more tense by the second, she waited for him to go on.

'I'm sure you're aware,' he began, 'that David has political enemies.'

'I suppose so,' she replied cautiously.

'Well, it turns out they've managed to unearth your connection to someone who was involved in a possible money-laundering scheme.'

For several moments she was too stunned to speak. Then, not sure what else to say, she told Miles, 'It was a mistake. He was released without charge.' She paused. 'I can't believe anyone's managed to find this out. As far as I knew it didn't even make the records.'

'Well, it seems it did, and obviously it could cause some embarrassment for both you and David if his enemies try to make something of it.'

Her mind was spinning. Surely to God Tony hadn't told anyone about it in some insane attempt to mess things up for her with David? He was capable of a lot of things, but she'd never known malice to be one of them. 'And you say David already knows about this?' she said, putting Tony on hold for the moment.

'I've mentioned it to him, yes, but he wasn't prepared to discuss it with me.'

'What did he say, exactly?'

'That he knew everything there was to know about your past . . .'

'Which is true, he does. I've told him about Tony, and how wild he could . . .' She stopped abruptly, realising she didn't have to explain anything to Miles. 'We all have a past, Miles,' she said tartly.

He nodded. 'Of course.'

When he said no more she filled the silence herself. 'You think this is what's bothering him?'

'Let's put it this way,' he said, shifting in his chair. 'I first mentioned it last Thursday, before he caught the train to Bristol, and we know what happened after. Having said that, no matter how angry and upset he was about it, I can't bring myself to believe it would stop him turning up for a TV programme.'

'Then what do you believe?'

'I wish I could give you an answer, but all I can

tell you is that he's been behaving quite oddly for a while now, and none of us has yet come up with a reason why.'

Knowing very well that they were blaming her, she said, 'Apart from grief?'

He nodded.

'Or . . . ?'

He shrugged, clearly reluctant to put his suspicions into words.

'What does Rosalind think?' she asked bluntly.

Loosening a collar that wasn't even buttoned, he said, 'She thinks he wants to break off his relationship with you, but can't find it in himself to hurt you.'

As her heart turned over she felt the blood draining from her face.

'But that's Rosalind,' he added hastily, 'so I don't think we can take it for granted that is the case.'

'But if it is?'

He shook his head, apparently unwilling to commit.

'She thinks her father's going to pieces over her mother,' Lisa said tightly, 'and to save him she wants me to call off the wedding? Is that how it goes?'

He didn't deny it.

'Well, you can tell Rosalind from me,' she said, throwing down her napkin, 'that if there is something wrong with her father then she should look to herself for the reasons, because if she knew how anxious and stressed he is about her she might do something about pulling herself together and damned well growing up,' and after tossing two twenty-pound notes on the table for a meal she wasn't going to eat, she walked out of the restaurant.

With Tony's card already in her hand, Lisa slammed the front door shut behind her and snatched up the phone.

'Sommerville Antiques,' a sulky female voice announced down the line.

Since it hadn't occurred to her that anyone else might answer, there was a beat before she said, 'Is Tony there please?'

'I'll check if he's in his office. Who's calling please?'

Picturing the little hottie with hair as long as her legs and eyes wider than her brain, she felt like slapping her down simply for being there, never mind for trying to block her. 'It's Lisa Martin,' she said coldly. 'I'm sure he'll speak to me.' If he didn't after that, she'd go down there and personally smash every fake antique in the place.

'Of course. Can I tell him what it's about?'

She was about to snap a cutting no, when she changed her mind and said instead, 'I'm calling from the Gloucestershire clinic for venereal diseases with the results of his recent test.' It was an old one, but it usually worked, and she had no reason to think it wouldn't this time, as a pregnant silence followed. After a few clicks on the line Tony was laughing as he said, 'She's the cleaner.'

'I don't care who the hell she is,' Lisa informed him, 'I want to know if you've been talking to anyone about the money-laundering incident.'

'What?' he said, sounding genuinely baffled. 'Why on earth would I do that? It was over three years ago – and, let me remind you, was . . .'

'All above board, yes, so you say, but was it really? Apparently it's gone on the record somewhere, presumably in Manila, and one of David's political rivals has managed to find it.'

'Ah, right. That's not good, except you weren't involved personally, and there were no charges, so as far as I can see you should have nothing to worry about.'

'But you know how sensitive that particular issue is these days, and I thought . . . Well, I want to be sure that nothing ever came of it for you either, because if my name can be connected to anyone or anything that's either criminal or in any way scurrilous . . .'

'It can't, at least not as far as I'm concerned, because contrary to popular belief, I have a squeaky-clean police record.'

'This is me you're talking to.'

'OK, then it's got a couple of grubby prints here and there where the wrong people have got hold of it, but I can promise you, my forays over to the other side of the law have all been accidental, or simply from being in the wrong place at the wrong time. So, my darling, you have nothing to fear from me – unless you consider my undying love to be a threat to your soon-to-be wedded bliss.'

'I do not,' she informed him crisply. 'So you're sure no one's been in touch with you, asking about me?'

'I'm sure I'd remember if they had. However, I admit I've been half expecting it, though I'd imagined it would come from the tabloids, rather than some government half-wit with a grudge.'

'And your answers if anyone does ask about me?'

'No comment, of course.'

'Why don't I believe you?'

He laughed. 'Would you rather I told them that I've turned my life around for you, only to find myself dumped in favour of a . . .'

'Don't you dare insult David.'

'Actually, I wasn't going to – or maybe just a little. The point is, you know I'd never deliberately say or do anything to hurt you, in spite of being broken-hearted that you've traded me in for an older model.'

'You're not funny.'

'You used to think so.'

'I used to think a lot of things where you were concerned, but I'm over them now.'

'So how come you can't get me out of your mind? You are thinking about me a lot, aren't you? I know, because I'm thinking about you all the time, and it's driving me nuts. Come back to me, Lisa. We belong together, you know we do.'

'What I know is that I'm marrying David in a little over three weeks, and nothing you or his daughter can say will change my mind.'

'Ah, so his daughter's not welcoming you into the fold?'

'Not exactly, but I'm sure she will in time.'

'Right,' he said dubiously, 'but if it doesn't work out the way you hope, you know where I am. And next time you call, please don't say anything to scare the cleaner. If she'd been feather-dusting something fragile when you impersonated a doctor, it might have cost me a lot more than my pride.'

She forced herself not to laugh. 'There won't be a next time,' she assured him, 'but thank you for putting my mind at rest about your role in what's going on,' and after ending the call she quickly connected to Polly.

'When you were over here the other night,' she said, 'you mentioned you had something to tell me.'

'Oh yes, that's right,' Polly replied. 'I had a call from someone the day before I saw you, asking about the time we were working as interpreters, and was it true it was all a front for some kind of international escort business.'

As the shock hit her Lisa's blood ran cold. 'Did they say who they were?' she asked.

'No, he just spun a line about investigating certain allegations that had been made, like he was some kind of detective, but I guessed he was most probably from the tabloids, so I told him he was definitely barking up the wrong tree as far as we were concerned, and please don't waste my time calling up again with his crap unless he wanted to speak to my lawyer. Bloody cheek. Do you think it's real, that someone is trying to make out that we – or you, I suppose, because that's who they're interested in – were being paid for another kind of service?'

'They no doubt wish someone was willing to cover us in such glory,' Lisa replied. 'It's all to do with the Foreign Secretary wanting David back on board at the next reshuffle. The guy who's most likely to lose his job is clearly fighting dirty to try and hang on to it.'

'Charming. And what does David say about it?'

'I haven't had a chance to speak to him yet. I've only just found out myself.'

'Well, if anyone's after any dirt on you, and I think it's despicable if they are, by the way, then it's Tony they should be looking to. He's got more skeletons in his closet than half a dozen graveyards . . .'

'Oh, don't worry, they're on to him, but I'll have to tell you about that another time. I've got more calls to make before I go for yet another fitting for my dress.'

A few minutes later she was relating her conversation with Miles to Amy, ending with her parting words about Rosalind needing to pull herself together and grow up.

'Good for you,' Amy declared. 'Let's hope he passes the message on. She is so manipulative – at least she's trying to be. Are you going to tell David?'

'I don't know. Probably not unless I have to. He's seemed quite down, or distracted, this past week, since the train incident actually, and what I'm more interested to find out right now is where the heck he actually was.'

The sunlight on the lake was like a glittering mass of diamonds floating on ink. The trees around the shores, limes, beeches, horse chestnuts and maples, swayed and rustled as a gentle breeze moved through them like a whisper, while the sky overhead formed a still, cerulean backdrop for the occasional white cloud that journeyed past. David was sitting amongst the clover and daisies of the meadow that sloped down to the water's edge, his eyes following the skittering progress of a dragonfly as it hovered and buzzed amongst the powdery flowers of cow parsley. All around him birds were chirping and whistling, a hidden musical chorus spread randomly amongst the leafy branches of their summer homes. Lawrence could name most of them, in Latin as well as their more common terms. He spent hours in the bird keeps dotted all around the lake, waiting and watching silently for his quarry. Today, however, he was more interested in throwing sticks for Lucy, who David had collected from Amy's on his way back from the Radstock surgery.

The bonding between dog and small boy was as touching to watch as it was amusing, since it was debatable which of them would tire of the repeated throw and fetch first. Lucy couldn't have wanted for a more steadfast companion; Lawrence had never known anyone, or anything, able to maintain his own single-minded level of absorption. Why, David wondered, had they never thought to get him a dog before? During the hours they spent together David had watched Lucy and wondered how she knew that Lawrence wouldn't welcome her wet nose pressing into his hand, or her large, furry body rolling against his. What instinct was telling her that this small person was different to most others she knew, and what had made her decide that he was every bit as worthy of her devotion?

He smiled as once again Lawrence sent the stick soaring through the air like an ungainly bird to plop soundlessly into the grass some twelve or fifteen feet away, where Lucy, who could move even faster, was already waiting to scoop it up and bring it back, tail wagging, eyes bright with eagerness for more. Back and forth, back and forth, a ritual whose end would probably only be found in exhaustion – or perhaps when it came time for David to take them home. There was no rush, though. Rosalind was at the company offices in town, and Amy wasn't expecting him back with Lucy until around seven.

'Will you be staying at Amy's tonight?' Lisa had asked when they'd spoken half an hour ago.

'No,' he'd replied, 'I've already promised Rosalind I'll stay with her, but I'll be at Amy's with you tomorrow.'

'That's good. I mean, I'll understand if you want to spend more time with Rosalind, but I think . . . Well, we need to talk and . . .'

'. . . the weekend will be a good time,' he'd assured her, summoning a warmth and sincerity to his tone that he hoped had masked the tremors of unease in his heart. He didn't want her to think, even for a moment, that his feelings for her were any less than they were, or that his desire to be with her had in any way altered, other than to grow. What was happening to him was no fault of hers, and the last thing he wanted was for her to share this torment of worry. Soon, perhaps in less than a minute, hopefully in no more than ten, his phone would ring and he would receive some answers, or at least an understanding of what was happening to him, and, more specifically, what had come over him after he'd left the train last Thursday night.

For now he was referring to those lost hours as an aberration that had left him in the station car park, sitting motionless behind the wheel of his car which he'd only found by pressing the remote control on his keys next to each vehicle, until finally the locks on a silver Mercedes popped up and the hazards flashed. Even then he'd been uncertain about getting in, but aware of some suspicious glances slanting his way, he'd opened the door and slipped into the driver's seat. Then he'd sat there, briefcase on his lap, keys still in his hand, time ticking by, moving on, vanishing into a distance and seeming to leave him behind.

He'd thought about Catrina a lot as he'd tried to decide what to do, and Rosalind; he'd wanted to call them but there was no power in his phone. He knew there was a way to charge it, but for some reason he hadn't done it. He knew he should drive away, but it was as though years had passed since he'd last driven a car, so he'd stayed where he was, afraid if he attempted it now he'd cause an accident, or lose his way. For a long time he hadn't even been able to remember where he should be going.

He recalled muffled voices calling out from somewhere, but they were either too broken, or too far away for him to understand them. Were they coming from his subconscious, his instincts, or somewhere outside? At one point he jumped, thinking someone had tapped on the window, but when he looked no one was there. He felt as though he was suspended in a void, neither falling nor fearing, only knowing that he was there with no way out.

How long had it taken him to collect himself? Long enough for him to realise, when he came to, that he'd either fallen asleep, or possibly even lost consciousness for a while. He'd known, when he'd registered the time on his watch, then checked his diary, that he'd let people down badly, and that Lisa, Rosalind, Miles would be frantically trying to contact him by now. He hadn't been able to speak to them right away; he needed to sort out what he was going to tell them, come up with a story that wouldn't alarm them, not because he wanted to lie, but because he had no idea how to explain the truth.

Karen Knoyle, his GP and an old family friend, had chided his gloomy outlook last Friday when he'd requested an emergency appointment. She'd even managed to tease him out of it for the time he was with her, but her sunny forecast that there would turn out to be nothing wrong with him that a little less stress and a relaxing honeymoon wouldn't put to rights, hadn't managed to keep the clouds from gathering during the ensuing days. He'd found it increasingly hard to concentrate as he'd worried about those he loved and how they would manage without him if his worst fears, that a tumour was developing on his brain or that he had somehow contracted some debilitating virus, were proved correct.

Now, as he sat in one of his favourite spots, warmed by the sunshine as he watched Lawrence and Lucy playing together, he was worrying about how devastated Lisa would be if he had to call off the wedding. If it turned out he really was as sick as he feared, he couldn't allow her to commit herself to him. It wouldn't be fair, she deserved so much more. Would life really be that cruel, to bring them together at last, only to wrench them apart like this?

A bolt of nerves collided with his heart as his iPhone started to vibrate with an incoming call. Feeling as though the world around him was slipping into another dimension of receding sound and fading colour, he tried to brace himself as he slipped the mobile from his pocket to read the screen.

It was Karen, and before his courage could fail he quickly clicked on. If she asked him to come to his surgery he'd know right away that the news was bad.

'Sorry I'm a bit later than promised,' she said, 'it's been a hectic day and unfortunately it's not over yet. However, you don't want to hear about my problems, you're only tuned in for these words, I hope – it's good news, my friend. You're all clear. Everything's working perfectly, no nasty intruders or weird infections to baffle the eggheads of medical science. Your blood pressure might be a little on the high side, but I'm putting that down to the same stress that caused the aberration which was all about stress. In other words, vicious circle.'

'So that's all it was,' he said, hardly daring to believe her. 'Nothing more than stress?'

'Far be it from me to say I told you so, but, I told you so. It can be a monster when it's got something to sink its teeth into, and let's face it, you've had a lot going on these last few years. Looking after Catrina wasn't easy, I know that better than most, and losing her hit you hard. In a nutshell, my friend, you've got a royal battle-field of emotions going on inside you, ranging all the way from grief to bridegroom elation, with liberal dashings of professional pressure, constituency problems, grandson issues, house moves, and trying to please all of the people all of the time . . . Wow! I'm starting to need time out myself just reciting it.'

Laughing more freely than he'd managed for days, he said, 'I'm not sure whether seeing my life through your eyes is comforting or scary, but if you're telling me that I'm not cracking up, or about to haul my boat down to the Styx, I might pop round there to sweep you off into the sunset.'

Chuckling, she said, 'Alas, I'm at least a stone heavier than your fifty-three-year-old spine can support – sorry, but that's true, for both of us – and you have a lovely lady waiting patiently in the wings to become your wife.'

'Yes, she is,' he said softly.

'You did right to come in,' she went on, 'if only so's I could tell you to stop tormenting yourself with guilt, because that's what I think is at the bottom of it all. If it had happened more than once, or over a sustained period of time, I might have been more worried, but from what you told me it hasn't, so all you have to do now is take my advice and start easing up on yourself.'

After thanking her again and promising to keep in touch, he ended the call and then, amazingly, there was the sunshine again, as rich and bright as if dust had been wiped from its face; and the birds as lively and melodious as though an orchestra had struck up an accompaniment.

Butterflies fluttered around him like confetti, and he wanted to laugh out loud.

As he got to his feet he felt more gladness and relief pouring over the remaining currents of unease in his heart. Soon they would disappear altogether, he was sure of it, because there was no reason for them to create an undertow to his happiness. Now that Karen had told him there was nothing to worry about, he was free to look forward again. He just couldn't help wondering, as he, Lawrence and Lucy began the trek up the hill, how long Karen had meant by a sustained period of time.

Chapter Ten

It was a hot and sultry Sunday afternoon. Everything in the valley was sleepily quiet until Rosalind suddenly shouted, 'Jerry! Jerry!' Running down into the hall as though there were a fire upstairs she burst into the TV room, where he was slouched on a sofa watching the cricket.

'Where are they?' she cried furiously. 'What have you done with them?'

Picking up the remote, he lowered the sound before saying, 'If you're referring to the boxes of your mother's things, I've put them in the attic where they should have gone months ago.'

'I'm the one who gets to make that decision,' she seethed. 'I told you last night I'd do it . . .'

'You say that every night, and I'm sick of them sitting there cluttering up our room like a bunch of damned ghosts, watching my every move . . .'

'Deal with your paranoia another way. Not by moving things around that don't belong to you.'

'Rosalind, when you're ready to go through them I'll bring them back down. Now, is that OK?'

Her temper was still at boiling point, but there was no reasonable objection she could make to that. She managed to force a brief nod before starting to leave the room.

'Where are you going now?' he asked.

Not being entirely sure, she had no reply.

'I have to leave in a couple of hours,' he reminded her, 'so if you've got some time free, why don't we spend it together?'

She swallowed hard, keeping her head down. She wanted to, more than anything, but she still wasn't finding it easy to say yes.

'We could go for a walk down by the lake,' he suggested. 'Or take a drive up to Priddy.'

'What about Lawrence?' she finally uttered, turning around.

'I'm sure he's fine where he is, but if there's a problem, we'll have our mobiles with us so Sally or Dee can get in touch.'

She still looked worried. They both were, because they hardly knew what else to be when Lawrence wasn't with them – or even when he was. Today, Dee and Sally had taken him to the cinema with a group of other children, including Sally's twelve-year-old daughter Gemma, who usually had more patience with him than the others.

'You need to relax,' Jerry told her. 'You're so wound up these days that I'm starting to worry about you going off the deep end and not coming back – and if I'm not here to dive in and save you . . .'

An unsteady smile started to soften her eyes. 'Why don't we go and sit in the garden?' she said. 'No talking, no rowing, no anything, just us being the way we used to be?'

Turning off the TV, he got to his feet, and taking her hand he led her out to the swinging hammock that looked down over the lake. As they sank into it, their hands still linked, they began to sway gently back and forth.

When eventually Rosalind felt some of the knots starting to unravel inside her and sensed that he was relaxing too, she let her head fall back and closed her eyes. If only it could be like this more often, with nothing to fear and no one to come between them. Sometimes their closeness seemed to her like a ghost wandering further and further away, soon to vanish over a far horizon. She didn't want to let it go, she desperately wanted to hold on to it, but having put her trust in him so completely once, she simply couldn't find the courage to do it again.

Feeling him move closer, she allowed him to slip an arm around her and rested her head on his shoulder. She wondered what he was thinking, if he was feeling happy to be here, relieved that they were able to share this time before he left for his next trip. Then, because she couldn't help herself, she began wondering if he was being affectionate because he knew that at some point in the next twenty-four, or forty-eight hours, he was going to betray her again. She tried to smother the suspicion and make herself believe that his motives were innocent and worthy with no artifice attached, but it was hard, so very hard.

'Are you OK?' he whispered softly.

'Mm,' she murmured, making herself sound sleepy.

It was comforting to know that his next trip was taking him to San Francisco, where they'd spent part of their honeymoon before flying on to Hawaii. How perfect everything had seemed then, how easy and true.

Why had he done it? What had made him turn to another woman, and how could it have gone on for so long without her even suspecting? It was that, more than anything – her own naivety – that continued to unnerve her, because if he'd been able to deceive her so convincingly once, what was there to say that he wasn't already doing it again?

She shifted to lie more comfortably against him, and brought his hand into her lap.

Last night, when she'd told him about her father's visit to Karen Knoyle, they'd ended up rowing again. It hadn't started out that way, of course, in fact he'd been quite concerned at first.

'Is he all right?' he'd asked.

'Apparently, yes, but the real reason he didn't turn up for *Question Time* was because he had a kind of aberration, was how he put it, brought on by stress.'

Jerry looked baffled.

'He didn't go into much more detail than that, apart from the fact that he's had some tests which have shown that he's fine, physically.'

'Well that's good. Isn't it?'

'Of course, but it's what's causing the stress that's bothering me. No, don't look at me like that, please hear what I have to say. I spoke to Miles this morning, who told me that she's lost her job.

This is obviously putting a lot more pressure on Dad . . .'

'Rosalind, you are jumping to conclusions . . .'

'*And*,' she cut in forcefully, 'there are things coming to light about her that could cause Dad some serious problems.'

'You told me that before, and I'll say the same again . . . Your father's not a child, or an imbecile. He'll know how to deal with the problems . . .'

'How do you know that, when you don't even know what they are?'

He threw out his hands. 'Do you?' he challenged.

'No, Miles still won't tell me, but if this information gets out . . .'

'If it does you won't need to worry, because no one will be able to accuse you of leaking it. Think of it that way,' and snatching up the paper he'd stormed out of the room.

She hadn't gone after him because there was no point. He didn't understand how she felt about Lisa Martin, any more than he understood how devastated she still was by his affair. He seemed to assume that because he'd told her it was over she could forget about it now, and carry on as though it had never happened. He'd even suggested they try for another baby, presumably to show how committed he was to staying. Though she wasn't entirely against it, she still couldn't decide whether it would be good for Lawrence to have a brother or sister, or if it would end up making him feel left out. Nor was she wholly convinced it was the right thing to do for them. What if the baby turned out to have the same problems as Lawrence?

Could Jerry stand to have another child he was unable to get close to? Could she? And was a new baby really any guarantee that he wouldn't stray again?

'That sounds like the phone,' Jerry murmured.

'You stay there,' she said, getting up. 'I'll bring you a cup of tea when I come back.'

By the time she walked into the house the answering machine had picked up, but she could hear Dee's voice leaving a message and quickly grabbed the receiver. 'Hi, I'm here,' she said. 'Is everything OK?'

'I'm afraid not,' Dee answered shakily. 'Lawrence ran out of the cinema and we can't find him.'

As fear exploded in Rosalind's heart she shouted, 'But he doesn't know his way home from there. It's too far. Have you called the police?'

'That's why I'm ringing, because I think maybe we ought.'

Lisa's eyes were filled with astonishment. She and David were upstairs in Amy's guest room, where he'd finally got round to telling her what had happened after the train ten days ago. It was bizarre, unimaginable, but he obviously wasn't making it up, so somehow she had to accept that it was real. 'Is it likely to happen again?' she asked, already alarmed that it might.

'I don't think so. It's hard to be sure, but as long as I find a better way to deal with stress, I guess everything should be OK.'

Still torn between shock and concern, she said, 'Well, clearly you shouldn't be bottling things up, and keeping them away from me as if I can't cope. I'm not some delicate flower whose petals are going to wilt at the first sign of rain. I understand, and I accept, that you still have feelings for Catrina, *and* that you sometimes feel guilty about loving me. OK, it's not great, but it's not surprising either. Apart from anything else, it shows you're human, and that you care.'

Apparently feeling the need to reassure her, he said, 'I'll get over it. It won't come between us, I swear.'

Picturing him again sitting alone in his car, baffled and afraid, then concocting an elaborate tale to cover his embarrassment, she still couldn't quite get to grips with it. It seemed so unlike him, and yet . . . Seeing how worried he looked now she felt an overwhelming tenderness come over her, and wrapped him tightly in her arms. The next instant he was sweeping her up off the floor and as they collapsed in a laughing, boisterous heap on the bed Roxy's voice sailed in from next door.

'I won't ask what's going on in there, but you're too old to be having so much fun. It's not decent.'

'And you're too young to be listening,' Lisa shouted back. 'Cover your ears, or play loud music like most normal people your age.'

'Who said I was normal?'

'Good point.'

After making himself more comfortable, with his hands behind his head and legs stretched out lazily, David watched her with wickedly gleaming eyes as she gathered up both their iPhones and switched them off. 'Mm,' he grunted disapprovingly, as she positioned herself cross-legged at the end of the bed, 'I was rather hoping you were about to ravish me.'

Tilting her head to one side, she narrowed her eyes as she gazed down at him. 'I will,' she promised, 'just as soon as we clear up the other little business you decided not to tell me about.'

He frowned, clearly confused.

'I had lunch with Miles on Friday and he told me how your enemies have been digging around in my past to try and embarrass you, or worse, so I thought I should tell you about the money-laundering incident myself.'

Though his eyes widened, he didn't say anything, so she pressed on with as much as she knew about what had happened the night Tony had found himself in a Filipino jail, and how he'd been released, without charge, the following day. 'Tony swears it was a mistake,' she assured him. 'I've spoken to him and he insists that nothing came of it afterwards. I guess we could check that out, if you like, but I don't think he's lying.'

'I see,' he said. Then, after a beat, 'So you're still in touch with him?'

Feeling herself starting to turn hot, she said, 'Only to find out if there was anything to worry about.'

He nodded slowly. 'And where is he these days? Still gallivanting around the globe in his usual irresponsible fashion, I suppose. You know it beats me how you could have got yourself mixed up with someone like that – and for so long.'

On the brink of defending both herself and Tony, she made herself pull back, knowing it would only turn into a row that she really didn't want to have. 'We can't always get things right every time,' she said, trying to make light of it.

Clearly not ready to let it go, he said again, 'So where is he these days?'

Realising that to tell him the truth would only make matters worse, she said, 'I'm not sure, and wherever I think he might be, by this time next week it's likely to be somewhere else.'

He nodded and continued to fix her with a look she was finding hard to meet.

Please don't let him ask if I've seen him, she was begging silently. It would be one lie too far if she denied that.

'Do you still think about him?' he asked.

'No, of course not,' she cried, plunging straight into the next lie. 'I mean apart from when something like this comes up. Anyway, even if I did, it's not the same way I think about you.'

It took a while, but eventually his mood started to show signs of lightening. 'I'll be having words with Miles about talking to you before he's brought the problem to me,' he told her gravely.

She was confused. 'But he said he'd told you and that you didn't want to . . . Oh look, it doesn't matter,' she said hastily, as the darkness returned to his eyes. 'Why don't we just let all this go and get on with the ravishing you were waiting for just now?'

As she swung round to lie beside him, he slipped an arm around her and pulled her in close. However, instead of turning to kiss her, as she'd expected, he lay staring at the ceiling until eventually he said, 'Do you wish it was Tony you were marrying in a couple of weeks?'

Stunned, she sat up sharply and looked down at him. 'Absolutely not,' she told him truthfully, 'and I can't believe you're even asking it.'

Raising a hand to her face, he cupped it gently. 'I'm sorry,' he said, gazing into her eyes, 'I didn't mean to make you angry,' and pulling her back into his arms he put his mouth to hers in a kiss that took a while to feel as intimate as it was.

Rosalind and Jerry were speeding up over Dundry, heading into the centre of Bristol. As Jerry struggled to keep out of the ditch, and avoid oncoming traffic, Rosalind was calling her father.

'His phone's off,' she cried furiously as she was diverted to messages. 'Dad! It's me!' she shouted into his voicemail. 'You have to call me back. Lawrence is missing! He was at the cinema with Dee . . .' Her voice broke on a sob. 'Call me back,' she choked, and snapping the phone shut, she gasped as Jerry braked hard behind a tractor.

'Bloody thing! Get out of the way,' Jerry growled, jamming a hand on the horn.

The farmer continued poodling along, shedding bits of straw like cares and woes as he went.

'Overtake,' Rosalind commanded.

'I can't. There are too many bends.'

'I'm going to try Dad again.'

'Why? There's nothing he can do.'

'He knows the Chief Constable. He can ask him to make sure every available officer is put on the case.'

'Let's try and calm down, shall we?' Jerry said shakily. 'They might have found him by now . . .'

'If they had they'd have rung.'

Her hand was clutching the phone so tightly she might have crushed it. 'Where would he have gone?' she cried. 'He's only ever been to Cabot Circus once, and he doesn't even know which bus to take home.'

'Someone will realise he's lost and take care of him,' Jerry replied, sounding more confident than he felt. Then, jamming his hand on the horn again, 'For God's sake, why doesn't this idiot pull over?'

Rosalind covered her face, unable to bear the snail-like pace they were being forced to keep to, when they had to find their son. Terrible, horrific images were tearing through her mind of a lawless, sadistic gang torturing him to death; or of him walking into traffic without realising it wouldn't stop; of some paedophile getting hold of him and subjecting him to unthinkable acts. She could see his face, so innocent and beautiful, confused and racked with pain. She had to get to him. She couldn't allow anything bad to happen to him. This was all her fault. She should never have allowed him to go to the cinema without her. If she'd been there, she'd have been after him the minute he ran away; she'd have caught him and he'd be safe now, but instead, no one knew where he was *and if this bloody tractor didn't get out of the way this minute she was going to SCREAM!*

As it turned into the next field, Jerry zoomed on and she tried to force herself to breathe. In, out. In, out. It was going to be all right. They'd find him, and before they knew it they'd all be on their way home as though nothing had happened.

Opening up her phone she tried her father's number again.

'He'll call as soon as he gets your message,' Jerry snapped.

Her eyes went down. 'I know. I just . . . I have to do something.'

Realising that his jealousy of the way she always turned to her father had no place now, he reached for her hand and gave it a squeeze. Then, putting his foot down, he sped through a set of lights as they were turning red.

'Let's try to get there in one piece,' she begged.

Easing off the accelerator he checked the mirror, willing a police car to come up behind them. Once they understood the situation they'd surely put on their sirens and get them through the traffic.

When finally they reached Cabot Circus Jerry pulled over for Rosalind to jump out, then drove on to find a safe, if not legal place to leave the car.

Still clutching her mobile, Rosalind ran between Next and La Senza into the glossy new shopping mall where Sunday shoppers were still meandering about, and a four-piece jazz band was playing outside a jeweller's. She looked around, turning in circles, searching the upper levels, while heading for the steps to the cinema. There was no sign of Dee, or Sally, so flipping open her phone she dialled quickly. No answer from Dee. Forcing down more panic, she tried Sally.

'Where are you?' she cried when Sally answered.

'Outside Boots, in Broadmead. Where are you?'

'Cabot Circus. Have you found him?'

'Not yet. Dee's still over there. We decided to split up. It'll be all right, Ros, we'll find him.'

Trying not to sob, Rosalind closed down the phone and looked frantically around for Dee again. She started shouting, 'Dee! Lawrence!' Her voice ricocheted around the terraces, and up to the glass-domed roof, causing people to stare down at her as though she were some impromptu theatre act. 'Dee!' she screamed. 'Where are you?'

'Are you all right?' someone asked. 'Can I help?'

She swung round to find an old lady looking concerned. 'I've lost my son,' she told her. 'He ran out of the cinema . . . Oh God,' she choked. 'I have to find him.'

Dashing up the steps she turned to the escalators, then slipped and fell, dropping her phone. Grabbing the pieces, she forced herself up and limped on. 'Lawrence!' she yelled desperately. 'Where are you?'

'Rosalind!' It was Dee, leaning over a balcony above. 'It's all right, we've got him.'

Such a wave of relief hit her that she had to cling to the railing to stop herself falling again.

Somehow she got up to the next level, and the instant she saw Lawrence with her aunt and two policemen a surge of unbridled fury overcame her. 'You silly boy!' she seethed, shaking him with all her might. 'What did you do that for? You'll never be allowed out again, do you hear me? Never. *Never.* You don't think . . .'

'Ros, stop,' Jerry said, panting for breath as he came up behind her. 'He's all right, that's all that matters.'

'He could have been killed,' she sobbed hysterically. 'Why doesn't he realise ...'

'Ssh,' he soothed, loosening her grip on Lawrence and pulling her into his arms.

'You're the parents?' one of the policemen asked.

'Yes,' Jerry answered. 'I'm sorry about this ...'

'No need for apologies, the important thing is we found him.'

'Where was he? Where were you?' Jerry asked Lawrence.

Lawrence's eyes were glassy as he stared at his mother.

'He was tucked inside a doorway, round the corner there,' Dee said, pointing. 'He wasn't there the first time we looked, so I don't know where he was till then.'

'Why did you run away?' Rosalind cried, turning back to Lawrence. 'Didn't you realise how much it would scare everyone?'

'They were going to kill Lucy,' he shouted.

Rosalind frowned in confusion. She looked at Dee, who shrugged, not understanding either. 'What do you mean?' Rosalind demanded. 'Was it someone in the film?' she asked Dee.

Dee shook her head. 'Not that I recall.'

Becoming aware of a crowd starting to hover, Jerry said, 'Come on, let's get him home.'

After providing all their details for the police, they waited for Dee to finish giving hers, then keeping an arm round Rosalind, Jerry put a careful hand on Lawrence's back to steer him towards the stairs.

When they reached the ground floor where the

jazz band was still strumming a lively tune, Dee said, 'I'd better call Sally to let her know everything's OK. What time are you leaving for London?'

'In about an hour,' Jerry replied, 'but I'll probably call in sick.'

'You don't have to,' Rosalind told him. 'We're fine now. Aren't we?' she said to Lawrence.

His only answer was to abruptly avert his head.

'We're taking the other kids for pasta,' Dee said, 'so I'll pop in and see you on my way back. Listen, I'm really sorry we didn't do a better job of taking care of him. I blame myself, I should have made sure he was sitting next to me . . .'

'It's not your fault,' Jerry assured her. 'He's been out with you plenty of times before and nothing like this has happened, so please don't give yourself a hard time over it.'

By the time Jerry drove them in through the gates at home, Lawrence was dozing on the back seat, while Rosalind, looking utterly drained, kept turning round to check on him.

'I'm going to call in now,' Jerry said, 'they should have enough time to get someone in from standby.'

'You don't need to,' she told him again. 'We'll be fine.'

'I don't want to leave . . .'

'It's OK,' she said more forcefully. 'I can manage, honestly.'

Realising to argue any further was pointless, at least for now, he got out of the car, and opening the back door he gently shook Lawrence awake. 'Come on, son, we're home,' he said, fighting back the urge to scoop him up and carry him in. If he did he'd probably start screaming, and that wasn't what any of them needed right now.

Bleary-eyed and tousled, Lawrence slid out of the car and with his head hanging down he walked to the kitchen door, where he waited for one of his parents to come and unlock it.

Once inside, Rosalind sat him down at the table. After pouring him a glass of milk she squatted down beside him as she said, 'Tell me again why you ran away. I'm not going to punish you. I just need to know.'

'They were going to kill Lucy,' he growled angrily.

'Who were?'

'They were going to kill Lucy,' he repeated.

'Who's Lucy?' Jerry asked.

'They were going to kill Lucy,' he said, banging a fist on the table.

Rosalind stood up. 'You'd better go and change,' she said to Jerry. 'You'll have to leave soon.'

Wondering if a day would ever dawn when he didn't feel next to useless where his son – and wife – were concerned, Jerry dropped her dismantled mobile phone on the table and went off upstairs.

Reaching for the battery, Lawrence tucked it under his arm and held it there as he rocked back and forth.

'Drink your milk,' Rosalind said brusquely, and going to the fridge she poured herself an enormous glass of wine.

By the time Jerry came down, wearing his uniform and looking as worried as he clearly felt, she was already on to her second glass. 'We'll be fine,' she told him again.

Jerry looked at Lawrence, who was still sitting at the table, swinging his legs and tapping his glass with the battery. He wanted to tell him to stop in case he broke it, but all too often when he reprimanded Lawrence a tantrum flared up, and that wasn't how he wanted to leave his family today.

'I'll come out with you,' Rosalind said, getting to her feet.

As she staggered he caught her and keeping an arm around her, he walked her out to where he'd left his holdall next to the car.

'Call if you need to,' he said, dropping it in the boot. 'They can always get hold of me.'

She looked up into his eyes, but as he put a hand on her face, ready to kiss her, the phone inside started to ring.

'I'd better go and see who it is,' she said. 'I'll see you next Monday.'

He nodded, knowing that her urgency to get away was in case it was her father on the line.

She was halfway back to the house when, seeming to realise she hadn't kissed him, she made a swift return and went up on tiptoe to press a kiss to his mouth. 'We'll be fine,' she told him once more, and after an unsteady smile she ran into the kitchen.

As the door closed behind her Jerry got into the car, trying not to mind that her father always seemed to matter so much more than he ever had. Every time there was a crisis, or a celebration, or anything at all, she'd call David first, almost as though she didn't have a husband. The day Lawrence's condition had been diagnosed it was David who'd been with Rosalind, holding her hand and seeing her through the dreadful trauma of it all, while Catrina was at a meeting in Taunton and he, Jerry, was flying back from Shanghai. And as if to punish Jerry for not being a worthy father, who had Lawrence developed his only attachment to – if such a grand word could be applied to something that never allowed touch, or teasing, or any kind of normal bonding? David, of course, because the heroic David had always been there, living less than ten minutes away, so constantly ready to tend to any mishaps or confusions, to sort the dramas and soothe Rosalind's nerves when Lawrence's tantrums became too much. In his bleaker, more self-pitying moments Jerry would tell himself it was no wonder he'd had an affair – who wouldn't when they were hardly appreciated, or even wanted, at home, and when a woman like Olivia, vivacious, uncomplicated and crazy about him, was so eager to take him on?

After starting the engine, he slotted his Black-Berry into the hands-free device and watched the messages come up. He wasn't surprised to see Olivia's name amongst them, because it was usually there, and as he envisaged her, petite and blonde with her laughing eyes and turned-up nose, he felt the familiar ache of loss and need come over him. If things didn't start improving at home soon, he knew in his heart that he wouldn't be able to ignore these emails for much longer.

*   *   *

Inside the house Rosalind was struggling to stop herself from crying as she explained to her father what had happened. 'It was awful, Dad,' she was telling him brokenly. 'I was so afraid, and when I couldn't get hold of you . . .'

'Darling, I'm sorry. We were having a nap, but he's all right, you say? You've found him now.'

'Yes, he's sitting right here, all in one piece, thank God.'

'So what made him run off?'

'He just keeps saying they were going to kill Lucy, but the only Lucy I can think of is the dog. Oh God,' she groaned as it finally dawned. 'Lawrence, was there a dog in the film?' she asked him. 'One like Lucy?'

Lawrence began to nod, up and down, up and down, long, deliberate movements that almost brought his chin into contact with his chest.

'All right,' she said, putting a hand out to steady him. 'That was it,' she told her father. 'Obviously something was happening to the dog in the film and he . . . Oh Lawrence,' she said exasperatedly. Knowing the retriever was *hers* was bad enough, that Lawrence must have, on some level, bonded so deeply with it, brought a rush of jealousy, like bile, to her throat. Yet how could she not be pleased to realise that her son was capable of feeling worried about and protective of someone – or something – other than himself?

As though echoing her thoughts, her father said, 'It was a dreadful thing for you to go through, darling, but it's very heartening to think that he cares about the dog.'

'Yes,' she mumbled. Then, to her surprise, since

211

Lawrence didn't much like phones, he suddenly stuck out a hand to reach for it.

'David,' he shouted into the earpiece.

'Like this,' Rosalind said, gently turning it around. 'OK, speak now.'

'David. Don't let them hurt Lucy.'

'No, I won't,' David promised. 'Would you like to see her next weekend?'

'Yes. That would be very agreeable. Where are you?' he added, looking around the room as though David might be hiding somewhere.

'Not far away,' David answered. 'I hope you understand that running away is not a good thing to do.'

Lawrence fell silent.

'Please tell me you won't do it again.'

'They were going to kill Lucy,' Lawrence shouted.

'It wasn't real. It was a film, and the dog you saw wasn't Lucy. It was an acting dog that looks like her.'

Lawrence shoved the receiver back at his mother, indicating he'd had enough.

'I should make him something to eat now,' Rosalind said, going back on the line.

'OK. Is Jerry there?'

'No, he left a few minutes ago.'

'I don't like to think of you on your own after such a shock.'

Wanting to tell him he could always come over, she said, 'I'll be fine. Dee's calling in on her way home, and I expect Sally will drop in later too.'

'All right. I'll call again tonight when I'm back in London, in the meantime, don't go blaming yourself for what happened. No one could have foreseen it, and thankfully it's turned out all right.'

If she was going to blame anyone, it would be his damned girlfriend for bringing a dog into their lives in the first place, but she managed to bite back the pettiness and say, 'I'll be here all evening, so don't forget, will you?'

At his end, as he clicked off the call, David was looking pensive. Lisa had already taken some bags down to the car, but he was torn now between going back to London with her and spending another night in Bristol with Rosalind. Opening up the calendar on his iPhone to check what he had scheduled for the morning, he was about to call Rosalind back when Lisa came into the room saying, 'I keep meaning to ask, have you decided yet where you're going to stay the night before the wedding? I mean, I know the official bit is at the registry office the day before, but if we're going to treat the Saturday as if it's the real thing, it's supposed to be bad luck for us to stay under the same roof, and we'll have moved into the house by then.'

With a twinkle in his eye as he slid his phone back into his pocket he said, 'I'll probably summon one of my harem to keep me company at the Hotel du Vin, so please don't worry about me.'

Laughing, she said, 'Just make sure she doesn't wear you out before we go on honeymoon. Have you found a hotel for us yet, by the way?'

He frowned. For the moment he couldn't seem to remember where they were going, much less if he'd booked a hotel.

She eyed him meaningfully. 'I know you're teasing me,' she smiled, 'but just tell me this, are we leaving on the Saturday or the Sunday?'

'Sunday,' he said confidently. He'd have it written down somewhere, he felt sure, so could always amend later if need be, and deciding not to start reading the same sinister reasons into his forgetfulness as he had before, he picked up the remaining bags and carried them down to the car.

Chapter Eleven

'David!' Lisa cried in despair. 'I know we need to make a list of the books we want duplicated in your library at the house, so instead of standing there repeating instructions, why don't you find a pen and paper and do it?'

Fighting back his own ill temper, David tugged open a drawer of the desk they shared, grabbed a pencil and was rummaging around for a notepad when Lisa growled, 'Where the hell are the scissors? I had them a moment ago and now they've disappeared.'

Glancing across the room, which was currently an obstacle course of packing cases, black plastic sacks and mountains of paperwork and magazines still needing to be sorted, he said, 'Try the fridge.'

She looked up in amazement. 'What?'

'Try the fridge,' he repeated, and swiping a sheet of paper from the printer tray, he set about making his list.

A moment later Lisa returned from the kitchen with the scissors. 'How did you know?' she asked.

He nodded towards a carton of milk on the table. 'You made coffee just now, and brought that back with you, so there was a good chance the scissors had been left to chill out next to the champagne.'

Laughing, she went to kiss him. 'Sorry, I'm really irritable today, aren't I? I don't know why. I suppose there's so much to do and such little time left to do it in that I'm afraid we'll forget something vital. When you've finished there, I'll have to go over everything to make sure the movers know what they're supposed to take and what to leave behind.' She glanced at the time. 'I hope Amy's getting on all right overseeing the deliveries at the house. I should give her a call. Actually, it'll have to wait because I have to go and pick up Roxy's dress. Are you expected back at the office today?'

Reaching for his iPhone to check the calendar, he said, 'No, this afternoon's meeting's been cancelled and tonight's announcement on spending reform has been . . . What does that say? Dlyd – delayed until Friday. I must remind Karen that I'm not strong on text-speak.'

'So that means you have to be in London on Friday?' With a sigh of exasperation, she said, 'I thought we were leaving tomorrow to spend our first weekend together at the house.'

'I'll just have to pop back to London for the announcement,' he assured her, and clicking on his phone as it rang, he said, 'Colin, to what do I owe the pleasure?'

Leaving him to chat with his buddy the Foreign Secretary, she returned to the box of photographs she was ready to tape up, but got no further than dropping to her knees before her own mobile started to ring. Managing to locate it down the side of the sofa, she quickly answered before the call went to messages, sounding impatient as she said, 'Yes? Hello?'

'Hey! It's me,' Roxy cried, her ebullience bringing an immediate smile to Lisa's face. 'You haven't forgotten my dress, I hope.'

'I'm going for it any minute. Where are you?'

'At the new house with Mum. It's so gorgeous, Lis. The ponds have got water in them already, and they're floating flowers and plants all over them as I speak. The landscaper told me they're turning on the waterfalls this afternoon to make sure they run down over the terraces to the courtyard the way they're supposed to, but then they'll be off again for more backstage work. It's going to be heaven, I can't wait for you to see it.'

'Nor can I. Has any of the new furniture turned up yet?'

'Yeah, loads. Mum's with the caterers at the moment, they wanted to check out what facilities you have in the kitchen. Hang on, she's saying something . . . She wants to know how the kitchen doors slide back . . . Oh, it's all right, they've worked it out.'

A beat later Amy came on the line. 'What are you doing about flowers on the steps going down to the courtyard?' she asked. 'Is the florist doing them, or do you want the caterer to take care of it?'

'I'm pretty sure I've discussed it with the florist,' Lisa replied, 'but I'll check and get back to you. Have you spoken to Mum today?'

'About an hour ago, so if it's about her shoes, I already know she doesn't like the ones we bought last week, she wants mauve to match her dress – thank you Mum, I know I can always rely on you to make my life easy. What time shall I expect you tomorrow?'

'Around midday, I guess. Listen, I'll talk to you again later, someone's trying to get through.' As she clicked off she found herself wondering, hoping, dreading that it might be Tony. She kept doing that lately and it was driving her crazy. It wasn't that she wanted to hear from him, but for some insane reason his silence was annoying her more than if he was calling every day.

It turned out to be Hayley on the line, wanting to know if she could drop round with a wedding gift.

'But we're not doing gifts,' Lisa cried in protest. 'It was on the invite. Donations to the new Bristol Children's Hospital.'

'I know, and I promise I've already made one, but there's a certain Indian abstract you've long had your eye on, and from what I heard about the new house I think it'll fit in perfectly. So the girls and I have clubbed together and I gave us a fabulous discount.'

'Oh Hayley, it's still too generous. I mean . . .'

'Just tell me when to bring it. It's already packed up, so the movers won't have to do anything apart from handle it with care.'

'I'll make absolutely certain they do. That's so wonderful of you all. It's going to get pride of place somewhere, that's for sure. Either in the entrance hall, or I think it might work best in the sitting room.'

'Your choice. Are you at the flat for the next hour or so?'

'No, I have to go out, but I can pick it up on my way back, if you like. Is it heavy?'

'Quite.'

'Then maybe David should come and collect it. I'll ask him, and perhaps you'll have time for a drink with us later so we can say a proper thank you.'

'Count me in.'

As she rang off, David said, 'So what have you roped me in for?'

After telling him, she set about the rest of the packing, while he disappeared into the bedroom to start sorting out what he was going to take from there.

'We should have done this days ago,' she groaned when she followed him in to track down her bag. 'Are you OK? What are you looking for?'

'I'm damned if I can remember,' he replied. 'Look at all this stuff. Where are you going?'

'To get Roxy's dress. Then I might pop into Fortnums to buy all the staples to ship down to Bristol. Anything you need?'

'Lime marmalade and the special blend tea we have. We don't want to be without that. What time will you be back?' he asked as she kissed him.

'I'm not sure. I'll call while I'm out. Don't forget to go to Hayley's. She's expecting you any time in the next hour. Did Colin want anything in particular, by the way?' She was already half out of the door.

When he didn't answer she turned back.

'Hello,' she said, waving a hand.

His eyes came to hers. 'Sorry,' he said. 'What did you . . .? Ah, Colin. He wondered why . . . It doesn't matter. We'll probably get together for a chat after the announcement on Friday, so don't count on me being back much before late afternoon.'

Though she wanted to protest, catching a glimpse of how tired he looked she softened her tone as she said, 'I'm sorry I woke you in the night. I tried not to make a noise when I got up . . .'

'I was already awake,' he assured her. 'That's what we get for eating late and drinking too much. Sleepless nights and hangovers when we could well do without them.' He looked behind him as his mobile started to ring.

Leaving him to take the call she went into the bathroom, and was halfway through rebraiding her hair when he came to find her. 'I'm sorry, I'm supposed to be at a meeting,' he said, 'but don't do any of the heavy stuff without me, and when I get back we have to make a list of the books to duplicate for my study in Bristol.'

Eyeing him meaningfully, she said, 'Will you please stop winding me up, and when you do go online to order them don't forget to add a new *Roget's International Thesaurus* for me, and the latest Chambers dictionary. It's time I updated, especially if I'm going to become a novelist,' and with a playful twinkle she blew him another kiss before sweeping out into the kind of blustery day that wasn't at all welcome, with not much more than a week to go to the wedding.

David's face was taut with anxiety when he returned to the flat an hour and a half later. It had been a short, but stressful meeting that had left everyone feeling frustrated and in many cases, he was sure, wondering why they'd bothered to come. The sense of failure and despondency he'd walked away with was still clinging to him like the spume of a wave, while the real rage of the tide was proving so elusive that he wanted to smash his hand against the front door as he let himself in. What the hell was happening to him? Were things going into his head and getting stuck there? Or were they just not going in at all?

When he'd spoken everyone had seemed to listen, then they debated, challenged, agreed, and planned. He knew what had to be done, how they should move forward, but then suddenly they were looking at him as though he was a stranger who'd said something outrageous or insane, when all he'd done, as far as he was aware, was ask a perfectly straightforward question.

'You've already asked that,' Colin Larch told him, 'and we've given you the answer.'

David had no idea now what he'd said in response, because looking back on the last hour or so was like listening to a badly tuned radio. Some events were clear, while others were so hazy he wasn't sure if they were there at all.

Still, at least he'd remembered to go and pick up the painting from Hayley, he was thinking as he let himself into the flat. And now he would go online to order the books he needed from Amazon. However, when he turned on his computer and called up his emails he saw, from the order confirmations, that he'd already done it.

* * *

'Dad, it's me,' Rosalind said into her mobile. 'Where are you?'

'At the flat, in London,' he replied. 'Is everything OK?'

She waited for a lorry to pass, feeling the draught of warm dusty air wrapping itself around her like a veil, then began crossing the iron footbridge towards the Mud Dock cafe. He didn't know. He hadn't clocked what day it was. 'Yes, fine,' she lied, managing to keep her voice steady. 'I was just wondering if you were coming for lunch on Saturday, that's all.'

The silence that followed didn't really surprise her, but it crushed her anyway.

'Darling,' he said softly, 'I'm sure I told you that Lisa and I are moving into the new house this weekend, but if you'd like to come over . . .'

'No, no,' she cut in. 'I don't want to get in the way.'

'You wouldn't be in the way. In fact, you'd be very welcome.'

'By you, I'm sure. Anyway,' she pressed on hastily, 'if you change your mind, Jerry's back tomorrow and Dee's around, so it would be a nice family get-together if you wanted to join us.' Had he really forgotten? She didn't want to believe that he had. 'It would make Lawrence's day if you came, obviously, especially if you . . . if you brought the dog.'

With the kind of chuckle he always used when feeling awkward and wanting to change the subject, he said, 'Has he gone on his trip to the museum today?'

'Yes, he has, and I'm sure he'll be full of it later.

You remember how he was the last time we took him to the zoo? He recited his list of animals so often over the next couple of weeks that we could all reel them off in the end.'

Laughing, David said, 'That was a lovely day out. Jerry was there too, as I recall.'

She swallowed hard. 'And Mum,' she added in a whisper. Then, summoning a stronger voice to try and quash her yearning, 'She got all squeamish in the Reptile House, which made Lawrence laugh so loudly that we were asked to leave because we were disturbing everyone else. Then we had to go back because she'd lost an earring.'

'Oh yes, the earring,' he laughed.

She was smiling too. 'You found it and clipped it to your ear and waited for one of us to notice.'

'And you all pretended not to, you horrors, so I was left walking round the zoo with a bright orange bauble bouncing off my ear thinking I was very witty and having a joke on your mother, when you were all having a joke on me. If my little champion Lawrence hadn't noticed, I might still be wearing it now.'

With a spluttering laugh, she said, 'Do you remember how he took to wearing the earring after? He got teased terribly about it at school.' She was at the Mud Dock now, climbing the stairs to the eatery. The morning-coffee drinkers had already left and lunch wasn't yet under way. Choosing a window table, beneath an array of hanging bicycles, she ordered a decaff latte and turned to stare out at the basin. 'I was wondering,' she said, turning her back so the milling staff couldn't hear, 'if you've been to Mum's grave lately.'

223

Though she knew already what the answer was going to be, it upset her even more than she'd expected when he said, 'Well, I confess, it's been a while since I was there, so I must go again.'

Yes, he must. 'Soon?'

'Of course, soon.'

She had to swallow again, and she was painfully tense inside as she said, 'When you go, don't take *her*, will you?'

There was a moment before he replied, and this time she felt sure the date was finally registering. 'Darling, I'm sorry you're feeling sad today,' he said gently. 'I should have called . . .'

But you didn't! 'She would have been fifty-two today,' she said, her eyes flooding with tears.

'Rosalind, what can I say? There's so much going on here . . .'

'Do you remember,' she cut in, 'how we always used to have double parties on our birthdays? Children in the day, adults at night, until I was old enough for us all to combine.'

'Yes, of course I do. They were wonderful times. Very special memories.'

So special you're not even thinking about them today. 'She used to love buying presents,' she tried to laugh. 'She even used to buy us one for her birthday so we wouldn't feel left out.'

'She was always very generous.'

'I know. Do you remember the party she threw for your fiftieth? There was even more to celebrate that year because she'd gone into remission.'

'Yes, she had, sweetheart, but unfortunately it didn't last anywhere near as long as it should have.'

'No,' she said brokenly.

'Darling, where are you? I think you should be with Dee, or Sally, if Jerry's not around.'

'I will be later. There's some business I have to attend to this morning. I'm interviewing a new decorator. Roland Swift's retiring at the end of the month.'

'Then we must give him a proper send-off. How about a gold paintbrush, or a magic ladder?'

Laughing, because she knew he wanted her to, she said, 'Don't worry, I've already got it sorted. He's never been abroad, apparently, so I talked to Joan, his wife, and they're going to spend a fortnight in Spain.'

'A very good idea. You know, your mother would be extremely proud of how much care you take of the people who've been loyal to us over the years, and of the way you make sure the properties are well kept and secure. She was always a . . . always a . . . Sorry, darling, just a moment.'

Guessing *she* had distracted him, Rosalind held on to the phone, the lump in her throat so large that she could hardly swallow. When he came back on the line she said, 'Do you think this is fair, Dad, what you're doing to Mum now?'

The line went quiet again, and she could almost see his face at the other end, tormented with misery and guilt, not knowing what to say that would make this any easier for either of them. 'Darling,' he said in the end, 'I know how you feel, and I'm sorry for it, truly I am, but . . .'

'It's all right, you don't have to say any more,' she cut in before he could start making excuses. 'I have to go now anyway, the new chap's just turned up,' and with a hurried goodbye, she clicked off the phone and stuffed it deeply into her bag. No one had come through the door since she'd sat down, but she'd needed to finish the call then or she'd have ended up disgracing herself in public. As it was, she was finding it difficult to push back the tears.

She should never have called him when she had. Why hadn't she waited till she got home, or at least done it while she was in the car? It was too late now to berate herself for bad timing. It was done and she should have known better than to have contacted him at all, because there had never been much doubt that she'd end up feeling even worse than she had before. He'd never forgotten her mother's birthday before, but she supposed he didn't see much reason to remember it now. Unable to bear even the thought of that, she pressed a hand to her mouth to stifle a sob. Sometimes she wondered if it wouldn't be best for them all if she were simply to take Lawrence away somewhere and never come back again. Everyone's problems would be over then – Jerry's, hers, Lawrence's . . . And her father and his mistress would be free to get on with their blessed and totally selfish lives without anyone bothering their consciences or standing in their way.

It really wasn't that Lisa wanted Tony to call. In fact, if he did, especially this close to the wedding, she'd be so furious she'd ring off before he even had a chance to get past hello. However, the fact that he hadn't made any attempt at all to be in touch since the day they'd had lunch – she had to concede she'd been the one to ring him over the money-laundering business – was starting to occupy almost as many of her thoughts as the wedding itself.

Actually, that was an exaggeration. Every moment of every day was taken up with the wedding now, but somehow, in some way he was managing to squeeze himself into the pauses, or roll around the questions, or move along with the decisions as though, God forbid, he was some kind of phantom guest who might, knowing him, morph into terrible reality at just the wrong moment.

'He wouldn't, would he?' she said to Brendan, her now ex-editor, who was the only person she could confide in at this late stage. Amy would go ballistic if she thought Tony Sommerville was even the whisper of a thought in her mind, and her mother would probably start worrying herself into some sort of funny turn. As for her other friends, she'd have so much explaining to do about why he was on her mind at all right now that it simply wasn't worth going there even if she had the time, which she didn't.

'Sweetie, he's on a buying trip in Beijing,' Brendan told her, 'and as far as I know he's there until the end of August, so don't worry, you're safe.'

'I can't let him ruin my wedding,' Lisa insisted. 'David's a wonderful man, and he doesn't deserve to have anything go wrong now when he's been so kind and generous and . . .'

'As I said, sweetie . . .'

'. . . I'm so lucky to be back with him. I know now that he's all I've ever wanted. Which isn't to minimise what I had with Tony, because that was wonderful too, at times, but with David . . . It's really special, you know the way things are when you go back such a long way?'

'Yeah, right,' Brendan answered, sounding vaguely baffled.

'So if Tony gets in touch with you to ask anything at all about me your answer is that you don't know how I am, what date I'm getting married, where I'm going on my honeymoon, where I'm going to be living. You know zilch, right?'

'Right. And you would be telling me this because?'

'Because . . . For God's sake, Brendan, you know Tony Sommerville and his stunts as well as I do, and any one of them would be totally inappropriate as well as unwelcome right now. I loved him, I admit it, but I'm over it, and I hope he is too. And if you happen to speak to him again before I do, please tell him I hope he'll be very happy with Mrs Overall, because . . .'

'Mrs who?'

'Overall – as in cleaner of an antique shop? I wasn't fooled, Brendan, and frankly, this conversation's gone on long enough. I don't want to waste any more time thinking, or worrying about him, because I've got more than enough to do about the . . .'

'Lisa, where are you?'

She looked around. 'Old Bond Street, by the flower seller, why?'

'Take yourself into the nearest cafe or wine bar, treat yourself to a nice hot cup of tea, or very large glass of the vino, and calm down, for God's sake.'

Stopping in her tracks, she said, 'You're right. I'm sounding hysterical, aren't I?'

'A bit. But I guess it's to be expected, pre-wedding nerves and all that.'

She looked around at the designer shops and tourists, and as the reality of her surroundings began sliding into focus she said, 'I am carrying my niece's bridesmaid's dress, together with a jar of lime marmalade and some special brew tea for my soon-to-be-husband, plus some fancy undies I've just bought for our honeymoon, and yet I'm standing here talking to you about Tony Sommerville. I've lost the plot, haven't I?'

'Sounds like it, sweetie.'

'Bren, do me a favour and forget I ever made this call?'

'Sorry, who are you?' he said. 'Must be a wrong number. Toodle-pip,' and the line went dead.

Lisa barely had a chance to click off her end or even gather her thoughts before the phone rang again. It was Miles.

'I hope this is a convenient time,' he said. 'If not I can always call back.'

'It's OK, now's fine,' she assured him, starting to walk on. 'What can I do for you?'

'Actually, if you were able to meet me,' he said. 'I'm on Piccadilly at the moment . . .'

She glanced at the clock outside the Rolex shop. She really didn't have time – however, since there was something she wanted to ask him, she said, 'If you can be at the Wolseley in the next ten minutes . . .'

'I'll be there,' he assured her, and quickly rang off.

* * *

It hadn't been Miles's intention to suggest they meet when he'd called Lisa. However, the words had materialised almost of their own accord, and now here he was, at the Wolseley, watching her weaving through the closely packed tables towards him looking as radiant and graceful as a movie star.

By the time she reached him he was already on his feet, holding out a hand to greet her. 'Thanks for coming,' he said, feeling a humiliating heat flooding his cheeks. 'I appreciate how busy you must be this week.'

'And some,' she laughed, 'but at least I'm not feeling quite as wound up as I was ten minutes ago. I'll have a fresh mint tea,' she told the waiter.

'The same,' Miles added. As they sat down he almost blurted out *Do you come here often*, but mercifully managed to swallow the abysmal cliché before it smothered him with yet more embarrassment.

'So,' she said, 'I hope this meeting is going to end better than the last one. I take it you didn't pass my message on to Rosalind.'

'No, I didn't,' he admitted.

Her expression became wry. 'I'm not sure whether that's good or bad,' she said, 'but let's presume it's good. So now I'm going to guess that you're here because David's instructed you to apologise for telling me about the money-laundering thing. If that is the case, then please don't, because you were right to tell me.'

'Actually, he hasn't mentioned it again,' he informed her, 'but I'm bracing myself for when he does.'

Appearing to appreciate his irony, she laughed

as she said, 'I generally find his bark is worse than his bite, so I wouldn't worry too much if I were you. So, as my guesses don't seem to be yielding much success I'm handing over to you to tell me why we're here.'

Deciding there was no other way than to come straight to the point, he said, 'I need to ask you about this "aberration" he had. Do you know any more than I do about what happened, exactly, and do you have any idea what caused it?'

She sat back as the tea arrived, and waited until it was poured before saying, 'To be honest, I'm not sure if you're the person I should be saying this to, but I know you have David's best interests at heart so I will. I imagine he told you that this "aberration" was caused by stress . . .'

He nodded.

'. . . and we both know that one way or another he's been under a lot of it lately, but what I think he's finding the hardest of all to deal with is how Rosalind is reacting to him getting married again.'

He didn't argue with that, because knowing what he did about Rosalind's almost pathological resistance to her father's betrayal of her mother, as she chose to see it, he couldn't.

'He's not sleeping well,' Lisa continued, 'actually neither of us is at the moment, but I guess that's only to be expected with so much going on, but David's insomnia . . . Well, what – *who* – else matters to him more than his daughter?' Her eyes became intent with feeling. 'You know her,' she said, 'so tell me, do you think there's anything I can do, anything at all, to help change her mind about me?'

Don't marry him were the words that burst from the bounds of his self-control. He would never utter them, of course, but even if he did he knew they'd ring falsely as advice on how to win over Rosalind. In their stark, humiliating truth, they would be a plea from him not to take herself even further from his reach. How fortunate it was that minds were as impenetrable as languages never learned, he was thinking.

'It would mean so much to David if she'd come to the wedding,' she continued. 'He'd never tell me this, I know, but a part of him is dreading the day because of how awful he's going to feel thinking of her at home on her own. Lawrence will be with us, and I think Jerry will too. I wish she wouldn't do this to herself. If she'd just give me a chance . . .'

'Lisa? Lisa Martin? Is that you?' a voice suddenly boomed across the restaurant.

As she looked up to see who it was, Miles could only marvel at how swiftly she was able to summon warmth to her smile, when he'd caught the flash of annoyance at being interrupted. 'Hannah Berinski,' she said, appearing as pleased to see the large American female in a pink straw hat and purple kaftan as the woman could wish for.

'Yes, it is you!' Hannah Berinski exclaimed, banging her plump bejewelled fists together. 'I told you, Hugo. I'd know that gorgeous braid anywhere. How are you, pumpkin? Come here, let me get a look at you.'

Glancing apologetically at Miles she said, 'Excuse me,' and dropping her napkin on her chair she threaded a path through to where the matri-arch of US stereotype was holding out a pair of quivering flabby arms with which to smother her.

As he waited for the reunion to reach its denoue-ment Miles sipped his tea and felt ludicrously jealous of the time they were stealing from him. How foolish and sad he was.

'Sorry about that,' she said, sitting down again. 'I'd have introduced you, but if I'd told them you work for David wild elephants wouldn't have kept them away. So I said you were my niece's new boyfriend who I'm vetting for my sister.'

His smile was faint. *Her niece's boyfriend. A nonentity kept at arm's length by the barrier of a gener-ation, and not even the whisper of suspicion that she might have a secret amour.* Was he losing his mind?

'Going back to what we were saying,' she said, picking up her tea, 'I've been thinking about writing a letter to Rosalind to try and persuade her to come to the wedding.' The expression on her face indicated she did not feel confident of success. 'She wouldn't have to speak to me if she didn't want to,' she explained, as though he might act as arbiter between them. 'It's just that it would mean so much to David to have her there, and surely his happiness matters more to her than the way she feels about me. I mean, I understand that she's still finding it hard to get over her mother, and as far as she's concerned I'm stealing him away, but . . .' She lowered her eyes and let her voice trail away.

Glad that putting a hand on hers was forbidden, since it would seem mawkish, or worse, camp, he remained as he was as he said, 'If you're asking do I think it's a good idea to write to her then I have to say yes, because if you don't you'll never know if it might have made a difference.'

She could hardly have looked more pleased. 'I'm so glad you said that,' she told him, a child-like colour suffusing her cheeks, 'because the very fact you think I should try gives me hope that I'll be able to come up with something, even if it's only a word or two, that will reach her.'

Rosalind was in her study, surrounded by paper-work, when she heard Jerry driving up to the house. It was late on Saturday afternoon, a week before *the wedding*, which she was doing her utmost not to think about. However, that was going to become increasingly difficult now that he had begun the leave he'd taken to cover it.

Remembering she still hadn't cleared away the remains of a boozy lunch she'd had with the girls, she got quickly to her feet, staggered as she turned, then made her way out to the terrace where the table was strewn with screwed-up paper napkins in greens and yellows that matched the summery plates and brightly painted bowls of leftover salad and fruit. There were also three empty wine glasses and a third bottle of wine only just over half full.

'Hi,' she said thickly, as he came towards her, 'you're earlier than I expected.'

'Not much traffic on the road,' he replied, draping his uniform jacket over the back of a chair before stooping to kiss her. 'Looks like you've had a bit of a party.'

'Just Dee and Sally. There's plenty more in the fridge if you'd like me . . .'

'I'm fine,' he assured her, sinking into one of the softly padded chairs and tilting his face up to the sun. 'I had a late breakfast. Where's Lawrence?'

She sighed irritably. 'In his tree house and refusing to come down unless Dad brings back the dog.'

Jerry glanced across the garden to where Lawrence's private dwelling was only partly visible from where they were sitting.

As she watched him Rosalind hoped that he might go and try to reason with his son, lost cause though it might already be, but when his eyes came back to hers with a strained, almost defeated look she knew he wouldn't, and wanted to scream or cry, she hardly knew which. 'Have a drink,' she offered. 'It's amazing how much better everything seems when you do.'

He appeared undecided for a moment, then said, 'Yes, OK.'

After fetching a clean glass from the kitchen she filled it almost to the brim, did the same with hers, and sat down too. 'So how was the West Coast?' she asked, taking a sip.

'That was last week,' he replied. 'I've just come back from Mumbai.'

'Yes, of course, sorry. Oh, and sorry I missed your call on Thursday night, I was over at Dee's, but I rang back.'

'I know, you left a message,' he reminded her. 'And as a matter of fact, you sounded as though you'd had a few then, and there are two empty bottles . . .'

'Please don't start getting on my case,' she said

tetchily. 'I'm in my own home, I'm not driving, I don't have to go anywhere or see anyone for the rest of the day, and after the week I've had I think I'm entitled to indulge myself.'

Lifting his glass, he said, 'Why? What's happened?'

Just like her father he'd forgotten, but there again why should he remember his mother-in-law's birthday? 'Oh, you know, tenants, estate agents, solicitors, cleaning companies,' she said, trying not to bite out the words. 'I don't know what's the matter with everyone these days. Nothing ever gets done on time, or in the proper way . . . And now Lawrence won't speak to anyone, or even eat, until the dog comes back. What am I supposed to do with him, that's what I want to know? It's not his dog. He can't just make up his mind he wants it here and expect it to happen.'

'Have you told your father?'

'Not yet, no.' She knew he wouldn't want to hear why, but she was going to tell him anyway. 'Frankly, I don't want *her* thinking she can use the animal to worm her way into our family, and that's what she's up to, I know it.'

His eyes remained down as he sipped his wine, then putting the glass back on the table, he said mildly, 'Much mail?'

'Some. It's on your desk, and I know you're trying to change the subject, but . . .'

'Rosalind, I've hardly been back five minutes . . .'

'I'm aware of that, and I'm sorry my issues are so irritating for you, but when it comes to my son and what's good for him . . .'

'You can't use him in this battle. It's not right, and it's not fair either. He likes the dog . . .'

'He's fixated on it. It's all he'll talk about. I want Lucy back. I'm not going to bed until Lucy comes back. I'm not getting up until Lucy comes back. I'm staying in my tree until Lucy comes back. It's driving me insane.'

'It wouldn't if the dog belonged to anyone else.'

Her eyes flashed. 'That's not particularly helpful, thank you very much. I could do with your support over this, but as we know that's in as short supply these days as your fidelity . . .'

'Oh for God's sake,' he snapped. 'You're like a stuck record sometimes, and as there's obviously no point trying to reason with you while you're in this state I'm going to take a shower.'

'No! Don't go yet,' she cried as he started to get up. 'I need to talk to you. It's not about that,' she promised, as he eyed her warily, probably assuming she was going to throw his affair in his face again. The monstrous jealousy and insecurity inside her wanted to, because it always did, but she needed to force it under control so she could ask his advice about her new concerns regarding her father.

'So what is it about?' he asked, sinking back into his chair.

After taking a breath to try to clear the grape fog in her head, she said, 'Dad was here this morning, going over the books. At least, that's what I thought he was doing, but when I went to check on him I found him standing at the window staring out.'

Jerry's eyebrows rose. 'And?' he prompted.

'Well, it just struck me as odd that he hadn't done anything yet, even though he'd been in there for over an hour, and when I asked if he was all right he didn't seem to hear me at first, so I asked again, and he shook his head.'

Jerry took another sip of his wine. Then, seeming to realise he'd missed something, he said, 'I'm sorry, you're going to have to be more specific.'

'OK, well, it was like he was miles away when he shook his head, and then he came to and said of course he was all right, but I just know he wasn't.'

Jerry almost rolled his eyes. 'So what do you want me to do?' he asked.

She took a breath. 'I was wondering if you'd have a chat with him, you know, to try and find out if he's . . . Well, if he's having second thoughts about things, because I'm sure that's what it . . .'

'OK, I've had enough,' he said, getting to his feet. 'I'm going to take that shower, and perhaps, by the time I come down, you'll have managed to sober up enough for us to talk about something else for a while. If you haven't, I'll be getting back into the car and driving away.'

'Well, wouldn't *that* be a responsible thing to do?' she shot after him. 'I don't expect you'd even bother to say goodbye to your son either. And why would you, when you can't even bring yourself to say hello?'

He spun round furiously. 'In case you hadn't noticed, no one in this house is interested in whether I'm here or not,' he raged. 'The minute I get in all you want to talk about is your father. You're so obsessed with what's going on in his life that you don't spare a moment's thought for me or what might be happening in mine.'

'You've hardly given me a chance . . .'

'You're not *interested*,' he yelled. 'Nor is Lawrence. He either wants David or apparently the dog now. That's it! I can go over there, if you like, and try talking to him, but we both know he'll just ignore me, or repeat what he's been saying to you.'

'At least you'd be making some kind of contact with him. Carrying on as though he's not there is hardly going to help matters, is it?'

'Maybe not, but right now I'm not in much of a mood to be treated like a nobody by my own son, any more than I care to sit here listening to you rant on about your father and Lisa Martin.'

As he stormed off inside, Rosalind snatched up the bottle and refilled her glass. It was more a gesture to spite him than because she wanted more wine, but now it was there she might as well drink it.

After downing half of it she closed her eyes and tried to bring herself down from the heights of anger. She didn't want to treat Jerry this way, and hated herself when she did, but it was as though she went into self-destruct mode when he was around, especially when she'd been drinking. But for God's sake, what did he expect when he'd forgotten her mother's birthday? He had to know how important it was to her, so how the hell was ignoring it supposed to convince her she still mattered to him, that's what she'd like to know? Maybe she should ask when he came down again, but if she did she knew they'd only end up in another blazing row, and with her father seeming more and more distant these days she had to start trying harder to hang on to Jerry, or she would end up losing him too.

'I'm sorry, Jerry, I wish I knew what to tell you,' David was saying as he and Jerry walked down through a freshly cut meadow towards the lake. 'I'm as worried about her as you are, but nothing I say ever seems to get through to her.'

Not having expected any other sort of answer, Jerry sighed and grabbed a strand of long grass from a tuft as he walked along. 'She's still adamant she won't come to the wedding,' he said. 'It seems wrong to go without her, but I have to be there for Lawrence. And for you,' he added quickly.

David's smile was fleeting. 'Thank you,' he said quietly. Then, 'I know I'm to blame for how unhappy she is. I should have waited before announcing my marriage plans, I can see that now in a way I wouldn't allow myself to before. Lisa kept saying we shouldn't be so hasty, but I wouldn't listen and it's too late now to turn back. Apart from anything else it wouldn't be fair on Lisa.'

'No, of course not,' Jerry agreed, 'and please don't think that's what I'm suggesting.'

David shook his head.

As they reached the lake shore Jerry stared down at the minnows darting about in the reeds, while David gazed out towards the house where he and Catrina used to live.

'She's got it into her head,' Jerry said after a while, 'that you want to . . . Well, that you want to change your mind about Lisa but you can't bring yourself to hurt her.'

When David didn't respond he turned to look at him, then followed the direction of his eyes.

'I forgot Catrina's birthday this week,' David told him.

Jerry almost groaned in dismay. Now he knew why Rosalind was behaving the way she was with him, because he'd forgotten too.

'I still miss her,' David confessed. 'Having Lisa in my life hasn't changed that.'

Not knowing what to say, Jerry continued to gaze at the house that held so many of their memories.

'I know Rosalind's telling herself that I want to change my mind,' David said, 'but I don't, because if there's one thing I'm absolutely certain of it's the way I feel about Lisa.' Then with a sigh, 'I only wish I could say the same about everything else,' and after clapping a hand on Jerry's shoulder he turned to walk back to where they'd left their cars.

Chapter Twelve

'Come here, Mrs Kirby,' David laughed, as a jubilant Lisa threw her arms around Amy and Theo. 'It's me you've just married, in case you'd forgotten.'

Flushed with happiness, Lisa flung herself from the doorway of Bristol Registry Office into his embrace and raised her mouth for a kiss. 'But we're not supposed to be making a big deal of it,' she reminded him. 'Tomorrow is when we really tie the knot. Today we've just been made official.'

'Let's get a move on,' Amy urged, glancing around to see if anyone was watching. 'If we don't someone's bound to recognise you, and the next thing we know it'll be in tomorrow's papers and that's definitely not what we want.'

Gripping David's arm as they hurried along Corn Street towards the Galleries where they'd left the cars, Lisa struggled with the urge to stop for some champagne. They couldn't risk it though, because they were all driving later, and besides there were still a million things to do. 'We should be just in time to get to the station,' she said, glancing at her watch. 'Heather's train is due in at four, then after we've taken her to the house we'll have to be back there by six for Sheelagh and Baz.'

'Remind me who they all are again,' David said, cocking a teasing eyebrow at Amy as she glanced over her shoulder. 'I'm hardly going to know anyone,' he told her.

'You know us,' Amy said comfortingly, 'and if you're feeling at a loss at all, there's always Matilda to keep you company.'

'Now you're talking,' he grinned. 'So, Heather is?'

'Only the celebrant,' Lisa informed him in a Roxy-type cant. 'For heaven's sake, don't forget who she is tomorrow. And Sheelagh and Baz are the singers. Royston and his wonderful jazz band are already booked into the Hotel du Vin – are you having dinner with them later?' she asked Amy and Theo.

'That's the plan,' Theo replied.

'Then Amy, you're coming on to spend the night with me at the house?'

'Correct,' Amy answered.

'How's Roxy getting there?'

'We're dropping her off before we go to dinner.'

'Great. The hairdresser and make-up artist are already there, we know that, and Izzy should have arrived with the dress by now. We left the florist doing her stuff, so that's under way, and the caterer was about to deliver the tables and chairs as we left – let's pray it doesn't rain tonight. The land-scaper's promised me the gazebo will be ready in time . . .'

'It will,' David assured her. 'It was already up before we left, so they only have to decorate it.'

Turning her focus on him, she said, 'You've got everything you need, haven't you? Your and Lawrence's suits are at Rosalind's?'

'Jerry picked them up yesterday, so yes, they're there.'

Trying not to worry about how at risk they might be in Rosalind's house, she said, 'How are you doing with your lines? Do you think you've memorised them yet?'

'I'm getting there. What about you?'

'About the same. We should have a couple more run-throughs before you leave tonight. What time are you going?'

'I'm not sure I've worked that out yet, but I expect you'll tell me if I look as though I'm hanging around too long.'

Laughing, she hugged his arm, then reached into her bag for the phone. 'Twelve text messages,' she cried as she turned it back on.

'Will that be in addition to the five hundred and sixty you've already received?' Amy enquired archly, 'or including?'

'In addition, of course,' Lisa retorted. In reality she'd received more than fifty good-luck messages by now, mostly by email, and could only imagine how many more might arrive tomorrow. Then there were the dozens of cards that had come flooding in during the past week, and the donations to the Children's Hospital had already gone over ten thousand pounds. Whatever the final figure turned out to be, she and David had pledged to match it.

She and David. Mr and Mrs Kirby. Lisa Martin Kirby.

Thrilling as it was, it was feeling strange to think she had another name now, as though there was a new part to herself that she hadn't yet had time to discover. She wondered what it was going to be like, being one half of a partnership after so many years of never having had to consult anyone but herself. She didn't seem to be doing badly so far, after all she and David had been living together for a little over eight months and apart from the odd lapse when he called her Catrina (only to be expected, but never welcome), or her annoying habit of not hanging up her clothes as soon as she took them off – apart from when they were about to make love – as far as she was concerned they were rubbing along very well together. Which was a lot more than she could say for the tempestuous attempts she and Tony had made at existing under the same roof, seven months being the longest stretch without a break, as she recalled. But his was a different personality altogether, and clearly one that didn't bring out the best in hers, at least not these days, so it was definitely a good thing that they'd finally gone their separate ways.

An hour later they were back at the house with Heather safely installed in one of the guest rooms and what seemed like an army of other people coming and going from a whole range of vehicles, with flowers, tables, linens, glasses, tureens, dishes of all sizes, silverware, menu cards, microphones, camera equipment and heaven only knew what else being transported back and forth in various trunks and trolleys.

'David! Where are you?' Lisa shouted, running

down from the bedroom where she'd left Izzy sorting out the dress.

'In here,' he shouted back.

She found him in the spa, watching a cascade of crystal water rushing into an already half-full swimming pool.

'It's a shame it won't be ready for anyone to use over the weekend,' he commented, as he put an arm around her, 'unless they want to brave it unheated, that is.'

'It'll be ready for when we get back,' she reminded him, thinking what heaven it was going to be having their very own pool to exercise in each day. 'I really love you for this,' she told him meaningfully. 'It's the most beautiful home anyone could ever wish for.'

He gazed lovingly into her eyes. 'And you're the most beautiful wife,' he said softly.

Wife. It sounded as though he was talking about someone else, someone who didn't fit her persona at all. *Wife.* She'd had no idea until now how much she'd enjoyed not being a wife, but on the other hand she had all the time in the world to start loving it. And slipping her arms around him, she murmured longingly as his mouth came to hers.

A moment later a crash outside brought them back to their senses. They waited for shouts of dismay or anger, but fortunately none came, so assuming there was no crisis, she said, 'OK, now, why was I looking for you? Ah, I know. Please don't go upstairs before we leave for the station, or if you do, no going into our bedroom, because my dress is hanging from one of the picture hooks and you're not allowed to see it . . .'

'. . . until tomorrow,' he finished. 'Don't worry, I haven't forgotten. In fact, if it's all right with you, I was thinking about leaving you to it now, unless you need me for anything else, of course. I'll leave the car for you to go and pick up . . . the singers . . .'

'Sheelagh and Baz. Why the rush?'

'No rush. It's just that Rosalind will be expecting me at some point, and I thought if you'd rather I was out of the way now . . .'

Understanding how torn he must be feeling, she smiled tenderly as she said, 'Go on, we can manage from here, and take the car if you like. I can always go to collect *the singers* in a taxi.'

'Sheelagh and Baz,' he said, tweaking her nose. 'Are you sure you don't mind?'

'Of course not. Will you tell her we're already married?'

He shook his head. 'I doubt it. It's probably best to let her think it's all happening tomorrow, that way she won't feel as though I've gone behind her back, which I have, of course, but hopefully by the time she finds out it won't matter any more.'

Tony's text came just before midnight, which was probably around nine or ten in the morning, Beijing time, Lisa calculated – she couldn't quite remember whether they were eight or nine hours ahead.

It wasn't a long message, nor was it at all what she'd expected. *Hey Babe, just to say I'll be thinking of you on your big day. My loss is his gain, but you know what they say, may the best man win. Please don't worry about me trying to mess things up for you (I bet that's what you're thinking). I've been a fool and now I'm paying the price. Be happy, my sweetheart. You'll always mean the world to me. Tx*

Though her heart swelled with feeling, she told herself that most of it was relief, because now she could be confident that he really wouldn't do something stupid, like sky-diving in at the crucial moment to try and whisk her away.

Her phone bleeped with another incoming text.

PS: It's not too late yet. You don't have to go through with it.

Smiling, she started to tap in a reply telling him she already had, but in the end she decided not to send it.

Rosalind knew she should have said no. When her father asked if he could stay the night before his wedding she should have come straight out and said that she was sorry, but it wasn't a good idea. Instead, she'd thought to use it as a last-minute opportunity to persuade him to change his mind.

It hadn't worked, of course, not because she'd tried and failed, but because Jerry had barely left them alone all evening, and even when he wasn't in the room Dee had been there with her son Wills and his girlfriend Daisy. Now it was Saturday morning and the three people closest to her, her father, her husband and her son, were all upstairs getting ready for an event – a farce, she'd rather call it – that couldn't possibly include her.

She was in her study going through the company accounts that her father had promised to check, but still hadn't. She could hear them moving about upstairs, the sound of voices, footsteps, showers going on and off, the news coming from a TV in one of the bedrooms. Beneath it all, as she was, felt like being in her own private hell.

Hearing footsteps on the stairs she reached for a tissue, and quickly blew her nose. Jerry would only become impatient if he saw she was upset, and she wasn't feeling strong enough to argue with him this morning. The fact that he was going to support her father, not only because of Lawrence, but to act as one of the ushers, was another betrayal on top of his affair. Lawrence, in his non-expressive, insular way, was proud of the special role the most special person in his world had asked him to play, and no doubt ecstatic that the dog was going to be there too. What more joy could her son wish for, apart from a properly functioning mind that would allow him to have friends and maybe a sense of loyalty towards his mother? She wouldn't dream of spoiling this for him though, she loved him too much for that.

'Doesn't your father fall into the same category?' Jerry had asked last night. 'Don't you love him too much to spoil it for him too?'

'Lawrence isn't old enough to understand what this is really all about,' she'd replied.

'And you think being older and who he is makes your father immune to the way you're behaving?'

She hadn't answered the question, because even if she'd tried to explain he wouldn't understand how devastating all this was for her – or how afraid she was that her father would wake up one day to realise that Lisa Martin had betrayed him the same way Jerry had betrayed her. She felt sure it was going to happen, and couldn't bear to think of her father going through something so shattering – losing his wife had been shattering enough.

Dee would be coming over later to keep her company while Wills and his girlfriend went to the wedding. She hadn't yet decided whether to tell Dee about the letter Lisa Martin had sent, but suspected she wouldn't. It had turned up in the mail at the beginning of the week, with the sender's name and address printed in grey ink on the back. When she'd seen it she'd felt sick, and had hardly been able to touch it. It was like an invasion, a rude and calculating attempt to break through her defences to . . . what? Persuade her to go today? Maybe it was to thank her for staying away.

It had been taken by the dustmen now, in shreds, unread and unable to be pieced back together or to contaminate her world any further.

'Ah, here you are,' Jerry said, putting his head round the door. 'Are you OK?'

'What do *you* think?' she replied, not bothering to look up. She could tell by his shoes and trouser bottoms that he was in his wedding attire now, and she didn't want to see him looking smart and dapper for an occasion that was nothing short of a travesty in her eyes.

'Have you had breakfast?' he asked.

'I'm not hungry.'

With a sigh he said, 'Rosalind, it doesn't have to be like this. If you'd just . . .'

'Please leave me alone.'

He stood looking at her, clearly torn, and she could almost feel his exasperation. In the end he left and though she'd told him to, it still hurt.

Reaching for her mobile phone, she opened a screen to send a text. For a long time she only stared at it, listening to the sound of Lawrence thundering down the stairs, and her father laughing as he came after him. They were in their own world, happy in a place where she couldn't go, because she didn't belong. Hearing them, imagining them going to join Jerry in the kitchen, was making her feel like a ghost in her own home. Neither her existence nor her feelings counted for anyone today, they were too caught up in the whirlwind of her father's ludicrous and disastrous romance.

It was only minutes before he was due to leave that her father came to find her. If he hadn't she didn't think she could have borne it, but when he swept her up into his arms she wasn't sure she could bear that either.

'I wish you'd come,' he whispered into her hair.

She clung to him as she sobbed, not caring that she might be staining his waistcoat, in fact hoping she was. 'Don't go,' she begged. 'Please don't go.'

'Oh darling,' he murmured, tightening his embrace. 'You're making this so hard for yourself.'

'No, it's you who's making it hard,' she told him, pulling back to look up at him. He was immaculately shaven, his thick silver hair neatly brushed back from his face. His eyes were what she loved most about him, smoky blue and always showing tenderness and humour when he was looking at her. This morning they were troubled, and she wondered again if he was really as certain about what he was doing as he was making out.

'Try to be happy for me,' he said, smoothing a stray strand of hair from her cheek.

'How can I when I know you're making a mistake?'

As a flash of irritation showed in his eyes, she felt her anguish deepen. It was rare he ever got angry with her, so what else could this be but yet more evidence of how they were drifting apart? She was braced for him to be short with her, but then seeing how heavily emotions seemed to be weighing on him she stood on tiptoe to press a kiss to his cheek. 'I'll always love you,' she whispered, 'and I'll always be here for you.'

'I know,' he said gruffly, 'and the same goes for me.' He was looking at his watch.

She started to turn away, but he pulled her back. 'What are you doing today?' he asked.

Wishing he wasn't sounding quite so curt, she said, 'Dee's coming over, we'll probably have our usual Saturday lunch, and then . . .' As her voice was strangled by a sob he drew her back into his arms and wrapped her up tight.

'David,' Lawrence said, coming into the room, 'Dad's brought the car round. We're ready to go.'

When she saw her son Rosalind felt her heart breaking apart. He looked so handsome and important in his grey tailcoat and paisley waistcoat. His cravat was leaf green, the same as his father's, and the pristine whiteness of his shirt made his glossy curls look darker than ever. She could imagine how impressed people would be when they saw him, and hoped they knew not to fuss him. Would *she* have warned them? Had her father thought to tell her? What was a child like Lawrence going to mean to someone like her, who probably only had time for herself?

'Say goodbye to your mother,' David said as Lawrence started to leave.

'Goodbye Mum,' he said obediently. 'I'm seeing Lucy today.'

Her father rolled his eyes, and because it was expected she attempted a smile. 'Bye then,' she whispered.

'Bye,' he said, and after giving her one last regretful look he left.

Turning back to her desk, she picked up her mobile to read the text she'd composed before he came in. She hadn't sent it yet, but now she would and with a flick of her thumb it went.

'Can I come in?' Amy demanded, sailing straight into Lisa's bedroom where her sister was seated in front of a wall-to-wall dressing table, with two sets of giant double mirrors at each end and a plasma TV screen in the middle. 'Oh look at you,' she cried emotionally, 'your hair's so gorgeous. You've done a fabulous job,' she told Melvina, the stylist. 'I'm so used to seeing it in a plait, but this is absolutely heavenly.'

Lisa was turning her head from side to side, her eyes glowing with pleasure as she admired the loose French roll that was curling in a seemingly effortless sweep over the back of her head, with random coils dropping around her face and neck. It was the casually elegant look that Melvina had spent four sessions perfecting these past few weeks. Now, as she tweaked and backcombed her finishing touches, and Amy stood watching, looking extremely chic in a bright fuchsia-pink dress with lavender swirls and a magnificent fuchsia hat, Lisa felt a fluttering of nerves wafting through her like a bunch of ribbons taking flight. She couldn't imagine why it was all feeling so enormous and unnerving today, but for some reason she was as skittish and queasy as a teenager, and the way her insides kept reeling every time her iPhone signalled an incoming text was wreaking havoc on her attempts at inner calm.

'I need to find my mobile,' she said to Amy. 'I can hear it, but God knows where it is amongst all this.'

'Let me track it down,' Amy offered, and as she started to plough through all the packing cases and other paraphernalia that was part move-in and part wedding, she said, 'Mum's arrived, by the way. She's with Roxy, whose dress looks absolutely divine. It made me want to weep when I saw her. She's almost like a bride herself.'

'Hold still!' Melvina ordered, as Lisa started to get up. 'We haven't put the crystals in yet.'

Tightening the towel she was wrapped in, Lisa obediently returned to her position, wondering what David was doing now, and if he was feeling as uptight as she was. But why was she feeling like this? She didn't understand it when they were actually already married. She knew it couldn't have anything to do with Tony, who was probably getting drunk with old friends by now, or losing himself in the arms of another woman, but she really wished that he'd stop staging unwelcome appearances in her mind.

Quickly switching her thoughts back to David she started to feel more agitated than ever, until she found herself recalling the conversation they'd had early this morning. He'd rung to say good morning and to remind her that it was too late to change her mind now. She didn't want to, but for some reason she wished he hadn't said it. Still, it had been a relief to hear him sounding upbeat and teasing after the way he'd snapped at her last night, when she'd rung to ask how he was getting on with his lines.

He hadn't mentioned them this morning, so she was going to assume he'd now memorised them, nor had he said anything about the letter she'd sent Rosalind, so she'd decided not to bring it up either. If Rosalind had trashed it, or returned it to sender, it would be likely to cause added tension between her and her father, which they could both do without today. She wondered what Rosalind was doing now and how she was feeling. She hated to think of her alone and unhappy, but at the same time, knowing how opposed she was to her father getting married again was starting to feel like a curse.

'Ah, here is it,' Amy declared, pulling the phone out from under a pile of lingerie boxes and tissue paper. 'My God, you've got fourteen texts and fifty-eight emails. Haven't you read any this morning?'

'I haven't had time,' Lisa reminded her, tilting her head from side to side to catch the glitter of Melvina's crowning handiwork, while Melvina held up a mirror to present the full effect. 'Perfect,' she murmured, loving the way the crystals sparkled in the sunlight that was streaming in through the open windows.

'Did you decide on a veil in the end?' Amy asked, opening up the first of the texts.

'No veil,' Lisa replied, kissing Melvina on both cheeks as she got up from the stool again. 'You've been an angel,' she told her. 'I can manage from here.'

'What about your make-up?'

'Honestly, I can do it. It's only the lip shimmer that needs to go on now, and you've shown me often enough how to do that.'

'OK, but don't forget to *step* into the dress. No pulling it over your head or God only knows what sort of mess you'll end up in.'

After assuring her she'd never dream of making such a mistake, Lisa waited for the door to close, then let her towel drop to the floor. 'Ah, that's better,' she sighed, loving the sensation of cooler air on her skin. 'I was so hot in that thing I was afraid I might start sweating off my fake tan. Is it OK? No runs or blotches?'

'Perfect,' Amy informed her as she gave a twirl. Then, returning to the phone, 'OK, so here goes with the texts: "Thinking of you today, don't forget to email photos, love Andrea."'

'Andrea Vavasour,' Lisa supplied. 'She's a journalist friend who lives in Rome.'

Moving on to the next, Amy read out, '"You've made the longest journey to what can only be the happiest destination. You deserve this, Lisa darling. Love to you both. Paulo and Jeremy."'

'You met them when you and Theo flew out to join Tony and me in Thailand.'

'Of course. How lovely that they're in touch today. You can read all these later yourself, but I'll carry on for now, shall I?'

'Yes, do,' Lisa said, starting to rummage through the lingerie boxes in search of the white silk body-shaper specially designed to blend invisibly under her dress, while helping to hold her up and in.

'"You're a lucky lady to have found someone so perfect,"' Amy read out, '"but he's an even luckier man. Enjoy your day and come see us soon, Evie and Joshua." Aren't they the couple who own that gorgeous hotel in Sicily?'

'Correct. Ah, here it is,' and sweeping up the body-shaper she sat down on the edge of the bed to start pulling it on.

'Is that all you're wearing underneath?' Amy asked, eyeing the flimsy-looking garment dubiously.

'It's all there's room for. I can't even wear stockings which is why my tan was so vital, but if I look at all lumpy I've got some passion-killing knicks with legs down to the knees to help smooth me out. Anyway, go on, who else has been in touch? I'm starting to enjoy this.'

'Am I likely to find one from Tony?' Amy asked darkly.

Lisa's heart gave a jolt. 'No,' she replied, as though amazed at such a suggestion.

Amy scowled at her knowingly.

Rolling her eyes, Lisa said, 'OK, he sent one last night wishing me well. Satisfied?'

Amy didn't look pleased.

'I didn't ask him to send it,' Lisa cried. 'Anyway, he's in China, and he has a new woman now, Mrs Overall . . .'

'Mrs Who?'

'Let's drop it,' Lisa said irritably. 'This is my wedding day, I'm marrying David and why you have to bring up Tony only you can know.'

Amy eyed her suspiciously, then getting back to the messages she scrolled to the next and started to laugh. '"RESULT! Nikki Freemason."'

Laughing too, Lisa said, 'A single friend from San Francisco.'

'"Divine justice for a divine spinster. Can't wait to meet the lucky man. Alfie and Jane."'

'They run a yacht-chartering company on Tortola,' Lisa said, wriggling the body up to her waist.

Amy was about to continue when the door burst open and Roxy bounced in, closely followed by Matilda. 'Wow, Lis!' Roxy exclaimed, coming to a rapid halt. 'That's a bit sexy, isn't it?'

'Just look at you,' Matilda clucked, almost colliding with her granddaughter as she regarded her daughter with mock disapproval. 'Hair all done to the nines and kinky undies, anyone would think you're about to get married.'

'She did that yesterday,' Amy reminded her. 'Roxy, darling, give us another twirl. You look heavenly.'

Obediently, Roxy held out her arms and rotated on her three-inch bronze heels to show off her strapless champagne-coloured silk dress with its softly ruched bodice shot through with sparkling thread, and filmy georgette skirts that swished and swayed wispily around her knees. One side of her copious blonde hair was held up by a glittering amber pin which perfectly matched the stones in the cream velvet choker around her neck.

'Has Daddy seen you yet?' Amy asked.

'No. He'll weep, just like you. They're a pair of wusses, my parents. I don't know where they get it from, oh silly me, it must be you, Granny. Have you seen her gloves?' she said to Lisa. 'Look at them, they're wicked.'

Lisa's eyes shone with laughter as her mother held out two purple-lace-clad hands, with a fake diamond on the third finger of one winking away like a risqué joke. The rest of her outfit was a taffeta short-sleeved suit in a more discreet version of the same colour, with a lavender pillbox hat, brushed-silver shoes and a matching over-the-arm bag.

'You look wonderful, Mum,' Lisa told her, going to kiss her. 'The gloves might be a bit OTT, but if you love them, then I do too.'

'Frankly, I think they're awful,' Matilda confessed, 'but they hide my arthritic fingers. All those knobbles and bumps make me look like an old witch. Is that string thing entirely comfortable when you sit down, darling? I don't think I'd like to wear one.'

As Roxy sniggered at the image, Amy said, 'I'm just reading out some of the texts that arrived this morning. If we didn't already know how many friends my sister has scattered all over the globe, then we're certainly finding out now.'

As she started reading again, Matilda began fussing around in the packing cases looking for only she knew what. Roxy wandered out on to the balcony to watch the musicians tuning up, while the helpers hired for the day arranged the chairs in rows ready for the ceremony.

Amy was still reading as Lisa turned to unzip the cover that was protecting her dress, and feeling more nerves starting to swirl and coast about inside her she had to pause for a moment to take a breath. All these reminders coming in of the life she used to lead, the unlimited freedoms she'd enjoyed, the way she'd never had to answer to anyone, were making her feel anxious about what might lie ahead. Or was her real worry that someone was going to mention Tony in their message? Maybe she was more upset by the fact that so far, no one had.

'Oh my God, David's arrived,' Roxy whispered excitedly from the balcony.

Lisa's heart somersaulted.

'He looks amazing,' Roxy told them. 'I guess that must be his nephew with him, who's kind of cute, and his son-in-law, the pilot, oh and you should see the little boy he's so gorgeous . . . Oh blimey, Lucy!' she choked. 'She's only made a beeline straight for Lawrence and knocked over some of the chairs. Honestly, Lisa, you should learn to control your dog.'

Behind her Lisa managed a smile, while Matilda went to peer over Roxy's shoulder.

'All the time I'm reading these there are more coming in,' Amy declared. 'We'll never get to the end of them before we go down.'

'Oh my God! I bet that's Miles,' Roxy gulped. 'If it is, then you're right, Lis, he's absolutely TDF.'

Matilda blinked.

'To die for,' Roxy explained.

'I said that?' Lisa said, barely paying attention as she peeled the silk covering away from her dress and let it fall to the floor.

'Oh, darling,' Matilda murmured, suddenly transfixed, 'it's absolutely stunning. Oh my, I'm feeling so proud of you I could cry.'

'Mum, will you please listen,' Amy scolded. 'I'm trying to provide a lyrical and nostalgic background for the putting on of the dress.'

Coming to watch – and listen – as Lisa began to unzip the dress, Roxy said, 'Hang on, what about something old, something new and all that? Have we done it yet?'

Lisa looked at Amy, surprised that they'd both forgotten such an imbedded tradition. 'Well, I think I qualify as old,' she twinkled, 'at least old for a first-time bride, and the dress is new, so we just have to sort out the borrowed and blue.'

As they racked their brains, while looking around the room for inspiration, another text message arrived.

'I've got it! I've got it!' Roxy declared. 'Granny, why don't you lend her your engagement ring for the day?'

Startled, Matilda looked down at her gloved hands as though something might have appeared there while she wasn't looking.

Coming to help, Roxy pulled back the lacy left glove to reveal the small but precious sapphire that Matilda had only removed a handful of times since her own wedding day.

'It's a marvellous idea,' Matilda murmured, looking up and touching Roxy's face. Then to Lisa,

'It'll be a bit like having Daddy with us, won't it? I think he'd like that.'

'Oh Mum, stop, you're starting me off,' Amy protested, as her eyes filled with tears.

'Are you sure you don't mind?' Lisa asked, her own heart flooding with emotion as she wished her father could be with them too.

'I made a donation to the Children's Hospital,' Matilda told her, sliding off the ring, 'but that was a wedding gift. This is something from me and Daddy to you on your special day.'

'Oh, that's me gone,' Roxy choked, grabbing a tissue. 'Granny, we've had professional make-up jobs this morning, and you're going to ruin them if you keep this up.'

Ignoring the rebuke, Matilda said tenderly to Lisa, 'He's worth waiting for, sweetheart, and I couldn't be happier for you today, so . . .'

'Mum,' Lisa protested, 'Roxy's right about the make-up, you've got to stop or I'll mess up my dress.'

Raising her hands in submission, Matilda went to perch on the dressing-table stool while Amy returned to the messages.

'"We understand you wanting to keep it to close friends and family, but please know when you're next in HK your friends here will want to throw a party,"' she read out. '"Our congratulations to the groom on winning himself such a beautiful bride, Pete, Sally, Janey and Frank."'

'We used to get telegrams in my day,' Matilda informed them. 'I've still got the ones Daddy and I received.'

'I'd love to see them,' Roxy told her, but her

eyes were on Lisa, who was drawing the dress carefully up over her hips. 'Oh, Lis,' she murmured. 'When you told me it was à la Vera Wang I was imagining the frothy *Sex in the City* number that Jessica Whatsit wore in the film, and it's nothing like it at all.'

Lisa smiled. 'At my age, Roxy, something like that would definitely be de trop.'

'Shall I help with the zip?' Matilda offered.

'That would be lovely, thank you. Keep reading,' she said to Amy, who was watching her, misty-eyed.

Swallowing the lump in her throat, Amy scrolled to the next text. '"What does he have that I don't?"' she read. '"Apart from good looks, great prospects and loads of loot in the bank? Have a great day and beautiful life. Love you always, Stevie B."'

Smiling, Lisa said, 'He was my fellow presenter for a while when I was doing the travel show. And, for the record, he's gay and has been with the same partner for at least ten years, and why am I defending myself? Does anyone here think I'm being unfaithful?'

'Oh Lis,' Roxy said in awe, as Lisa turned round. 'When David sees you he's going to fall in love all over again.'

'He's already done it twice,' Matilda muttered.

'What jewellery are you wearing,' Roxy asked, 'apart from Granny's ring?'

'It's here,' Lisa said, pulling open a bedside drawer.

'OMG, it's only Tiffany,' Roxy gasped.

Amy was watching, so was Matilda, their eyes

widening like children's in a sweetshop as Lisa removed the signature blue box to reveal a white leather case containing a brilliant cut-diamond-studded choker with matching bracelet, and two simple diamond drop earrings.

'I've never been this close to something that must have cost so much,' Matilda murmured. 'I feel like we've floated off into a fairy tale, don't you?' she said to Amy.

Nodding, Amy said, 'Would you like some help putting it on?'

'I can do it,' Roxy told her. 'You carry on with the messages.'

'Oh my, listen to that voice,' Matilda swooned as Sheelagh Rayne sang a few notes to start warming up.

'Isn't it heaven?' Lisa agreed. 'And you wait till you hear Baz, her husband, when he comes in with her. If you're managing not to cry now, you will when they get started on "Morning Has Broken".'

'I'm losing it, just to think of it,' Amy assured her. 'Remind me why you chose that particular song for your entrance?'

'It was one of David's favourites when we were together before,' Lisa replied. 'He doesn't know that I'm walking in to it, so I hope he doesn't lose it when the moment comes.' She was putting in her earrings now, and feeling a surge of euphoria suddenly breaking free from her nerves, she gave a gasp of laughter.

Laughing too, Amy looked down as the mobile bleeped again. 'Two more,' she said, scrolling on, 'then I think Mum and I should go and mingle.'

Taking a pair of white satin slingbacks from their Jimmy Choo box, Lisa lifted the hem of her dress while Roxy set the shoes in position for her to slip on.

'"I want you to know that if you go ahead and marry . . ."' Amy stopped abruptly and a wash of colour spread over her cheeks. 'Oh, for heaven's sake,' she mumbled, and started to scroll on quickly, but Lisa took the phone from her hand.

'Who's it from?' she asked, before looking.

Amy visibly braced herself. 'It can only be Rosalind,' she told her, 'which is why I think you should give me back the phone and let me erase the message.'

Clicking it open, Lisa read, *I want you to know that if you go ahead and marry my father today, the next time he sees me it will be with my mother in heaven.*

Chapter Thirteen

'She's lost her mind,' Matilda declared, aghast.

'This is a monstrous thing to do,' Amy murmured.

'They're already married,' Roxy pointed out. 'Doesn't she know that?'

Lisa shook her head. 'David hasn't told her,' she mumbled. Then, 'I have to think. What are we going to do?'

'She doesn't mean it,' Matilda said confidently. 'Apart from anything else, she's got a little boy to consider.'

'Let me call her,' Amy suggested.

Her face pale, Lisa looked at the message again. Though anger and pity were starting to emerge through the shock, it wasn't Rosalind she was feeling sorry for as much as David, and everyone who'd come so far and already put so much into this special day. What were they going to do now? How could they possibly go ahead with this sort of threat hanging over them? 'I have to talk to David,' she decided.

'No!' Amy protested, leaping from the bed. 'He can't see you like that. No one can yet.'

'What does it matter?' Lisa cried angrily. 'There can't be a ceremony now.'

'Yes, there can.'

'Are you crazy? How can we . . .'

'Let *me* talk to David. We might still be able to work something out,' Amy urged.

'What about her husband?' Matilda piped up. 'Shouldn't he be dealing with her?'

'Too right,' Roxy agreed.

Lisa's eyes were blazing into Amy's. 'If she carries out this threat . . .'

'She won't,' Amy growled. 'Now wait here. Don't do anything rash. Stay with her, Rox, and you Mum. I'll be right back,' and snatching the phone she swept out of the room and ran swiftly down the stairs, holding on to her hat.

As she reached the hall she quickly assumed a happy, welcoming smile ready to greet the guests, most of whom were gathered now and sipping champagne on the sitting-room terrace. In the courtyard below fifty chairs were meticulously assembled, like brackets, each side of the flower-strewn gazebo, while a half-dozen round tables regally adorned in crisp white linen and silver settings were positioned around the courtyard borders, like the second act waiting to take centre stage. After the ceremony, while photographs were being taken and more champagne was consumed, the helpers and catering staff were to carry in the tables, rearrange the chairs and finish off the place settings ready for the wedding banquet to begin.

All that was supposed to happen, and two rehearsals earlier in the week had proved it could, weather permitting. Certainly there was no sign of wind or rain now, and none was forecast. No one, however, could have foreseen this sort of last-minute drama.

'There you are,' Theo said, as Amy began weaving through the throng towards David. 'Everything going all right upstairs? We should be getting started . . .'

'Look at this,' she whispered, showing him the phone.

As he read the words Theo's face froze with shock. 'What are you going to do?' he said quietly.

'I need to speak to David.'

'Yes, but not here. Go into the sitting room. I'll send him in.'

Moments later David appeared through the open French windows, looking faintly puzzled, and even, she thought, a little strained. 'You can't tell me she's changed her mind now,' he joked. 'It's already . . .'

'It's not Lisa,' Amy broke in, 'it's this.' She handed him the phone. 'I'm really sorry,' she said as he started to read. 'Lisa says you have to see it, and I don't know what we're going to do . . .'

David's face had turned white.

'What is it?' Jerry said to Amy, coming into the room. 'Your husband said to . . .'

'It's Rosalind,' David told him, handing him the phone, and taking out his own he scrolled to his daughter's number and clicked on to connect.

Rosalind was sitting at the kitchen table, listening to the phone ringing on the counter top behind her. She knew it would be her father, or possibly Jerry, but whoever it was, she was too afraid to pick it up.

Eventually the machine kicked in and her father said, 'Rosalind, I know you're there, so please answer.'

Her eyes went to her aunt, who was sitting with her.

'Why won't you speak to him?' Dee asked softly.

Rosalind shook her head, unable to admit what she'd done, even to Dee.

'Rosalind!' David said more firmly. 'Please pick up the phone. I need to know you're all right.'

Appearing puzzled, Dee said, 'He sounds worried . . .'

'Speak to him if you must,' Rosalind said, getting up from the table. 'I can't.'

As she walked outside, Dee managed to grab the phone before David rang off. 'David, it's me,' she said. 'What's going on?'

'Is Rosalind there?'

'Yes, but . . .'

'Please put her on.'

'She's saying she doesn't want to talk to you.'

'I'm sure she doesn't, but I need to talk to her, now if you . . .'

'Maybe if you tell me what this is about,' Dee suggested, watching Rosalind walking down to the lawn.

As David explained, Dee's face went pale. 'Oh no,' she murmured. 'What was she thinking? She doesn't mean it, you must know that.'

'I'm sure she doesn't, but she's upset Lisa and we both need . . . We need . . . an . . . an . . . Oh God, what's the effing word?' he growled, sounding most unlike himself. 'An apology! Please, put her on.'

'OK, I'll see what I can do. Wait there,' and setting the phone down, she followed Rosalind outside. 'He told me about the text,' she said, going to slide an arm round her niece's shoulders.

Rosalind lifted her head and gazed out at the mountainous distance and wide, empty blue sky. Was her mother watching? Did she know what was happening? 'Is he angry?' she asked.

'He wants you to apologise.'

Though Rosalind's insides were churning with regret and shame, she was only sorry for upsetting her father, not for ruining Lisa Martin's day. In that, she profoundly hoped she'd succeeded.

'He's waiting,' Dee said softly.

Realising to carry on refusing was going to hurt and upset him even more than she already had, she turned back to the house.

Picking up the phone she said nothing, only listened to the happy burble of voices at the other end, and the sound of a jazz singer crooning 'Sugar Blues' into the summery afternoon. Suddenly she wanted very badly to cry.

'Are you there?' her father said.

'Yes,' she whispered. 'I – I know what you're going to say . . .'

'No you don't, so I want you to listen.' His tone was sharp, confirming that he was as angry as she'd feared. 'I should have told you this last night and I'm sorry I didn't, but Lisa and I got married yesterday at the registry office so she's already my wife, and you, my darling, will always, *always*, be the daughter I love more than my own life.'

'Then why are you doing this?' she said brokenly.

There was a pause, and more laughter in the background, before he said, 'Lisa and I got married yesterday at the registry . . .'

'You just told me that,' she snapped. 'I'm not deaf.'

'I'm sorry – I . . . Look, darling, please, send a text to Lisa telling her you're sorry . . .'

'No! I will not do that.'

'Rosalind, she hasn't done anything to deserve this . . .'

'How can you say that? You know very well she couldn't wait for Mum to die, so if I could I'd ruin every day of her life, because that's what she's doing to mine.'

'No, Rosalind, you've got it all wrong . . .'

'This conversation is over.'

'OK. Then at least apologise to me before you ring off.'

'If I've upset you, I'm sorry, but I'm not going to send a text to *her*, so please don't ask again.'

There was another interruption his end before he said, 'Jerry's on his way back . . .'

'No! I don't need him here.'

'He's already left. Now, could you put Dee on again, please?'

Passing the phone back to her aunt, Rosalind slumped down at the table and buried her face in her hands. If she'd ever wanted her mother more she couldn't remember it, because all of a sudden the need was so urgent and consuming that she wanted to scream out loud with the sheer unrelenting force of it.

'OK, I'll do my best,' Dee was saying, and hanging up she came to sit down too.

'Please don't try to persuade me to send that text,' Rosalind said, having guessed what her father had asked Dee to do.

'Then let me send it. You won't even have to know what it says if you don't want to, but, sweetheart, they're already married; the wedding's going ahead anyway . . .'

'In which case, she doesn't need an apology.'

'But you *are* sorry you sent it, I can tell. So if it's too difficult for you to say so, let me say it for you.'

Rosalind shook her head.

Ignoring the refusal, Dee said, 'Where's your mobile?'

'Why is everyone on her side?' Rosalind suddenly raged, banging her fists on the table. 'She's no one to us, do you hear me? *No one,* so if you want to do something, why don't you get her out of our lives?'

As she stormed off Dee remained where she was, looking as helpless and troubled as she felt. Time wasn't doing much to heal her niece's grief, and now that her father had married again, Dee couldn't help fearing for how much worse Rosalind's despair might become.

Upstairs in her bedroom Rosalind opened her mobile phone, and after one or two false starts she managed to compose a message to her father saying, 'If you want to tell her I won't do anything stupid, you can, because I won't – at least not today.'

In the end she forced herself to erase the last four words out of concern for him, and after pressing send, she turned her face into the pillows. Scrunching them as tightly as she could, she willed her mother with every fibre of her being to reach out to her in some way, because she couldn't take any more of this emptiness, or silence, or terrible, frightening loneliness that was all her life was now, and had been ever since Catrina had gone.

Lisa was on the phone to David when Amy came back with four glasses of champagne on a tray. Taking one, Lisa sipped it gratefully as she listened to David saying, 'I'm truly sorry it happened. If I'd had any idea she was going to do something like that . . .'

'Darling, it's not your fault,' she interrupted softly. 'Just as long as she's all right.'

'Dee's there and Jerry's on his way back. I know she's sorry, even though she can't bring herself to say so. Has Amy arrived with the champagne yet?'

'Just. Thanks, I really needed it.'

'I thought you might. So, do you feel OK to continue? If you want to delay or . . .'

'I'm fine as long as you are.'

There was a tremor in his voice as he said, 'Then let's try to put the past few minutes out of our minds and concentrate on what today is all about.'

Taking another restorative sip, she wanted to say it would be hard to stop thinking about Rosalind, but that wasn't going to help either of them.

'Shall I tell everyone we're ready?' he asked.

As her insides flipped with nerves she turned to the mirror and wondered again why she felt so anxious, when they were already married. Then, allowing herself to see how lovely she looked, she said, 'Yes. Why don't you do that?'

After ringing off she took one more sip of her drink, then looking at the others she whispered, 'OK, girls, first positions.'

A few minutes later, as the laughter and clinking of glasses dissolved into a murmur and the jazz band rested on their instruments ready for their next cue, Roxy came out of the sitting room carrying her small spray of white sweet peas inside a floating cloud of verdant fern. Quietly descending four of the wide stone steps leading down to the courtyard, she took her position.

Standing at the centre of the gazebo with Lawrence and the rosy-cheeked celebrant whose name had escaped him again, David was smiling past the terrible tension inside him. He was thinking of Rosalind, and Catrina, and wondering how he had come to be here, and whether he could get through the next hours without shaming himself, and Lisa. He'd been awake most of the night trying to memorise the poems they'd combined to celebrate their vows, but if he was asked to repeat any one of them at this moment he knew he would be unable to.

He felt Heather – Heather, that was the celebrant's name, and relief poured over him – he felt her hand on his arm, and as he glanced at her she nodded for him to look up at the house.

Lisa was standing at the top of the steps, and in her ivory silk taffeta dress with its softly sculpted bodice that accentuated her waist and breasts and clung like a caress to her body to fan out in a mermaid tail from mid-thigh, she was a vision that was so captivatingly romantic she almost seemed ethereal. And as a murmur of approval spread through their guests, he knew he'd never felt more anxious or elated in his life.

Seconds of stillness passed, with the sound of trickling water carrying over the garden along with the exquisite scent wafting from Lisa's trailing bouquet of lilies of the valley. Then, emerging from the silence with all the beauty and grace of a swallow taking flight, Sheelagh's haunting voice began to fill the summer air.

Morning has broken, like the first morning,
Blackbird has spoken, like the first bird
Praise for the singing, praise for the morning
Praise for them, springing fresh from the Lord.

Remembering the song from their early days, David felt a lump forming in his throat. Knowing it was one of his favourites, and presenting it to him this way, was a gift more precious than he could have imagined and way beyond anything he deserved. He should let her go now. He couldn't tie her to him like this when the fears were haunting him again and in truth had never really gone away. He wasn't the man he used to be, he was a fraud, a coward who should have backed away yesterday, or long before, but instead he'd kept clinging to the vain hope and delusion he'd spun for himself out of the half-truths he'd given the doctor.

As Baz's hypnotic tenor took the second verse and Lisa started forward, David was aware of everyone rising to their feet.

Sweet the rain's new fall, sunlit from heaven
Like the first dewfall on the first grass
Praise for the sweetness of the wet garden
Sprung in completeness where his feet pass.

It was as though the alchemy of the words, the arrival of the bride, and the whole poignancy of their lives were bringing them together in a way nothing else could. He watched her descending slowly, radiant and happy, and knew he could never do anything to spoil this day for her.

As Roxy reached the gazebo she smiled at him and moved discreetly aside. Then, as both singers and the band joined to escort Lisa for the final few steps, it was as though everything and everybody were blending into one, and the effect was so rousing that Lawrence's were perhaps the only dry eyes in the garden.

Mine is the sunlight, mine is the morning
Born of the one light Eden saw play
Praise with elation, praise every morning
God's recreation of the new day.

Lisa was gazing into David's eyes as he reached for her hand, and in that moment she could only feel thankful that Rosalind hadn't come, because now they could speak the entirety of the vows they'd created without having to spare her feelings.

Gesturing for everyone to sit, Heather waited for them to settle, and once the rustling had stopped, leaving the simple sounds of birdsong and crickets, she began by saying, 'Thank you all for coming, and thank you, Lisa and David, for allowing me the honour of blessing your marriage. Lisa and I go back many years, which I hope qualifies me to say that the moment she got in touch to tell me about David, I knew from the very timbre of her voice that she had found her soulmate at last.'

So she never thought it was Tony? Lisa was thinking.

'In fact, she had *reconnected* with him,' Heather was saying, 'because as many of you here already know, they first met in this very city as much younger people than they are today.'

After waiting for the wave of amusement to ebb, she continued. 'It's because of what went before that I like to think that we are now being shown by this union how those who belong to one another will, if parted, always manage to find each other again. And how true love, no matter how severely tested either by circumstance or time, will never die.' She paused again, to allow the gentle sincerity of her belief to resonate with them all.

'Though between them,' she went on, 'Lisa and David could have put on a wedding for three or four hundred guests, they have chosen instead to celebrate this special day with you. So I think we can be sure that the very spirit of this occasion is being created by the love you all bear them, and that when combined with the love they have for each other it will carry them into a happy and rewarding future together.'

As David's hand tightened on hers, Lisa, feeling oddly empty and displaced, returned the pressure.

'I shall step aside now,' Heather said, 'to allow Lisa and David to speak the words they have in part written themselves, and in part drawn from our most celebrated poets. I think you will all agree when you hear the selection that it is very beautiful and fitting, and I hope Lisa, David, that you feel I've served you well with this opening contribution I have chosen from George Eliot.

'*What greater thing is there for two human souls,*' she recited, looking from Lisa to David, '*than to feel that they are joined together to strengthen each other in all labour. To minister to each other in all sorrow, to share with each other in all gladness, to be one with each other in the silent, unspoken memories.*' She smiled as she finished, and took a step back.

How could she know? Does she know? David was asking himself, his head seeming to spin as he and Lisa turned to one another and gazed into each other's eyes.

Several seconds ticked by.

'You first,' Lisa whispered.

He swallowed drily and took a breath. TS Eliot. He knew the poet, but where were the words?

'*In my beginning,*' she prompted.

'*In my beginning,*' he repeated, '*is my end, And over the dark water . . . speak to me with your love.*' He knew he'd missed some, but Lisa was still smiling and holding on to his hands, so could he assume he hadn't disgraced himself?

'*Yes, yours my love,*' she recited from Edwin Muir, '*is the right face that I in my mind had waited for this long.*'

She paused and he felt a cold sweat trickling down his back.

'*I mourn no more my lonesome years;*' she continued

from Elizabeth Akers Allen. *'This blessed hour atones for all.'*

David's vision was blurred as he tried to absorb her declaration, and then, in an almost blinding moment of clarity, he found himself quoting Christopher Marlowe. *'Come live with me, and be my love, and we will all the pleasures prove.'*

With the ghost of a smile, she allowed a pause before saying, *'If ever two were one, then surely we; If ever man were lov'd by wife, then thee.'*

Making everyone smile, David said, *'Love me not for comely grace, For my pleasing eye or face, Keep, Lisa, a true woman's eye, and love me still but know not why; So hast thou the same reason still to dote on me ever.'*

Humour was shining in Lisa's eyes as she glanced at Heather, who nodded for them to continue with the words they'd written themselves.

David's throat was dry, but he could sense the words coming, ready to be spoken. 'When my eyes first on you did light, true love in me stirred with glorious might. Though I have loved another and loved her true, always in my heart there was you.'

Gazing into his eyes, Lisa said, 'I loved you then, I love you now; and all the many years intervened, my journey long and aimless seemed. But now aside my wanderings and wonderings go, for today I come to rest where I have always belonged, with you.'

The next lines were his, but they had flown.

'On this, our wedding day,' Lisa said for him, 'let our loved ones rice and confetti throw. Let fireworks soar, champagne flow and music play;

let old friends meet new and family gather round, all to bear witness that I give myself to you . . .'

He felt the squeeze of her hand, telling him it was for him to speak now. 'And I to you,' he heard himself say.

'And know that our vows will be spoken true,' Lisa added.

'David,' Heather said, stepping forward again, 'do you, of your own free will and consent, choose Lisa to be your beloved wife, and do you promise to love, honour and cherish her always?'

Looking at Lisa, and almost shaking with relief that the most difficult part was over, David said, 'I do.'

'Lisa,' Heather continued, 'do you, of your own free will and consent, choose David to be your beloved husband, and do you promise to love, honour and cherish him always?'

Knowing this last would surprise David, a mischievous light leapt into Lisa's eyes as she quoted from *Ulysses*, saying, '. . . and then he asked me would I yes . . . and yes I said, yes I will, yes.'

As a murmur of laughter spread through the guests, David's eyes showed so much emotion that Lisa's smile faltered in the force of it.

Heather nodded to Lawrence, who'd barely taken his eyes from her as he waited for his cue with the rings. Stepping forward with the two brushed-platinum bands on a black velvet tray, his fathomless eyes held firm to hers in case there was anything else he needed to do. At a discreet distance, Lucy sat watching, oblivious to her fetching collar of fresh cut flowers.

With Lawrence and his tray now in place,

Heather said, 'Lisa and David, these rings symbolise the love that joins you, spirit to spirit. Just as they have no beginning or end, nor points of weakness, may your union be the same, and may you be blessed with great joy as you journey through life together surrounded by the circle of your love.' She waited for David to pick up the smaller of the two bands and slide it to the knuckle of Lisa's third finger.

As he started to speak his voice fell into a void, so Heather helped him recover by whispering the words for him to repeat.

'I give you this ring,' he said, looking at Lisa, 'as a symbol of my love.'

He pushed the ring fully on to her finger, and Lisa said, 'I receive your love as my greatest treasure.'

After pausing to allow the sense of connection its completion, Lisa took the other ring from Lawrence's tray, and slipping it on to David's third finger, she said, 'David, I give you this ring as a symbol of my love.'

Visibly moved by her use of his name, he paid her the same compliment, saying, 'Lisa, I receive your love as my greatest treasure.'

Holding out her arms to include the gathering, Heather said, 'Let us give thanks for this union that is bringing us together in love and joy.'

Speaking almost as one, they said, 'We give thanks.'

Heather's eyes moved to the upper terrace, where Baz and Sheelagh were standing, ready to sing, and taking their cue Wills and Theo carried chairs into the gazebo for David and Lisa to sit down to watch the performance.

The Berlin Philharmonic came courtesy of a backing track being played through specially erected speakers. However, the effect of the voices was undiminished, as Baz's profoundly resonant tenor opened the way into one of Lisa's favourite operatic duets, *O Soave Fanciulla*.

The audience were soon spellbound as the drama of the music began to build, filling the garden, the whole valley with the rousing crescendo that, at its peak, reached out to sweep Sheelagh's voice into its force and to create such a magnificent fusion of sound that the rush of feeling to Lisa's heart pushed tears to her eyes.

It wasn't a lengthy piece, but it felt sorely too soon that the music began to fade with the words, *'Amor! Amor! Amor!'* As it drifted through the air like a magical spell Miles lowered his head, unable to support it any longer. Behind him Hayley was trying to smile through her own tremulous emotion, until Nerine lost a sob in a splutter of embarrassment and Polly joined in at the moment of permissible amusement.

When Lisa and David returned to their feet, still moved by the performance, they stood facing Heather for her closing words.

'I wish you courage and happiness from this time on,' Heather said, holding out her hands for theirs. 'May your love forever nourish you and keep you strong, and may it fulfil you in every way. Please take this, my blessing, on your union. Go in peace. Live in joy, for you are now husband and wife.' She smiled tenderly, and leaning forward whispered, 'You may kiss.'

As David turned to her, Lisa looked up at him

with wet, troubled eyes. Then his lips came to hers in a gentle but passionate sealing of their connection, and all her misgivings and annoyance that he'd forgotten his lines did nothing more than melt away.

Chapter Fourteen

It was just over a week since David and Lisa had set off on their honeymoon, leaving Amy and Theo to continue entertaining their overseas guests, and Rosalind was doing her best to carry on as though nothing in any way remarkable had happened.

Watching her moving around in a shell of silence, Jerry could feel the distance growing between them. Since the day of the wedding they'd barely spoken, so he could only guess at how she was feeling about the way he'd come home to give her a piece of his mind for sending such a terrible message to Lisa.

All she'd said when he'd finished was, 'Why don't you go back there? Lawrence shouldn't be left on his own, and I don't need you here defending her, thank you very much.'

By the time he'd brought Lawrence home it was after midnight and she was in bed. Since she was clearly in no more mood to talk then than she'd been earlier, he'd slipped quietly between the sheets next to her, and turned out the light, thankful that she wasn't going to quiz him about the day. The fact that he'd struck up a rapport with Lisa's sister and brother-in-law would quite possibly prove the final straw for their sorry wreck of a marriage, and if that didn't do it, then the blinding revelation that Polly, one of Lisa's closest friends, was a second cousin of Olivia's would undoubtedly blow it away altogether. How had his mistress's name even come into the conversation, Rosalind would want to know, and if he were to admit that he had mentioned it himself, almost as soon as Polly had told him she'd grown up in Cape Town, that would be proof enough for Rosalind that Olivia was always on his mind.

And she was, more now than ever.

He'd truly believed it would get easier in time; that after eighteen months the longing would have lost its intensity and the wrenching guilt would have faded to nothing more than a vague discomfort in his conscience. He wondered if it was Rosalind's inability to forgive him that was keeping his feelings for Olivia alive, or was it a weakness in him that couldn't let go of his marriage, even when there was nothing left to hold on to?

Such difficult thoughts burned like heat on open wounds. Though Rosalind gave him little reason to want to stay, and Olivia, he knew, would welcome him with open arms, to walk away from his marriage would mean walking away from his son, and in spite of how little he seemed to mean to Lawrence, he really didn't think he could do that. Yet Lawrence would always have David, and perhaps if he, Jerry, was no longer there, Rosalind would have to make more of an effort to get along with Lisa, if only to keep her father in her life.

All these thoughts, and so many more, were

whirling through his mind as he left his car in the long-term car park at Heathrow airport to make his way to the Crew Report Centre in Terminal 5. It seemed that no sooner had his decisions formed than a rush of doubt would send him spinning again, and by the time a new way forward started to show itself, the cracks in his conscience were opening up to destroy that too. He felt sure that if he weren't flying to Cape Town today his confusion wouldn't be fraught with such immediacy, as though a decision had to be made now and adhered to, or he'd end up . . . End up what? He couldn't say with any kind of clarity, it was simply a pervading sense of having to do something soon before it was too late for them all.

This was definitely not rating as the most successful honeymoon of all time. In fact, it was so far from achieving such a lofty status that it might be coming close to ranking as the worst. Almost nothing had seemed to go right from the minute they'd turned off the M6 on day one, when David had lost his temper because he couldn't remember where they were going. *How could he not remember where they were going on their honeymoon?*

'But you must have a record of it somewhere,' Lisa had protested, irritable enough already thanks to the rain, which had started around Birmingham and hadn't stopped since. And if it turned out they didn't have somewhere to stay for the night, she was going to be royally pissed off.

'If I did then we'd know where we were headed,

286

wouldn't we?' he snapped back. 'I must have left it in my briefcase.'

'So what are we going to do?'

'I don't know.'

Biting back a choice retort, she turned to stare out of the window as they continued in the direction of Windermere.

'Are you sure that's where you booked a hotel?' she asked after a while. 'There are a lot of lakes . . .'

'I'm aware of that, thank you very much.'

'Don't speak to me like that. It's not my fault you've screwed up.'

'So you think it's mine?'

'You were the one in charge of . . .'

'All right, all right, I've screwed up. Having my face rubbed in it isn't helpful.'

In the end he'd called the local MP, who had apparently recommended the hotel. The Miller Howe turned out to be exactly what she'd asked for – a small and romantic hotel at the edge of Lake Windermere with no fuss and frills, just an intimate atmosphere and an excellent restaurant.

As soon as they were alone in their room he'd apologised for his outburst, and accepting that they were both tired after the long journey and huge adrenalin rush of the wedding, she'd readily forgiven him. However, they hadn't made love that night, a disappointment she'd put down to tiredness again, but the following night there had been no kind of intimacy either. By the third night she was no longer in the mood anyway. The dismal weather was getting her down, and sightseeing in driving rain was no more her idea of fun than being stuck in endless traffic jams, or jostling with a bunch of fat, anorak-clad tourists to get off a cruise boat. The way they trod on her toes and elbowed her out of the way, anyone would think they were trying to chuck themselves off the *Titanic*.

In truth, she could probably have stood it all, possibly even laughed it off, had David not been so short-tempered and, it had to be said, maddening. It turned out it wasn't only the name of the hotel he'd forgotten, he'd left his phone charger at home so they'd had to go out and buy another; and for some unknown reason he'd padlocked his holdall and no longer had the key, meaning they'd had to rip it open with a penknife. There was still, in her opinion, a chance all could have been rescued with humour, but he'd flown off the handle at both mishaps, and had then promptly decided to punish himself – because that was how it seemed – by refusing to speak for almost a day. Or maybe he'd been trying to punish her, it was hard to tell when he was being so uncommunicative and childish, and it had really started to get on her nerves.

'I'm sorry, I'm sorry,' he said when she demanded an explanation. 'It's not you, it's me. I don't know where my head is these days, and I should have insisted we go somewhere hot for our honeymoon, because this wind and rain in the middle of November . . .'

'August.'

He chewed air. 'August,' he repeated, 'is . . . Well, it's not what you'd expect.'

A banal tailing-off like that wasn't what she'd expect from him either, and to her mind the weather seemed a pretty lame excuse for so much impatience and intolerance, but since she'd already guessed that Rosalind and her pathetic suicide threat was behind it all, she'd done her best to go along with his charade.

This morning, however, she'd come close to the end of her tether when, on the first fine day they'd had so far, she'd managed to trip on the front step as they left the hotel, possibly spraining her ankle, and now here she was, fed up, in pain and marooned on the balcony of their room with her foot propped up on a facing chair while she waited for Amy to come back on the line.

It was the middle of the afternoon, and though no rain had doused the lake yet today, the bulbous clouds forming overhead were clearly threatening a magnificent performance. She just hoped David managed to get back from his walk before the storm broke, because the last thing they wanted was both of them laid up on their honeymoon – at least not with a mildly sprained ankle and man flu.

Sipping from a glass of lemonade as she continued to wait, she tried entertaining herself with another soaking-up of the stunning vista, and being so spectacular it was really quite uplifting. With the lake stretched out before her like something from Avalon, winking and shimmering in the misty sunlight, and the trees roaming and foaming down to the water's edge, it was no wonder so many poets had chosen to live here. Her eyes moved over to the far shores, where cloud shadows were gliding over the mountains like giant birds and glistening bands of sunlight were bathing them in a vaporous glow. Amongst their rise and fall were two craggy peaks known as the Lancaster Pikes. According to her guidebook, when you could see them it was about to rain, and if they weren't visible it was already raining. She'd enjoyed what she'd assumed was typical northern irony, until David had asked her to repeat the folklore no less than three times this morning, at which point she'd started to wish she'd never mentioned it.

'Are you just not listening, or are you trying to wind me up?' she'd demanded, managing to throw the book down instead of at him.

He'd frowned as he looked at her. 'I'm sorry,' he said. Then, sighing heavily, 'It's amusing, of course, but I . . . Well, I had a call earlier from Rosalind. She sounded quite low.'

Failing to hide her exasperation, she said, 'Has she forgotten you're on your honeymoon? Oh, no, that's right! She's in her own little world where nothing matters but her, and we haven't happened.'

'Actually,' he said, looking away, 'I think she's rather lonely at the moment. Jerry's not due back till the weekend, and Dee's at her apartment in Spain with Wills and Daisy.'

'So why doesn't she call one of her friends? She must have them, she's lived there all her life.'

'Of course she does, but sometimes . . .' He shook his head, indicating that it was probably best they didn't discuss it any more, but Lisa was able to guess what he'd been about to say, that sometimes only family would do. And it wasn't that she begrudged Rosalind's call on her father, or at least she was trying not to and starting to fail miserably, she'd just rather it wasn't happening during what was already proving a very sorry excuse for a honeymoon.

Hearing Amy click back on to the line, she said, 'And about time, I thought you'd forgotten me.'

'As if. So, where were we?'

'I've completely forgotten, but something I keep meaning to ask you is if anyone's still staying at the house.'

'You mean your house? Of course you do. Sheelagh and Baz left this morning, so the place is now officially guest-free and the cleaners are blitzing it tomorrow. Theo and I are going over most evenings to make sure everything's watered and taken care of, or that's our excuse, because the landscapers are clearly in charge of all that, but we're doing a stellar job of testing the pool to make sure it's up to the right temperature and I have to tell you, it's a hard slog having to do all that swimming.'

Laughing, Lisa said, 'We haven't even had a chance to use it ourselves yet, which is making me wonder why the heck we're here, but don't let's get started on that.'

'I take it the weather's still bad.'

'Actually, it's better today, if you can call a few escaped sunrays and one degree rise in temperature better, but I suppose we should feel lucky it was so gorgeous for the wedding. It's getting us both down, though. I've never known David this tetchy. I've even started to wonder if we shouldn't just give up and come home.'

'Seriously?'

She sighed heavily. 'No, I suppose not. It would

be a bit defeatist to write off the entire two weeks when we haven't even been over to Ullswater yet – and I think the forecast is quite good for when we're there.'

'You're not sounding very enthusiastic.'

She sighed again. 'Frankly, it's hard to get worked up about anything while I'm stuck here with a great big fat ankle and feeling ready to wring Rosalind's neck for the way she's getting to her father. Or maybe it's his neck I should wring for allowing it. You probably won't be surprised to hear that there's been no more mention of that awful text she sent. It amazes me the way he can put these things out of his mind, as if they've never happened.'

'It's probably best that you do too.'

'Maybe. In fact, what else can we do? And I suppose I have to take some of the blame for things not going well, because I'm the one who chose to stay in England for our honeymoon. What the hell got into me, I want to know? Why did I imagine it would be fun to be here when I know what the weather's like? At least if I'd bust my ankle in Lampedusa, which was where I really wanted to go, I'd be getting a tan and cocktails on tap as it healed.'

'If that's where you wanted to go, why didn't you say so? You know he'd have taken you.'

'Why do you think? Tony flew me there for my thirty-fifth birthday, and it was hardly going to seem right taking David somewhere I'd already been with another man. I know I wouldn't like it if he'd chosen somewhere that had been special to him and Catrina – except I'm going to be living in the very valley they called home for the last thirty years, and having a very intense non-relationship with their daughter. Can you remind me how I ended up agreeing to that?'

'You fell in love with the house, and the man, and it's in his constituency.'

'Oh yes, and it's close to you, which frankly sealed it. Actually, I never thought I would say this on my honeymoon, but I wish you were here now to keep me company, because I'm starting to get the feeling my new husband is doing his best to avoid me.'

With one of her sisterly groans, Amy said, 'You're so prone to exaggeration. He'll be back soon.'

Lisa glanced at her watch. 'Well, let's hope so. He left over two hours ago, and surely even Rosalind can't keep him on the phone for that long, because I know that's what's really going on. I should probably give him a call, just to remind him I'm still here, because the way he's been carrying on lately there's a good chance he's forgotten.'

Amy chuckled. 'OK. So, if I don't talk to you before, I'll see you when you get back. Actually, I have some news, but it can wait till then.'

An hour later Lisa was sitting on the bed, wondering who to call next, because David still wasn't back and his phone was right here in the room. She'd only realised that when she'd tried his number and heard it ringing on the chest of drawers next to the TV. Now she was stuck here, unable to go and look for him thanks to her foot, and the storm outside was already sluicing the landscape with such fierce needles of rain that it had to be painful to be out in it.

Deciding he must be taking shelter somewhere until the worst of the weather had passed, she picked up a book to carry on reading, but her concentration was so poor that she soon put it down again. Why hadn't he taken his phone, she wanted to know. It didn't make any sense, when the whole purpose of him going out was to call Rosalind, or so she'd thought. Even more baffling was why he hadn't rung. It couldn't be that difficult to find a phone, there were sure to be boxes in Windermere and Bowness, or in one of the water-sport kiosks along the lake.

Her irritability was growing by the minute, along with the throbbing in her ankle, and because she was starting to become nervous about another explosion of temper when he got back, as though whatever was keeping him would somehow end up being her fault, she found herself wondering if this was the life she really wanted to lead. Was it always going to be like this, him running off to deal with Rosalind every time she threw the least little tantrum, constantly putting her first no matter what other commitments he might have? Maybe she'd made a mistake in marrying him – or at least she shouldn't have let him rush her into it. As it was, she'd been so caught up in the excitement of the wedding for the past few months that she hadn't allowed herself to believe anything could go wrong, while Rosalind had apparently been making sure it would.

Except he wasn't talking to Rosalind now, because his phone was here, and over three hours had passed since he went out, which was two more than he'd said he'd be, so what the heck had happened to him?

'What if he's had another of those aberrations?' she said, her voice not quite steady when she rang Amy again. 'Maybe I should start calling the local hospitals.'

'Actually, why don't you speak to someone at the hotel first, see what they advise?'

'Of course. Good idea. I'll call back as soon as there's some news.'

After being put through to the manager, who assured her he'd come up to her room straight away, she limped over to the window to stare out at the mist. The landscape had vanished now; everything was shrouded in an impenetrable mass of cloud, as though to remind her of how hostile this territory could be when it chose. 'Where are you?' she murmured, using anger to try and smother her fear. 'Why don't you find a phone and ring?'

Hearing a rap on the door, she called out that she was coming and hobbled as fast as she could across the room. The manager, looking worryingly young, introduced himself as Phillip, and the girl who was with him as Gemma.

'I'm sure it's nothing to be alarmed about,' Lisa told them, as though to forestall any premonitions of doom, 'but there was an incident a few weeks ago . . .'

'Let's start at the beginning,' the manager said kindly. 'What time did he leave? Where did he say he was going? And what did he take with him?'

Doing her best to answer the questions, Lisa watched Gemma jot her answers on to a notepad, while Phillip took out his mobile as it started to ring.

'I see,' he said, his eyes coming to Lisa. 'Thank you. I'll let her know,' and ringing off he said, 'Apparently your husband's on his way up.'

Relief unravelled her so fast that she started to laugh. 'Thank goodness,' she gasped. 'Is he all right? I'm so sorry to have bothered you. I over-reacted. I'm afraid it's not unusual for me . . .'

'Please don't apologise,' he interrupted. 'You were right to call us. It's what we're here for, to help in any way we can.'

Before Lisa could answer Gemma was opening the door, and the next instant David came dripping into the room. Had she really forgotten how handsome he was, even when looking as drowned as the proverbial rat?

'Darling, I'm sorry,' he said, scraping his fingers through his hair. 'What a fool . . .'

'We'll leave you to it,' the manager said. 'If there's anything you need, just give us a shout.'

The instant Phillip and Gemma had gone Lisa said, 'We have to get you out of those clothes and into a hot bath. Look at you, you're soaked to the skin.'

'And don't I know it,' he groaned, starting to peel off his shirt. 'What a bloody nightmare.'

'Where did you go? What happened? I was so worried, and why didn't you take your phone?'

'I thought I had it, but it turns out I picked up the camera instead.'

Having done the same herself in the past, she

gave him a kiss and hobbled off towards the bathroom to start running a bath. As soon as it was under way, she scooped up a couple of towels and took them back into the room. She found him naked with his wet clothes creating a puddle on the floor and his shoes, caked in grass and mud, dangling from his hands as he carried them out to the balcony.

'So what happened to you?' she asked, as he closed the door. 'Where did you go?'

A shadow of annoyance crossed his brow. 'If I knew that I wouldn't have got lost, would I?' he retorted.

Though she bristled at his tone, being unwilling for this to develop into yet another row, she sat him down on the bed and started to towel his hair. 'I was really worried,' she told him. 'I was afraid you'd had another of those blackouts . . .'

'Ow! You're rubbing too hard,' he snapped.

'Sorry. Here, you do it. I'll go and check the bath.'

A moment or two later he came into the bathroom behind her and turned her to face him. 'I'm sorry if I scared you,' he said, managing to look both contrite and guilty.

Relieved to have him sounding more like himself, she said, 'It's OK, as long as you're all right.'

'As you can see,' he said.

She managed a smile. 'From now on you can consider yourself banned from going anywhere without me.'

Gazing at her tenderly, he said, 'Are you happy to be here?'

Wondering how he could ask that when this first week had gone so badly, she decided it was best not to remind him, so simply said, 'I guess, if you are.'

'Don't I look it?' he asked, apparently meaning it.

She hardly knew what to say when actually he did right now, but how long would it last? 'We haven't got off to a great start, have we?' she said.

He seemed surprised, then concerned. 'So you're *not* happy to be here?'

Since it would achieve nothing to hurt him, or point out how difficult he'd been, she put a hand to his face as she said, 'I'm fine.' Then turning as her iPhone started to ring, she said, 'It'll probably be Amy wondering if you're back. Why don't you get into the bath and I'll order you a brandy?'

Catching her hands to delay her, he said, 'Next week will be better, I promise. When we go to Windermere . . .'

'We're at Windermere, you mean Ullswater.'

'Of course. We'll start again, as though it's the beginning.'

A few minutes later, after assuring Amy that everything was fine, she sat down on the edge of the bed to wait for someone from room service to deliver their drinks. There was something about his unwillingness to go into any detail about why he'd been gone for so long, and the way he'd brushed over his bouts of ill temper as though they'd never happened, that wasn't feeling right at all. It was as though he was in some kind of denial . . . Or that he was hiding something from her. Perhaps he was hiding it from himself, because he surely had to know how difficult he'd been since they got here. He seemed to think that if he pretended something hadn't happened she would too, which was bizarre and unsettling, and starting to make her worried about how naive she'd been to assume they knew one another inside out simply because they'd been close twenty years ago.

They were different people now, with histories, temperaments and even secrets that neither of them knew anything about. It felt suddenly daunting to realise that. But he was still David, she told herself. He was a good man, kind and generous and unfailingly supportive. But there seemed to be another side to him that she either hadn't noticed before, or he'd managed to suppress, and she was fairly sure it was a side she wasn't going to like very much.

However, no one was perfect, she reminded herself, only too aware of how critical and contrary she herself could be at times, and since he'd promised that next week at Ullswater would be better, she was ready to trust that he'd be as good as his word.

Rosalind could count on the fingers of one hand how many times she saw Lawrence laugh in a week, perhaps even a month. His amusement was often expressed in loud staccato bursts that rang as hollow and dry as the spaces between them, yet it still warmed her to hear it. He was laughing now as he sat in the TV room replaying the DVD Jerry had made of him throwing sticks for the dog at the wedding. Realising that Jerry must have edited the recording to make sure it contained nothing of the actual event, simply Lawrence and the dog, had surprised her when she'd first seen it. It conveyed a sensitivity to her feelings that she hadn't expected when she knew how strongly he disapproved of her decision to stay away, and how angered he'd been by the text she'd sent. So in spite of it all, on some level he seemed to understand that for her, watching her father committing to his new life surrounded by people she didn't know, in a place she would never visit, would have been like standing alone on a platform watching everything she treasured leaving on a train that had no room for her.

The loneliness she'd felt since that Saturday was only surpassed by the remorse that smothered her in shame every time she thought about that text. Her intention had been to rob Lisa Martin of the smugness of her victory and ruin her day – what she'd succeeded in doing was scaring her father and diminishing herself even further in the woman's eyes. Knowing that she must now view her with contempt was driving Rosalind's humiliation to even greater depths, which in turn was making her hate Lisa Martin all the more.

However, right now the woman was only in her thoughts because of her connection to the dog Lawrence was so passionate about. Having long guessed that the animal was going to be used to try and bridge the gap between her father's two families, she was already working on how to avoid that cunning little trap. She hadn't discussed it with Jerry yet, but she felt sure he'd approve of her decision to get a dog of their own once she told him, and she would as soon as he came home. He was due back later today, and she was eager to make his homecoming as special as she did in happier days.

From now on, she'd decided, she was going to put all her efforts into rebuilding their marriage, which meant she must force herself to let go of the fear that he would hurt her again. There was a time when she'd considered him her best friend, as well as her life partner, and she felt sure he was as keen to recapture that closeness as she was. In fact, she probably felt ready now to start trying for another baby.

'Again,' Lawrence stated, as the video ended on a full shot of his and Lucy's faces staring into the camera, and snatching up the remote he reset to the beginning.

'I was wondering,' Rosalind said, going to sit on an adjacent chair so she could see him without crowding him, 'if you'd like to have a dog of your own.'

Lawrence looked at her and blinked.

She smiled. 'That would be nice, wouldn't it?' she prompted.

'I want Lucy,' he said.

'But you know she belongs to somebody else.'

'I want Lucy.'

'You can still visit her, or she can come here, but think how lovely it would be to have your own dog here all the time.'

His expression was starting to darken. 'I want Lucy.'

'Stop that now,' she snapped as he began banging his feet into the sofa.

'I want Lucy.'

With a sigh she got up to go and answer the phone.

'I want Lucy.'

Closing the door behind her, she scooped up the cordless she'd left on the hall table and clicked on as she carried it into the kitchen.

'Hi, it's me,' Jerry said.

Though she'd expected it to be him, she experienced a fluttering of nerves that wasn't unlike the excitement she used to feel when they were dating. 'Hi,' she said, opening the fridge to take out some wine. 'I guess you've landed.'

'Mm, yeah, you could say that,' he replied.

She smiled. 'A bumpy one?'

His half-hearted laugh told her she was probably right and he was still cross with himself for not achieving perfection. 'What are you doing?' he asked.

Deciding not to mention the wine as she filled a glass, she said, 'Not much at the moment, but now I know you're on your way home I'll get cooking. Actually, I've already prepared quite a bit, because I'm making an Indian with all the trimmings, spicy poppadums, bhajis, chicken rezzala, pilau rice.' They were all his favourites, so he'd know without her having to say so that she had romantic plans for the evening.

There was a moment before he said, 'Actually, I'm not coming home. It's why I'm calling. I'm . . . Well, I'm not coming home.'

Her heart seemed to stop as his words rang with a meaning she didn't want to understand. She tried to laugh. 'I thought you'd landed,' she said. 'Has there been a delay? Oh no, don't tell me there's a problem with the same . . .'

'There's not a problem,' he interrupted. 'Not of that sort, anyway. What I'm saying is . . . Well, I think you know what I'm saying.'

No she didn't. She didn't want to, so she told him she didn't.

'I'm sorry,' he said quietly. 'I've tried, I swear I have, but you know as well as I do that we can't go on the way we are, so I think it's best all round now if we call it a day.'

A wrecking ball was coming at her so fast that there was no way she could avoid it. Any moment now it was going to smash her apart. 'But that's not what I want,' she said shakily.

'It's not what I wanted either, but we both know you can't let go of the past, and I can't go on trying to make it up to you.'

Grasping at what felt like a last straw, she said, 'I understand that, truly I do, but I've been thinking and I realise now how difficult I've been, always going on about what happened, never allowing myself to trust you, but I can change. In fact, I've already made up my mind that I will. I want us to start again. I'm cooking dinner tonight to show you . . .'

'Please don't do this,' he broke in gently. 'It's too late, Rosalind.'

'No! Don't say that. It's because I love you that I've found everything so difficult. If I didn't care it would make no difference to me who you slept with or how often, but I do care, Jerry. I care more than I know how to put into words. You must know that. I'm just so afraid of it happening again . . .'

303

'No, what you're afraid of now is being on your own. Your father has chosen Lisa in spite of all your efforts to stand in his way . . .'

'This isn't about him,' she cried. 'It's about us and how I feel about you. And it's about Lawrence, your son. He's been watching the DVD you made, over and over. He loves it. I told him we'd get him a dog of his own. Jerry,' she choked, desperately, 'if you won't think about me then please think of him. You're his father. He needs you too. I know he can't show his feelings, but that doesn't mean he doesn't have them. Please come home. I've got bhajis and masala and poppadums and . . .'

'I'm not in England,' he told her quietly.

As the words he didn't say started to register she became very still. 'So where are you?' she asked hoarsely.

He didn't answer, but the silence was answer enough.

'Oh my God, you're with her,' she sobbed. 'You've gone back to her . . .'

'Rosalind!'

'No! I don't want to hear any more. I always knew I was right . . .'

'Please don't hang up.'

'You know what's really sad about this?' she shouted. 'It's that you didn't have the guts to come and tell me in person. You're a coward, Jerry,' and with a slam that could have broken the handset she ended the call.

'I want Lucy. I want Lucy,' Lawrence yelled from the doorway.

'Shut up! Go away!' she sobbed, and grabbing her mobile she pressed in her father's number.

'Daddy! Oh God! Jerry's left me. He's in South Africa with his mistress and he's not coming back.'

'Just a moment,' a woman's voice said at the other end, 'I'll put you on to him.'

Chapter Fifteen

There had been no point in arguing, so Lisa hadn't even attempted it. Rosalind needed her daddy, so Rosalind's daddy was abandoning his honeymoon along with his promise of a better second week at Ullswater to speed back down the motorway to rescue his little princess's troubled marriage. Never mind about his own, all that mattered was that Rosalind shouldn't be alone at such a difficult time.

It was the middle of the afternoon now and they were already on the M5, south of Birmingham, so they should be home in less than an hour. Lisa could only hope that he remembered to drop her off before charging on to the rescue, because she was certainly in no mood to deal with his daughter the way things were.

'I'm sorry,' he said, casting her a quick glance, 'but you have to understand . . .'

'Will you please stop saying that?' she cut in angrily. 'I heard you the first time and the second and the third. I understand perfectly, thank you, so you don't have to explain it again.'

Appearing contrite, he said, 'I didn't realise I was repeating myself. How very annoying.'

'Yes, it is,' she confirmed, 'but not nearly as annoying as the fact that I'll probably be spending tonight on my own, and for all I know the entire second week of our honeymoon.'

She noticed his hands tighten on the wheel. 'Lisa, please try to have some compassion. Her husband's left her . . .'

'It's not that I don't feel sorry for her,' she cried, 'because actually I do, but tell me this, what consideration is she showing anyone else? Does she care that you're on your honeymoon? Did she stop to think that she might be spoiling a wonderful time for you? Not for a second. In fact, she probably hopes she is, because God forbid that you should enjoy yourself with anyone but her, or her mother, and especially not me, your new wife of one week and two days who she's decided to turn into her own personal bête noire without even meeting me.'

For a moment it seemed as though he might respond, but in the end he evidently decided not to and kept his eyes on the road as he continued to drive.

'What's the matter with you?' she suddenly snapped.

He frowned. 'What do you mean?'

'I mean why are you allowing this to happen, and why aren't you arguing back? This past week you've hardly stopped biting my head off or getting worked up over nothing, and now I can barely get a word out of you. So, what's the matter with you?'

'There's nothing the matter with me,' he said quietly.

Stifling the urge to scream, she turned to stare out of the window, resolved to pass the rest of the journey in silence unless he spoke first. It lasted until they were rapidly approaching their turn-off.

'Where are you going?' she shouted. 'Start indicating to pull over or we'll miss the exit.'

Seeming to come to, he quickly signalled and made a hasty swerve across the slow lane on to the slip road. 'Lucky nothing was in the way,' he said, glancing sheepishly into the rear-view mirror.

'Too right,' she muttered, still holding on to the edge of her seat.

He looked at her, and when she looked back she finally felt herself beginning to thaw. She really didn't have to be making this so difficult for him when it was clearly difficult enough already. 'I'm sorry,' she said, reaching for his hand. 'In fact, it's a bit perverse of me, isn't it, to be making such a fuss when we weren't having a particularly good time anyway. Will it make you feel better if I say I'll be glad to get home?'

'Would you mind if I said me too?' he replied with a smile. 'It's just a shame I have to go straight out again.'

Though she was tempted to remind him that Rosalind didn't actually know they were back yet so he could at least come in for a cup of tea, she realised it would only make him feel more torn than he already did, and since nothing she said was likely to change his mind, she might as well let it go.

'Honestly,' she said to Amy when she was finally back in the house and on her own, 'I'm beginning to wonder who he thinks he's married to, me or her? And if it ever came to choosing between us, I'm pretty sure she'd win . . . What am I saying? It just happened and she did. He had the choice of staying in the Lake District with me, or coming home to her, and look where we are.'

'Well, at least he didn't leave you there,' Amy commented drily.

Not being in the mood to laugh, Lisa said, 'I've a good mind to call a cab and come over to you for the night. Let him see what it's like to feel dumped on his honeymoon.'

'You know you're always welcome, but I don't think it's a good idea.'

Sighing, Lisa replied, 'No, I suppose not. It would just serve him right, that's all. I wonder what time he'll be back.'

'I never imagined myself defending Rosalind,' Amy said, 'but try to remember how you felt every time you thought Tony had left you. You were pretty devastated and then, when it really did come to an end . . . Well, you don't need me to remind you how hard you found it to get over. That's what she's going through now.'

'OK, you don't have to make me feel any worse than I already do. It's tough for her, I know that, horrible, one of the worst things that can happen. I just wish David weren't so . . . I don't know what he is . . . Yes I do, he's weak with her and I don't think I'm ever going to find that very easy to deal with.'

'Most fathers are jelly when it comes to their daughters, you know that, and I see it every day. So I'm afraid one way or another you'll have to get used to it, because he's not Tony who comes with no ties or responsibilities, and who was free to make you the centre of his world . . .'

'Let's not talk about Tony,' Lisa muttered, 'because right now he's starting to seem like the better option. At least he never used to pull Jekyll and Hyde stunts on me the way David has this past week. Tell me, was he moody before the wedding, and I was too busy to notice, or does being married do something to a man that I was never aware of?'

Sighing, Amy said, 'He's still the wonderful man you married, but now all the fuss and hoopla has died down reality's starting to kick in, and part of that is facing up to the fact that he has other commitments. So, let him deal with Rosalind, and while you're at it support him all you can, because it's the only way he's ever going to feel comfortable about getting the two of you together, and that's what needs to happen. Once she gets to know you she'll be as mad about you as I am.'

'But will I be mad about her, has anyone given a thought to that? No, of course not, because it's always about her. Well, I'm damned if I'm going to let my life revolve around someone who's spoiled rotten and way too cosy in her role as Daddy's girl.'

'Lisa . . .'

'No, I mean it. She did her best to ruin my wedding, she's managed to break up my honeymoon, now I'm starting to wonder what the hell she's going to pull off next.'

* * *

310

Rosalind was laughing as she dabbed tears from her eyes and settled in more comfortably against her father's shoulder. They'd been sitting together on the sofa for over an hour now, talking a little about Jerry and what had happened, but mainly they'd been reminiscing about her mother, which was something she'd so desperately needed to do with someone – and who better than him? Next week it would be a year since her mother had gone, but Rosalind hadn't got round to asking him yet if he was going to spend the anniversary with her. She would when she was feeling strong enough to deal with the rejection when it came, as she felt sure it would.

She continued to smile as she listened to him recounting the 'earrings at the zoo' story, which was clearly one of his favourites. The way he was telling it made it sound as though he'd forgotten all about it until today, with his surprises and chuckles and fake horror, reminding her of how he used to tell her stories when she was small.

When he'd finished she was ready with a special memory of her own, as much to keep him there as to place Jerry into their pictures of the past. 'Do you remember the first time I brought him home to meet you?' she said, a bubble of unsteady laughter rising up through her pain. 'You and Mum had been out for lunch and were completely legless when you came back to find us waiting for you. You'd only forgotten about us! What kind of parents were you? Then you started hiccuping like a horse and Mum couldn't stop laughing ... I was so embarrassed and furious, then I realised Jerry was laughing too ...' Her eyes closed as she started to cringe. 'Oh God, I'd made him wear his new uniform to try and impress you,' she groaned. 'He looked so ridiculous sitting there with his cap on, which I wouldn't let him take off because I thought it made him look so dashing and important.'

'It did,' David assured her, 'but it has to be said, ridiculous too, which was part of the reason your shamelessly inebriated mother couldn't stop laughing.'

'Poor Jerry,' Rosalind intoned wistfully. 'It's a wonder he ever came back after that. I was so ghastly and uptight, and you two were so out of control.'

'You tried to send us to bed, which made us laugh even harder, and as for Jerry, I don't think he ever really left after that, because apart from when he was in the air he always seemed to be with us.'

She sighed shakily. 'Yes, he practically moved into our house, didn't he?' she said. 'We were so mad about each other then and you were great parents, making him feel so welcome, and even letting us share a room.'

She waited for him to remind her that it had been her mother's decision to allow that, because he'd never approved of his little girl sharing a bed with a 'big hairy bloke, even if you were nineteen by then', but he didn't say anything, and as the awfulness of where she and Jerry were now descended over her like an avalanche she could feel herself becoming smothered again. 'What am I going to do, Dad?' she whispered. 'I don't want to lose him, but he said it's already too late.'

Pulling her in closer, he said, 'Would you like me to have a chat with him? I'm sure we can get this sorted . . .'

'No, I mean yes, I would, but you can't, because he's always saying I'm too dependent on you as it is. But I have to try to get him to come home so we can talk, face to face. I'm sure that'll make a difference, except if he's gone back to her . . .' Her words were swallowed by a wave of pure wretchedness. 'He can't go back to her, Dad,' she sobbed. 'He just can't . . .'

'Sssh, ssh,' he soothed, pressing a kiss to the top of her head. 'Would you like me to have a chat with him? I'm sure . . .'

'No, I just said, he thinks I depend on you too much already. I need to try and sort this out for myself, but what am I going to do if he really has gone back to her? I won't be able to bear it. I know I won't.'

'Did he actually say that's what he's done? Do you know for certain that's where he is?'

'He didn't answer when I asked, but he didn't deny it either.' Her eyes closed as the image of a beautiful, mischievous blonde of twenty-five or less, with no grief issues, or difficult children, or any baggage at all to make her appear less than attractive, came up to taunt her. 'He was flying to Cape Town last week,' she choked, unable to stop another deluge of tears. 'He's obviously decided to stay there. Oh God, Dad, I'm such a mess. I shouldn't be letting him get away with this, I know I shouldn't. I ought to be telling him that I'll never take him back, no matter what, but I couldn't bear it . . .'

'Sssh, ssh,' he whispered again as she fought for breath.

'Do you think I ought to go over there? I should, shouldn't I? But what if he refuses to see me? It would be so awful to be there on my own, in a place I don't know and with no one to talk to.' She turned to look at him, her eyes bright with hope and tears. 'You could come with me,' she suggested tentatively. 'He wouldn't have to know you were there ... We could check into a hotel and you could wait while I go ...' Already the energy was draining from her words. 'You wouldn't be able to get away, would you? She wouldn't let you. Anyway, he'd find out somehow and then ... No, forget it, it was a stupid idea. I just can't think what else to do.'

Stroking her hair as she rested her head on his shoulder again, he said, 'Would you like me to have a word with him? I could ...'

'Dad, please don't keep saying that. I've already told you why it won't work. I've got to figure this out for myself.'

They sat quietly then, listening to the rain beating the windows and the sound of Lawrence's PlayStation bleeping and roaring in the TV room next door. Thinking of him in there alone, all shut up in his own little world, untouched, misunderstood and abandoned by his father, brought more tears flooding from her heart. 'How can he do it to Lawrence?' she sobbed. 'I know he's difficult and not the kind of son he wanted, but he's still a human being ...'

'Jerry loves Lawrence very much,' David assured her, 'but it's not always easy to show it, as you know very well.'

'If Mum were here she'd know what to do. Oh God, Dad, what's happening to my life? First Mum goes, then Jerry, and I'm losing you too . . .'

'You are not losing me,' he told her firmly.

'Do you swear it? You won't let *her* come between us? Lawrence needs you . . .'

'Shush now. I'll always be here for you. Nothing will ever change that, even when I'm married you'll still be . . .' He swallowed and put a hand to his head. 'Lisa has no intention of trying to come between us,' he said faintly. 'She understands how important you and Lawrence are to me.'

'Will she let you spend the day with me next Wednesday? I don't want to be on my own for the anniversary, Dad. Please say you'll come?'

He didn't know what to say.

'Oh, please don't tell me you've forgotten . . .'

'Of course not, I'm sorry. I wasn't thinking . . .'

'We can do something special, the three of us? Lawrence will like that. Maybe we could go and find him a dog? He keeps saying he wants Lucy, but if we got him one of his own . . .'

'That sounds like a good idea.' He made a surreptitious glance at his watch. 'Actually, I should probably pop in there and see him before I go . . .'

'You're not leaving yet,' she protested.

'I'll have to go soon . . . No, not if you don't want me to. I should call Lisa though, to let her know I'm still here.'

'Why don't you stay for dinner? I haven't seen you for ages and in the circumstances . . .'

'Darling . . .'

'I made an Indian meal for Jerry yesterday . . .'

315

'I'd love to stay, but Lisa and I have only just got back and . . .'

'It's OK. I'm sorry, I keep forgetting that she has to come first now, I just need some time to get used to it. She knows you've promised to help me with the business this summer?'

When he didn't answer she turned to look at him. 'Dad! You promised . . .'

'Of course I can help you,' he assured her. 'It had just slipped my mind . . .'

'Please don't back out. There's such a lot going on and I need your advice, especially now all this has happened with Jerry. My head's going to be all over the place and the accountant's . . .'

'It's all right,' he interrupted. 'I'm going to help. I was just . . .' He broke off as Lawrence suddenly burst into the room.

'David,' he cried. 'Where is Lucy?'

'She's at home,' he told him.

'I want Lucy.'

'Well, first of all, that's no way to ask, and second you know very well that she's not yours. But guess what, we're going to get you a dog of your own.' He threw out his arms as though he'd just performed a conjuring trick.

'I want Lucy,' Lawrence insisted, stamping a foot.

With a sigh, David got up, saying, 'Come on, let's go and search the Internet to see if we can find some retriever puppies.'

Loving the way her father rarely seemed fazed by Lawrence, Rosalind said, 'Shall I bring you another drink? We might as well finish off the bottle now.'

Seeming not to have heard, David walked Lawrence into the study to sit down at the computer, while Rosalind, feeling suitably guilty about what she was intending to do, went ahead anyway and poured her father another very large glass of wine. If he drank it all he'd be over the limit, so unable to drive home. And she wouldn't be able to take him herself, because she'd already had too much.

Lisa was in the pool, swimming languorously back and forth with a mellow jazz tune drifting from the surrounding speakers, when her iPhone started to ring. Speeding up to reach the edge, she got there before it went through to messages.

'Hi darling,' she said, seeing it was David. 'How's it going?'

'I'm afraid she's pretty cut up,' he replied, 'and Lawrence isn't helping much by being a pain about Lucy. We're going to try and get him a dog of his own next week, hopefully that'll keep him quiet. What are you up to?'

With a smile she said, 'Right now, I'm sitting on the edge of our wonderful swimming pool staring out at the rain and thinking how much more wonderful it would be if you were here too.'

His voice was jagged with awkwardness as he said, 'Believe me, there's nothing I'd like better, but I think I'll have to stay here tonight. Rosalind's not coping too well and she's had quite a lot to drink. To be honest, I've probably overdone it too.'

'Oh, David,' she groaned, trying not to sound angry, but not quite succeeding. 'I don't mean to be unsympathetic, but this is our first night back . . .'

'I know, I know. It'll just be tonight. I'll be home in time for breakfast.'

'Will you?' she said tartly. 'Or will she have come up with another way to keep you there by then?'

'I promise I'll be back by nine at the latest. Why don't you invite Amy and Theo over tonight?'

'First of all, don't patronise me. And secondly, because it's too short notice. Actually, they've invited us for dinner next Saturday. Apparently they have some news.'

'Oh? Any ideas?'

'Not really.' In fact that wasn't true, because she half suspected Amy was going to announce she was pregnant, and if she was, thrilled as Lisa would be for her, she knew she'd feel deeply envious too. 'You know,' she said shortly, 'I'm trying very hard not to be fed up about you staying there tonight.'

'I'm sorry,' he sighed. 'I'll make it up to you when I get home, but I really wouldn't feel good about leaving her now.'

Sighing too, she said, 'So what's the news on Jerry? Has he gone back to this other woman?'

'Um, uh,' he mumbled.

Guessing Rosalind must have come into the room, she felt a spark of sympathy for Jerry as she considered how long he'd been trying to deal with his wife's dependency on her father. 'Well, I suppose I'd better get used to the fact that I've lost you for tonight, and go and prepare my lonely supper,' she said, not liking how sour she sounded, but hell, why shouldn't she? 'Will you call again to say good night?'

Silence.

'David?'

Still no reply.

She glanced at the phone to check the connection. 'Are you there?' she asked. 'Can you hear me? I can't hear you.'

Though he said nothing she could hear noises in the background, and she was sure one of them was him breathing. 'Have there been any calls?' he asked suddenly.

She frowned with annoyance. 'No, we're supposed to be away,' she reminded him snippily.

'Ah, yes.' There was another drawn-out silence before he said, 'Lisa, I'm sorry. I'm very ... I'm very sorry,' and before she could say any more he left her with a dead line and no clear way at all of trying to get a grip on what had just happened.

At his end David was standing in the study next to Lawrence, unable to focus or even think through the clouds of confusion that were forming at the backs of his eyes. A part of him wanted to cry, but self-pity was something he despised, while helplessness was something he didn't understand. Whatever he was feeling he couldn't allow it to go on. He'd have to call Karen Knoyle tomorrow, before things got any worse. He must tell her the whole truth this time, because he knew he'd omitted parts before, though now he was no longer sure what they were. Other things had happened since, while he and Lisa were away, during meetings he'd had before the wedding, phone calls he hadn't returned or didn't remember receiving. He'd seen too much frustration and bewilderment in other people's eyes, or heard it sharpening their tones, to be able to go on ignoring it. He had to face up to whatever was happening, for Lisa's sake, if not for his own. He'd feel so unworthy and ashamed if he'd landed her with a husband who wasn't as fit and healthy as she deserved. She was his wife now. They'd had a wedding. He remembered almost everything about it, including the fact that he'd been unable to deliver all of his lines. He'd loved her, or at least the memory of her, since she was in her teens. He mustn't let her down. Not now. They had so much to live for, mostly each other, so he must find the courage to face the demons that were prowling around inside him and might, if he didn't confront them soon, end up driving him out of his mind.

Dr Karen Knoyle's plump, oval face was showing little expression as she listened to David talking her through the reasons why he was in her surgery for the second time in as many months. Though much of what he was saying was becoming elliptical and occasionally tangential as he went through it, she didn't feel inclined to interrupt. She was interested to hear the way he expressed himself and, perhaps more importantly, to find out how far he would go with an explanation before backing away from its conclusion.

As he moved on to describing his bouts of anxiety and forgetfulness, which, he confessed, sometimes led to outbursts of frustration and anger, or self-enforced silence, what she was finding the most intriguing was the way he kept referring to the notes he'd apparently made for himself.

When he finally came to a stop she waited to see if there was anything more he'd like to add, and when there didn't seem to be she said, 'The last time you were here . . .'

'This isn't to do with Catrina,' he interrupted.

Hiding her surprise, she regarded him steadily, then backing up a little, she said, 'What exactly do you remember of the last time you were here?'

He took a while to reply. 'I guess we were quite regular visitors,' he said, 'so it's hard to be specific.'

Her eyes stayed on his as she tried to gauge whether he really had forgotten the last occasion he'd come here and the tests they'd run afterwards, and decided that for the moment anyway, he apparently had. 'Tell me, how do you feel physically?' she asked. 'Any headaches, nausea, dizziness?'

He shook his head.

'And in yourself? Would you say you're in good spirits? Or could you be feeling a little down?'

The irony she knew well made a fleeting appearance. 'I've just got married,' he reminded her.

She smiled too, finding herself relieved to know that he remembered that. 'That still doesn't answer my question,' she reminded him.

The light in his eyes dimmed as he seemed to sink from good humour into a place of discomfort. 'Well, I suppose I have been feeling a bit down lately,' he admitted, 'but if you're asking if I'm happy with Lisa, then the answer . . .' He trailed off, as though not sure what to say next. 'Since you asked,' he said finally, 'I'm finding it a little difficult to be up in my spirits when I know . . . Well, when I know I'm not . . . When I think there's . . .'

His eyes came directly to hers. 'How would you feel if you thought there was something wrong with you?' he asked.

She held his gaze while waiting for him to say more. When he didn't, she hedged for a moment, saying, 'Have you discussed any of this with Lisa?'

There was only the briefest hesitation before he replied, 'No. I want to try and get things sorted out without worrying her.'

She nodded, understanding his reasoning. 'Usually,' she said, sitting back in her chair, 'when someone visits a doctor they have their own theories on what's wrong with them, so I'm interested to know what yours might be.'

He started to answer, but whatever he'd been about to say ended up staying with him.

'I'm going to venture a guess,' she said, 'that you're scaring yourself witless with all the biggies like brain tumours and CJD, maybe mini strokes, schizophrenia . . .'

His eyes stayed on hers.

'. . . but what if I told you we could be looking at something like a kidney infection, or a thyroid-gland deficiency . . .'

He was already shaking his head. 'I think we both know what it is,' he said quietly.

Certain now of what was really in his mind, which unfortunately was what was in hers too, she said, 'Actually, we don't know anything yet, but here's what we're going to do . . .'

Chapter Sixteen

How could a month go by so quickly, yet still manage to feel like an eternity, Lisa was asking herself as she and David drove over to Amy's. Instead of a prolonged honeymoon period spent settling into their new home and enjoying a relaxing summer, it had turned into the strangest and most stressful time she could ever remember. It was as though David was actively trying to avoid her, as he spent more and more time out of the house, either on constituency business, or supporting Rosalind with the company and through the break-up of her marriage. Jerry wasn't coming back, it seemed, though according to what little she could get out of David, it didn't appear that anyone was entirely sure yet whether Jerry was with his girl-friend in South Africa, or even where he was living. David said he called now and again, but he never went into any detail about what had been said, or how Rosalind was feeling.

Possibly pretty smug in some ways, Lisa frequently reflected to herself, since she now seemed to be having her daddy to herself most days, and by the time he came home at night he was so tired and uncommunicative that Lisa was starting to wonder why he bothered. She'd stopped complaining now, she didn't even risk asking him to explain why he was being so difficult, because every time she did they ended up in some kind of row that hardly made any sense, nor was anything ever resolved at the end of it. He wouldn't even give her a reason for not wanting to socialise, or for refusing to answer his own phone at times. He simply left the calls to go through to messages, and her to wonder how often he did the same to her when she was trying to contact him.

To her dismay, it was starting to feel like one of the loneliest times she'd spent since breaking up with Tony. She'd even, occasionally, found herself tempted to call Tony, not only because of how uncomplicated he was starting to seem by comparison, but simply for company. Had Amy been around it might have been easier, but two days after she and David had returned from the Lake District their initial plans for dinner had to be put on hold as Theo's mother had been burgled, so Amy had been staying with her to try and help her deal with the police and insurers, and recover from the trauma. Of course, she and Lisa spoke on the phone most days, but it wasn't the same as actually spending time together, and Lisa sorely missed her. Her only reprieve from the loneliness was when she was on her computer either trying to sort out some future employment, which wasn't going terribly well so far, or attempting to draft the first chapters of her new novel. However, if David happened to be around when she shut herself away, he was as likely as not to start becoming suspicious of what she was really doing.

'I can't imagine what you think it is,' she'd cried, when he'd accused her for the second time of trying to hide things from him. 'If you don't believe me, then read what I've written. It's still very rough, but at least you'll see for yourself that it's happening.'

He hadn't taken her up on the offer, had simply disappeared into his own study and closed the door. Half an hour later he was back with two glasses of champagne, insisting they celebrate their three-week anniversary. He'd taken her out to dinner that night, and had been so like his normal self that she'd risked asking him why he was behaving so erratically. To her relief he hadn't flared up the way he often did when she commented on his moods, instead he'd apologised for upsetting her, and then tried brushing it off by saying he had a lot on his mind.

'Like what?' she'd implored. 'If you'd tell me, at least we could discuss it.'

'It's not important,' he assured her. 'I'm sorting things out, so don't let's spoil the evening.'

And that was all she could get out of him, that he had a lot on his mind and whatever it was he didn't want to discuss it. So she was left wondering what on earth was bothering him, and dreading the next time he flew off the handle over the least little thing. What did it matter that he couldn't remember which drawer they were using for cutlery? It took time to find one's way around a new kitchen, and with half the boxes still not unpacked she didn't always know where everything was either, but was she throwing a fit every time she had to go on the hunt for this or that? Was she heck!

'I've looked this up on the Internet,' he told her one night, 'and it recommends labelling cupboards and drawers so that you know what's inside.'

It seemed so preposterous that she'd hardly known what to say. In the end all she'd managed was, 'If that's what you want, then do it.'

He hadn't, thank goodness, but nor had he stopped getting irritable when he opened the wrong door, or tripped over a box which was where he had left it.

Now, at last, Amy was back, and Lisa couldn't have been more relieved to see her. However, minutes after they arrived Theo's mother rang, so Amy had to go and deal with her, while Theo sorted out the drinks and David went off into the garden to take a call from the constituency chairman. As she watched him from the conservatory Lisa was thinking about how little intimacy they'd shared since the wedding, which was as baffling as everything else when they'd been so close before. She'd even started to wonder if he still loved her, or indeed how much she loved him, because when he was withdrawn or irritable she was finding herself tempted to walk away and not bothering to come back.

'Oh, heavens!' Amy winced, coming to join her, as Roxy let out an ear-splitting shriek.

Amused, Lisa turned to look at her niece, who was in the sitting room bouncing up and down in euphoric paroxysms, apparently so blissed out by what she'd just heard down the phone that she couldn't sit still – or, equally as likely, she might be desperate for the loo.

'Theo'll be through any minute with the drinks,'

Amy told her, 'and his mother seems to have settled for the night, so finally I'm all yours, or at least for the next few minutes.'

Lisa smiled and tucked an arm through Amy's, as she turned to continue watching David. 'I'm going to be really interested to hear what you think of him,' she said quietly, 'because something's definitely not right. It's like there's some other side to him that I neglected to spot during the run-up to the wedding. I really thought I knew him . . . I mean, of course he's changed, we all have, but the way he's been since the wedding . . . Well, you'll see for yourself. He can go from being completely stressed and hostile one minute, to the wonderful man we all know and love the next. And somewhere in between he might just go silent, like he doesn't want to speak at all.'

'He doesn't seem to be having too much of a problem now,' Amy commented, as David laughed at something the chairman was telling him.

'Thank goodness, but if you could have heard him yesterday when I told him he obviously had a screw loose, so maybe he ought to go back and see the doctor . . . I admit, it wasn't the most sensitive thing to say, but I was angry at the time and then I got even angrier when he started accusing me of being the one with problems. Apparently I don't know anything about the real world, I've got my head in the clouds only ever thinking about myself and how everything has to run to my rules and in my time frame . . . Actually, I'm making this sound a whole lot more coherent than he did, because most of what he was saying seemed to go nowhere. He wasn't making much sense at all, but by then we were both yelling and I don't think either of us had any idea what it was about in the end.'

'But you've made up since?'

'I think so. Once again I was the first to apologise, but then he did his usual thing of insisting it was all his fault, which it was, and that he was sorry I'd lost my purse, as if that was the reason we'd blown up at each other.'

'You didn't tell me you'd lost your purse.'

Lisa gave a growl of annoyance. 'Can you believe it? We turned the house and the car upside down yesterday and called the shops I'd been to, but no one had handed it in. I must have dropped it when I was in the car park, or maybe I was pickpocketed, who knows? I had to cancel all my credit cards and go through the extremely tedious rigmarole of contacting everyone . . . Anyway, it's done now, and he's finished his call, so we'd better change the subject. Who's Roxy talking to?'

'Oh, that'll be Mabel, her new best friend. They're clearly discussing Sven, the latest TDF in their world.'

With a smile, Lisa watched David waiting for Lucy to bring back her ball as she said, 'So poor Freddy is already history? He was the last one, wasn't he?'

Having overheard as he carried a tray of his speciality cocktails out of the kitchen, Theo said, 'And he could be back on the scene before the evening's out, she's so fickle. Oh, *Roxy*!' he winced, as Roxy shrieked again. 'Is she too old to be sent to her room?'

Laughing, Amy planted a kiss on his cheek, and

went to link David's arm as he came up from the garden. 'Perfect timing,' she told him. 'The screaming orgasms have just turned up.'

'Ah, something I'll never tire of,' David quipped, sending Lisa's eyebrows skywards as the others laughed.

'I should think they'd have worn you two newly-weds out by now,' Theo teased.

'Theo!' Amy reprimanded, throwing a sheepish look Lisa's way.

'What?' Theo protested innocently. 'They're practically still on honeymoon, so I don't think that's inappropriate.'

Keeping her eyes down, Amy picked up two giant Martini glasses filled to the brim with the cocktail and passed one each to Lisa and David.

'So, here's to you two,' Theo declared when they were all holding a drink, apart from Roxy who was still breaking decibels on the phone. 'May all your orgasms be screaming.'

'I'm sorry,' Amy mumbled, glancing awkwardly at Lisa, 'I'll find his off button in a minute.'

Feeling David coming to stand next to her, Lisa leaned affectionately in to him and was about to speak when he said, 'So, has my lovely wife told you her news yet?'

Amy's eyes widened, all intrigue.

Lisa was baffled. 'I have some news?' she said.

David was smiling proudly. 'She has a publisher for her novel,' he announced. 'Isn't that marvellous?'

As Amy blinked in amazement, Lisa did a double take and turned to David. 'You're presumably referring to what I told you in the car on the way here?'

He nodded happily. 'It's very good news,' he assured her.

'All that's happened,' she informed Amy and Theo, 'is that I had a chat on the phone yesterday with Marcia Edmonds, who's an editor at one of the big London publishers. We go back a long way, so it's no big deal that she suggested we have lunch when I'm next in London.'

David continued to look thrilled. 'It's an excellent story,' he told Amy and Theo, 'so I'm not surprised this editor . . . What was her name?'

'Marcia.'

'Yes, I'm not surprised she wants to see you. She knows she's got the next bestseller on her hands.'

Not bothering to point out that she hadn't even told Marcia what the book was about yet, Lisa kissed him briefly on the cheek as she whispered, 'Let's not get too carried away, mm?'

His eyes came to hers, but before he could say anything she gave his arm a squeeze and turned back to Amy and Theo. Roxy then came skipping out on to the terrace, and grabbing herself a cocktail, she said, 'So! What do you think, Lisa and David? Isn't it brilliant? I mean, I'm going to miss them, obviously, but I'll be at uni from . . .'

'Roxy,' Amy broke in sharply, 'we haven't told them yet.'

'Oh my God,' Roxy gulped, going up on tiptoe as she wagged a hand, as though erasing her words. 'I'm sorry, I'm sorry. I heard someone mention news, so I assumed that's what you guys were talking about. Ignore me, pretend I never said anything.'

'If only,' her father muttered.

Though Lisa's smile was already a ghost of its former self, she was somehow managing to hang on to what was left of it, in spite of her insides dissolving into turmoil. *Please don't let this be true*, she was thinking. *Please let me be misunderstanding what I think is going on.*

Her eyes were on Amy and it was clear, from the colour creeping over her sister's neck, that Lisa's worst fear was about to be confirmed.

'Well,' Theo declared manfully, 'that certainly wasn't how we'd intended to break it to you, but I guess it's out now, so there we are, Amy and I are off to Oz.'

As Amy put a hand to her head, and Lisa started to reel, David said, 'You mean Australia? For a holiday?'

Amy shook her head and seemed to wince as Lisa took David's arm and said, with a terrible smoothness, 'Australia. How lovely. It's one of my favourite places.'

Rising gamely to the occasion, David proposed a toast. 'To Oz,' he announced, while managing not to sound as bemused as he looked.

'Thank you,' Theo cried, too loudly.

Roxy was looking sheepishly at her mother. 'Oh God, I feel terrible,' she wailed. 'I'm really sorry if I've put my foot in it . . .'

'Of course you haven't,' Lisa assured her, unconsciously tightening her grip on David's arm. 'Mum and Dad were about to tell us anyway, so now perhaps they can give us the back story, such as how long have you been planning this, Amy, and why is this the first I'm hearing of it?' Her eyes

331

were glittering a challenge as she glared at her sister, who seemed to be shrinking by the second.

'Lisa, I'm sorry,' Amy said with feeling. 'I wanted to tell you, and I came within an inch of it so many times, but you've had so much going on what with the wedding, and then . . .' She stopped at the edge of the faux pas. 'I didn't want to spoil anything, or make things about me when . . . Well, you know what I'm saying.'

Even though she could see how dreadful Amy was feeling, Lisa was still finding it hard to be forgiving. 'We're not supposed to have secrets, remember,' she said brusquely.

'Lisa . . .'

Lisa waved a hand to stop her. 'So when are you intending to go?' she asked, unable to keep the edge out of her voice.

Retaking her role as the dropper of bombshells, Roxy said, 'At the end of October, after I've gone up to Oxford.'

Lisa couldn't take her eyes off Amy. This was feeling like the worst imaginable betrayal, yet she had no right in the world to feel that way. 'So, what brought it on?' she demanded. 'When did you decide this was what you wanted to do?'

Amy glanced at Theo as he said, 'You may remember Charlie Goodson, one of my partners, who went to Oz about ten years ago to set up an office in Sydney?'

Lisa nodded. 'Yes, vaguely,' she replied.

'Well, the old chap's retiring at the end of the year, and when he was last here, in Bath, at a partners' meeting, it was decided that I would take over the position, subject to Amy agreeing, of course.'

Lisa looked at her sister again, and as Amy began trying to lighten things by reminding them how easy it was to stay in touch these days with emails and Skype, Lisa was struggling with a growing surge of panic. *Please no*, she was crying inside. *You can't go now. Please don't leave me.* She wanted to remind Amy that she knew no one in the area and was relying on her to help her feel settled. She wanted to grab hold of her and make her understand how afraid she was of what was happening to her marriage, that she wouldn't be able to cope without Amy's support. Of course she wouldn't speak out, because she understood that Amy had her own life, and her husband had to come first, but wretched as Amy was clearly feeling, Lisa could tell that she was as excited about starting a new life as she, Lisa, had been during the times she'd done the very same thing.

'. . . so we've already rented this house to a retired couple from Newcastle,' Amy was explaining to David, while casting anxious glances at Lisa. 'They're due to move in at the beginning of November, by which time our furniture will have gone into storage . . .'

'Hang on,' Lisa interrupted, taking heart from the word 'storage', 'how long did you say you're going for?'

'Two years initially,' Amy replied, 'but if we like it, and feel that it suits us . . . Well, who knows,' she said, evidently feeling the need to downplay things again, 'anything could happen between now and then.'

'Have you told Mum about this yet?' Lisa wanted to know.

'Actually, yes we have,' Amy confessed, 'and she's fine with it, especially now you're going to be close by. I'll miss her, obviously, but she's already planning to fly out with Roxy for Christmas.'

Christmas! They weren't going to be here for Christmas.

Lisa's head was reeling again. What if her mother decided to stay in Sydney too? She'd always been closer to Amy than she had to her, so she might. How was she going to cope without either of them? OK, she'd managed for years while she'd been globetrotting with her career and Tony, but she'd known they were here, in England, the place she always came back to because it was *home* ... Feeling David's arm sliding around her shoulder, as though to remind her she'd always have him, she found herself taking another gulp of her drink.

Theo was speaking again. '. . . and the apartment they've taken for us has four en suite bedrooms apparently, so there'll be plenty of room if you two decide to come with Matilda and Roxy. You obviously know the city quite well, Lisa, so it would be great to have you to show us all around.'

Lisa looked at Amy as she went on chattering about the kind of fun they could have spending Christmas in the sun, which would be a first for them, but instead of listening Lisa became caught up in a glittering panoply of Christmases past, mostly with Tony, not only in Sydney, but Bangkok, Singapore, Argentina, Barbados, Zanzibar, so many exotic hot spots that she'd almost lost count now. Had she ever stopped to wonder what her family was doing on those days, or how much they might be missing her? The truth was no, she hadn't, and now she was receiving a taste of what it was like to be forgotten in the grand plan.

'We'd be delighted, wouldn't we, darling?' David was saying, as he gave her a squeeze that felt like a prompt. 'I can't think of anything we'd like better.'

'Do you have a long enough break at that time of year?' Lisa asked him. And what about Rosalind? Would he seriously consider leaving her at that time of year? She didn't think so.

'Try to keep up,' David teased. 'We're talking about Roxy making her home with us for the time her parents are away.'

Amy quickly came in with, 'I swear it wasn't why we were choosing rooms when you first showed us the house. That was a joke. We didn't know anything about this then. Obviously, she'll come to us for the longer breaks . . .'

'But of course Roxy can stay with us,' Lisa interrupted, grasping the one small glimmer of light flickering on a black horizon. 'Where else would she go?'

'Oh fab!' Roxy cried excitedly. 'I promise I won't get in the way, and if you want some private time you just have to say the word and I'm gone, aren't I Mum?'

'Really? Not so's *I'd* ever noticed,' her father cut in.

'Oh, it'll be such bliss,' Roxy gushed on, 'having that pool to swim in, and spending time with you, Lis. I won't miss Mum half as much as long as I know I've got you. Oh, and I'm going to have the

335

old VW Polo they use for the garden centre and stuff, so you won't have to worry about ferrying me around or anything like that.'

This was still happening too fast, yet was clearly already so well planned that Lisa barely knew what to say.

'My Smart is on offer, if you want it,' Amy told her. 'I know you always laugh at it, but don't forget, it's environmentally friendly, zero road tax, and parks on a sixpence, which you'll need going in and out of Bristol, especially Clifton.'

Lisa turned to David, but seeing how thrown he was now looking too, she buried her face in his shoulder, giving herself a moment to turn the urge to cry into a laugh. 'All this is acceptable,' she said, bringing her head up again, 'as long as I get my dog back too.'

'Ah, well, we thought that went without saying, didn't we, Luce?' Roxy said, stooping to give the watchful Lucy a bruising hug.

Lisa turned to David again, and this time found herself wondering if the prospect of her niece and her dog moving into the house was making him feel as trapped as he was suddenly looking.

'Well, I have to admit, from what you've been telling me I was expecting him to be practically schizo or something,' Amy commented, as Theo left her and Lisa alone in the kitchen. The meal was over now, and the men were catching up on the Ashes while Roxy went off to check her emails. 'I mean, I can see that he's a little . . . how would I describe it? Distracted? Yes, distracted now and again, but we're all like that at times.'

Since they'd spent most of the past two hours discussing Amy's move Lisa guessed there was nothing left to be said about it at this stage, so why not let Amy return the subject to David? 'I take it you noticed that he hardly spoke,' she said, continuing to rinse the plates. 'That's what he does these days when we're in company. He just sits back and lets everyone else do the talking, and if you ask him anything he gives the briefest possible reply. Is that the David you know?'

Amy was shaking her head curiously. 'I suppose not,' she replied, 'but he's always been a good listener, and Theo and I were jabbering on so much about ourselves it was difficult for anyone to get a word in.'

This was true, but Lisa didn't blame her for it. 'So you think I'm worrying about nothing?' she said.

'I wouldn't say that, exactly, because obviously you're not making up all the arguments and stuff, but it's hard for me to be a judge when he seems perfectly normal to me.'

Turning as Lucy came skidding into the kitchen, apparently having only just woken up to the fact that leftovers might be going into the bin instead of her bowl, Lisa tried to smile past the lump in her throat. 'There you are, you rascal,' she said, catching Lucy's face between her hands and planting a kiss on the top of her head. 'I wondered when you were going to show up.'

'There are some scraps over there,' Amy told her, pointing to a plate on the dresser.

'It's clear you've been completely spoiled living in this house,' Lisa informed the dog as she gave her the scrumptious addition to her Pedigree supper. 'Things are going to change when you come to me, so be warned.'

'Oh yeah?' Amy said mockingly. 'This from you, who's always slipping her a little something when you think no one's watching.'

Forcing a laugh, Lisa handed over the plate to go in the dishwasher, and leaned back against the counter top as she said, 'I haven't had much time to think this through yet, but I was wondering how you'd feel about Lucy going to Lawrence?' Though the mere thought of it was making her ache with longing for Lucy's faithfulness, she had to consider how much time she and David would be spending in London.

Closing the machine, Amy reached for a towel to dry her hands and turned to look at her. 'Actually, I had a feeling you might suggest that,' she said, 'so I suppose my first answer is, she's your dog, so it should be your decision.'

'Yes, but we both know she's yours really.'

'Well, whoever's she is, we both love her to bits . . .'

'This isn't about not wanting her,' Lisa interrupted hastily, 'please don't think that, because it couldn't be further from the truth. I'm just thinking about the amount of time we'll be away, and when we are she'll probably have to go into kennels, which she'd hate, and considering how attached she and Lawrence have become to one another . . . Well, you know what I'm saying.'

'Of course I do, and in principle I think it's a good idea. He's a sweet boy who obviously doesn't have many friends, and when I saw them together at the wedding and how much they've bonded . . . Well, to put it bluntly, Lisa, it's not him I'm worried about. It's his mother.'

Sharing the same concern, Lisa drew in her breath.

'She'll obviously know where Lucy's coming from,' Amy continued, 'and I'd hate to think of her being cruel, or neglecting her, just because she was ours – or more particularly yours.'

'I understand what you're saying, but would she really take out her prejudices on an innocent dog? Especially one as loving and daft as Lucy.'

Amy was still looking worried. 'How can we say when we don't actually know her? The question is, do we want to take the risk?'

Lisa was very far from sure. 'I'll have to talk it over with David,' she said, 'but if we do end up convinced she's going to a good home, you never know, she might not only become Lawrence's best friend, she could go some way towards lessening hostilities between me and Rosalind, because I'd call her a pretty special sort of olive branch, wouldn't you?'

'I certainly would, but I don't think you should do it unless you're certain it's for Lawrence, and not for you.'

'You're right,' Lisa agreed, with a sigh, 'but I would sorely like to know if she's finding her father as difficult as I am – or maybe she's used to it because this is what he's like all the time. How would I know? Actually, he's probably completely different with her.'

'Listen, you two will sort it out one of these days,' Amy said comfortingly.

Lisa was too tired to sound convinced as she said, 'I hope so, because she surely can't keep this up for ever. Or maybe it won't matter, if David and I end up not working out.'

David was alone in the constituency office, sitting in front of the computer with his head buried in his hands and his phone turned off. He was unable to speak to anyone for the moment, and too afraid to do any more research into what was happening to him. There would be no point to it anyway, because he'd downloaded so many specialist websites and read so much expert opinion over these past few weeks that he couldn't fail to know the answers by now. He matched all the symptoms, and the kind of tests he'd been put through since his last visit to Dr Knoyle had left little room for doubt, or hope, in spite of the fact that he'd had no results yet.

He'd always been disgusted by self-pity, it wasn't an indulgence he'd ever allowed himself before, not even during the darkest hours of Catrina's ordeal. His feelings had all been for her then, and Rosalind, but now he was drowning in a welter of sorrow for his pathetic, blighted self. Why was this happening? What was the point? How could anyone, least of all him, benefit from this terrible disease? He wanted to smash his computer, kick out at the walls, rage and rant at the malicious fate that was striking him down. It made no sense. He was a normal, healthy man in every other way. He had a new wife, the woman he'd loved passionately and quietly over so many years. Why had they been given a second chance only to have it crushed like this?

When he finally lifted his head to look at the computer screen again, he felt the claws of terror digging so deeply into him that he almost cried out in a rage of denial. Dear God, no. Anything, *anything* but this.

Unable to look at any more, he closed the screen down and got to his feet. He had to leave now, and by the time he got to Rosalind's he must somehow summon the inner strength and courage to continue as though none of this was happening. It wasn't applicable to him, he would tell himself. Somehow he'd got it wrong and the tests that were still to come would prove it. He would grasp that final sliver of hope, as intangible as a ray of light, and use it to keep himself steady, or feeling as he did right now he'd never be able to hide his fears from his family, much less be brave enough to go through what still had to be faced.

Had Rosalind not been so strung out following a bitter and frustrating call to Jerry, she might have been able to muster more pleasure in Lawrence's whoop of joy when he spotted Lucy jumping out of her father's car.

In a flash he was out of the house, dashing towards the dog, teeth bared in one of his biggest smiles, arms jutting out behind him in what Jerry called his aeroplane run. When he wrapped Lucy in a boisterous embrace and allowed her to lick his face, Rosalind barely felt the surprise of this rare gesture, merely registered it through blurred, bloodshot eyes, which she then turned to her father. He was clearly enjoying the reunion, while trying to dodge the whip of Lucy's tail.

After he'd exchanged some words with Lawrence, who'd appeared on the point of taking off with Lucy before saying hello, David started towards the house, giving her a wave as he spotted her watching from the window.

Remembering the glass of wine she'd left on the draining board, she quickly emptied it into the sink and was just closing the dishwasher when her father came in.

'I didn't realise you were bringing the dog today,' she said as he kissed her.

'I hope it's not a problem,' he replied, going to help himself to a cold drink from the fridge, 'because I'm about to say she can stay if you'd like her to.'

Rosalind gave a distracted murmur. 'That's fine,' she said. 'For how long?'

'For good,' he told her. 'I've got her bed and . . .' he frowned as he took a breath, 'so she can be Lawrence's dog if you're prepared to take her on.'

With a dismissive wave of her hand she said, 'OK, why not? It's what he wants . . .'

Regarding her more closely, David said, 'Has something happened? You've been crying.'

She shook her head, but tears welled in her eyes. 'I just spoke to Jerry,' she said raggedly. 'He's still refusing to come home, or even discuss where we should go from here.'

Before David could respond the phone rang, and she grabbed it so quickly she almost dropped it. 'Hello?' she said, clearly hoping it would be Jerry.

'Hello, darling, it's me,' Dee announced. 'Just letting you know we're back from Spain, so any time you want to come over . . .'

'That's lovely,' Rosalind mumbled, so crushed by the disappointment that it was almost impossible to get the words out. 'Will you come for lunch on Saturday?' she invited, almost by rote.

'Of course. I'm looking forward to it. Now, how are you? Any news from you know who?'

'Not really,' Rosalind answered thinly, putting a hand to her head. What was her father looking for? Why did he have to open every damned drawer?

'Oh dear,' Dee murmured. 'I'm so sorry I was away when it happened, but I'm sure it can all be sorted out, you know.'

'Yes,' Rosalind said, feeling no such certainty.

'And how's Dad? Have you seen much of him?'

Actually, she hadn't seen him anywhere near as often as he'd promised for the summer, but she wouldn't say that while he was standing there, because she wasn't up to a row. All she said was, 'He's here at the moment. I can put him on if you like.' She'd like to tell her aunt how frustrating he'd been lately, upsetting the accountants, accusing them of getting things wrong when, according to them, he was the one at fault. He never used to question them, had always considered their word to be final as far as the company finances were concerned, so now she didn't know who to believe, and wasn't even sure how much she cared, with everything else that was going on. Maybe, if Dee spoke to him, she'd be able to get some sense out of him.

'Oh no, it's OK. Just say hi from me,' Dee said. 'I'll catch up with him once I've had a chance to unpack and get myself straight. Wills and Daisy are staying till tomorrow, so if you'd like to pop over this evening they'd love to see you.'

'Thanks,' Rosalind mumbled, and after ringing off she glanced briefly at her father. He seemed to have given up the hunt for whatever he'd been looking for, or maybe he'd found it.

'Sit down, and have a drink if you want one,' he said, surprising her as he pulled out a chair and pressed her into it. 'Is there a bottle open?'

'It's in the fridge door,' she answered dully. 'That was Dee, in case you didn't guess.'

'I did,' he replied, and putting a glass of wine in front of her he sat down too, taking out the notebook that he often had with him these days. After casting a quick look through it, as though making sure he had enough time to deal with this before having to go on to wherever he was due next, he said, 'Right, about the dog. I need to know . . . Before I say . . . There are . . .'

'Dad, please come to the point,' she cried.

'I'm trying to ask,' he said quickly, 'if you . . . I don't want to say . . .'

'I can't deal with this,' she choked, getting to her feet.

'Are you happy to have the dog?' he asked in a rush. 'Before I tell Lawrence . . .'

'It's what he wants, so why not?'

'But dogs are a big tie.'

'I know. It's fine. We'll work it out.'

'Rosalind, sit down!' he suddenly snapped.

Obediently she dropped back into her chair, and when she saw the anger in his eyes giving way to concern her heart flooded with guilt. She shouldn't take her frustrations out on him.

Reaching for her hand, he held it comfortingly as he said, 'You know who the dog belongs to, so please tell me . . . I need to know that it won't affect the way you treat her.'

After taking a moment to understand what he was saying, she regarded him in complete bemusement. 'You can't really think I'd ever treat an animal badly,' she said. 'It's not Lucy's fault she belongs to *her*. She didn't get any choice in the matter.'

'No, she didn't,' he agreed, 'but Lisa and I have talked it over, and she wants to do this for Lawrence. If you have a problem with it . . .'

'Dad, I don't want to talk about this now,' she said, pulling her hand away. 'The dog is welcome, if that's what you want to hear. I'm sorry, I just can't seem to get my head round anything else while this is going on with Jerry.'

With a sigh he sat back in his chair. 'Actually,' he said, glancing at his notebook again, 'I have some news.'

She looked up, expectantly. He'd seen Jerry. He was making everything all right, the way he always used to.

'He rang me last night,' he told her. 'He's going to be in London next week and he wants to see me.'

Rosalind's heart started to thud in a clash of hope and dread. 'What did you say?' she asked, trying and failing to imagine what this might mean. 'Are you going to go? Oh Dad, please tell me you'll go.'

'Of course I will,' he promised, and capturing both her hands he squeezed them tightly. 'I'm going to take the train to London and get off at

Paddington,' he said playfully, 'and we all know the name of the bear who lives there.'

Realising that treating her like a child might make everything all right for him, she tried not to show her annoyance as she tugged her hands away and went back to the fridge.

Lisa was standing at the front door watching David at the end of the drive. He seemed to be trying to open the gates, but if he was, she couldn't understand why he wasn't using the remote control. Perhaps he'd discovered a fault and was trying to repair it. Deciding to go and find out if there was anything she could do, she put the door on the latch and started towards him.

'Is there a problem?' she asked when she was in earshot.

Without turning round he said, 'I can't seem to open the gates.'

Her heart gave a twist of unease as she saw the car keys in his hand, which he seemed to be trying to use. 'They're electric,' she reminded him.

Looking angry and strained, he turned and stared at her.

'Where are you going?' she asked.

'I just want to go out,' he informed her, and grabbing the upright bars he started to pull with all his might.

'Don't do that, you're going to injure yourself, or damage . . . David, the gates are electric. We open them with a remote control. You do it every day, so why are you . . . ?'

'Will you please just open them?' he cut in fiercely.

'Not until you tell me where you're going.'

'What is this?' he cried. 'I want to go for a walk and suddenly I'm locked in my own home, like a prisoner. Now, please, open the gates.'

Realising that to carry on arguing was only going to inflame him further, she took the car keys from him and walked over to the Mercedes. After turning on the ignition, she pushed a button on the underside of the mirror and the gates started to slide apart.

Without another word David walked through and set off down the lane.

She felt tempted to go after him, but since she didn't much relish the idea of dodging in and out of shadows and hedgerows trying not to be seen, she watched the gates glide together again and went back into the house.

After pouring herself a coffee she stood staring at the phone, needing to tell Amy what had just happened, but since Amy had announced her plans for Australia Lisa had decided to stop confiding in her as much. It wouldn't be fair to burden her with her problems when her sister had so much else on her plate, and it might be a good idea to start getting herself used to not having Amy within easy reach.

The other person she longed to call was Rosalind, but if Rosalind were to slam the phone down on her, or worse, tell her father the reason Lisa had been in touch ... Well, given David's unsteady temper these days, Lisa didn't particularly want to think about the kind of scene it might cause.

Eventually she decided to return to her study,

where she'd been trying to focus on the second chapter of her book when she'd heard David letting himself out of the front door. This morning they had been like strangers in the same house, which had been more disconcerting and distressing than usual, coming so soon after the wonderful evening they'd shared last night. He'd cooked, she'd lit candles, they'd opened an expensive bottle of wine, and he had complimented her on the beautiful home she was creating. She hadn't told him, because it wouldn't have been appropriate then, that she was starting to lose her passion for the place. Though she'd never deny it was exquisite, or that it was the kind of home anyone would be proud to own, there were days now when she found herself almost overwhelmed by a sense of it closing in on her, as though it was going to crush and bury her inside its walls. Even knowing these feelings were tied up with the uncertainty of what was happening between them didn't make them any the less unnerving, since it seemed like one more thing that was driving her away.

She was almost at her study when she noticed that the door to his was open, and without any clear idea of what she intended to do, she walked inside and went to sit down at his desk. Everything seemed to be in its place, files of pending constituency cases piled at one corner, photographs of her, Rosalind and Lawrence forming a triangle in the other, and his laptop, open and on, in the middle. Putting her coffee on the coaster next to the keyboard, she pulled open the top right-hand drawer of his desk and found, to her surprise, the small black notebook that he generally took every-where with him. Closing the drawer again, she slid open the next one and felt a sudden jar in her heart at what she saw. Surely he hadn't found her purse and not bothered to tell her? Perhaps he'd forgotten?

Picking the purse up she opened it and found all her cards in the wallet, and around forty pounds in cash tucked inside the zip. Nothing was missing – even the receipts from the shopping she'd done the day she'd lost it were still there.

Feeling faintly peculiar, she put the purse on the desk, and returning to the top drawer she took out the notebook. Written on the inside cover, in clear script, were both his addresses, in London and in Bristol, and all three phone numbers, followed by a list that struck some oddly discordant notes as she read it. Next to 'Wife' he'd written Catrina (dead); Lisa. Below that was written: 'Daughter' Rosalind; 'Grandson' Lawrence; 'Son-in-law' Jerry; 'Sister-in-law' Dee; 'Head of Staff' Miles, and so on through all the key people in his life. Had it been written by a child she'd probably have considered it sweet, but that it had been written by him felt unsettling and even ridiculous.

At the top of the facing page was a large note saying: Date and time at bottom right-hand corner of computer screen. Beneath that was a date in August which seemed to be heading up every-thing he needed to do that day. The next page was the same, and so on, much like a diary, but with far more explicit notes than she'd have thought necessary. They were more like instructions than reminders, with things like: Dog = Lucy; belongs

349

to Lisa, Lisa giving to Lawrence but needs to be sure Rosalind will treat her well. Or: Call Miles to discuss party conference arrangements including hotel, how to get there and make clear no interviews or speeches.

It was when she came upon an entry for the Monday of the week they were in – today was Thursday – that she felt her heart slowing to a standstill.

Sitting back in the chair she pressed a hand to her mouth and tried to persuade herself that she was misunderstanding, except it was so clear that it simply wasn't possible to read it any other way. Her head started to spin as she imagined him going through the motions he'd so carefully written down. It was so shocking that she almost couldn't bear it. Why hadn't he told her? What had made him think he must do something like this alone? Unless Rosalind had been with him, but there was no mention of her, and given how detailed everything else was it didn't seem likely he'd have overlooked that.

Opening up his email box, she began searching for messages that might tell her more about Monday's entry, but she couldn't find anything, so she tried Google and his search history to see if that might throw more light on matters. A few minutes later she was staring at the screen, unable to move as she realised she'd rather have found porn than what she was looking at now. It wasn't making any sense – and yet at the same time it was explaining everything in a way that was completely terrifying.

It wasn't as though nothing like this had ever

entered her head, because she had to admit that it had, but she'd always dismissed it, knowing it was what everyone said, or thought, when people became forgetful or behaved out of character. It wasn't real. It couldn't be, because he was too young. It was an old person's disease, not something that struck down men like David in the prime of their life.

With shaking hands she went back to the notebook and opened it to today to find out if it might tell her where he was now. Though the date was carefully written at the top of the page, there was nothing else until the following Monday, where he'd written 'BRACE' and next to it a time: ten thirty, followed by specific directions and where to park.

Quickly typing BRACE into Google, she felt herself starting to panic as the results began downloading. There were several options, dental braces, neck braces and even a pop singer called Brace, but she knew right away which one was relevant to David.

'What are you doing?' he said from the door.

Starting, she turned to look at him. She tried to speak but no words would come out, then seeing how angry and afraid he was, she quickly went to him and wrapped him in her arms. 'Why didn't you tell me?' she choked through her tears. 'I thought . . . I didn't know . . . Oh David, you should have told me.'

For a moment he stood rigid and unmoving, but then his arms came round her crushing her to him as he buried his face in her neck.

*   *   *

A while later David was standing at the sitting-room window, staring out at the rain that was sweeping in from the hills. Lisa was watching him from the sofa, feeling her heart breaking with the fear that must be weighting his own. She wondered what was going on in his mind now. The doubt, the dread, the torment of what he could be facing must be terrible, even crueller than she could imagine. To think of what he'd been putting himself through over these past weeks, the strain and anxiety, the tests, scans and interminable waiting that still continued, made her want to weep for how foolish and uncaring she must have seemed all this time.

As if he sensed her watching him, he turned to look at her. 'I didn't know how to open the gates,' he said. 'Can you believe that? I didn't know how to open the damned gates.'

She felt so helpless she barely knew what to say. 'It doesn't matter,' she told him gently.

'But it does, everything does, I just . . .'

When he trailed off she let the silence rest for a while, then steeling herself, she said, 'I read your notebook, so I know you've had tests, including a CT scan.'

Though he must have heard what she'd said, his thoughts seemed to be drifting as his eyes moved past her.

'When you go to your next appointment on Monday,' she said, 'I'm coming with you.'

His eyes flicked to hers, then away again. 'I don't need any more tests to tell me what's wrong,' he replied gruffly. 'You've seen the way I am, you've read what the websites say . . .'

'You can't just not go . . .'

'You know what this is, Lisa,' he cried angrily. 'You're as capable of understanding the symptoms as I am, so why don't you save me the trip and spell it out for me? It has a name, so say it.'

'David stop . . .'

'I want to hear you say it.'

'No, I will not, because I don't know what it is.'

'No, it's because you're afraid to. Well I'm not. I have some form of dementia, Lisa, and whichever one it is we both know there's no turning back from it. So no, you can't come with me on Monday. It's not your problem. It's mine, and I will deal with it.'

Going to him, she grasped his hands tightly in hers and forced him to look at her. 'If what I read in your notes is accurate,' she shouted, 'then we don't know anything for certain yet. So please, let's stop jumping to conclusions about what's wrong with you. That's what the specialists are for. And no matter what you say I will be coming with you on Monday, so don't waste your breath trying to argue any more.'

Chapter Seventeen

Blackberry Hill Hospital was a complex of austere grey stone buildings that in too many ways still resembled the eighteenth-century prison it originally had been. In more recent years the place had become a centre for mental health, as well as a secure unit for the criminally insane. These days only the latter were still housed there, in a block not visible from the road and set apart from the rest of the site. Now, appearing as eerie from the outside as its empty wards and corridors did within, the rest of the hospital sat sprawling over a vast acreage of the Fishponds area of Bristol, surrounded by deserted car parks, towering trees and signposts directing infrequent visitors to places no longer in use.

The BRACE unit – Bristol Research into Alzheimer's and Care for the Elderly – was a newer and slightly friendlier-looking single-storey building with its own car park. The entrance boasted a small porch, allowing David and Lisa to step in out of the rain as they waited for someone to answer their ring on the bell. Though this unit was no longer used for memory tests, apparently arrangements had been made for David's to be carried out here instead of at a more public clinic, where he probably would have been recognised.

'Ah, you'll be Mr and Mrs Kirby,' said a large, casually dressed black woman with merry eyes and a broad smile, opening the door wide. 'I'm Melinda, one of the nurses. We've been expecting you.'

The waiting room they stepped into was full of the usual stacking chairs pushed up against the walls, with a couple of coffee tables strewn with out-of-date magazines, a water cooler and a portrait of Princess Anne with a brass plaque beside it commemorating the date she'd opened the unit.

'Fiona's already here,' Melinda informed them. 'That's Dr Milton, but we tend to use first names, if that's all right.'

'It's fine,' David assured her, 'provided it works both ways.'

Melinda beamed. 'Can I get you a tea or coffee?' she offered. 'Kettle's just boiled.'

'I'll have a coffee, thank you,' he replied.

Starting to wonder which of them was the more nervous, since he seemed to be handling himself so well, Lisa said, 'Me too, thank you. My name's Lisa, by the way.'

After Melinda had gone off to rustle up the drinks, Lisa and David sat side by side beneath a notice-board full of information on how to deal with various mental health issues, and a clock that was five minutes slow.

Slipping a hand into his, she whispered, 'OK?'

'I am, question is, are you?'

No, she wasn't, but she was hardly going to admit it when she was supposed to be here as a support for him.

They sat quietly then, listening to the silence and gazing blankly at a young Princess Anne. It seemed disorientatingly surreal to be there, as though they'd wandered off the wide, sunny road they were supposed to be on to find themselves lost in a backwater with no apparent way out. How could they have got here? Where had they gone wrong? They didn't belong here. Their lives were somewhere else, in a world that had somehow become mixed up with this one, so they must do something to try and straighten it out.

'Aha, I know you're David, because I recognise you,' announced a plump, pretty little woman with huge brown eyes and a glorious shock of red hair. 'I'm Fiona Milton, aka the psychologist who's conducting your test today.'

David and Lisa rose to their feet. 'It's good to meet you,' David told her politely as he shook her hand. 'This is my wife, Lisa.'

'Lisa,' she said cheerily. 'Ah, I see Melinda's got the coffee going. Great show, Mel. Shall we take them into the office?'

A few moments later Lisa and David were seated in a room whose only redeeming feature, as far as Lisa was concerned, was the doctor herself. Her vibrant hair lent the only colour to a setting that was otherwise as drab and dated as it was depressingly medical.

'Not exactly the Ritz, is it?' Fiona commented wryly, 'but believe me, it's a lot better than some of the places where we have to carry out our clinics.'

After taking a sip of her coffee, she set her cup aside and turned to the computer on the desk that was pushed up against the window. 'OK,' she said, reaching for the mouse to scroll down the screen, 'I think I have everything I need . . . Yes, looks like it,' and from a drawer she took a file containing some official-looking forms. After filling in David's name and the date at the top of one, and assigning a visit number, she said, 'Right, I guess we can get this show on the road. I'll start by explaining that the test battery, as we call it, is designed so that it can be modified as we go along, either to include more detailed tests if I think they're necessary, or to exclude those that don't seem relevant. There's nothing to worry about,' she assured them, 'it's true to say that some of the tests are difficult, so you should expect to make mistakes, and some are easier. This is so we can stretch everyone, including very bright people like your good self. So, are you ready?'

Lisa looked at David as he nodded, and wondered how he was managing to stay so calm.

Fiona smiled. 'Nice and simple to begin: I'd like you to rate your memory for me. How do you think it compares to other people your age? For example, would you say yours is poorer than average? About average? Better than, or very good?'

David took a breath and blew it out slowly. 'It always used to be very good,' he told her.

She waited a moment, hand poised over her form, then seeming not to mind that he hadn't given a direct answer, she asked, 'How much time, would you say, have you spent feeling a bit low, or sad, over the past month?'

Lisa looked down at David's tightly bunched hands. 'More than I'd like to admit in front of my new wife,' he replied.

'So you'd say a good bit of time?' Fiona prompted. He nodded. 'Probably.'

'And how anxious are you feeling about this assessment? Extremely? Moderately? Just a little? Or not at all?'

'I guess that would have to be extremely,' he replied, trying to make it sound wry.

Fiona's smile was sympathetic. 'OK,' she said, after circling something on her form. 'Can you tell me what year it is?'

'Two thousand . . . Oh, crikey, twenty . . .' He stopped, shaking his head in frustration.

'Month?' she asked.

'September.'

'Date today?'

He started to respond, but then didn't.

'What day is it?'

'Monday.'

'Do you know which season we're in?'

'It could be winter, but it's autumn.'

'What's the name of this hospital?'

He seemed uncertain again.

'Which floor are we on?'

'Ground.'

'Do you know which city we're in?'

'London.'

'Which country?'

'England.'

'OK, I'm going to say some words now which I'd like you to repeat. Are you ready?'

David nodded.

'Ball. Flag. Tree.'

'Ball. Flag. Tree.'

'Starting with one hundred, I'd like you to work backwards, taking seven away each time. Do you understand the question?'

'I think so. That would be ninety-three, eighty-six, seventy . . . eight? Seventy-one. Sixty-five . . .'

'That's enough. Can you spell the word "world" backwards?'

He frowned. 'D-R-L-O-W.'

Noting it down, she said, 'I asked you to repeat some words earlier, can you tell me what they were?'

'Uh, yes. Ball. Tree . . .' A frown again crossed his face.

Next to him Lisa's heart was beating wildly. It seemed incredible that he couldn't remember flag, when he'd only just heard it. He'd got the backward spelling wrong too, and some of the subtraction, as well as saying they were in London instead of Bristol and becoming confused about the year. Was it normal to make these mistakes? Did everyone when they were under pressure? What exactly were these answers saying about him?

To her relief the next few minutes proved more encouraging as he successfully identified a watch and a pencil, and repeated the phrase 'no, ifs ands or buts' correctly, but when it came to a paper-folding exercise he became so frustrated with his clumsy attempts that he bunched the paper in his fist, and only just managed to stop himself slamming it down on the desk.

'I'm sorry,' he apologised, clearly embarrassed.

Fiona simply smiled, then asked him to compose

a short sentence about anything he chose. Taking the pen he wrote, 'How am I doing so far?'

With a meaningful look that made him smile, she handed him another sheet of paper, saying, 'I want you to carry out the instruction printed here.' It said, CLOSE EYES.

David looked at her.

Lisa tensed.

Fiona nodded for him to continue and he promptly closed his eyes.

Next he had to draw a pentagon, which was fine, but when Fiona took out a clock with no hands and asked him to pencil in one forty-five Lisa could hardly believe her eyes. After seeming uncertain he ended up drawing the small hand pointing towards the one, and the other pointing between the four and the five.

She was so thrown that it took her a few minutes to catch up as Fiona launched into a whole series of questions about the time and clocks, some of which he got right and some he didn't.

Then came a range of other tests in which he had to remember as many single words as he could; recall a story Fiona recited; sort colours into groups and explain how he'd sorted them; grade similarities; name the missing part of a picture, such as legs, from a man, when he bizarrely named the man; then he had to perform each of the tests again half an hour later.

It was gruelling, and Lisa could see how tired he was becoming. God knew her own head was spinning by now, but there was still more to come.

In the end, after providing basic descriptions of words such as 'rhinoceros', 'escalator', 'stilts', 'compass' and 'abacus', not all of which he managed accurately, then failing to name any animals beginning with S, Fiona brought the ordeal to a close.

'I'm sure you've had enough now,' she said, 'so tell me, how did you find this assessment?'

David inhaled a deep breath and puffed it out with an unsteady laugh. 'Tougher than I expected,' he admitted. 'How did I do?'

She smiled. 'We'd expect someone with your IQ to score fairly highly,' she informed him, 'and you did.'

Realising how skilfully she was avoiding being pinned down, Lisa felt a fresh stirring of unease and reached for David's hand. 'What happens next?' she asked.

Fiona finished making another note and looked up. 'Now, I'm afraid, we play the waiting game while the results of your bloods and the CT scan, together with my report, are sent to a consultant psychiatrist. As soon as that's happened you'll be given an appointment to come in and see her – I say "her" because it's almost always a woman.'

'At which point we'll have a diagnosis?' he said.

'She'll want to do an assessment herself, but yes, that's when you should receive the diagnosis.'

'Is there any chance . . .' he began hoarsely. 'Does the CT scan happen to show any signs of a tumour?'

Feeling the tragedy of wishing for something so awful, Lisa wanted to wrap him in her arms as though it might make everything go away.

'I'm afraid I don't have the results,' Fiona told him. 'They'll go to the psychiatrist.'

Lisa had to swallow before she could speak. 'How long will we have to wait?' she asked.

Fiona's hand rocked back and forth. 'Usually it's around two to three months,' she replied apologetically. 'I'm afraid we're short of doctors, but I'd hope, in your case, that it won't be as long as that.'

As Lisa drove them home, taking it slowly through the teeming rain, she was struggling to attach a sense of reality to what David had just been through, and to the way she was feeling. It was as though she'd somehow fallen out of step with normal life, lost a sense of where or even who she was as she drifted along in the wake of what felt like someone else's dream. It didn't seem possible to be where she was now, in a car returning from a test that might render David's future null and void when it was less than six weeks ago that they'd married, surrounded by friends and loved ones and with, they'd thought, only happiness in store. It was as though she'd crash-landed into someone else's world. She didn't belong here, it had nothing to do with her, wasn't conforming at all to the heady promises and rewards life had led her to believe would be hers. And yet she had no idea where else she would want to be, other than at David's side.

She'd have liked to think he was glad she'd been with him today, but he hadn't said so, nor had he yet made any comment on the test itself. The ignominy of being treated like a child, of having to answer such straightforward questions and then not getting all of them right, must be terrible. Perhaps he was waiting for her to reassure him that he'd done well. To think he might be made her wretched with guilt, because though she couldn't be sure she'd have done any better under such pressure, she couldn't tell him anything while she was afraid of how hollow her words might sound.

Aware of him leafing through his notebook, presumably to reassure himself that he didn't have to be anywhere else today, she considered reaching over to take his hand, but then he was closing the book and saying, 'I have to go to London tomorrow.'

She cast him a quick glance. Just like that? Somehow he was making himself carry on as normal. 'Can you change it?' she asked, not feeling comfortable about him being away from home.

'What for? I'm perfectly capable of getting there, if that's what you're thinking.'

Was he capable? Knowing it wouldn't be a good idea to ask, she said, 'Will you take the train? I know, I'll come with you. There are plenty of things . . .'

'I'd rather you didn't.'

She looked at him again, aware of a growing tightness in her chest. 'But if I want to go anyway . . .'

'You didn't until a moment ago, and I would prefer to go alone.' Then, after a pause, 'But thank you for coming today. I hope you're not regretting it.'

Swallowing drily she replied, 'Why would I regret it? I don't want you to go through this alone.'

His tone was tetchy as he said, 'This isn't a journey you can embark on with me. It's in my head, remember? Not yours.'

'David, please don't talk like that. You still haven't had a diagnosis, so . . .'

'Let's change the subject,' he interrupted sharply. And with no more preamble than that, he said, 'Are you still in touch with the chap you used to live with? I've forgotten his name. The one who . . . You know who I mean.'

She didn't answer.

'What's his name?' he persisted. 'Come on, you know who I'm talking about.'

'You mean Tony Sommerville.'

He frowned, as though not entirely sure. 'I suppose that's him,' he said. 'Is he still free?'

'What?'

'Is he married to someone else now?'

'I don't think . . . Actually, I'm not sure I want to find out where this is going.'

For several seconds there was only silence, charged with the words he wasn't saying, then with a sigh that sounded like an irritated defeat, he let his head fall back and closed his eyes.

Relieved that she'd managed to steer them clear of an argument, she leaned forward to put on some music in the hope it might go some way towards relaxing him.

'The reason I'm going to London,' he said, either waking up or suddenly deciding to speak as they turned in to their gates, 'is to see Jerry. My son-in-law.'

'Does Rosalind know?'

When he didn't answer she cast him a look and felt a twist of pity as she realised he wasn't sure.

'You don't have to stay with me, you know that don't you?' he said abruptly.

Understanding what he meant, she said, 'I'm not having this conversation.'

'Well, that's a shame, because I am, so I suppose we can now add talking to myself to my list of . . . of . . . Whatever the fuck they are. Aberrations! What kind of word is that, anyway? It doesn't mean anything . . .'

Leaving him to rant on as he got out of the car, she went to let herself in the front door and after checking the answerphone, more out of habit than expectation, she decided to take refuge in her study. It wasn't that she wanted to shut him out, she simply needed some space to think and to attempt to get a grip on what was happening to him, to them, as a couple, and she couldn't do that while he was trying to drag her into a fight.

As she sat down at her desk and put her head in her hands she wanted desperately to cry and scream and rage at the fate that was doing this to them, but once she'd done that she'd still have to face what they were going through and somehow deal with it. But how was she going to do that if he really did have an early onset dementia? What the hell was it going to mean for their marriage, their life together, his career and hers? She knew from the websites that his behaviour was typical of someone with certain types of dementia, so much as she might want to pretend it wasn't a possibility, she couldn't. Nor could she be entirely sure how much of his behaviour was an act to try and push her away – and how much was him already losing the sense of the wonderful man he really was.

* * *

365

After spending three days in London, mostly at the office with Miles preparing for the Party conference, David was now back in Bristol and on his way to see Rosalind. He knew she was waiting to hear how his meeting had gone with Jerry, but if she hadn't sounded so upset when she'd rung a few minutes ago, he'd have tried to put her off. Maybe he still should, not only for Lisa's sake, who was waiting for him at home, but for Rosalind's too, because though he knew he'd seen Jerry at a cafe in St James's Park, he hadn't written anything down about what had been said, and now he was struggling to remember.

Bringing his car to a stop a few yards from Rosalind's gates, he did the only thing he could and took out his iPhone. As he searched for Jerry's number a flash of memory sliced out of the darkness – he'd forgotten Jerry's name that morning, yet he was having no difficulty with it now. There was no logic to that, so he wouldn't try to find any.

'Jerry. You're there, good. It's David.'

'David. I'm so glad you rang,' Jerry said. 'I've been thinking since our chat . . . Have you spoken to Rosalind yet?'

'No. Actually, I'm just about to, but I was hoping . . .'

'That I would do it? You're right, I should. As her husband, it's my place to tell her what's happened, how things have changed. I didn't mean for you to shoulder the responsibility. I know it's mine. I just wanted . . . Well, I guess I wanted you to hear it from me.'

David didn't know what to say.

'I never meant to hurt her,' Jerry insisted. 'I hope you understand that.'

'Yes, of course,' David replied. Did he? His son-in-law wasn't a bad man, so it seemed reasonable to believe that.

'I'll drive down there tonight,' Jerry said. 'It's not going to be easy for her, I know that, but I'll try to break it as gently as I can. Do you think I should bring the photographs?'

Photographs?

'Maybe I'll put them in the car and make the decision when I get there.'

Fearing for what they might be, David said, 'If you think they're going to hurt her . . .'

'I swear that's the last thing I want to do. In fact, I won't show them unless she asks. I don't suppose she will.'

David's mind was starting to spin as he said, 'No, maybe not.' *What was Jerry talking about? If he just focused a little harder . . .* 'I'd better ring off now,' he said, hating how weak he sounded.

After ending the call he made no attempt to restart the car, only sat where he was, unable to see or think through the frustration that was forming at the backs of his eyes. He wanted to cry, sob and rage, but surely he wasn't sunk so far that he'd allow himself to do that. He needed to speak to Catrina. She would understand what was happening and find a way to make it less than it seemed. She'd always had a knack of doing that. How cruel it was that he could no longer speak to Catrina.

It was the middle of the afternoon by now, and David was feeling too tired and strained to take very much more. He wasn't sure if he'd been sleeping, he only knew that he hadn't wanted to carry on driving so he'd left the car at the end of the trail.

Taking a walk was always a good way to alleviate stress, he'd known that for a long time, which was why he was on foot now, ambling along the country lane towards the gates leading up to the house. Finding them open he pressed on along the drive, glancing down towards the lake and registering the flowers he hadn't seen before. Then a woman he didn't know came bounding up over the lawn towards him.

'Hello?' she cried. 'Can I help you?'

Not being quite sure what to say to that, he ended up saying nothing at all.

On reaching him, the woman tilted back her hat and said, 'Oh my goodness, Mr Kirby. What a lovely surprise. Do excuse me, I was just sorting out the roses.'

Baffled, he glanced in the direction she was pointing and said, 'Are you the new gardener?'

She laughed as though he'd made a hilarious joke. 'No, no, no, I'm Jessie Lamb,' she told him. 'No make-up, scruffy clothes . . . Sorry. My husband and I bought the house from you.'

Once again he didn't know what to say.

'Would you like to come in?' she offered. 'You'd be very welcome.'

'Where's my wife?' he asked.

She didn't seem to know what to say to that until finally she pointed down the drive, muttering, 'Perhaps I should get my husband.'

He didn't argue, only watched her tooling off

towards the house, then turning around he went in the opposite direction.

Rosalind had no idea what to say. Though she could feel herself falling apart, as if an implosion was pulling silently through her, for the moment shock seemed to be holding her together, a binding, resilient force keeping her stable and sane, like a straitjacket, or a coffin in which she could bury her pain. Her eyes were large and glassy as she stared at Jerry, seeing him, and yet not. He was a stranger, an intruder, someone pretending to be the man she loved.

Or perhaps she was seeing him for who he really was.

Her breath caught on a sudden sob, and she turned her head to one side.

He had a child, a daughter, another family. All this time, when he'd been swearing he would never betray her again . . . He'd said he didn't know, that he'd only learned about it a month ago, but could she believe that? Did it even matter what she believed? It wouldn't change anything, or make them go away, or stop him wanting to be with them. He'd already moved them to London, he'd said, and in her mind's eye she could see them in their beautiful home overlooking a park, where they played together on sunny days. A perfect little family, two bubbly females filling him with happiness and pride, making him feel loved and valued in a way she apparently never had. Her commitment and loyalty, and everything else she had brought to their marriage clearly hadn't been enough, or he wouldn't have felt the need to turn to another woman in the first place.

Chloe. That was the little girl. It wasn't a name she particularly liked, but what difference did that make? She felt sure she was a pretty, lively little toddler with heart-stopping eyes and winning ways. They all were, so why should she be any different? Olivia was no doubt a great beauty, but even if she wasn't he was still choosing to be with her rather than stay here. A twist of pain dug through her heart. It was as though she and Lawrence were being shut away in a darkened room, the relatives who didn't matter any more.

She heard Jerry's voice, but his words were no longer reaching her. She glanced at him, then away again. Was he really going to leave and never come back? Could he actually do that? She'd feared it for so long that now it was happening it felt like a dream. She started to wonder what her father had said when he'd found out, then her heart churned with more pain. Her father had let her down earlier. He'd said he'd come, but he hadn't, and when she'd called to find out where he was he hadn't even seemed to remember that he'd spoken to her. His mind was full of Lisa now, and Jerry could think only of Olivia. And Chloe.

'Please say something,' Jerry implored.

She took a breath, but no words emerged. She put a hand to her head, and as her breathing started to shudder he came to take her in his arms.

'Don't,' she said, turning away. 'I'd rather you . . . Actually, I think you should go.'

He looked surprised, and hurt. 'But there's so much to discuss . . .'

'I don't have anything to say to you, so please, just go.'

He ran a hand anxiously over his face. 'Can I at least take some . . .'

'No. Not today.'

'But . . .'

'You've chosen a new life,' she reminded him, 'and everything here is part of the old one.'

Apparently not ready to dispute that, he said, 'I don't want to think about you sitting here alone.'

'Then don't think about me at all.'

His face was turning as pale as the wall behind him. 'Shall I call your father?' he offered.

'Why? What difference is he going to make?'

'I just thought . . .'

'Jerry, I'm not your concern any more so please, just go.'

'Of course you're my concern. You're still my wife and though you might not want to hear it, I love you.'

She flinched, and turned her face away.

'What about Dee?' he said. 'Shall I call h—?'

'I don't know how to make myself any plainer,' she cried. 'I want you to leave, so please stop trying to shunt me off on to someone else so you can ease your conscience.'

'Come on, that's not fair . . .'

'Don't talk to me about *fair*,' she shouted. 'None of this is fair.'

'I'm sorry. That was the wrong thing to say, I just don't want you thinking that I don't care, because I . . .'

She clapped her hands to her ears.

'Rosalind, we need to talk . . .'

'There's no "we" any more, Jerry. Now, please don't make me repeat myself again . . .'

'OK, if I leave, what are you going to do?'

'I fail to see what business that is of yours.'

'Will you call your father?'

'All right, if that's what you want to hear, that's what I'll do.'

'I'm trying to find out what *you* want.'

'OK, then I'll tell you. What I want, Jerry, is for none of this to be happening. I want that child not to exist, or her mother. I want you to go back to being the husband I used to love and trust, the man I respected and felt proud to be with. I want this home to be ours, the way it used to be. I want my father to be married to my mother again. I want Lawrence to be like other boys . . . I want a lot of things, Jerry, but you can't make any of them happen, because there's no way you can unbreak my heart, or bring back my mother, or change the way our son is. All you can do, Jerry, is get on with your life now, because that's what you've chosen to do. So at least have the courage to face up to your decisions and stop hanging around here as though you can make everything all right, because you can't,' and rather than have to go through the awfulness of watching him leave, she walked out of the kitchen and closed the door behind her.

It was a long time later, an hour, maybe more, that she realised she wasn't sitting alone on the floor in the drawing room. Lucy, the dog, was lying next to her with her head in her lap, and a little apart, but not too far away, Lawrence was sitting like a small guardian angel staring quietly into space.

* * *

Lisa came awake with a start, her heart thudding hard and her skin breaking out in a sweat. She wasn't sure what had disturbed her, perhaps a noise outside, or a bad dream. She glanced at the clock. Two twenty in the morning, and David still hadn't come to bed.

When he'd finally arrived home this evening he'd looked so haggard with exhaustion that she'd simply poured him a drink and sat with him quietly, understanding that he wasn't yet ready to talk, though half expecting to be told to leave him alone. However, he'd seemed if not pleased that she was there, then less troubled by it than he sometimes was, and had even, at one point, taken hold of her hand.

She'd said nothing about how worried she'd been while he was gone. It wouldn't help him to know that, or her to go over it again. Nor had she asked what had happened with Rosalind this afternoon. He'd told her he was going there straight from the train, but she hadn't expected him to stay for so long, nor had she imagined it would leave him so drained. She still didn't know what Jerry had told him when they'd met, though it seemed clear now that Jerry wasn't coming back. The extra strain that was going to be put on David was already showing, and troubling her deeply. It could hardly have come at a worse time, and since David was unlikely to have told Rosalind about the tests he was having, Rosalind wouldn't be aware of how much more difficult she was making things for him.

Should I tell her, or shouldn't I, Lisa kept asking herself. It hardly seemed her place to do so, and yet, as David's wife, what more right could she have? It was highly probable that Rosalind would turn more hostile than ever, and possibly even find a way to blame her, and that wouldn't help the situation for anyone. Nor could she imagine David reacting kindly to finding out that she'd gone behind his back to speak to his daughter. So for the moment she guessed it would be best to wait for the results, and then let David decide how he wanted to handle it. She just hoped to God the wait wasn't as long as three months, because if it was she dreaded to think what kind of state they'd be in by then.

When David still hadn't returned to bed by three she decided to go downstairs and look for him, hoping it wouldn't make him angry to feel she was fussing him. She needed to be sure he was all right and was actually still in the house, and not outside somewhere wandering around in the dark.

Everywhere was quiet as she went downstairs, with only a silvery glow from the moon lighting the way. The kitchen and sitting room were empty, but there was a chink of light showing beneath his study door. She hung back, anxious about how he would treat her intrusion, and wondering, helplessly, how they were going to carry on living like this, with her so afraid of upsetting him, and him doing his best to increase the distance between them.

Moving as quietly as she could to the door, she put an ear against it, and when she heard what was happening inside she no longer cared how angry it might make him, she went in and gathered him in her arms.

He didn't object or try to push her away, instead he buried his face in her waist and continued to sob as though his heart was breaking.

'Ssh,' she soothed, tears rolling down her own cheeks as she held him close. 'It's going to be all right, I promise. We'll work it out . . .'

'But how can we? It's irrev— irr— For God's sake, listen to me.'

'You're upset now,' she said uselessly. 'That's why you can't find the word.'

He was shaking his head. 'Read that.' He turned to the computer. 'It'll tell you . . .'

'No, I won't, and you shouldn't torture yourself like this. We still don't know . . .'

'But we do!' he exclaimed. 'I do.' He grabbed her hands. 'You have to get on with your life, Lisa. You can't . . .'

'Stop! I don't want to hear you saying those things. Whatever's wrong with you, you're still the man I love, the man I . . .'

'But I'm not,' he cried angrily. 'He's gone and he won't be coming back. This is who I am now, someone with an atrophying brain and no future that any right-minded person . . .'

'David, I'm not going to let you do this.'

Pulling her down to his level, he said, 'Look at you. You're still so young and beautiful, you have so much life ahead of you, you surely can't think I want to steal it from you.'

Hardly able to speak through her own tears, she said, 'And listen to how rational you're sounding, even though you're talking nonsense.' She gave a splutter of laughter as a spark of humour showed in his eyes. 'You see, you're still there,' she told him. 'I know you are and I'm not going to let you go.'

Drawing her into his arms he held her tightly, as though it was him comforting her now. 'My darling, my wonderful, beautiful Lisa,' he murmured. 'I'm so sorry. I'm so, so sorry.'

'It isn't your fault, and please don't make everything sound so final. We still have a long way to go, probably a lot longer than you think, because there are drugs now, if it does turn out to be what we're thinking, and we still don't know for sure that it is.'

Holding her face between his hands, he let his tears roll as he gazed at her with all the love and anguish in his heart. 'I want to stay hopeful,' he told her, 'but the evidence . . . There's nothing to say . . .' He started to break down again. 'Please don't leave me yet,' he gasped, pulling her to him. 'Stay with me at least until we know.'

'Of course,' she cried, wrapping him fiercely in her arms. 'And I'll still be here after that. I'm not leaving you, David, so please, *please* stop trying to make me.'

Chapter Eighteen

The next four weeks passed in an agony of nerves and frustration as Lisa and David tried to go about their day-to-day lives as normally as possible. After the night he'd gone to pieces in his study, David had seemed calmer and less prone to tormenting himself with online research. However, now Lisa was looking for it she was seeing evidence of his problems manifesting all the time, in ways that were mostly heartbreaking, but occasionally alarming, or even mystifying, such as when he took something of hers and hid it. It was hard to accept that someone as intelligent and lucid as he'd always been was now more given to silence than to talkativeness more out of fear of losing what he was saying before he could reach the end, than because he had nothing to say. It was as though he was locking himself up inside and throwing away the key when he had no need to go there.

Though they'd started to share tender moments again, there was still his anger and helplessness to deal with when he fumbled to perform tasks that should have come naturally, or struggled to remember something that he knew shouldn't be difficult. It was proving as big a strain for Lisa as it was trying to stay positive for him. Were she able to offload on to Amy once in a while it might have helped, but Amy was so engrossed in her departure plans and getting Roxy ready for uni that she rarely seemed to notice that Lisa wasn't her usual upbeat self whenever they spoke on the phone. It was easier to pretend when they weren't face to face, Lisa had decided, which was why she was avoiding seeing her – a state of affairs Amy would never have allowed had she not been so busy herself. As it was, she was prepared to accept that Lisa was making good progress with her book, and that the situation with David had started to settle down.

It was only when he went to Bournemouth for the Party conference, and during the short trips she made to London, that Lisa was able to relax a little, but even then the dread of what they could be facing was always with her. His incessant checking in his notebook and dwindling confidence were their own constant reminders. Sometimes she wanted to scream at him to pull himself together, as though he was doing it deliberately to provoke her. Then he'd say, or do something that was so like him that she found herself shedding tears of relief, along with her fears for the future, and taking heart again. It was a punishing, unending roller coaster of emotions that was keeping her awake at night, and occasionally driving her thoughts into places that were so black and shameful she'd never want to admit them to anyone. She came close many times to calling Rosalind, but knowing how hard Rosalind was struggling with the end of her marriage, she couldn't bring herself to shatter the rest of Rosalind's world.

But surely she must know something's wrong, she kept saying to herself. *She must see the change in him, and wonder why it's happening.* But even if Rosalind did, she was saying nothing, at least not to Lisa. Very possibly not to herself either, which Lisa could hardly blame her for when it was only a year since she'd lost her mother. The fear that there might be something wrong with her father wouldn't be one she'd even want to consider, never mind have confirmed.

It was during the fourth week of waiting that Jerry rang to ask David if he'd speak to Rosalind about the midnight calls she was making to Olivia. Apparently she was often drunk and usually abusive, and Jerry was starting to worry that she would do something stupid like turn up at the house while he was away.

'It's not that we're thinking of calling the police, or anything drastic like that,' he assured Lisa, who'd answered David's phone. 'I'd never do that to her, but Olivia's starting to get worried, and with Chloe in the house and the things Rosalind's saying . . . I'm sorry to bother you with it, but she won't speak to me.'

David went round to see Rosalind the next morning, but Lisa had no idea what he said to her, because he didn't mention it when he came back. She even wondered if he'd remembered why he'd gone. If he hadn't, then it was highly probable nothing had been said. Or perhaps it had and he was finding it too difficult to recount, either out of wishing to keep Rosalind's confidence, or because he couldn't find the words. Whichever, Jerry didn't call again, so Lisa decided to presume that Rosalind was now leaving Olivia alone.

Then finally, five excruciating weeks after the appointment with the psychologist, and only a week before the start of the new parliamentary term, a letter arrived giving them a time and date to see the consultant psychiatrist, Dr Isabelle Manning. It was to be in the more private surroundings of the BRACE clinic at Blackberry Hill again, at eleven o'clock the following Wednesday.

Now that day was upon them, and as they drove through the hospital's mostly deserted site to park outside the BRACE centre Lisa could only wonder how, outwardly at least, David was managing to appear so together when she knew how fearful he was inside. Earlier, he'd said it was a relief to be finally getting on with it, but when she'd seen how afraid he'd looked it had made her want to cry.

This time it was the doctor herself who let them in, with the same warm greeting as they'd received before. She was a tall, grey-haired woman with horn-rimmed glasses and softly sagging cheeks that dimpled when she smiled.

'It's a pleasure to meet you,' she said, shaking David's hand first, then Lisa's. 'Do go through. I'm using the office straight ahead. Coffee's on its way, unless you'd prefer tea.'

David looked at Lisa.

'Coffee's fine,' Lisa assured her.

Moments later they were seated in the same

office they'd been in before. Nothing had changed. It was almost as though there had been a warp in time, and the past weeks of waiting, pretending and dreading had been sucked into a bubble that had now burst and vanished, leaving them exposed to the cruel reality of ongoing life.

'Right, well, I'm sure you're keen for us to get started,' Isabelle Manning said, after their coffees had been delivered. 'I know these waits for appointments can be very stressful, but luckily yours hasn't been quite as long as some. Now, before I begin, is there anything you'd like to ask?'

Lisa looked at David as he said, 'You have the results of the CT scan?'

The doctor nodded. 'Yes, they're here,' she confirmed.

'So is there a tumour?'

Her tone was gentle as she said, 'No, there's no tumour.'

As David seemed to collapse beside her, Lisa's heart rose to her mouth. It was their last hope. A tumour was treatable, the nightmare it was possible to wake up from. She could hardly bear to look at David. How on earth must he be feeling to have had this last terrible straw snatched away?

Clamping a stethoscope around her neck, Isabelle Manning said, 'OK, I'm going to give you a quick check-over first, then we'll have a chat about your symptoms and medical history.'

Understanding that all this had to be gone through, but still wishing she'd just give them an answer, Lisa bit back her frustration and took David's cup as he stood up. As she watched him undress she felt a disorienting, surreal sense of distance come over her, as though she was detaching from where they were, moving away, losing perspective, and she could only think how strange, even terrifying, it must be feeling for him.

It seemed an eternity, but was probably no more than ten minutes, before the stethoscope and other instruments were put away, and David started to dress again. Lisa could see how strained he was, and so had to admire how well he'd managed to rise to Isabelle Manning's polite chatter throughout the exam. Then he gave her a smile and she felt her heart stumble and fall. He was managing to be so brave, and here was she on the verge of falling apart. She had to pull herself together. She was of no use to him at all in this pathetic, self-involved state.

Registering that he was about to put his shirt on inside out, she got up to take it from him, then stopped when Isabelle said gently, 'It'll be good for me to watch David do this.'

Lisa sat down and felt humiliated and wronged for David as he took far too long to sort out the shirt and put it on. Then he gave her a wink before sitting down and she wanted to fold him in her arms and protect him from everyone and everything, especially this horrible ordeal.

Over the next few minutes Isabelle Manning led a discussion through his general well-being, such as whether he felt depressed at all, or overly anxious about anything apart from the tests. Once satisfied with that she moved them on to the results of his memory test, but as she started to explain how the conclusions had been drawn David said, 'We can do away with all that if you like. I know it's early onset dementia.'

Lisa stopped breathing. Please God Isabelle Manning's answer wasn't going to prove their worst nightmare. Please *please* God, it just couldn't.

The doctor's eyes were gentle as she said, 'Yes, I'm afraid you're right, David.'

Understanding now what it felt like when the world fell apart, Lisa's mind went reeling, until feeling the shudder of David's shoulders as he started to break down she quickly turned to him.

'It's all right,' he said raggedly, as she tried to hold him. 'I'm sorry,' he apologised to Isabelle. 'It's just . . . I couldn't help hoping . . .'

'I understand,' Isabelle said softly as she passed over a Kleenex.

Taking it, Lisa handed it to David and sat holding his hand as he used the other to dab away the tears. His devastation was so apparent it was hard to look at him. Having no hope now had already turned out a light inside him, and she wondered if he'd ever be able to find it again. She wished she could think of something to say, or do, but knowing that life was treating him this wretchedly was making it impossible to find any words.

Eventually he was able to look at Isabelle again. 'I'm sorry,' he said, 'I don't normally . . .'

'Please don't apologise,' she interrupted gently. 'I know what a shock this must be for you.'

'I tried . . . I thought I'd prepared myself.'

Her eyes were filled with compassion.

'Is it . . . I suppose it's Alzheimer's,' he said.

She shook her head. 'No, you have what's called multi-infarct dementia,' she told him, 'which is a form of vascular dementia. This means that you are experiencing lots of tiny strokes which

383

you possibly don't know anything about, but they are interrupting the flow of blood to the brain, which in turn is affecting the way your memory is functioning.'

After taking a moment to digest this, David said, 'Is there – ?' He cleared his throat. 'Is there anything you can do?'

Her eyes remained on his as she said, frankly but gravely, 'I'm afraid that the damage already done cannot be reversed, but we generally find that people suffering with MID – multi-infarct dementia – have a much better insight into their condition than those with other dementias such as Alzheimer's. This means that the deterioration in the brain will be more noticeable following a stroke, but then you will quite probably stabilise for a while and even show signs of improvement, until it happens again.'

'Is there anything we can do to prevent the strokes?' he asked, sounding more defeated by the second.

'We can certainly reduce the risk by keeping a close eye on your blood pressure, and cholesterol, and by making sure you're fully informed about the symptoms that lead up to one. I'm also going to prescribe aspirin to help prevent the blood from clotting, and donepezil, which you might know better as Aricept.'

Hearing herself speak, as though from the end of a tunnel, Lisa said, 'I thought Aricept was for Alzheimer's.'

'Yes, it is, but we're finding it has some bene-fits for people suffering with other types of dementia too.'

David cleared his throat again. 'So how . . . How long are we talking?'

Understanding what he meant, Lisa tensed as Isabelle said, 'It's hard to be precise, because each individual is different, but early onset, as you probably know, can show itself to be more aggressive . . .'

'How long?' he repeated.

With no more prevarication she said, 'It could be as little as five years, or I've known people to go on for twenty or more, provided of course we do everything we can to minimise the risk of further strokes.'

David took an unsteady breath. 'And in what kind of state would I be for these five or twenty years?' he asked.

'Again, each individual is different, but as you know it is a progressive condition that I'm afraid will only get worse with time.'

His head went down, but as Lisa put a hand on his arm he lifted it again. 'Well, so now we know,' he said, with a finality that suggested he didn't need to hear any more. 'Thank you for your trouble, Doctor. We probably shouldn't take up any more of your time.'

'Please sit down,' Isabelle said kindly as he made to get up. 'There's a great deal we need to discuss about where we go from here, not least of all on the practical side, which is actually very important and probably best dealt with straight away.' Her eyes moved to Lisa. 'This is where you come in, because I'm afraid we can't be sure how much of this David will remember later.'

'Oh God,' David groaned.

Taking his hand in an effort to steady him, Lisa said, 'What do I have to do?'

Seeming to appreciate how pragmatic she'd managed to sound, Isabelle said, 'First of all you will need to inform the DVLA of the diagnosis.'

At that David's head came up. 'You can't take my . . . take my . . .' His eyes closed in frustration.

'You'll probably be able to keep your licence for a while,' Isabelle reassured him, 'but I'm afraid they do have to be informed, as do your insurers. It's also important to decide who you'd like to have power of attorney,' she continued, addressing David now rather than Lisa, 'because there will come a time when you won't be able to handle your own affairs, particularly finances.'

He said nothing, and Lisa found that she couldn't speak either.

'You might also want to draw up a living will,' Isabelle told him. Then she said to Lisa, 'There are lots of information leaflets and brochures I can give you on all of this, I'm just making you aware now of what steps you can take to prevent any legal or medical difficulties in the long run.'

Lisa looked at David, and seeing how glazed his eyes had become, as though he was no longer listening, she realised she must think of something to say. 'How long will it take for the drugs to start working?' she asked.

'The Aricept will take eleven to twelve weeks.'

Could she ask her next question in front of David? If she didn't she wouldn't be able to ask it at all. 'How much is he likely to deteriorate in that time?' she said.

'I'm still here,' he reminded them shortly. 'Please

don't talk about me as if I'm deaf or already brain-dead.'

Isabelle's eyes moved to his. 'A very common complaint from people with dementia,' she told him. 'As for the progress of deterioration, it's hard to say when much depends on the frequency and level of the mini-strokes. I'm sure you will already have noticed what probably seem like mood swings, or erratic behaviour?'

Lisa nodded.

'I need the bathroom,' David suddenly said.

As the door slammed closed behind him Isabelle looked sympathetically at Lisa. 'It's not un-common for someone in his position to become angry and go into denial at first,' she told her. 'It's a means of self-protection, and quite frankly, it's more important for you to understand what's going on than it is for him, since you'll presum-ably be the one taking care of him.'

Feeling herself teetering on the edge of denial too, Lisa said nothing, only waited for the doctor to continue.

'It might help to know,' Isabelle said, 'that someone with David's condition finds it increas-ingly difficult to learn anything new. We've seen examples of this in his failure to remember meet-ings, or what was said at them. This means that new information isn't always getting through. What's already learned is still there, and it won't, or shouldn't go anywhere for a while yet. However, accessing it can prove problematic.

'But let's deal with the new information first, because his difficulties in retaining it are what you're going to find the hardest to cope with.'

Picking up a pen and pad she began to sketch a diagram. 'Here's a rough look at the way the memory brain functions,' she said. 'Verbal into working memory takes around forty-five seconds to a minute. From working into short term is between five and twenty minutes. The information then goes into the recent memory store, which directs it through to the executive brain where the major processing is done – in other words what we're going to retain for future use, or what we can just dismiss. What concerns us at the moment is the working to short-term memory. The working is functioning, meaning that he's taking information in, but the short term isn't always sending it on down the line the way it should, so this is where things are getting lost.

'Over time, the short-term memory will cease to function altogether, while the rest of the memory brain starts to break down too. This is when the problems of remembering something as fundamental as the names of his family, or the timing of certain events in his past, or how to perform everyday functions will start to kick in. You saw the problem with the shirt just now – that could have been nerves, but in a man like David I'm afraid it's not a good sign.'

Lisa's face was bloodless as she regarded the doctor. If only her own memory-brain could let this information go, she was thinking, maybe then none of it would be happening. 'I know he'll want to carry on working,' she said, 'but is that going to be possible? Perhaps I should be asking, how long will it be possible?'

'That will be largely up to him. For the time

being there will continue to be the same sort of problems he's already experienced, but unless you tell me differently he's still able to function on most levels?'

Deciding that in the main he was, Lisa nodded.

Isabelle smiled. 'I'm going to give you my mobile number,' she said, taking a Post-it pad from a drawer, 'so please feel free to call any time. There's a lot to take in, and you'll find all sorts of questions coming up over the next few weeks that you'll need answers to.' After jotting her number down she handed it over, saying, 'You'll be contacted by a memory nurse as a follow-up to this diagnosis. She'll come to your home to advise you on what to expect, how to proceed, what kind of backup there is . . . Basically everything you need to know.'

Lisa looked up as David came in.

'I think we should go home now,' he said shortly. 'The doctor must be very busy.'

Lisa looked helplessly at Isabelle.

'You have my number,' Isabelle reminded her. 'Don't hesitate to use it.'

Moments later they were walking silently out to the car with the echo of Isabelle Manning's terrible words still ringing in their ears, and the spectre of what was to come already dancing before them.

'You drive,' David said, handing her the keys.

Wanting to show she had confidence in him, she said, 'Are you sure you don't want to?'

He didn't answer, only waited for her to unlock the doors, then sliding into the passenger seat he fastened his seat belt.

It was a while before he spoke; they were already heading up the ramp to join the M32 back into town. 'This isn't fair on you,' he told her. 'You shouldn't have to be . . .'

'Stop,' she interrupted. 'It's not about me. It's about you.'

His head came round to look at her. 'Actually, it's about both of us, which is what I'm trying to say . . .'

'I know what you're trying to say, but now isn't the time to have a sensible conversation about anything.'

He didn't argue any further, simply turned to stare out at the passing landscape of terraced houses and rows of shops that he'd never visited and probably never would.

Did that matter? Did anything any more? Of course it did, but right now it was as though he was turning slowly numb inside. Since his brain apparently was, he guessed it was hardly surprising he felt that way. It was the most humiliating and enraging thing to know that he was letting himself down. *He* was responsible for what was happening. *He*, David Kirby, who existed, like all men, because of his brain, was shrinking in memory, identity, even purpose. Nothing was the same any more, or ever would be again. From now on, until his brain failed him altogether, or a massive stroke tore it apart, he would have to live with the gradual disintegration of his world. How much longer would he be able to understand what was going on around him and respond to it in a normal, socially acceptable way? How many weeks and months would pass before he stopped recognising the people he knew and loved?

Turning to look at Lisa, he felt himself collapsing inside. Would he forget her name in time, who she was, and how much she meant to him? Was it worth continuing to live if all he was going to bring her was heartache, embarrassment and regret? What kind of man would he be if he kept her trapped in a marriage that could never now bring her joy?

'I'm hungry,' he said suddenly, 'are you?'

Managing a smile she said, 'Would you like to stop somewhere, or shall we go home?'

'Let's go home,' he answered, and attempting to rein in the rage and self-pity that was threatening to engulf him he turned to look out of the window again. He must back away from his emotions, keep a careful distance from them and somehow treat them as though they belonged to somebody else.

He began wondering what it would be like when he had no more memory, when he could no longer express himself at all. How would he feel? Afraid? Impotent? Alone in a crowd? Would he be cowering in the shell of his body, like a small, shrunken version of himself? How much was he going to understand? Would people treat him like a fool? Would youngsters poke fun at him, the way some did with the elderly and infirm, particularly those who were confused and afraid? How much control would he have over his actions? Would he harm people, or run from them? Would he even understand what they were saying, or doing?

So many questions, and there was no one to ask, because those who were afflicted were unable to tell how it really was. They were watching the world from a prison of damaged cells, there but not, alive, but gone. Did their thoughts make any sense to them? Did the words form coherently in their minds, only to be jumbled on the journey to their tongues? Were they shouting inside with no sound coming out? When they laughed, did they know why? When they cried, were they grieving for who they used to be? When they ate was there a sense of fulfilment? When they slept did their dreams give them cheer, or even have any kind of meaning? What was it like to want to go home, when there was no home to go to any more?

How many of these thoughts, and how much of this fear would he remember tomorrow? Would it all come back as something new to put him through this harrowing angst all over again? What was his life going to be like now he knew the truth? Was there even any point to it any more?

They were at home now, eating a snack lunch of mozzarella cheese and fresh tomatoes. The rain was beating an incessant tattoo against the windows; the garden outside looked windswept and forlorn.

'We have to talk to Miles,' David declared, making it sound like an order. 'Let's invite him here, to the house.'

Topping up their wine glasses, Lisa said, 'If you like.'

There was a flintiness in his eyes as he said,

'I'm sure you'll be glad of some intelligent company.'

She took a mouthful of food, then made herself smile in the face of his belligerence. 'It's not making a difference,' she told him, managing to sound unruffled when actually she was fraught with all kinds of conflicting emotions. 'I know you think it is, but you're wrong.'

'What are we talking about?' he demanded.

'You think, because of the diagnosis, that my feelings have changed.' *Had they?* How could she know when she was still so far from processing it all?

'Well, it's good that you know what I'm thinking,' he retorted, 'because it'll help no end when I've forgotten how to speak.'

As a curl of dread wrapped around her heart, she said, 'What do you want to discuss with Miles?'

Sitting back in his chair, he said, 'I'm glad you asked, because if I tell you now, and then forget, you'll remember when he gets here.'

Still managing not to engage with his ugly mood, she said, 'So tell me.'

'Do you want to take notes? I usually do. They recommend that, you know, but maybe you should do it from now on, it would help us both.'

'I'm not your secretary and nor am I going to treat you as an incompetent when you're far from it.'

'It'll be good practice for when I am, and who says I'm not already?'

'You, apparently.'

'Because you're too polite or . . . or whatever the hell you are.'

Putting her cutlery down she said, 'David, stop it. I understand this is difficult . . .'

'Do you? You know how it feels to have your brain turning on you . . .'

'If you can speak as coherently as you are now, then there can't be too much wrong, can there?'

'But there is. The doctor just told us.'

'That's right, and the good thing is that the diagnosis has clearly got past your short-term memory.'

'Great. To sit and fester in the big brain like a . . . like a . . .' He slapped a hand against his head. 'What is it going to take to make you understand that you can't stay here?' he barked angrily.

The answer that shot to her tongue hovered nervously for a moment, then daring to go with it, she said, 'Whatever it is, you don't have the words.'

He glowered dangerously, but then a hint of amusement began to shine through a chink in his anger. 'That's not kind,' he told her.

'No, but nor is the way you're trying to push me away. You're my husband, I love you and if being with you means having to deal with this crotchety, antagonistic old sod you've apparently decided to become, then so be it.'

'He's going to be a doddle compared to the bedwetting drooler coming up behind him,' he snapped, and throwing down his napkin he walked out of the kitchen.

Lisa continued to sit where she was, unable to argue with him, or defend herself, or even to try and comfort him, because she had no idea how to handle this in a way that would make any kind of difference at all. In fact, she was completely lost in a world where she'd never in her entire life imagined she'd be, a world that she was already struggling to stop herself thinking of as a chasm with no way back to the top.

He was right, she was still young, not yet forty, but fifty-three wasn't old either, and anyway, no matter what their ages, neither of them deserved to have this unassailable cruelty flung upon them.

Later in the day they were lying in each other's arms on the bed after making love in a way that had seemed almost desperate in its passion, and yet so profound in its tenderness that the sheer power of it was still reverberating through them. It was as though they'd joined more completely and deeply than they ever had before, and feeling his arms so strongly around her, and the full sense of the closeness they shared binding them more tightly than ever, was almost breaking her heart. How could a man who was so vital and healthy in every other way be falling victim to such a terrible disease? It wasn't right. It made no sense at all. She could hardly bear to imagine what must be going through his mind now. Was he wondering how often they'd be able to share this sort of physical closeness in the future; how long it would be before he'd forget the desire and so no longer need the release? She wanted to tell him that it wouldn't matter, she'd be here anyway, loving him and caring for him in every other way, but she knew it wouldn't be what he wanted to hear.

How would he react, she wondered, if she told him that she felt something very special had just happened between them, something bigger and more lasting than ever before? With all her heart she longed to be right, but there had been too many times in the past when she'd felt certain she'd conceived and had been disappointed. She wasn't going to allow herself to get her hopes up now, especially when it meant so much. Instead, she turned her face into his neck and inhaled the wonderful male scent of him, feeling it moving through her with the same stirring potency as the most intimate caress.

David, David, David, she was crying inside. *Don't leave me yet. Please don't go.*

Feeling him press a kiss to her head, she gave a soft moan of protest as he gently disentangled himself and got up from the bed. When he returned from the bathroom a few minutes later, belting his robe, she could see the terrible angst he was trying to hide. 'I need to talk to Miles,' he said gruffly.

Though she understood the fear that was compelling him to try and put a distance between them, she wasn't going to let it happen, so using her own strength of will to bring him back to her she reached out her hand and waited for him to take it. When he did she pulled him to her and wrapped him in her arms. They'd have to deal with the rest of the world sooner or later, she accepted that, but when the time came, which wouldn't be today, there was no doubt in her mind that his daughter needed to be told before anyone else.

Rosalind was surprised to see Dee getting out of David's car. The last she'd heard her aunt was unable to make lunch today, because she'd agreed to help an old friend at an antiques fair in Yeovil. Not that Rosalind minded about her coming, in fact she was quite relieved, since she was still half afraid each time she saw her father these days that he was going to start giving her a hard time over the calls she'd made to Jerry's mistress.

She only knew her father was aware of them because Jerry had told her he'd asked him to make her stop. So far, to her surprise – and relief – David hadn't mentioned it. However, he'd been quite distant with her lately, which in itself suggested his disapproval, even if he didn't come right out and express it.

'You should be ashamed of yourself, stealing another woman's husband,' was one of the things she'd shouted down the phone to Olivia at one o'clock in the morning. Or, 'He has another child, you know. A son, and if he can leave him just like that, what makes you think he's going to stay around for your child after the novelty's worn off?'

Far worse than that though, in fact so bad that it made her cringe with shame even to think of it now, was the night she'd said, 'I'd watch out for your daughter if I were you, or something bad might happen to her.'

That was when Jerry had contacted her father, and in all honesty Rosalind didn't blame him. She must have frightened the life out of them. It had even left her feeling unnerved when she'd woken the next morning – with an unspeakable hangover – and remembered what she'd done. She'd toyed with the idea of calling again to apologise, but then Jerry had rung to let her know that he'd asked her father to intervene, which had sent her flying off the handle, and the call had ended with him threatening to inform the police if she ever did anything like it again.

The police! Her own husband was threatening to set the law on her and in spite of how furious she'd been at the time, she had to admit she bloody well deserved it. She'd made herself stop drinking after that, because the last thing she wanted was the ignominy of some kind of restraining order being slapped on her. Or for Jerry's mistress to think she was some dangerous madwoman who'd stalk her daughter and kidnap her, or feed her poisoned sweets, or strike her down in some other grim and newsworthy way. Now she was going to bed at nine o'clock most nights, and watching the TV in her room. More often than not she cried herself to sleep, which was absurd, she kept telling herself, when she wouldn't take him back now even if he wanted to come.

'Hi,' she said forcing a cheeriness as Dee came in the door. 'This is a nice surprise. What happened to the antiques fair?'

Dee was scuffing her feet dry on the mat even though it wasn't raining outside. 'Oh, that,' she said airily. 'She got someone else to help. Is there enough for me? Sorry, I probably should have rung to let you know I was coming.'

'Of course there's enough for you. I've found a new recipe for boeuf bourguignon which is usually one of Lawrence's favourites. Let's hope it still is after today. Help yourself to a drink. There's plenty in the fridge. Hi Dad, are you OK?'

she said, hugging him warmly, maybe too warmly, but was there anyone else she loved more? Apart from Lawrence. 'We've already heard back from the planners about the Long Ashton project,' she told him. 'It's not bad news, but not great either. You can take a look after lunch if you like.' Was he starting to get fed up with the company now he had a new wife? He wasn't paying it as much attention as he once had. If anything, it seemed to get on his nerves.

'Are you all right?' she asked again as he closed the door. 'Headache all gone?'

'Headache?' he echoed.

'When we spoke yesterday . . .'

'Ah, yes. No, it's fine. All gone.'

Rosalind turned to her aunt. Something wasn't right, she could sense it. They didn't seem themselves, and though she had no idea what was happening, her instincts were already telling her that it wasn't good. 'What is it?' she said tremulously. 'Why are you both looking so . . . serious?'

'Your father has some news,' Dee told her, folding her coat over the back of a chair. 'I think we should probably sit down.'

Becoming more alarmed by the second, Rosalind said, 'Shall we have some wine? Am I going to need it?'

David went to the fridge, and after filling three glasses he brought them to the table where Rosalind and Dee were already seated. 'Where's Lawrence?' he asked.

'In the TV room with Lucy. He's got a new DVD he wants to show you.'

David nodded, and when his eyes went down

399

Rosalind suddenly felt like running out of the room as though to escape whatever was coming. 'Is it Jerry?' she said, all kinds of horrible images starting to flash through her head. 'Has something happened to him?'

'No, it's not Jerry,' Dee answered.

Rosalind turned to her father. 'Dad?' she cried. 'For heaven's sake, what's going on?'

Closing the notebook he'd been looking at, David said, 'You might . . . Well, I'm sure you've noticed that I've . . . Well that I haven't been quite on top of things lately.'

Her heart was starting to pound. 'Not really,' she lied.

His eyes came up to hers. 'I think you have,' he said softly, 'and it turns out that the reason for this is that I am suffering . . . Well, I have been diagnosed with a form of early onset dementia.'

Rosalind's heart shuddered to a stop. She looked at Dee, then back to her father. 'That's not true,' she protested. 'Of course you're not suffering with *dementia*. You're too young for one thing, and . . .'

'It's early onset,' Dee said gently.

Seeing the pain in her father's eyes, Rosalind shot to her feet. 'I'm not listening to this nonsense,' she told him. 'There's absolutely nothing wrong with you, so I don't know why you're saying there is. It's cruel, Dad. I love you, and the last thing I'd want . . .'

'Darling, I'd never tell you this if it weren't true.'

'I don't think you know what dementia is,' she cried. 'I mean, look at the way you're sitting there now, speaking to me quite normally. People with

400

dementia can't do that. You're not someone who's losing his mind.'

Keeping his voice calm, he said, 'I'm afraid I am, and whether we like it or not, sweetheart, somehow we're going to have to come to terms with it.'

Not knowing what else to do, Rosalind glared at Dee.

'It's terrible news,' Dee said quietly. 'I feel quite devastated.'

'Is no one listening to me?' Rosalind demanded furiously. 'There's nothing wrong with you, Dad. If there were I would know, and I'm telling you there isn't.'

'Darling, please come and sit down . . .'

'No! If you're going to carry on . . .' She stopped suddenly, as understanding dawned. 'Oh my God, I know what's going on here,' she declared shakily. 'I know exactly what's happening. Lisa Martin is behind this, isn't she?'

'Oh, Rosalind,' Dee murmured.

'It's you who's talking nonsense now,' David told her.

'Why are you believing what she's telling you?' Rosalind demanded angrily. 'God, I knew she was evil, but to do something like this . . .'

'Lisa isn't evil,' David interrupted, 'and nor are you incapable of accepting the truth. I know you don't want to, but . . . It's . . .' He looked at Dee as she said, 'He's had all the tests, darling, and the doctors wouldn't lie.'

Rosalind stared at her aunt helplessly. In her heart she knew, *she knew*, but she couldn't let it be true.

'Come here,' David said, holding out his arms.

Rosalind shook her head. Her eyes were flooding with tears and as a sob erupted from her turmoil, David got to his feet and went to hold her.

'It'll be all right,' he soothed, his own voice thick with emotion. 'We'll work things out, and nothing's going to change very much for a while. I'm on medication now that should help to slow things down.'

Looking up at him, she put her hands each side of his face and gazed fiercely into his eyes. 'I'm not going to let this happen to you,' she told him earnestly. 'I don't care what they're saying, they've got it wrong.'

'Darling . . .'

'Stop!' she spluttered.

'Poor love,' Dee whispered, as Rosalind clung to her father again. 'She's been through so much lately.'

Bringing her back to the table, David sat her down next to him and took her hands in his. 'There are still several practical things to sort out,' he said, 'but I want you to know . . .'

Rosalind shot to her feet again. 'Shall we have some lunch now?' she said briskly. 'I expect Lawrence is hungry, and he'll be cross that I haven't told him you're here.'

David glanced at Dee, who shook her head sadly.

'I'll go and get him,' David sighed. 'We can talk about this another time.'

Lisa was in the hall, waiting for David to come home. He was much later than she'd expected.

Usually when he went to Rosalind's on a Saturday he was back by four at the latest. It was now almost five, and she'd received no call yet to let her know he was on his way. Was he lost, or was he still at Rosalind's, helping her come to terms with this new turn in their lives?

Pacing, pacing. She must make herself stop.

Finally seeing the gates start to open and his car coming through, she heaved an enormous sigh of relief and rushed off to her study, not wanting him to know that she'd been fretting about his return. On the other hand, he'd had a difficult task ahead when he'd left earlier, and he was late coming back, so he'd probably expect her to be at least a little bit concerned. So abandoning her desk again, she went back to the hall just as he was coming to a stop outside the front door.

'Hi, how did it go?' she asked, as he got out of the car.

He shook his head, and seeing how ashen he was, told her that it hadn't gone any better than he'd feared.

'I should put the car away,' he said, starting to turn back.

'It's OK, I'll do it. Go in and sit down. You look exhausted.'

Not even attempting to argue, he kissed her briefly as he passed, and after taking off his coat he went to slump down on a sofa.

'I expect it was very difficult for her,' she said, when she came back.

He frowned as though his head was aching. 'Right now she's not accepting it at all,' he replied.

403

'I wanted to talk to her about the . . . what's it called? The legal thing?'

'The Lasting Power of Attorney.'

'That's right, and about my will, but she doesn't want to listen.'

'It's too soon,' Lisa told him, repeating what she'd said before he left.

'But we don't know how long it's going to be before these things start to matter.'

'No, but it won't be this week, or even this month, so there's no need to rush. Just give her some time, she'll have to accept it sooner or later and when she does . . . Well, she'll find her own way of coping.'

He sighed wearily and let his head drop forward. 'I keep thinking about Lawrence,' he said bleakly. 'We watched his new DVD this afternoon, twice, and I couldn't help wondering if our brains might end up communicating on some other kind of level at some point. That's a daft way to think, isn't it? But his stands a chance of improving as he gets older, whereas mine . . .' He looked up at her, then he held out a hand for her to come and sit with him. 'Are we doing anything tonight?' he asked.

'It's Amy and Theo's leaving party,' she reminded him, 'but we don't have to go.'

His eyebrows rose in amazement. 'I think we do,' he corrected, 'and it'll probably do us good to get out, instead of sitting around here tormenting ourselves with what a bugger of a hand we've been dealt. What time do we have to be there?'

'Not until nine. I've booked a taxi so we can both have a drink.'

'Good idea.' He settled in more comfortably. 'Did Miles call back?' he asked.

She'd told him already this morning, but it was OK, she could say it again. 'Yes, we're seeing him in London on Thursday, after we've dropped Amy and Theo at the airport.'

'Good. Where are they going?'

'Australia.'

He made no comment about that, only yawned and pulled her in closer. This tenderness was a complete reversal to the way he'd been earlier, when he'd shouted at her to start packing up her things to move back to London. She wondered now if he even remembered it.

'Roxy's bringing all her stuff over tomorrow,' she reminded him. 'Amy and Theo are taking her to Oxford on Tuesday.'

'Lovely,' he murmured. 'She's going to have the time of her life.' Then, 'Do you remember how we met at Bristol Uni?'

'Of course,' she smiled. 'Actually, it was at the Colston Hall, but I'd seen you around lots of times before that. I don't think you'd noticed me until then, but you were so dashing and full of yourself and all the girls were dying to get off with you.'

'But there was only one I wanted,' he said, 'and lucky me, I got her in the end.'

'You did,' she agreed, knowing it was true then, but seeming not to know anything now. How possible was it to love a man whose brain was ceasing to function? What kind of person was she even to be asking herself the question?

'Am I in dreamland,' he muttered a while later,

'to be hoping that you and Rosalind might find a way to get along? You're going to need one another when things start to go downhill.'

'You know that's not my decision,' she answered.

'No, I suppose it isn't,' he sighed. Then, 'She hasn't taken it well. She really hasn't.'

Since the only good thing about that was that he'd remembered it, all she said was, 'I don't think it's going to be very easy for Miles, either.'

'Mm, maybe not. When did you say we're seeing him?'

'Thursday. It's in the diary.'

Stifling another yawn, he closed his eyes and resettled his head on hers. 'There's something else I want to discuss with you,' he said, 'but I'm damned if I can remember what it is.'

Several more minutes ticked by, then going to fetch his notebook he came back into the room and showed her an entry he'd made the day before. 'We need to talk about this,' he said.

As she read what he'd written Lisa felt her mind reel. 'No,' she whispered, looking up at him. 'You can't be serious.'

The severity of his expression told her that he was, but as he sat down to start discussing it, she got to her feet and left the room. It was never wise, she was thinking as she stifled a sob, to assume things couldn't get any worse, because as far as she was concerned they just had.

Chapter Nineteen

'Can you imagine how terrible I feel just for being here?' Lisa wept as she dabbed her eyes with a ragged tissue. 'I know I shouldn't have come, but I had to speak to someone and with Amy so close to leaving . . . You were the only person I could think of.'

'Well, I suppose I should feel flattered,' Tony responded drily, as he took the sodden tissue and replaced it with a fresh one. 'And that wasn't the kind of answer you were looking for.' His expression was solemn as he continued to absorb all that she'd told him, while in the car park around them people came and went from the motorway services. 'Poor guy,' he murmured, 'he must be totally devastated.'

'It's a nightmare,' she said, her voice sounding nasal and quivery as she blew her nose again. She still wasn't sure she'd done the right thing in turning to Tony, except he didn't know David, so it was less like breaking a confidence than if she'd gone to her mother, or one of her friends. She didn't want their pity or constant phone calls asking how David was, or if she was managing to cope, it would only make everything seem worse. Tony wasn't like that. As wayward and unpredictable as he could be at times, he'd always been good in a crisis and ready with lashings of moral support where it was needed.

'I keep reliving the day the doctor told us,' she said hoarsely, 'the way I wanted to scream and make her take it all back; then I wanted to run . . .' As her words were swallowed by a gulf of shame her head fell forward. 'I keep telling myself I can handle it,' she said, 'that being with him is all that matters, but what happens when it isn't him any more? He's already changed, and apparently every time he has one of the mini-strokes, which we might not even know he's had, it's going to get worse. Then he'll improve for a while until it happens again . . . How am I going to handle that? How is he? He keeps trying to hide how afraid he is, but I can see it all the time, and when he started to talk last night about going to Switzerland "to put a dignified end to it all" . . .' She covered her face with her hands. 'I didn't know what to say, because obviously I understand why he'd want to do that, but how can I allow myself to go along with it?'

Tony was still looking shell-shocked himself, but nevertheless he tried to be objective as he said, 'Well, I can see it would be hard, but maybe you should be thinking about how you'd feel if you were in his shoes.'

'I'm sure I'd want to do the same,' she admitted, 'but lately . . . Well, I have to be honest, I've started to question how I feel about him anyway, and if . . . Oh God, that sounds so awful, doesn't it? What kind of person am I that I could even think about leaving him when he's facing what he is?'

Tony frowned. 'Are you thinking about it?' he asked doubtfully.

She shook her head. 'No, I don't suppose so. I mean, no, I'm not. I want to be there for him, to do everything I can to help him, but when I read about what it entails . . . It takes a very special sort of person to be a carer, Tony, and I just know I don't have it in me. I wish I did. I swear to God, if I could bestow those qualities upon myself right now I would, but the very thought of having to deal with incontinence and . . .'

'Stop, stop,' he said gently. 'You're going so fast that you've just gone straight to jail without passing go and . . .'

'That's just it! I'm already starting to feel trapped, so how much worse is it going to get? Will I be able to stand it?' More tears were dropping on to her cheeks now, and as he passed her another tissue she said, 'I promise I'll stop in a minute. I just . . . I suppose I've kept it all bottled up, feeling so ashamed of what's going on in my head, and trying not to think about it when actually I'm never thinking about anything else.'

'Listen,' he said, 'I'm not going to try and pretend this isn't a scary thing you're facing, because it is, but you have to try and stay focused on the present, because honestly there's no telling what the future might hold. For all we know you could get run over by a bus tomorrow . . . Oh, now there's a happy thought, Tone. Glad you came up with that one, it's sure to cheer her up.'

With a splutter of laughter, Lisa attempted to dry her eyes.

'What I should have said,' he continued, 'is that he's still got a lot of good years in him if he's only just been diagnosed, and he's not short of money, so when things do start getting tough you can always bring someone in to help you.'

'I know, you're right, and every time I tell myself that it does make me feel better. He needs to have the best sort of care, and he'll get it because I'll be there to make sure he does.'

'Unless,' he added carefully, 'he takes himself off to Switzerland.'

As her heart turned over, she said, 'No, I can't let him do that. His daughter won't allow it either, I know she won't. He'll only be doing it to stop us sacrificing the next five or however many years of our lives taking care of him . . .'

'Or so that he doesn't have to spend the next five or however many years suffering one of the longest and cruellest sorts of deaths there is, because that's what dementia is. It has no mercy for anyone, least of all its victim, or the carer.'

Turning to look at him, she said, 'You sound as though you know about it.'

He shook his head. 'Only from things I've read, or talking to friends who are going through it with their parents or grandparents. It's not something I'd wish on my worst enemy, and believe it or not, I don't view him as that.'

Swallowing as she looked away, she said, 'What am I going to do, Tony? How am I going to cope with this?'

'You'll find a way,' he assured her, 'because I

410

know you, no matter how afraid, and cheated you might be feeling right now, or how hard he tries to push you away, you don't have it in you to walk out on him.'

Surprised by his answer, she turned to gaze into his eyes as she said, 'You know, I was afraid, when I told you that you might be . . . Well, that you'd see it as a way . . . Sorry, that's a horrible thing to think.'

'I don't blame you,' he replied, 'and I have to confess I do still want you back, but not like this. I'd never be able to live with myself, thinking of him struggling on in his private hell while we get merrily on with our lives, and you wouldn't be able to either. No, what I'd rather do is try to find a way to help him, but God knows how I'm going to manage that when even the experts don't have the answers.'

Keeping her head down, she said, 'You could be there for me. Once Amy's gone . . . I'll . . .' Biting her lip as more emotion swept over her, she brought the Kleenex back to her eyes.

'You'll need someone to lean on,' he finished for her, 'and I'm sure I can be that.' Then, with a wryness that was more typical of the Tony she knew, he added, 'I admit, I never envisaged myself as your brother or best friend, but it's plain that's what you need right now, and so that's who I'll be. Any time you need to offload, day or night, my door will always be open.'

'Thank you,' she whispered. Then, looking down at the tissue she was shredding, 'So you really don't think I should do as he seems to want and leave him?'

Brushing her hair back from her face, he replied, 'OK, what if I said I think you should?'

Her head came round in surprise. Then her eyes narrowed with suspicion as she asked, 'You're not serious, are you?'

'What if I am? Would you leave him?'

Keeping her eyes on his, she shook her head. 'Never,' she murmured. 'I know I keep thinking about it, but . . .'

Putting a finger over her lips he said, 'I just wanted you to see what it felt like to get the permission you're seeking.'

She was still looking at him as she gave a tremulous smile. 'You know, I never realised you could be so wise,' she said, and taking his hand she held it between her own as she turned to gaze out at the rain. 'I can do this,' she told him quietly. 'Whatever's expected of me, I can do it, because he's a wonderful man who deserves to be loved and cared for in the same way he'd love and care for me if I were in his position. And I could be, any of us could, even you.'

'Too right,' he agreed.

She turned to look at him again. 'David's much stronger and more honourable than I am,' she said, 'but I'm going to be there for him, Tony. I really am.'

'In any other circumstances,' Tony whispered, 'I'd say he was a very lucky man, in these I'm going to say that in whatever way I can I'll be there for him too.'

'Is this really happening?' Amy was murmuring excitedly, as they approached the airport terminal

412

building. 'Am I seriously leaving my little sister behind, and my daughter and my mother? How could I do that? How on earth are you all going to cope?'

As Theo laughed and David smiled, Lisa said, 'Oh, I'm sure we'll manage somehow.'

Grinning, Amy squeezed her hand and kept it bunched between her own as David steered them on to the ramp leading into the short-term car park.

It was impressive, Lisa was thinking, how he'd managed to drive all the way here as though nothing in the world was wrong with him. She felt proud of him, and at the same time resentful that she was now viewing something so normal as a particular achievement.

'Don't look so upset,' Amy wailed. 'I know it's hard. I feel awful too. Are you ever going to be able to forgive me?'

'Probably not, but please don't let that stop you.'

Piping up from the front, Theo said, 'I don't think anything could now, bar death or disaster. The new tenants are moving in on Monday, the apartment's ready for us in Sydney, the company has even sprung for business-class flights.'

'Isn't that fantastic?' Amy trilled. 'We really wouldn't want to go all that way scrunched up in cattle class.'

'It's true, you wouldn't,' Lisa agreed, having never done it herself. 'Now, I hope you've got the list I gave you of people to look up when you get there. They'll take care of you royally, make sure you know all the best places to go and right things to do. I've already sent emails so they're expecting to hear from you.'

'Did I mention that my cousin in Cairns is going to invite you up there?' David asked for the second time that day. 'I haven't seen him for decades, but he's a proper sort of bloke, as the Aussies would say.'

'Is that what they say?' Lisa teased.

'Isn't it?' he asked, catching her eye in the mirror.

Realising the joke might misfire she squeezed his shoulder, saying, 'It's exactly what they say.'

Ten minutes later they were wheeling two trolleys loaded with cases into the vast and frenetically busy departure lounge of Terminal 5 to check in for the Hong Kong flight, which was where Amy and Theo had decided to spend four days before completing their journey.

'Are you getting itchy feet?' Amy asked, as the men started to heft the cases on to the weighing belt.

Lisa was watching the milling crowds, feeling strangely as though she were a ghost returned from another time. 'I guess so,' she said, unwilling to consider her former life when she'd been free to jet off anywhere in the world at any time.

Amy smiled. 'Chances are you'll be doing plenty more travelling with David. Think how fantastic that'll be . . . You know, I could quite fancy being a top politician's wife myself. Oh God, what's happening? What is it?' she cried, noticing David starting to load the cases back on to his trolley.

'We can't check in until three hours before take-off,' Theo told her, 'and we've still got four and a half to go.'

Though the early arrival was deliberate so they could have a late lunch together, they hadn't expected to be stuck with the luggage, and Lisa could see Amy starting to boil up ready to do battle with the check-in clerk.

'It's OK,' she said, stepping in quickly, 'they'll allow you to park the luggage at the entrance to the restaurant. I've done it a dozen times, so let's just do that.'

'Good, I'm famished,' David said, rubbing his hands. 'Where are we going?'

'Carluccio's,' Amy reminded him. 'So where is it, Lis?'

'Right there,' Lisa replied, pointing to behind the check-in desks.

'OK, here we go,' Theo said, and wheeling his trolley round to lead the way, he raised an arm to marshal his troops.

'Hey, isn't that Jerry?' Amy suddenly exclaimed. 'Jerry, is that you?'

Jerry, in full uniform, broke his stride and turned around.

Amy's face lit up. 'Yes it is you,' she declared. 'How are you? You remember us, don't you? Well, you remember David, obviously.'

From the readiness of Jerry's smile it was impossible to tell how awkward he might be feeling at running into his father-in-law, but he had to be at least a little uncomfortable, Lisa felt sure. However, that was nothing to what she was experiencing, because slim though the possibility might be, there was still a chance Rosalind had told him about David's condition and if he mentioned it now, with Amy right on the verge of leaving . . .

'Amy,' he was saying warmly, 'how lovely to see you. And Theo. Where are you guys off to?'

415

'This is our big move to Sydney,' Theo told him.

'But we're only going as far as Hong Kong today,' Amy added.

Jerry laughed. 'If you're on the 1835 then we're going the same way.'

'That's the one,' Amy cried, clearly thrilled. 'How fab, knowing the captain.'

Chuckling, Jerry turned to Lisa and David. Now Lisa could see his discomfort, and in spite of feeling sorry for Rosalind, her heart went out to him. 'Hello,' he said, shaking David's hand. Then to Lisa, 'I guess this is a big day for you too, saying goodbye to your sister.'

Lisa grimaced. 'I don't know about big, but it's definitely not one I've been looking forward to.'

'So how are you?' he said to David. 'I hear you've . . .'

'Oh, *excuse us*,' Amy snapped as someone careered their trolley into Theo's.

Lisa hardly noticed, she was so tense. Surely to God Jerry wasn't about to mention it, even if he did know.

Turning back from the scuffle, Jerry was on the point of continuing, when Lisa suddenly blurted, 'How's Olivia and your little girl?'

As Jerry's cheeks burned with colour, Lisa felt David draw back and wanted to bite out her tongue. She'd only said it to stop Jerry triggering all sorts of explosions, and now here she was setting them off herself.

'They're fine, thank you,' he answered quietly. Then, turning to Amy and Theo, 'I don't know how full the flight is, but I'll see what I can do about an upgrade. Which cabin are you in?'

'Business,' Theo told him, 'so we're pretty good.'

'First is better, if I can swing it.' He glanced at his watch. 'I should be going now, there's a meeting I have to be at. If I don't see you before, I'll catch up with you in Hong Kong.'

'Perhaps we can have dinner, or something,' Amy suggested, just as Lisa was thinking they were off the hook. 'We're staying at the Mandarin Oriental, do you know it?'

Jerry's smile was wry. 'I believe I do,' he replied, and after a brief nod towards Lisa and David, he went on his way.

Looking appropriately shamefaced, Amy turned to David. 'I'm sorry if I put you on the spot,' she said, linking his arm. 'I just saw him, and I didn't think until it was too late.'

'It's fine,' David assured her. Then to Lisa, 'What was that about Olivia and a little girl?'

Lisa's heart turned over. He'd obviously forgotten. 'It just came out,' she said, hoping to fudge the issue. 'I thought I should . . . Oh great, look, there's a table coming free, let's see if we can get it.'

As Amy and Theo surged forward, she took David's arm and held him back. 'Olivia's Jerry's new partner,' she whispered, adhering to their new pact that she should tell him when he'd forgotten something. 'They have a little girl called Chloe.'

His face was starting to pale. 'I see,' he murmured. 'Does Rosalind know about this?'

'Yes, she does, but that's enough, we don't want to spoil our last lunch with Amy and Theo.' She eased him forward. 'My concern now,' she said, 'is that Rosalind might have told Jerry about you, and if they see him in Hong Kong and he tells them . . .'

'Does Rosalind know about me?'

Almost too late to swallow her despair, she said, 'Yes, you told her last Saturday.'

'Come on you two, we're in,' Amy called out. 'Shall we have a glass of Prosecco to start?'

Lisa looked at David. 'If you want to drink, I'll drive,' she offered.

'I'm fine. One glass won't do any harm.'

'But you drove here. I think that's enough. If you get tired . . .'

'I'm not an invalid.'

'No, but we don't even know if you're supposed to be driving. We still haven't heard back from the DVLA.'

'I hope you two aren't bickering on our last day,' Amy chided, coming to get them.

David smiled broadly. 'I'm being bossed around by your sister and trying to . . . Well, I'm not . . .'

'Oh, I know what a toughie she can be,' Amy teased. 'I'm glad to be getting away from it myself.'

'Believe me, that's not what she said last night,' Theo informed them, as they sat down at a window table.

'Oh, please don't get me started again,' Amy protested. 'The truth is, I'm absolutely dreading going, but on the other hand, if you told me I could change my mind now I know I wouldn't. How's that for contrary?'

'It's called being a woman,' Theo quipped. 'So, have we decided? Proseccos all round?'

'Proseccos all round,' David confirmed.

Happy to go along with it, if only to avoid

another dispute, Lisa settled herself next to Amy and was just reaching for her hand when Amy's mobile rang. It turned out to be Roxy, who had to speak to everyone, one by one, returning to her mother at the end, and by the time she rang off their first courses had arrived. Within minutes of getting started Matilda was on the line wanting to speak to everyone too, including David who assured her they hadn't forgotten they were driving her to the airport at Christmas. Whether he had or not, Lisa couldn't tell, but she felt proud of the way he'd handled it if he had.

Amy's and Theo's phones hardly stopped after that as more friends and family called to wish them bon voyage and good luck, but annoying and disruptive as it was, Lisa couldn't help feeling relieved to have Amy distracted. If her whole attention were focused on what was happening in front of her, Lisa knew she'd pick up on something right away.

Two hours later they were back at the check-in desk, reloading the luggage on to the weighing belt as the boarding passes were issued. By now Lisa was struggling so hard to keep herself together that she was finding it difficult to speak. Saying goodbye to Amy would never have been easy, but needing her as much as she did now, it was starting to feel like the hardest thing she'd ever had to do. She only had to look at her dear, lively face as she took in everything the clerk was saying, before glancing up at Theo to make sure he was listening too, to want to hug her to within an inch of her life. Everything about her sister was seeming so precious in these moments that it was as though she might be seeing her for the very last time.

The worst of it, she realised, as she watched Amy embracing David at the departure gate, was that this was very probably the last time she would see David as he was now. Heaven only knew how he would be a year or two down the line, unless he persevered with his determination to go to Zurich . . . Unable to think about that now, she pushed it quickly from her mind.

'Come here,' Amy said, tears shining in her eyes as she held her arms wide for Lisa to step into them. 'I love you so much,' she murmured, her voice brimming with emotion. 'I'm really going to miss you, but promise me you'll come. Soon.'

'I promise,' Lisa said, keeping her fingers tightly crossed. 'Just take care of yourself, OK? And don't worry about the time zones, if you want to call, pick up the phone.'

'Same goes for you. Any time, day or night. Keep me in touch with everything you're doing, because I'll want to know.' Then, seeing that David was talking to Theo, she said quietly, 'Is everything all right between you two?'

Lisa feigned surprise. 'Of course,' she replied. 'And what a time to ask!'

'I know. I guess you just seem a little tense with each other today, but hey, that happens.' Cupping Lisa's face in her hands, she said, 'You'll call, won't you, if anything's ever bothering you?'

'I'll call,' Lisa promised. Amy had to go now, because if she didn't there was a very strong chance she'd start begging her to stay.

'OK, are you ready?' Theo said, seeing Amy still clinging to Lisa.

'Go on,' Lisa whispered raggedly. 'Call when you get to Hong Kong.'

'I will,' Amy assured her, and turning to take Theo's hand she started to walk in through the fast track, keeping her eyes straight ahead, unable to look back.

Feeling David's arm go around her, Lisa stifled a sob and leaned in closer to him. 'There's nothing to stop you going too,' he told her.

As her heart expanded with too much emotion, she turned to look at him. 'Yes there is,' she whispered, gazing into his eyes, 'there's you, and I wouldn't have it any other way.'

His smile was tender as he put a hand on her cheek. 'I want you to know,' he said, 'that you're free to change your mind at any time, and if you do I will completely understand.'

Chapter Twenty

Miles was feeling as though he'd been struck. In spite of this being the very fear he hadn't wanted to name, the worst possible explanation for David's aberrant behaviour, hearing it, knowing now that it was a reality, was too hard to take in. He wanted to rage out loud in protest, punch someone, kick life in the bollocks and howl with despair. David wasn't just his boss and mentor, he was his friend, his confidant, his rock-solid, one-way ticket to the top. He couldn't lose him now, and certainly not to this vile, malevolent disease that had no business afflicting anyone, least of all men with brains as capable and worthy and *needed* as David's.

'I'm sorry,' he said weakly, as David put a drink in his hand. When he looked up and saw the sadness in David's eyes he almost couldn't bear it. 'I'm so, so sorry,' he mumbled. 'I was afraid . . . It . . .' He took a breath to try and straighten his thoughts. 'You're sure?' he asked croakily. 'There can't be any mistake?'

'I'm sure,' David told him, sitting down with his own drink.

They were in his and Lisa's London flat, but

there was no sign of her, so Miles was left to wonder how she had taken the news. 'This must be very hard for . . . for your wife,' he said.

'Yes, I think it is,' David agreed. His smile was briefly edged in bitterness, but there was no hint of it in his tone as he said, 'She doesn't talk about it much. I wish she would, but maybe she thinks telling me anything is a waste of time now, I'll just forget, so what's the point?'

Miles's eyes were incredulous. 'I can't believe she feels like that,' he argued.

David sighed. 'No, I'm sure you're right, and self-pity isn't commendable, is it, so let's try to forget I said that.' His eyebrows rose ironically. 'Probably easier for me than for you,' he joked.

Even if it had been funny, Miles knew he'd never have been able to laugh. 'Where is she?' he asked. 'I thought you were both going to be here this evening?'

'We were, but she's had a tough day. Her sister left for . . . Hong Kong this afternoon, which is something she's been dreading. She said she was going shopping, but I'm hoping she'll have dropped in to see one of her friends.'

Miles nodded. 'So what happens next?' he asked. 'Are you going to carry on . . . ? I mean, do you have . . . ?' Was it OK to ask these questions? '. . . any idea how much longer you'll be able to?'

'No, not yet.'

Though David's expression had become impenetrable, it wasn't difficult for Miles to imagine the sense of outrage and helplessness he must be feeling, knowing that all his dreams and ambitions were being snuffed out like candles. What must it be like to see all the doors closing before you could even reach them? To know that life would continue along the same path for everyone else, while for you there was only an irreversible downward spiral to the end?

David's eyes seemed to soften as they returned to Miles. 'I hope you understand this is . . . Well, it's . . . A man of your talents and experience . . .' He clenched a hand in frustration. 'I can think of several Ministers already who'll be fighting over you once they find out you're . . . you know.'

Miles could hardly respond. What was there to say? As far as he was concerned no one else came even close to David's unselfconscious style of politics and lightning understanding of a situation, though he had to admit it was a while since he'd seen this in full operation. Quite suddenly it felt as though all the light was draining from his life. He didn't know what to do, or where to go from here.

'We'll need to work out how we're going to handle my departure,' David was saying, after glancing at the notebook he'd just opened. 'I admit it's not something I'm looking forward to. If I could I'd make myself disappear, if only to spare my loved ones. No, that's not true, I'd like to spare myself too. And you. Do you think you're up to dealing with it? Maybe you'd rather get out now, rather than be . . .' His voice broke on a wave of emotion and he pressed his fingers to his eyes. 'I'm sorry,' he said raggedly.

'I'll be there for you, David, for as long as you need me,' Miles told him, his voice thick with feeling.

David swallowed hard and nodded. 'I hope you

realise that I'd never have got as far as I have without you,' he said. 'Of course you know that, but I want you to know that I know it too. You've been like a son to me, Miles. I'm a very fortunate man to have had you heading my team. Am I embarrassing you?'

'No, yes,' Miles answered, 'but it works both ways, and it's a long way from over.'

At that David's eyes went down. 'Is it?' he said quietly. 'Who knows?' Then in a stronger voice he said, 'Back to my departure: obviously we should make Ted Astley, the Party chairman, our first port of call, so a decision can be made on the best date for a by-election.'

Was he reading aloud? Or just making it sound that way? Then the word by-election registered, and though Miles knew he should be handling this better than he was, it was hard when he kept seeing so many repercussions heading their way.

Realising David had fallen silent, he looked up to find himself being regarded with David's habitual amused curiosity. It was so familiar and reassuring that Miles almost heaved a sigh of relief. None of it was real. It was an elaborate joke, albeit in very poor taste.

'How would you feel about that?' David prompted.

'I'm sorry . . . I didn't catch what you said. Something . . .' He cleared his throat. 'Something about the by-election?'

'I asked if you'd be interested in standing,' David repeated.

Miles went very still as the world seemed to tilt and dip away from him.

'You'd have my full support, of course,' David continued, 'and I can't imagine there being too many objections from the Party bigwigs.'

Aware of a distant stirring deep inside him, Miles said, 'But this isn't the time to be . . . I mean OK, maybe one day, further down the line . . .'

'We all have to change our plans when circumstances dictate,' David reminded him, 'and I believe you'd make a fine MP. In fact, I wouldn't be surprised to see a swift rise through the ranks, knowing your skill and . . . mm yes . . .' He glanced at his notebook again. 'We've got a couple of very good . . . I don't . . . It . . .' He looked down the hall towards the front door as though expecting it to open.

'Are you OK?' Miles asked, feeling a horrible coldness coming over him. Could he be experiencing one of the mini-strokes he'd mentioned? If he was, what should he do?

David nodded distractedly. Then, appearing to register the book in his hands, he looked at it again, but whatever was written there didn't seem to be helping any more.

Miles couldn't think what to say. This was the last thing he'd expected when he'd come here this evening. In fact, all he'd prepared himself for was a preliminary chat about the parliamentary agenda for the next few weeks. 'Would you like me to call Lisa?' he offered.

David seemed puzzled. 'No, her sister left today,' he said, as though it were an answer. 'She needs some time alone. Will you have another drink? I think I will.'

Miles thought he would too.

Several minutes later, with two more large Scotches in front of them, Miles was watching David fiddling about with his iPhone.

'I've made notes here,' David told him, turning the phone so Miles could see. 'It's part of my backup to be sure I've covered everything. I've started to make a habit of doing this. It's recommended, you know, for people with dementia.' There was the bitterness again, as fleeting as it was understandable.

Miles said, 'Can I ask . . . ? Are they giving you any treatment?'

David nodded. 'Yes, but there's no cure. I expect you know that though, don't you?'

As David's eyes dropped back to his notes Miles's heart was pounding with horror. 'Yes, I do,' he answered quietly. 'My grandmother has Alzheimer's.'

David looked up, appearing surprised and confused. 'Have you told me that before?' he asked.

Miles shook his head.

'Oh dear. Well, I'm very sorry to hear it. Where is she?'

'In a care home not far from my parents. They go to see her a couple of times a month. She doesn't know who they are, though.'

'A care home,' David repeated. Then, after writing something in his notebook, 'Shall we start drawing up some plans of how we proceed from here?'

It was over an hour later that Lisa returned to find them engrossed in their 'extrication strategy', as they were calling it, with David looking at least a couple of sheets to the wind.

'Hello Miles,' she said, as he shot ridiculously to his feet. 'How are you?'

She looked exhausted, he was thinking, and wished there was something he could do to make her feel better. 'I'm fine, thank you,' he replied, 'but very upset by the news, of course.'

She nodded, and going to drop a kiss on David's head, she said, 'I think you've had enough for today, my darling. Time to shower and think about dinner.'

'But we're in the middle of things here,' he protested.

'It's OK, I can come back tomorrow,' Miles assured him.

'Why don't you stay for something to eat?' David invited.

Miles's eyes went to Lisa, but she wasn't giving him a lead, so he said, 'I've already got plans, thank you.'

'Are you going by taxi?' Lisa asked. Then, without waiting for an answer, 'I'll walk down with you.'

As soon as they were out on the street Miles said, 'I'm so sorry this is happening.'

Her smile seemed distant. 'Did he talk to you about standing in the by-election?' she asked.

'Yes, he did.'

'Good. So what do you think?'

'Well, I'm flattered, of course, but filling David's shoes . . .'

'We'll give you our support.'

'Thank you, but . . .' He was embarrassingly close to tears. 'I'm finding it hard to talk about this now,' he confessed.

At that she seemed at a loss and only dropped her head.

Resisting the urge to reach for her hand, he said, 'I'm sorry. Your sister going probably couldn't have come at a worse time. Does she know about David? Yes, of course . . .'

'No, she doesn't. I'll tell her after she's been there for a while. It would have made it too difficult for her to leave if I'd told her now.'

He swallowed hard, searching for something else to say. 'You seem . . . very alone,' he blurted and immediately felt himself starting to colour. 'I'm sorry, that was inappropriate. I . . .'

'It's all right,' she said with the ghost of a smile. 'I'm just tired, but not alone.' Then, after taking a breath, 'I should probably let you go now. I just wanted to be sure he'd remembered what he needed to discuss with you, and to ask if you'd mind keeping, you know, all this to yourself for now, until we're ready to go public.'

'Of course,' he assured her. 'You know you can rely on me for discretion. Like you, I have his best interests at heart.'

Seeming to appreciate his words, she put a hand to his cheek as she said, 'I don't know how much you'd guessed before he told you, but even so, this has been a blow for you, hasn't it? I know how fond you are of him.'

With his throat tightening, Miles put his hand over hers and held it. 'We'll do our best for him,' he said softly.

She managed another smile. 'Yes, we will,' she said. 'He'll be in your hands while he's in London. It gives me confidence to know that.'

With feeling, Miles said, 'And I won't let him down. I promise. Or you. If there's ever anything you need, if you want to talk, or you think there's something I can do, you only have to pick up the phone.'

'Thank you,' she whispered hoarsely. 'That's very kind.' She turned to glance up at the windows, but there was no sign of David. 'I should go up now,' she said, 'he'll know we're down here talking about him and he'll want to hear everything we said when I go back.'

Wishing he could use her hand to pull her into his arms, Miles looked up at the windows too, and said, 'I meant what I said, if you need a friend . . . I know you probably have dozens, but I'd be honoured to count myself amongst them.'

With a more genuine-seeming smile, she turned back to him, saying, 'You're very sweet, thank you. To tell you the truth . . . Well, I hope you don't mind me saying, but I think Rosalind could be more in need right now than I am.'

Though it wasn't the answer he'd hoped for, he had no trouble believing it. 'I'll give her a call,' he promised.

When she started to move away he kept hold of her hand. 'There is just one thing before you go,' he said.

She turned back, but he could tell that wherever her thoughts were, they were no longer with him, and realising he was right on the verge of making a fool of himself, he let her go. 'It's nothing,' he said, and after watching her walk back through the front door he went on his way to hail a cab.

She really didn't need to know now that David's enemies were once again at work trying to discredit him, or how they were, once again, using her to achieve it. The fact that they'd dug some woman out of the past to accuse Lisa of stealing her husband was scheduled, he'd been told, to make the front page of one of the Sunday tabloids this week.

It wouldn't happen, he decided. He was going to make sure of that, and taking out his mobile he connected to one of his sources. 'Tell the editor,' he said, 'that if he pulls the story, I'll have a much bigger exclusive for him further down the line,' and clicking off he went on walking, feeling very uncomfortable about using David's condition to try to protect him and his wife, but what else was he to do?

It was just over a week later that David threw open Lisa's study door saying, 'Put on your coat, I want you to come with me.'

Looking up from the email she was writing to Amy, Lisa said, 'Where to?'

'You'll see,' he replied mysteriously, and after throwing her one of his more roguish smiles he went off to get in the car.

To Lisa's relief, apart from a few absent minded moments and a heated exchange with a telemarketer the day before, he'd been in quite good spirits recently, indicating, she'd decided, that there had been no dreaded infarcts in his brain lately, so he was, for the time being at least, seeming much more like his normal self. Even the post-diagnostic visit from the memory nurse two days ago hadn't seemed to get him down. If anything, the way she'd arrived wreathed in smiles and as pregnant with information as she was with a baby had seemed to lighten his mood, which had come as a relief because she'd fully expected the awful reminder to send him crashing into a depression. For her part Lisa had found it difficult to get the visit out of her mind, in particular the outrageous way both she and David had behaved. It was the mention of a dementia cafe that had done it. Lisa had sensed straight away that David was about to laugh, and when he started to lose it there was nothing she could do to hold herself back.

Amazingly, the nurse, Jackie, hadn't been in the least bit fazed. In fact she'd dutifully chortled along with them, saying, 'Yes, it can be lots of fun at these monthly get-togethers, you just wait and see.'

By then both Lisa and David were close to helpless, and the way Jackie was bouncing around so joyously wasn't helping matters at all.

'It can be a great source of support and comfort to laugh and chat with others,' she chuckled on. 'They'll all be experiencing the very issues that, sooner or later, you'll have to be dealing with too. They'll explain how they're coping, and give you some handy hints on the best ways to distract someone who's pacing, or wandering, or trying to express themselves without much success.

'It's important,' she ran on, apparently still not in the least flustered by their childish hilarity, 'to know how to create a safe haven for your husband, because there will be times when he feels disoriented and insecure and won't be able to say why.'

Lisa looked at David and when he gave her a wink she lost it again.

'The people at the cafe will have come across all sorts of things that you probably can't even imagine right now, or don't want to,' Jackie burbled on in her bizarrely jolly way, 'and I wouldn't blame you for that. It's a very good idea to appreciate this time you have together, especially with David being so lucid and understanding of his own situation. But at the same time we have to be mindful of the things that need to be done. For example, have you contacted the DVLA yet?'

'I have,' Lisa assured her.

'And what about a solicitor to organise the power of attorney and living will? I expect Dr Manning explained about that, did she?'

Since David seemed to have stopped listening, Lisa said, 'Yes, we've been to see someone, so it's all in hand.'

Jackie then went on to inform them about future visits and how regularly they'd happen, plus the importance of going to their GP whenever they felt worried or baffled by a new turn of events. She concluded with another upbeat sell of all the support groups and websites they might find useful, by which time David had ceased to find anything funny and was looking distinctly fed up with it all.

However, he'd bounced back in next to no time, and now, apparently jazzed by his secret mission, he was driving them out of their lane and down the hill to head deeper into the constituency, instead of towards town which was what Lisa had been expecting.

'I'd really like to know where we're going,' she told him as they motored on through the villages and out into open countryside.

'I want to introduce you to some friends of mine,' he replied. 'Well, I've only met them a couple of times, but I think it will be good for you to meet them too.'

Turning cold as the suspicion of what could be happening crept over her, she turned to look at him. 'David, I don't think this is a good idea,' she said darkly.

'But you don't know where we're going.'

'I think I do. You're taking me to Burnham Down, aren't you?'

He cast her a quick look, apparently impressed. 'Yes, I am,' he confirmed. 'I didn't know you'd heard of it.'

She didn't tell him she'd heard of just about every care home around since checking them all out on the Internet, she only said, 'I think you should turn round.'

'Absolutely not. I want you to see for yourself what dementia does to a person.'

'David, you can't treat people like that. They're not animals in a zoo to be gawped at as though they don't know any better.'

'We won't be gawping,' he corrected, 'we'll be visiting, and my whole point is that most of them don't know any better. They're gone, Lisa. We don't know where, no one can tell us that. All we know is that they're no longer who they used to be . . .'

'David, please turn round,' she said, starting to get upset.

'We can't. I've already told them to expect us and I'm not going to let them down now.'

Realising she wasn't going to win, she turned to gaze out at the passing fields, understanding why he wanted to do this, but still desperately wishing he wouldn't. And as Burnham Down finally appeared on the horizon, she felt herself starting to put up barriers as though trying to keep out any sense of this becoming a future reality. 'Do you remember the matron's name?' she asked, as they approached the gates.

He frowned. 'No, but I'm sure it'll be in my book.'

Reaching for it, she leafed through to that day's notes and though she was faintly baffled by some of what was written there, the words Matron: Sally Gosling stood out clearly enough, so fortunately that answered that.

'Does she know about you?' she asked, putting the book back in his folio case.

'Mm, I don't think so.'

'You mean you can't remember whether or not you told her?'

'I'm going to presume I didn't, because we're not telling anyone yet. Are we?'

Since it sounded like a genuine question she said, 'No, not yet,' but after speaking to Miles yesterday when he'd told her about the deal he'd struck with one of the tabloids to get her off the front page, she knew it was only a matter of time now before some clever hack managed to work it out for her or himself.

One day at a time, Lisa, she reminded herself as they pulled up outside the sprawling old stately

435

home with its towering Gothic windows and glistening russet facade. The gardens were exquisitely kept, with lots of walkways and benches and some impressive examples of animal topiary. Was this where he wanted to come when she wasn't able to manage any more?

'Before we go in,' he said, coming round to open her door, 'you know the reason we're doing this, don't you? It's because I want you to fully understand the journey we're on and where it's going to end.'

'I already do,' she told him, spotting a cheery old face watching them from a downstairs window, and giving her a smile. Touched by how excited the old lady seemed, she smiled again and gave her a wave.

Even before they could knock on the front door it was swinging open, and a slight, rosy-cheeked woman with a sprightly thatch of curls clamped to the top of her head and an infectious smile was emerging in a gust of hot air.

'David, how lovely to see you,' she cried. 'Come in, come in. And you must be Lisa. I hope it's OK to call you that? I'm Sally, one of the matrons here. Everyone's looking forward to meeting you. This is quite an event you know, to have our MP dropping in for a visit with his new bride.'

There was so much friendliness oozing from Sally Gosling's compact little person that Lisa couldn't help liking her on sight. She was clearly someone who loved what she did, and that alone made her special, but so did the delightfully heart-shaped face and the kindly blue eyes that must surely be able to make even the most insecure of her charges feel valued and safe.

'We've organised tea in the drawing room,' she said, leading them through a brightly painted entrance hall where a rogues' gallery of presumably past and current residents was keeping good company with the Queen and some of her family. 'Terry will take your coats,' Sally was telling them. 'Where is she? Ah, there you are, dear. Our visitors have arrived so you can do the honours, but do make sure you put them under the stairs, won't you? Remember, you took them outside the last time and I don't know how long we spent trying to find them.'

Bent with arthritis, very wrinkled and probably the wrong side of ninety, Terry all but snatched their coats and bundled them up like old rags.

'I'm sorry,' Sally said in a whisper. 'Believe it or not, she'd kick up a terrible fuss if I didn't allow her to do it. She spent thirty odd years at the Savoy, taking care of people's coats. That's quite something, isn't it?'

'Should we tip her when we leave?' David asked, while Lisa wanted to laugh at the way Terry slung their coats at the bottom of the stairs and started back again.

'Oh I'm sure fifty p would be very welcome,' Sally replied, having a chuckle as she caught Lisa's smile. 'One of the staff will pick them up when she's not looking. Now, here we all are,' she said, turning to where the other residents and a few visitors were waiting to be introduced. 'We're mostly girls here. Twelve to be exact, with only three boys, but Harold's not feeling too good today so he's up in his room. Christopher and Bob have joined us though, as you can see – and going round the rest of the circle, we have Gracie with her daughter, Jacqueline; Anita, Norma, Sarah, Ivy and Beat. Oh, and we mustn't forget Lizzie who's brought little Oliver to meet his granddad Bobby, who's one of our longest residents. Oliver is how old now, Lizzie? Six weeks?'

'That's right,' Lizzie confirmed, blushing slightly as she smiled down at the bundle of her tiny sleeping son.

'The other girls are either out with relatives, or at hospital appointments,' Sally continued. 'Oh, and as you can see we're all wearing badges to help you with our names. This was Sarah's idea.'

As Lisa looked at Sarah she felt her heart churn with pity. The way the old lady was sitting, slumped off to one side in her chair, her hands clenched almost like paws in front of her with her eyes moving vaguely from side to side, it was hard to credit her with managing a thought, much less an idea. Had she heard what Sally said? Was she able to appreciate being included?

Once the introductions were over and cake and tea had been brought in, Lisa and David separated to go and speak to each of their hosts in turn. Lisa started with Sarah, pulling up a chair next to her, and gently touching one of her hands as she said, 'Hello, I'm Lisa. I'm very glad to meet you, Sarah.'

Sarah's eyes slid to the bottom corners of their sockets. Had she forgotten how to direct them?

'I can see you're wearing a wedding ring,' Lisa said, already struggling to keep her emotions at bay. 'I got married quite recently. It was a lovely day. I expect yours was too, when you got married. Did you have any bridesmaids? I had one, my niece, Roxy, who's recently started at Oxford. We're very proud of her.' She continued to gaze into the lonely pale blue eyes and had to fight an urge to hug her.

'You'll probably be surprised to hear,' Sally said, coming up behind her, 'that she's only sixty-eight.'

Lisa could hardly have felt more shocked. She'd never have said so, in case Sarah could hear her, but she looked at least ninety.

'That's early onset for you,' Sally murmured sadly. 'If I showed you a picture of her ten, even five years ago you'd never know it was the same woman.'

Lisa was finding it hard to catch her breath. 'Does she . . .' She tried again. 'Does she have any family?'

'Oh yes. Her husband comes every Sunday to give her some tea, and her son drops in from time to time, when he's in the area. They used to come more regularly, when she knew who they were . . . Maybe she still does, but she can't communicate any more, and that's very upsetting for her loved ones.'

Even so, Lisa was thinking, how could they just leave her here, all but abandoned as she waited to die?

'Come and say hello to Beat,' Sally said. 'She's very excited about meeting you.'

As she rose to her feet Lisa stooped to kiss Sarah gently on the cheek, then paused to watch David who appeared to be flirting with Norma and Ivy.

It was very touching, she was thinking, to watch two such elderly ladies giggling and nudging each other with girlish delight.

'My daughter never comes to see me,' she heard someone wailing behind her.

Lisa turned round to see Anita sitting with a younger woman, who must have arrived while Lisa wasn't looking.

'Mum, I'm here,' the younger woman said.

'Where's my daughter?' Anita wept. 'She said she'd come.'

'Oh, Mum, you're being difficult again. Why don't we have a cup of tea and you can tell me what our MP was saying to you when I came in. Isn't it lovely that he's brought his new wife to see you?'

Starting to feel emotional again, Lisa followed Sally over to where Beat was sitting in an armchair, holding a cup of tea and smiling vacantly as Sally began chatting to her. 'Hello, Beat,' Lisa said. 'Do you mind if I join you?'

'Oh no, not at all,' Beat assured her. 'You're very pretty. I used to be once, and I do my best to keep myself up together. A girl shouldn't be seen without her make-up, is what I always say.'

Since her sunken mouth had been transformed into a startling ruby-red gash between her colourless cheeks, there was no mistaking her love of lipstick, or eyeshadow, given the electric-blue streaks on her papery lids.

'Getting old's not much fun,' she told Lisa chattily, 'but I'm very lucky. They take care of me ever so well here. Nothing's too much trouble. She's an angel, our Sally, aren't you, dear?'

Sally grimaced. 'I wouldn't mind a pair of wings, that's for sure,' she retorted.

'I've been here for nearly ten years now,' Beat rattled on, 'but I shall be leaving soon.' She glanced at her watch. 'My mother's on her way to pick me up.'

Lisa's expression showed no more than tenderness as the old lady glanced at her watch again. The chances of her mother still being alive had to be less than zero.

As Lisa made to get up, Beat suddenly gasped, 'Oh my goodness, I'm feeling very unwell, Sally. I think it quite possible I'm going to die.'

'Oh dear,' Sally said, patting her hand. 'That's a pity, but would you mind waiting until we've finished our tea, dear?'

'Oh no, no, not at all,' Beat assured her.

Not sure whether she wanted to laugh or cry, Lisa said, 'How about another piece of cake?'

'Goodness, no, I have to think of my figure.' Then with a mischievous twinkle, 'Oh, go on then. 'Tis my birthday, after all.'

'Really?' Lisa said, suspecting it probably wasn't. 'Then I should wish you a happy birthday.'

Beat's face lit up. 'Lovely, lovely,' she cooed. 'My mother will be here to pick me up in a minute.'

After leaving Beat devouring a third piece of cake as she waited for her mother, Lisa went to stand beside David who was with Bob, trying to coax him to lift his head so he could see his new grandson.

'Look Dad, it's Oliver,' Lizzie was saying. 'He's awake. Can you hear him snuffling? Dad?'

Bob's head continued to loll forward, his chin almost resting on his chest.

'Would you like some help, my friend?' David offered, and taking Bob's face gently between his hands he tilted it up so he could see the baby. Though Bob's eyes were open, the lids were drooping and he appeared to be gazing off to one side.

Moving round to get in his eyeline, Lizzie said, 'Here he is, Dad. Can you see him? He's lovely, isn't he? Daphne's thrilled to bits about having a little brother. I told you, didn't I, this one would be a boy? We're christening him Oliver Robert, after you, only you're Robert Oliver. Do you like that, Dad?'

Bob made no response at all, then a single tear rolled from the corner of his eye, and Lisa had to turn away to hide the tears that rushed to her own. What did he know? How much could he understand?

They stayed for over an hour, chatting with each of the residents, or simply sitting with those who were unable to respond, until several of them started to doze off, and after bidding a fond farewell to the others Lisa and David crept out quietly and got into the car.

For a while they simply sat staring at the gardens, too shaken up to say very much.

In the end it was David who broke the silence. 'It affected me before when I came here,' he said. 'Today it was . . . Well, it was pretty sobering, to say the least.'

Lisa nodded. Her throat was still tight, and her heart so weighted with pity and dread it was hard to breathe. 'Is this where you want to come? Is that what you're trying to tell me?'

'No,' he replied. He pressed his fingers to his eyes to relieve some of the tension. 'I want to spend whatever lucid time I have left doing everything I can to make a difference for the people in there, and others like them. If I can do that, then what's happening to me . . . What's happ— Won't be for nothing.' He turned to look at her. 'Do you think . . . Can you . . .' His eyes closed as he lost his words.

'Of course I'll help you,' she said, certain that was what he'd been about to ask. 'I was thinking about it while we were in there, and I was wondering . . . Maybe we should start by trying to get young people more involved. We're all going to be old one day, but no one ever wants to think about it. It's as though the elderly and infirm have stopped mattering, or have become an embarrassment, when they're so dear and sweet and in such need of being loved. If we could enlist the help of some young celebrities . . .'

'That's it,' he said. 'That's what we should do. Try to bring the generations together.'

'We'll make a list of sporting heroes, soap stars, you name it, when we get home,' she told him. 'We're going to make it trendy to help the aged, and raise more money than they'll know what to do with.'

He smiled into her eyes, and reached for her hand. 'It must have scared you to see what I'm going to become,' he said softly.

Unable to deny it, she said, 'Yes, but if you think it's changed my mind about standing by you, you're wrong.'

He continued to smile. 'To be honest, I wasn't

sure whether it would, or not,' he confessed, 'but what I am hoping is that it's given you some understanding of how important it is that we all have a choice. Without wishing any disrespect to . . . Mm, I don't want to end up . . . Or have you and Rosalind . . .'

'David, no,' she said, taking her hand away. 'I know what you're going to say, and I can't . . .'

'Darling, please listen.'

Lisa sat staring at nothing, waiting for him to go on, but he didn't, and when she turned to him she couldn't hold back her emotions any longer, because his eyes were shining with tears. Whatever he'd been about to say had apparently vanished, leaving behind only the residue of urgency for it to be said, and the knowledge that he'd failed to make his point.

Chapter Twenty-One

David was standing at the foot of Rosalind's garden, his hair being tousled by the wind as he watched Lawrence throwing a ball for Lucy in the meadow below. Several weeks had passed since the day he'd had his worst fears confirmed, the day he'd felt as though a part of him had gone to wherever Catrina was now and hadn't come back. The ache, the confusion, the rage, were only easily set aside during the hours he slept, or when he was waiting for Catrina to call, or walk in the door. To wait for Catrina was easier than to know she was never coming back.

Her funeral was an event he remembered only fitfully, as though it were a film with batches of dark frames passing through a projector. The coffin of a woman too young to lie in it; hands shaking and comforting; voices joined in song; curtains closing for a final time. He'd spoken, but how well, or what he'd said, he was unable to recall. He suspected he'd lost his words at times, but perhaps the other mourners would have put it down to the wrenching sadness he'd felt, and the overwhelming sense of loss.

He guessed they'd all know by now, if they

watched the news or read the papers, that his other great loss was under way. After the announcement, delivered in a press release from his office, because when the time had come to face the cameras he'd lost his confidence, they'd been inundated with requests for interviews which he'd had to decline, and messages of sympathy and moral support. Cards, emails, letters and texts had come flooding in from around the world. He had little recollection of what they said, but he'd read most and helped Catrina reply to those that required it. Except it wasn't Catrina, it was Lisa. His new wife Lisa, who was having to bear this burden after knowing him for not much more than a year. How much easier it would be if he were able to turn to Catrina, who'd been such a vital part of his life for so long.

He'd started to wonder lately if his perception of himself was different to the way others perceived him. Did they, like him, see a man whose body was in good health, and whose wits were slightly blunted from time to time, but were on the whole as sharp and as fast as ever? Or were they seeing a man whose shell was intact, but whose mind was disintegrating invisibly and whose actions were slow and erratic, annoying and disruptive? Was he both of those men? Were things happening to him during moments of emptiness or misunderstanding that he was later unable to recall? How would he know unless he asked? And then for how long would he remember?

He wasn't yet losing a sense of who he was, or where he belonged, or of what was going on in his brain, that was probably still a long way off, but he did know that sometimes it was as though a tight lid was crushing down on his thoughts. He could almost feel them being trapped at their roots, having the air squeezed from between them so that they melded one into the other and became an alphabet soup of no thoughts at all. He didn't speak then, it was best not to. At other times he was like a conductor who'd lost control of his orchestra; percussion and brass were suddenly colliding with woodwind and strings; pianos were sounding like drums and clarinets like violins. A grim, relentless symphony of tangled sounds and malfunctioning plaques. He could write that down, given time, but he'd never be able to say it.

He realised now that many thoughts didn't need words, only perception and feeling. For instance, he knew where he was standing, and that the weather was cold and the ground underfoot was wet. He didn't need to utter the words to himself, he just knew it. Operating with instincts as opposed to thought was a natural process that required no decisions or explanations. It just was, and reminded him that he was still aware, still functioning, still alive. When he looked at the natural world he understood that it only existed for him, for everyone, in their minds, because if the senses couldn't absorb and evaluate it, and if no one had the wit to admire or fear or tend it, it would be as though it wasn't there. What would a world be like without trees and fields, no sky, no sun, no sea, no stars? Time would have no meaning once he lost the ability to read a clock, but what would that change in his mind?

His brain was shrinking, his memory was

rolling away like a wave – brainwave? – from the shore, never to return. He'd come to understand now, in a way he'd never considered before, that life was only possible because of that part of the brain called a memory. It was where everything was stored, to be recalled when the eyes saw something, or someone, familiar. If it was a person, or an object, or an event that he'd never seen before, he'd rely on someone else's knowledge, which came from their memory, to explain it, and then it would be locked away in his. The same with things he heard or touched or smelled. Everything had to be remembered, or there was nothing. If he couldn't recapture words he had learned he'd have no language, if he couldn't remember how to walk, he'd go nowhere, if he forgot how to feel he'd be no one.

He believed that most days, and most hours of the day, he was lucid. Lisa assured him he was, and he believed her, because he had no reason not to. He'd experienced shifts in his consciousness, however, when he'd either lost track of time, or failed to recognise straight away where he was. How long did those lapses last? Where did he go, exactly, when they occurred? Was he suffering a stroke? Was his grasp on reality draining away, like sand through his fingers? When there was no more reality, what then? Hallucination? Confusion? Chaos?

'Dad? Dad, what are you doing standing there?'

Turning around he saw Rosalind coming down through the garden towards him, looking pretty in her dusky pink wool coat and scarf. He put on a smile as he held out his arms. She used to run into them as a child and he'd swing her up so high that she'd shriek and laugh and cling to his face with all her might.

'You used to flatten my nose,' he told her, bringing her into a hug.

'I what?' she said, kissing his cheek. 'Where's Lawrence? Did you collect him from school?'

A wasteland appeared before him, with no stones to pick up and turn into words.

'Ah, there he is,' she said, spotting him in the meadow. 'You shouldn't allow him to go so close to the lake unless you're down there with him. What if Lucy's ball ended up in the water? Lawrence,' she shouted. 'Come on, time for tea.'

Hearing her voice Lucy began bounding up to the garden, leaving Lawrence to fetch the ball from where it had landed.

'How long have you lot been out here?' Rosalind demanded, trying to tamp down Lucy's enthusiasm, while ruffling her ears. 'You must be freezing. I know I am.'

'Oh, you're just a girl,' David teased. 'We boys don't feel the cold, do we, Lawrence?'

'No,' Lawrence agreed. 'We're tough and strong and even if the temperature was absolute zero, which is the lowest it can possibly go, we could stand it.'

'And what is absolute zero?' David asked, falling in beside him as they started towards the house.

'Minus two hundred and seventy-three point fifteen centigrade,' Lawrence replied without hesitation. 'Mum, can we have pizza for tea and Coca-Cola?'

'No, we're having shepherd's pie with a very small helping of apple crumble to follow.'

'A big one!' Lawrence demanded. 'Are you having tea with us?' he asked David.

'I was hoping I might, if there's enough,' David replied.

'Of course there's enough,' Rosalind called back over her shoulder. 'There always is for you.'

'Can Lucy have shepherd's pie?' Lawrence asked. 'It's her favourite.'

'You say that about everything, except her proper food, and I suspect that's because you can't share it.'

'Yes I can, yes I can. She'd let me have some if I wanted it. Harry Clark says that if you rub a dog's tummy long enough it will have a puppy, but that's not true, is it?'

Rosalind scowled at her father before opening the door. To her that sounded as though the other children had been teasing Lawrence again.

'No, it's not true,' David replied, sounding amused. 'But you can tell Harry Clark that if he wants to rub Lucy's tummy to give it a try, I'm sure she wouldn't mind a bit.'

'Do you have homework?' Rosalind asked, unwinding her scarf as she unbuttoned her coat.

'Maths and History. We're doing Roman numerals and Roman emperors ... Augustus, Tiberius, Caligula ...'

'All right, all right, get some juice and off you go upstairs. Tea should be ready in about an hour.'

'Can I show you my homework when I've finished?' he asked David.

'I should hope so,' David assured him.

While Rosalind took their coats into the utility room, David put on the kettle, then glanced through his notebook as he waited for her to finish playing back her messages.

'Oh Dad, you haven't got that thing again, have you?' she complained, catching sight of it before he put it away.

'If I'd forgotten it I might not have remembered to ask . . .'

'If you're going to mention Jerry, please don't,' she jumped in. 'I haven't spoken to him for over a week, but I'm sure he hasn't changed his mind about wanting a divorce.'

David nodded slowly, realising this was possibly something she'd told him before. 'And what do you want?' he asked cautiously.

With a sigh she shook her head uncertainly. 'I don't suppose there's any point trying to hang on to him, is there?' she said. 'In a way I wish he'd gone when I first found out about the affair, if he had I'd probably be over it by now. Anyway, I don't want to talk about it, it still upsets me and he isn't worth it. Tell me about you, and what you've been up to since I last saw you.'

'Well,' he said, sitting back in his chair, and allowing a few moments for a memory or two to stir. His eyes went down as he considered taking out his book, but if it annoyed her . . . He was searching for answers, but though his thoughts were forming, trying to turn themselves into words, when they came to be spoken they were like snow falling on warm ground.

'. . . then you might as well give up now,' he heard her saying.

'Mm?' he said, looking up. How long had she been speaking? 'Give up what now?' he asked.

She glanced at him suspiciously. 'Do you ever listen to anything I say?' she demanded. 'If you ask me, you only ever hear what you want to hear, so I don't know why I bother wasting my breath.'

'Give up what now?' he pressed.

'OK, give up being an MP. Now you've told the world you've got dementia no one trusts you any more. They're not coming to the surgeries or town hall meetings unless they're fellow sufferers, or someone in their family is, so what's the point?'

'The point,' he said carefully, 'is that these people need to be heard too, and they feel, understandably, that I will be more sympathetic to their issues than someone who's fortunate enough not to be sharing their world.'

'Oh, for heaven's sake, listen to yourself,' she cried. 'I've told you before, you wouldn't be able to speak the way you do if you had any form of dementia.'

'And you know this because?'

'Because I do. Everyone does . . .'

'Rosalind, you don't know anything about it, other than what you've heard or seen on TV. Now, I'm not going to waste our time arguing about it,' he pressed on, taking out his book to steal another glimpse. 'There's something I want to discuss with you that's . . .' Seeing what it was, he hesitated. This was going to be too difficult for her. He didn't know how to begin. Would he even be able to carry it through? His eyes moved up to an earlier note, which he read quickly, and then said, 'Lisa and I went to see a lawyer, mainly to sort out my will and who is going . . .'

'And you've given her power of attorney,' she broke in snappishly. 'Yes, you told me, and why not? It's what she's after . . .'

'Rosalind, stop,' he said irritably. 'What I'm trying to tell you is that I want to exercise my right to choose when I die.'

As her face drained, he realised he'd been too abrupt and made to reach for her hand as though to soften the words, but she whisked it away.

'I've – I've tried to discuss this with Lisa,' he stumbled on, 'but I . . . Please listen,' he said, as she started to walk away. 'I've read a lot about it now, and I . . .' Even though he was moving forward the ground was disappearing. 'I don't want you or Lisa to have to cope . . . Your lives are too precious . . .'

'Hers might be,' she snapped, 'but you can't speak for me when I . . .'

His hand went up. 'Lisa feels . . . from my point of view.' What was his point of view? What was he talking about? The wind was blowing, but nothing was moving.

'. . . I mean it with all my heart, Dad, I'd rather kill myself than help her to kill you – and please don't forget they are both mortal sins.'

His eyes briefly closed. 'Darling, you are not a practising Catholic. Your mother . . .'

'But I am still a Catholic, and there is nothing in this world that will induce me to help you or *her* to do what you're asking. There's nothing wrong with you, Dad. OK, you're a bit absent-minded at times, but you always have been, it's part of who you are, we all know that, and love you for it, so to start buying into all this crap she's feeding you . . .'

'Rosalind, that's enough. I'm not going to allow you to speak about your mother like that . . .'

'She's not my mother.'

'No, no.' His head was hurting. There was something he needed to do now, but he couldn't think what it was. It was vital, he had a sense of that, so why wasn't it coming to him? He was the conductor who'd lost his orchestra again. He put his head down and forced himself to breathe. His instincts were begging for words. He was going to do this. He had to . . . He was in charge of his mind. It wasn't the other way around . . . And yet who was he, if he wasn't his mind?

He wasn't sure how much time had passed, how could he know? If he'd looked at the clock before, then he'd forgotten now what he'd seen. He couldn't even be sure, immediately, of how long he had been here, but he was in Rosalind's house and looking at her . . . That was all that mattered . . . His daughter. She looked worried, ready to cry, or shout, or shake him . . .

He put up his hands. He needed to laugh, or smile. Was he doing that? He must have been, because her expression was showing relief.

'You were outside in the cold for too long,' she told him.

He tried to remember when that was, but couldn't. Then like threads being whisked away in the wind, he managed to catch hold of the tail end of some and remember what he'd been saying, why he was here. He knew instinctively that he had something to help him, but he couldn't think what it was.

'I'm sorry, what did you say?' he asked, hoping she would guide him back on track.

'I didn't say anything. It was you who started talking about Mum . . . Oh please don't start that again.'

He'd found his notebook. Ignoring her, he turned to the most recent entries and quickly scanned them. It was no good, he couldn't marshal his thoughts. He was too tired, too stressed . . . He'd rather go and sit with Lawrence. He was peaceful and undemanding. With a sigh he said, 'You're angry, so I'm going to let it drop now, just please try, for my sake, to find it in your heart to . . .' To find what? What was he attempting to say?

Since David had left for London that morning, with the instruction 'get off train at Paddington, Miles will be waiting,' written in his notebook, Lisa had been trying not to worry about whether he'd arrived safely and was coping all right. If he wasn't she was sure she'd have heard, but even so she'd been in her study for over two hours now, struggling to compile a list of young musicians and sports stars who might be willing to become involved in their awareness campaign, and had still achieved next to nothing.

She'd imagined, when she'd dropped David at the station, that it was going to be a relief to spend some time alone, but it wasn't happening like that at all. Instead she couldn't seem to get past her edginess, or the guilty conscience that kept telling her she should have gone with him, even though he'd ferociously insisted he wasn't such a bubble-head yet that he couldn't get himself to London alone.

She glanced at the time and wondered if it was too early to call him. Perhaps she should try Miles instead, making it clear that he mustn't let David know she was checking up on him. Deciding that was a good idea, she picked up the phone and pressed the auto dial to Miles's mobile. After being diverted to voicemail she left a brief message asking Miles to call when he had a chance.

He rang an hour later to let her know that everything was fine. David was over at the Foreign Office with Colin Larch at the moment and was, as far as Miles knew, still intending to catch the three thirty train back to Bristol.

'Will you go to the station with him?' Lisa asked.

'Of course, but I don't think he'll like it. He says we're treating him like an imbecile and he hasn't reached that stage yet.'

Easily able to imagine it, Lisa said, 'Please don't let him bully you into leaving him alone. We don't want him to end up on the wrong Tube, or train, being whisked off to the middle of nowhere.'

'Don't worry, that's not going to happen,' Miles assured her. 'I'll call again when he's on the way back so you'll know what time to be at the station.'

After ringing off, Lisa returned to her study and this time managed to get the entire way through an email to Roxy asking for some suggestions on the best celebrities to contact for a charitable project. Then she sent another to Amy, with whom she'd spent hours on the phone the day David had gone public with his dementia, explaining and apologising and promising never to keep something so crucial to herself again. It was a relief not having to hide anything any more, but it still wasn't the same as having Amy there. Her mother had taken the news badly, as though it was going to impact on her life and plans for the future, when, as Lisa had told her in a snappish moment, it actually wasn't about her. Unfortunately that was becoming typical of Matilda these days, always thinking of herself first – maybe it was a symptom of getting old.

She didn't want to be in touch with her other friends at the moment, all of whom had tried contacting her after hearing the news. She knew they meant well, but talking about David to people he barely knew, especially when it concerned something so sensitive, always left her feeling wretchedly disloyal. She hadn't even called Tony again, in spite of the many times she'd wanted to. At least he had a way of raising her spirits and would no doubt remind her that there was a life beyond this diagnosis, but it wasn't right to lean on him the way he'd offered. David would hate it if he knew and given the way Tony felt about her, it really wasn't fair on him either.

Feeling a tight band closing around her head, and an ocean of unshed tears flooding her heart, she looked at the phone that was lying on her desk next to her coffee cup. There was one other person she could call, but she really didn't know if she had the courage to. Feeling so vulnerable and afraid of whatever trick fate would play on her next, did she have what it took to set herself up for another blow?

In the end, without allowing herself any more time to dither, she picked up the phone and pressed in Rosalind's mobile number.

After three rings Rosalind's answer came cautiously down the line. 'Hello?'

Lisa's eyes were closed. She was so tense that her voice sounded ragged as she said, 'Is that Rosalind?'

'Yes. Who's this?'

Lisa took a breath. 'It's Lisa,' she said. 'Please don't hang up on me. We need to talk about your dad and what . . .'

'I can't believe . . . ! I'm sorry, I have nothing to say to you,' and the next instant the line went dead.

Putting the phone back on the desk, Lisa took a shuddering breath and buried her face in her hands.

Rosalind was at a window table in Zizzi's, the restaurant she and Sally often ate at when they were both coming into Clifton. Her mobile was still in her hand, and she was shaking with anger and shock.

Of all the nerve, calling her as though she had every right to discuss her father when, of course, she did as his wife, or she might have, were she not, as far as Rosalind was concerned, damned well responsible for whatever was going on with him – if indeed anything was, and for her, at least, the jury was still out on that. He'd been absolutely fine before Lisa Martin came along – OK, stressed, in grief denial and overworked, but that was normal for him. So if that woman thought she could grab control of David Kirby's assets using some trumped-up assumption of dementia, then she was not only gravely mistaken, she was going to have a serious legal battle on her hands, because Rosalind had consulted a lawyer too.

'Hey, is that you, Ros?' someone said cheerily.

Though her pretty face was drawn with rancour, an inherent politeness was already forcing its way to the surface as she looked up to find one of the architects she often worked with beaming down at her. Since he was someone who she and her father – and mother – had always had a lot of time for, she was even able to inject some warmth into her tone as she said, 'Ben. This is a nice surprise. What are you doing here?'

He laughed. 'My office is just around the corner,' he reminded her.

'Of course,' she said, feeling herself starting to colour. 'It's lovely to see you. Did you get the new contracts we sent through last week?'

'I'm sure we did. I can check with my secretary . . .'

'Oh no, it's not urgent. So how are you? It seems ages since I last saw you.'

He pulled a face. 'I've been a bit off the scene for a while,' he admitted. Then, gesturing to the empty place at her table for two, 'Are you expecting someone?'

'I am, but I'm early and she's running late, so do sit down if you have time.'

Pulling up a chair, he said, 'I'm on my way to the solicitor's to sign most of my worldly wealth away to a wife who deserted me and took my kids into the bargain. Don't need to be in a hurry for that, huh?'

Feeling a huge wave of empathy, Rosalind said, 'Oh Ben, I'm so sorry. I had no idea.'

He flipped a hand as if to say no big deal, but obviously it was.

'Why don't I buy you a drink?' she offered. 'A bit of Dutch courage to see you on your way?'

He twinkled. 'Sounds good to me,' he said, checking his watch. 'Let them wait, why not?'

Feeling herself warming up inside as she laughed, Rosalind turned to catch the eye of a waiter, and after giving their order, she said, 'So where did your wife take the children, if you don't mind me asking?'

Raising a sardonic eyebrow, he said, 'About three streets away, to someone who's actually not a bad bloke – if I can get past wanting to punch his lights out – and who's way better off, financially speaking, than I am, but hey, why not use my income to bolster the whole new-family thing? What the hell else am I going to do with it?'

'Oh God,' she groaned, wondering if she might have to pay Jerry off at some point in the future and knowing she'd rather burn the money first. 'It doesn't sound very fair. Are you able to see your children at all?'

'Two weekends a month and occasional holidays, apart from when I'm required to babysit. I don't complain, because at least it means I get to spend more time with them.'

'How old are they now? They were tiny the last time I saw them.'

'Would you believe Justin's going to be fourteen

soon, and Sadie's already twelve going on twenty. Boy, does she like to boss me around, but I suppose that's girls and their dads for you.' Grimacing as he realised what territory he'd just trodden on, he sounded genuinely regretful as he said, 'Ros, I heard about yours. I'm so sorry. He's such a great . . .'

'Oh, he's fine,' Rosalind quickly assured him. 'Absolutely fine. He'll be pleased to know I've run into you. Now tell me, what do you think of this wine?'

Lisa had cried so hard and for so long that her eyes were sore and her ribs ached. Damn Rosalind, she was thinking as she blew her nose and picked herself up from the bed. Or maybe she should actually be thanking her, because after releasing so much emotion she seemed to be feeling less edgy now, and hopefully more able to deal with David – and whatever mood he might be in – when he came home. Miles had woken her up about fifteen minutes ago with a call to let her know that the train had left on time, but she still felt groggy and vaguely nauseous. It would soon pass though, probably once she'd had something to eat, and since it was usual for her to ring David during his journey back to check there were no hold-ups and to assure him she'd be waiting when he arrived, she reached for the phone.

After being bumped over to his voicemail, she told him to call when he could to let her know if he'd like to go out for an early dinner, and if so, she'd try to get them into Lockside. That might make his homecoming feel more inviting, she decided, just in case he was in one of his more difficult moods. Then, taking her mobile into the bathroom ready for when he rang back, she put it down on a shelf and didn't notice until she picked it up again twenty minutes later that there was a text message waiting. Opening it, she read, *I won't be home tonight, but please don't worry. Dx*

Feeling a beat of alarm she quickly rang his mobile, but found herself being diverted to messages again.

Without bothering to leave one, she tried Miles. 'Do you have any idea where he might be going?' she asked, after repeating the text.

Sounding equally baffled, Miles said, 'As far as I knew he was on his way home.'

'Are you sure he got on the train? Did you actually see him . . . ?'

'I boarded with him because we were still talking, so he was definitely on it, and it was ready to pull out when I got off.'

'So where is he now?' she cried. 'He's not answering his phone.'

'It's not even four o'clock, so he must still be on his way home.'

'But he's not coming home! That's what he said, so where else would he go?'

'Have you tried Rosalind? Maybe he's going there for the night.'

'If he was, why wouldn't he say so? Oh God, why anything with David these days? I can't call her. She won't speak to me. Would you try?'

'Of course.'

While she waited Lisa tried David again, but there was still no reply, so she replied to his text begging him to tell her where he was, if only to put her mind at rest.

When Miles rang back he said, 'I didn't want to alarm her, so I tried to be vague about him mentioning he might go there from the train, but if that is what he's intending, she's not expecting him.'

'Oh God,' Lisa murmured, both angry and worried. 'What the hell is he doing? How are we going to find him?'

Miles said, 'OK, let's try to think about this rationally. We know he was on the train, so where else might he get off between London and Bristol? Bath?'

'Did he have his station written down?' Lisa asked.

'I saw it there. He even showed me, Bristol Temple Meads.'

'Then I should go to the station to see if he turns up. Yes, I'll do that, but it's not due in yet, so just in case, let's carry on thinking about what that text might mean. He's saying that he's not coming home tonight, so are you sure he didn't mention anything today that might give us a clue to where he might be intending to go?'

'I'm racking my brains, but like I said, I thought he was on his way home. The only other stations he can get off at are Reading, Didcot, Chippenham and Bath. You know, I'm going to try and get hold of Colin Larch to see if anything came up while David was with him today.'

As he rang off Lisa fought a wave of dizziness as an awful suspicion started to emerge from her fear. It didn't seem rational or even possible at first, but only a few seconds of considering it were enough to send her running downstairs to David's study to turn on his computer. It took moments to call up his emails and there, in the three most recent messages, were the confirmations she'd been dreading. A reservation at the Baur au Lac hotel in Zurich; an invitation from BA to check in online; and a message from a Herr Jorge Wengle detailing the date and time of their meeting – *tonight at 2030!*

Grabbing the phone she pressed in David's mobile number, so afraid now that she was practically screaming as she left him a message. 'I know where you are,' she cried furiously. 'You can't do this, David! It's insane. Please, please call me.' Cutting the connection she raced back to the kitchen and scrolled through her mobile for Tony's number. 'You have to help me,' she begged. 'David's gone to Zurich. He's got an appointment with someone at Exit for tonight . . .'

'Hang on, hang on,' Tony interrupted. 'Try to calm down . . .'

'How can I when David's about to take his own life?'

'Lisa, they don't let people just walk in off the street . . .'

'He's got an appointment!'

'But there's still a procedure you have to go through. Has he been in touch with them before?'

'I don't know. I can check his emails again . . .'

'Listen, before you do that, why don't you give me the number and I'll try to speak to someone there . . .'

'No, I can do that. I want you to go to Zurich and stop him.'

'Are you crazy? Even if there's a flight out tonight, I'll never get there before his appointment, unless it's at midnight.'

Putting a hand to her head, Lisa said, 'No, of course not. I'm sorry. I just . . . They won't let him do anything, will they?'

'You can be sure of it, but I'll tell you what, call and get them to put your mind at rest, and if there is a flight to Zurich tonight, I'll be on it. OK?'

Starting to breathe again, she said, 'OK. He's booked into the Baur au Lac hotel. What are you going to say to him?'

'Well, I was rather hoping you were going to give me some ideas,' he replied.

After asking the taxi driver to wait, David put away his notebook and gave a cursory glance around the quiet, rather bland suburb of Zurich he'd been brought to. Then walking up to the front door of a white flat roofed building with blue blinds at the windows, he found the single word 'Exit' next to a bell at the front door. The irony of that wasn't lost on him.

'Mr Kirby?'

Turning around, David saw a lanky young man with swept-back shoulder-length hair, a pierced ear and designer stubble approaching him from across the street. 'Mr Wengle?' he said.

'That's me,' Wengle confirmed, reaching to shake David's hand.

Though he was nothing like the image David had created of him, his smile was infectiously friendly, and on closer inspection his eyes showed the sensitivity which someone in his line of work would certainly need.

'Come on up,' Wengle said, unlocking the door. 'And by the way, call me Jorge.'

'Jorge,' David echoed, to try and plant it in his mind.

'There's no one else around this evening,' Jorge went on as they walked up a flight of stairs most remarkable for its lack of atmosphere, 'apart from the guy who mans the overnight phones, but he's up on the third floor.'

'Are you American?' David asked. 'You sound it.'

'My mother is,' Wengle – Jorge – told him.

At the top of the stairs Jorge led the way through a small waiting room that boasted a few bucket seats, a water cooler and a built-in tank of tropical fish drifting dreamily around their exclusive domain.

'Can I get you anything?' Jorge offered, as they entered a conference-style room and he closed the door.

'No, I'm fine, thanks,' David replied, sitting down at one end of the long table.

Wengle pulled up a chair to face him, and clasping long, bony fingers together, he smiled kindly as he said, 'I have to admit I'm surprised you wanted to come. You got my emails, right?'

'I did,' David confirmed.

'So you understand that our organisation is only licensed to help Swiss nationals or foreign residents, meaning you have to have an address in this country?'

David nodded.

'Then can I ask,' Jorge continued, 'why you got

in touch with us, rather than Dignitas, who I think are better known in your country?'

Remembering the answer to that, or at least in part, David said, 'I tried contacting them, but they . . . They didn't want to help me.'

Jorge grimaced. 'It'll probably be because of who you are. They've had some bad publicity lately, and given your position they could be afraid that you're conducting an investigation rather than a genuine enquiry.'

'Bad publicity?' David echoed.

'Mainly here, in Switzerland, because they're pissing off the locals. It's all to do with money not going to the cantons, and certain codes of practice that don't precisely conform to regulations, but they do still operate a service that is open to non-nationals.'

Again David nodded. *Cantons, codes of practice, regulations.* He understood what they all were, but it was hard to respond the way he'd like to. However, there was a question he knew he wanted to ask. 'If I had an address here?' he said.

Jorge's eyes stayed on his. 'Then we could probably help you,' he said.

David continued to meet his gaze. 'I sent an email outlining my reasons . . .'

When he stopped, Jorge seemed to read where he was going, because he said, 'Would it surprise you to hear that by far the majority of people who come through our doors are suffering from some kind of dementia?'

David indicated that no, perhaps it didn't surprise him.

'The difficulty with it is deciding when is the right time,' Jorge went on. 'I'd say, out of every hundred sufferers we see, we probably end up helping no more than two or three.' He eyed David closely, apparently assessing how well he was following. Presumably deciding David was on board, he said, 'It's almost impossible to determine when a person moves from being capable of making decisions for themselves, to being incapable, and all too often the time passes before they're aware of it.'

'I – I understand that,' David said hoarsely. 'But what if I wanted to do something now, while we know I'm still able to think for myself? How long would I have to have an address here?'

'Well, there are no actual time constraints,' he said, 'but there are a lot of medical and legal requirements that need to be met before we can discuss allocating a time. You would also need to become a member of our organisation.'

David felt bemused. 'Is that . . . ? Can I?'

'Anyone can join,' Jorge told him. 'It's forty-five Swiss francs per year, which I think translates into around twenty-six pounds sterling.'

David took out his wallet. 'I have some currency,' he said, and after handing over the correct amount he took a moment to consult his notebook. 'Going back to an address. If I rented an apartment, here in Zurich, would that qualify me for your services?'

Jorge nodded.

David made a note.

'Would it be where you'd want to spend your last days?' Jorge asked.

David wasn't sure how to answer that.

'The alternative would be to do it here,' Jorge explained. 'We have a room next door to this one that I can show you, if you like. It doesn't get used often, because most of our members prefer to leave from their own homes. Tell me, have you discussed any of this with your family? Are they supportive of your decision?'

David swallowed. 'Not yet,' he admitted, 'but I'm hoping . . . I . . . I don't need their permission?'

'No. We're all about *your* right to choose,' Jorge reminded him, 'but when you're ready to take the step, you will be urged to consider how distressing your actions are likely to be for your relatives if you act without their knowledge.'

David's eyes began drifting around the room. Simply being here felt surreal, to be having this conversation was proving almost impossible to grasp. 'What . . . ?' He swallowed again. 'How does it happen?' he asked.

Jorge's elegant hands locked and unlocked. 'It's all in the documents I emailed across,' he said, 'but to precis, once we have all the requisite confirmations from your doctors that you are suffering with this illness, you will be able to select your own date of death, which can be postponed or cancelled at any time. Once you've selected your date, a physician here in Zurich will prescribe the medication that's necessary, and either an Exit assistant or a doctor will collect it from one of the specially designated pharmacies and bring it to you.'

'What . . .' David cleared his throat. 'What is the medication?' he asked.

'It consists of two tablets of Dramamine, which

469

will help you to relax. Then around half an hour later you'll be given ten grams of sodium pentobarbitone, dissolved in water. Usually no more than five minutes after you've taken the drink you will fall asleep, and within the next hour or two, without regaining consciousness, you will pass peacefully away.'

Feeling oddly dizzy, David took in some air and blew it out slowly. 'And then?' he asked.

'Then we call the police, who will make sure no Swiss laws have been violated.'

'And my . . . after . . . my remains? What will happen if I come alone?'

'Cremation is generally recommended in Switzerland, which we can organise for you. The urn and the ashes can then be sent on to whomever you have chosen.'

Thinking of Lisa and Rosalind, David raised a hand and rubbed his eyes.

'We would always urge you to discuss everything with your next of kin,' Jorge told him kindly, 'and if possible to have them with you for the time of passing. To borrow from an overused American phrase, it helps to bring closure.'

As the words and images blurred together to make an abstract kind of pain for his conscience, David sat staring at nothing. He wasn't ready for this yet, he knew that, but on the other hand if he waited too long . . .

Oh Catrina, Catrina, he was saying to himself when he finally returned to the taxi. *Am I crazy? Is this what I should be doing? I know you never considered it an option yourself, but I'm not Catholic and nor do I know if I have your kind of courage to suffer through to a natural end.*

The next morning Lisa was in the arrivals hall waiting for David to come through from his flight. She'd learned from the operator at Exit when she'd rung last night that David wasn't a member, so couldn't possibly be scheduled for an assisted suicide, so at least she'd been able to set that fear aside. It was merely a consultation, as David himself had explained, when he'd finally got in touch after his insane mission was over. They hadn't discussed it then, had simply gone through the details of his return journey, and had wished one another a tender goodnight. Afterwards, she'd spent over an hour on the phone to Amy, pouring her heart out, while Tony, who'd almost made it to Heathrow by the time she rang him, had turned around and gone home again. The apology and thanks she owed him were so huge now that she needed some time to work up to them, but for the moment, what mattered was getting David home.

The instant she saw him, looking so together and distinguished amongst the crowd, she was caught by such a conflict of emotions that she barely knew whether she was laughing or crying or seething with anger as she embraced him.

'Promise me you won't ever do anything like that again,' she demanded, as they walked, arms around one another, to the car park. 'I was so afraid. When I realised where you'd gone . . . What the hell were you thinking?'

When he didn't answer she turned to look up at him, and her heart jarred against a bolt of dismay. 'David, please tell me you know where you've been and what you were doing,' she urged. 'You can't have . . .'

'I haven't forgotten,' he interrupted quietly.

'So why did you go without telling me? Don't you understand how inconsiderate that was?'

'I knew you wouldn't come . . . I wanted the information . . .'

'But you got it in an email. I read it last night.'

'I wanted to see the place . . . The people . . .'

Though she was still reeling from it all, she guessed that was a reasonable enough excuse, so decided to let it go for now.

On reaching the car she asked him if he'd like to drive, but he shook his head and slipped into the passenger seat. Going round to the other side she got in, planted her bag next to his feet and was about to start the engine when he said, 'Catrina would understand.'

Feeling as though she'd been punched, Lisa turned to look at him. 'Well, I'm sorry I'm not Catrina,' she said, barely containing her anger, 'but I'm doing my best here and frankly you're not making it easy.' Hot tears started to burn her eyes as more outrage and frustration overcame her. 'That was a terrible thing to say to me,' she cried. 'If you knew how worried I was, Miles too. We were going out of our minds trying to find you, and Tony was nearly on a damned plane before you finally deigned to give anyone a call. Don't you realise how difficult this is for the rest of us? It's not just you, you know. We're all affected by it, because we care for you and we don't want to lose you – and certainly not in the way you seem to be planning.'

472

His eyes remained straight ahead as he said, 'So turning into a vegetable with no faculties or memory or anything that makes a human life worthwhile, would be better?'

'That's not what I'm saying. I understand why you want to go on your own terms, I swear I do, but flying off like that was so . . . selfish, and extreme. It's hardly been two months since you were diagnosed . . .'

'But we don't know how much time . . . I have to do it while I still can.'

'Time is not running out that fast. We need to discuss it, to be sure it's the right answer . . . And what about Rosalind? Have you thought about how hurt she'd be if she had any idea where you've been?'

Averting his head, he said, 'I can't argue with you now.'

Since she didn't want to carry this on either, she took his hands in hers and leaned over to kiss his cheek. 'I love you,' she told him softly, 'and I don't mean to . . .'

'Who's Tony?' he asked.

Tensing as she remembered what she'd said, she turned away to start the engine, hoping he'd let the question go.

It was as they joined the M4 that he asked it again.

'It's Tony Sommerville,' she answered briefly.

'Do I know him?'

'No, you don't.'

'So why was he . . . ?'

'I called him last night because he was the first person . . .' How could she tell him that her ex

473

had returned to being her first port of call in a crisis? 'Because I thought he would be able to stop you.'

'But who . . . ?'

'He's the man I was involved with before I met you.'

For a long time he said nothing, then taking out his notebook he asked her to spell Sommerville.

Chapter Twenty-Two

It was on Christmas Eve that David informed Lisa he would be going to Rosalind's for lunch the following day.

'I'll be back for dinner,' he assured her, 'but . . .'

'Absolutely no way!' she cut in furiously. 'This is our first Christmas as husband and wife so the hell am I going to let you leave me here on my own.'

His face was pinched. 'I said I'll be back . . .'

'And I said *no*. My mother and niece have gone to Australia and all my friends will have made other arrangements by now . . . Anyway, that's beside the point. I want to spend Christmas Day with *you*, *here* in our new home, next to our lovely tree . . .' Tears were blurring her eyes, making her angrier than ever, and slamming a hand on the counter top she cried, 'I can't believe you're putting her first. I'm your wife, for God's sake. Don't I count?'

'Of course you do, and it's . . . I'm not putting her first. I need to be with you both and this is the only way I can see of doing it.'

In spite of how torn and helpless he looked, or maybe because of it, she felt her frustration deepening. 'We'd all be together,' she shouted, 'if you'd put your damned foot down and stop letting her control you.'

'She's my daughter,' he said quietly. 'I have to spend some time with her.'

'Then go on Boxing Day. Better still, invite her here and make her talk to me, because we – *you* – can't go on like this. It's crazy, insane, and I don't think I can take much more of it.'

Putting a hand to his head, he said, 'I know you're right but . . . I still don't think she's ready for it yet. She can be very . . . I don't want her to hurt you.'

Lisa was shaking with outrage. 'So you'll do it for her by leaving me on my own tomorrow,' she yelled, 'while she's got her aunt and cousin and son and heaven only knows who else around her table?'

'Dee's gone to Spain with Wills and . . . his girlfriend.' His eyes were pleading for her to understand as he said, 'It'll only be for a couple of hours, and I'll try to talk to her then about us all getting together.'

She wanted to fight this and win, to make him see that this wasn't the right decision, but she felt suddenly too exhausted to go on. 'Don't think this is over yet,' she warned him angrily, and snatching up her mobile she stormed upstairs to shut herself in the bedroom.

She knew it was the relentless strain of it all that was making her overemotional and weighing her down physically, but knowing it wasn't helping to prevent it. She'd even considered going to the doctor to get some sort of tonic to boost her energy, which in turn might help her morale, but she'd been so busy lately trying to set up David's new charity, researching how she was going to get them both through the weeks, months, years to come and sorting out a romantic Christmas *à deux*, that she hadn't even had time to make an appointment. Maybe she would once the holiday was over. Meanwhile, she was damned if she was going to let Rosalind ride roughshod over her plans for tomorrow. For all she knew this could be the last Christmas David would be functioning this well – though she didn't really think he'd decline that quickly – but who knew? And anyway, there was no getting away from the fact that this was their first Christmas as a married couple – and in this house which she'd decorated so beautifully – so it surely couldn't be unreasonable, or selfish, to want him to spend it with her, especially when Rosalind had had him for the last twenty or more Christmases without a break, thank you very much.

By the time he came up to bed Lisa was in such a deep sleep that she had no idea he was there, until she woke in the early hours to find him lying next to her, staring into the darkness.

Forgetting for the moment that they'd argued, she reached out to touch his face. 'Are you all right?' she murmured.

'Mm, I'm fine,' he whispered, raising an arm for her to snuggle in closer. When she was settled he pressed a kiss to her forehead and said, 'Go back to sleep.'

Though she could tell he was upset and worried, and she was now remembering that she'd caused this, her eyes were so heavy and the tiredness inside her so dark and consuming that she couldn't manage another word before sinking back into oblivion.

When she woke up in the morning she still felt tired, and her muscles ached so badly that she could hardly make a move to get up. When she tried, such a powerful wave of dizziness swept over her that for one awful moment she thought she was going to faint. Then, realising her throat was on fire and her head was throbbing, she sank back against the pillows and pulled the duvet up to her chin. She had no idea what time it was, or where David might be, but for the moment she hardly had the energy to care. All she wanted was to go back to sleep.

When she finally woke up again David was sitting on the edge of the bed, fully dressed and looking concerned.

'Are you OK?' he asked gently. 'I tried to wake you, but you were dead to the world.'

'I think I might have flu,' she rasped.

He nodded agreement. 'Can I bring you something?' he offered.

She shook her head. 'What time is it?'

'Almost midday.'

Startled, she turned to look at the clock.

'Merry Christmas,' he whispered with a smile.

Feeling her heart somersault as the memories of yesterday came flooding back, she said, 'Are you still going to Rosalind's?'

'I am, but . . .'

She put up a hand. 'I don't want to hear your excuses,' she told him hoarsely. 'This is where you

478

should be today, with me, not with her. You can always go there tomorrow, or the next day . . .'

'She's expecting me now.'

'And of course, we can't let her down, can we?' she retorted, the bitterness exacerbated by the soreness in her throat.

'I'll be back by six,' he promised.

'*Six!*' she tried to shout. 'I thought you were going for a couple of hours, and in case you hadn't noticed I'm not very well.'

He looked suitably guilty. 'You need to sleep,' he told her, 'you won't even know I've gone.'

'Yes I will, and six o'clock isn't acceptable.'

With a sigh he said, 'We probably won't eat until three, and I can't just get up and leave as soon as I've finished.'

Realising if he ate that late she'd be wasting her time if she tried to force herself up to prepare something for when he came back, she could only wish she had the strength to shake him, or scream at him, or damned well walk out and leave him. But she was too incapacitated by the heaviness in her limbs, and so very close to tears that all she could do was say, 'You're weak, David, and insensitive, and if you cared about me at all you wouldn't be doing this.'

'I care about you more than anything,' he said softly, 'but please try to understand that I care about my daughter and grandson too.'

Accepting that she wasn't going to change his mind, she turned her back and pressed her face into the pillow, wishing she was anywhere right now rather than here.

'I'll bring you some hot water and honey,' he

told her, and getting up from the bed he quietly left the room.

Several minutes later she heard the front door closing, followed by the garage doors opening. Apparently he'd forgotten about her drink and for some reason that upset her even more than the fact that he'd gone, and as tears streamed down her cheeks she felt so sorry for herself and furious with him that if she had had the energy she would have rung Tony to ask him to come and collect her. Except he was skiing in Gstaad, and she wished to God that she was there too, living it up in their old carefree way, anything rather than be trapped here by a fever and self-pity and the whole damned nightmare her life had become.

'This isn't a marriage,' she rasped down the phone to Amy when she got her on the line later. 'It's just a joke that someone up there is having on me – and now I feel utterly terrible for saying that, because how can my problems even begin to compare to his?'

'It's not a contest,' Amy reminded her, 'and for what it's worth, I think he made a wrong call today by going to Rosalind's, but that's where he is and frankly, you sound so terrible I think you should just get yourself back into bed.'

'That's where I am, but I'm so hungry I could eat an entire turkey all to myself. Oh God,' she wailed as her eyes welled up at the thought of the day she'd planned. 'Why am I sitting here on my own and you're over there and he's chosen to be with his daughter? Nothing's making sense any more and I wish I'd never got married, which isn't to say I don't love him, because I do, but I'm so angry with him about today . . .'

'Lisa, you're so obviously not well that you have to try to forget it's Christmas Day and get some more sleep.'

'I haven't spoken to Mum yet, or Roxy.'

'OK, I'll put them on, but promise me when you've finished you'll do as you're told.'

In a wavery voice Lisa said, 'OK, I promise. I wish you were here.'

'I wish I was too, but I'm not, so just call whenever you want, but get some more sleep first.'

It was almost three o'clock by the time Lisa woke up again, achy and hot, but after taking a few minutes to assess how she was feeling – apart from horribly neglected – she decided she might have the strength to go downstairs. She had to eat something or she really would faint, and right now she'd trade her own mother for a slice of toast.

After pulling on an old tracksuit and wincing painfully as she dragged a brush through her hair, she went down to the kitchen to raid the fridge. To her surprise she found a plate of smoked salmon, covered in film, laid out on a tray with a cup of water, now gone cold, smelling of honey and lemon. So he had made her drink, and had even thought to bring her something to eat, he'd just forgotten to take it upstairs.

Feeling herself back at the brink of tears, she tore off a sheet of kitchen roll to dab her eyes and blow her nose. Then, opening the card he'd left for her, she read what he'd written and started to sob.

I don't wish to make you sad, or to force you to think of days beyond today,

But while clarity is still my friend I have a favour to ask:

When I go, would you mind if I took a little something of you with me?

Nothing that you would miss, or couldn't easily spare;

Just the memory of your smile, or the scent of your skin, or a precious little soupçon of that magical something that is the essence of you?

It wasn't the first note he'd written her like this, but it was certainly the most beautiful, and remembering how angry she'd been before he left was making her cry all the harder. This was the strangest and loneliest Christmas she'd ever spent, and she could only hope that she never had another like it, especially as her stomach was now starting to churn and she was very much afraid she might be about to throw up.

However, the nausea soon passed, leaving her with a raging hunger again, so after making another drink and forgoing the toast because of her throat, she carried the plate of salmon into the sitting room where she found the fire set, ready to light, and the tree lights on, so the place looked wonderfully seasonal and cosy. It seemed everything was going to make her cry today, so she simply let the tears roll and reminded herself that at least the time was passing, and he'd be back soon. She just hoped he remembered he'd said six and didn't come any later, but even if he did she must try not to start another row about being left on her own, or the day would be ruined completely.

Finding nothing she wanted to watch on TV she rang Amy and the others again, then rather morbidly, or even masochistically she decided on reflection, she put on their wedding video. Strangely this didn't make her cry, probably because it was like watching some bizarre episode in a drama that had lost its way. How had so much happiness and so many dreams managed to turn to dust in such a short space of time?

Ho! Ho! Ho! Happy Christmas, Lisa and David. How are you enjoying this crazy new journey life is taking you on?

When David finally came home, at a quarter to six, Lisa was fast asleep again, curled up under a blanket on the sofa with an old black and white film playing on the TV. She didn't hear him come in, nor did she register the TV going off, or stir when he covered her with a duvet. She only knew he was there when she finally woke up around two in the morning to find him standing at the window, gazing out at a moon that was little more than a smudge in the sky.

Wrapping herself in the duvet, she forced herself to her feet and went to stand next to him. 'You shouldn't be up,' he told her, pulling her against him.

She tried to say she was fine, but it turned out her voice had gone.

'I wonder if that's what's happening to my mind,' he said, still gazing at the moon. 'Everything getting hazier and hazier until finally it isn't there any more.'

Unable to speak she simply stood holding him, feeling the ache in her heart growing with each minute that passed. She'd have given anything to be able to take back how angry she'd been earlier, because she'd known then and was being reminded now that even after their follow-up visit to Dr Manning a week ago, when she'd assured him that the latest CT scans were indicating that the medication had started to work, his depression hadn't shown any signs of lifting. Ever since his trip to Zurich he'd become increasingly withdrawn, with precious few moments like this scattered like jewels over the darkness.

Chapter Twenty-Three

David was in the waiting room of the Kirby
company offices in the centre of Bristol. After being
laid low with the flu virus that had kept Lisa in
bed for most of Christmas and him until after the
New Year, he was finally up and about again and
able to get on with the reason he was here. He'd
chosen a day and time when he knew the staff
wouldn't yet be back from their seasonal break,
and while Lisa was at Heathrow collecting her
mother and Roxy. This way he wouldn't have to
tell her where he was going, or whom he was
meeting.

He'd given a great deal of thought to what he
was doing, and had made copious notes in order
to keep himself on track. At first he'd considered
asking Miles or Jerry to help him, but realising
they'd feel compelled to talk to Lisa or Rosalind
before committing themselves, he'd decided that
there were actually many more reasons to turn to
the man who was staring at him now as if one or
other of them had gone mad.

Having only got back from Gstaad the night
before, Tony might not have made this meeting
had Mrs Overall, his cleaner, not popped a note

through his front door to let him know that there were messages on the shop answerphone. On finding one from David asking him to call between ten and eleven this morning, he'd done just that, and after jotting down the address of these offices he'd driven into Bristol mightily intrigued to know what David wanted to discuss.

Now he knew, he was sorely wishing himself back in Gstaad, or at least in the land of ignorance.

In the end he was the first to break the silence. 'You're serious, aren't you?' he said, holding David's earnest gaze.

'Yes,' David confirmed.

Tony shook his head. 'Then I'm afraid the answer has to be no,' he said, meaning it. 'You can't ask me to do that. For God's sake, I don't even know you . . .'

'Please,' David interrupted.

Tony threw out his hands in frustration. 'Look, I understand where you're coming from,' he assured him, 'and in your shoes I know I'd want to do the same thing, but think of the position you're putting me in . . . If Lisa or your daughter ever found out I'd helped you . . .'

'I understand why you're worried, but I know without asking that neither of them will rent the apartment for me . . .'

'Which is exactly why I can't. It's not my place to go behind their backs. I'm not even family, and think how your daughter would feel if she knew that Lisa's ex had helped send her father on his way. Jesus, no! It can't happen, David. I'm sorry. I really am, but I just can't do this.'

As David's head went down, more in defeat, it

seemed, than despair, Tony watched him and longed to be able to make this easier for him, but what the hell could he do? Given his connection to Lisa, there was just no way he could enter into the assisted-suicide thing, and if David were thinking straight he'd surely understand that. Then realising, to his horror, that David had started to cry, he felt more wretched than ever.

'Come on, man,' he said, grasping David's shoulder. 'I know this is hard, and I want to help, I swear it, but not like this.'

Taking out a handkerchief to blow his nose, David apologised and got up to help himself to a drink from the cooler. 'I can't do anything until I've been a member for . . . for . . .' How long was it?

'I believe it's three months,' Tony said, having read the emails Lisa had forwarded to him when David had gone off on his lone trip to Zurich.

David took a while to look through his notebook. 'I joined in November,' he said eventually, 'and today is January 4th.'

Tony said nothing.

'They've let me keep my driving licence,' David said, apropos of only he knew what.

'That's good,' Tony responded. 'It shows you've still got a long way to go, so to be talking like this now . . .'

'It's because I can talk like it that I have to . . . I don't want to end up finding out it's too late. It won't be fair on Lisa, or my daughter. If I . . . If you . . .' He pressed his fingers to his eyes, digging in hard. 'They won't want to think of me being alone at the end, but I can't ask them to go through it.'

Tony's insides churned with despair. 'Look, I'll

tell you what,' he said, 'if you can get Lisa and your daughter to agree to it all, then I'll be there for you, OK? I'll find the apartment, I'll book the flights, I'll even, God help us both, hold your hand as you go – that's provided they don't want to do it themselves, but you have to give them the chance.'

For a long time David simply stood staring towards the window, where a flashing neon sign outside was turning the panes from blue to red and back again. In the end he said, 'Thank you, Tony, for coming.'

Realising that there probably wasn't any more to be said, and feeling next to useless for all the support he'd been, Tony picked up his keys and got to his feet.

'You won't tell Lisa about this, will you?' David said, his back still turned.

'No, that's for you to do.'

Attempting a smile, David turned to look at him. 'When it . . . After I . . .' He swallowed. 'You'll take care of her, won't you?'

Feeling a lump forming in his throat, Tony said, 'You can count on it, my friend, you can count on it,' and after shaking David by the hand, he left, wondering when in his life he'd felt more choked up, or if he'd ever admired a man more.

Having Roxy around was helping to lift Lisa's spirits no end. It wasn't only that her niece seemed to be injecting life back into the house, it was the way she'd managed to get David's enthusiasm going again for their charitable project. He was keen to have as much in place as quickly as he could, he'd said, in order to be able to participate in the early crucial decisions. And Roxy's patience with how often he asked the same questions or mislaid some information was, Lisa decided, nothing short of saintly. She didn't even seem to mind when he shouted at her – always because he was frustrated with himself – and on the one occasion he'd reduced her to tears they'd been for him, not for herself. She was remarkable, and Lisa could only have felt prouder of her if she'd somehow managed to pull off the impossible by bringing on a cure.

'He is so amazing,' Roxy would purr. 'He's not all talk. He really wants to make a difference to people like him, and I'm going to get all my friends involved in it as soon as I go back to uni. I've already emailed them, so they'll know what it's about, and wait till they check out our list of celebs! It's getting more impressive by the day, thanks to you. I had no idea you knew so many famous people.'

'Not just me, David too,' Lisa reminded her. But she had to admit her own address list, now she'd found her iPhone in David's bedside drawer, did seem to contain quite a lot of glitterati, and she could hardly feel more gratified by the responses they'd received so far.

Now, as she listened to the noise Roxy was making in the pool, apparently challenging David to yet another race, Lisa felt her heart warming all over again. He'd seemed quite down again this morning, and he hadn't slept too well either, which was why she'd suggested taking him to Dr Knoyle for a check-up. In his usual fashion he'd brushed her concerns aside, telling her he was perfectly all right, or he would be if she'd only stop fussing. Fortunately, he sounded better now, and thrilling quietly to herself as she recalled the cherished secret that she hadn't yet confided in anyone, she decided to run upstairs to make sure that her wildest dream really was coming true.

It was – *it was!* She was going to have a baby, and if it was possible to feel any happier or more thankful or more disbelieving that it had finally happened, then she truly didn't know how. The little white tube with its double blue line was like a magic wand waving away all her doubts, and conjuring up the most precious gift in the entire world. David's baby was growing inside her. He wasn't leaving her after all, not yet, not ever, because this tiny little life that she was going to treasure above all else was a link between them that could never be broken.

Thank you, thank you, thank you, she gushed inside, her eyes blurring with tears. All the years of fearing that she would never be a mother, were over. David had turned her into the woman she'd always longed to be. She felt a sense of completion that she could scarcely begin to quantify or even comprehend. She could hardly wait to tell him, yet at the same time she was nervous of it too, because though she was certain he'd be happy for her, she couldn't help being anxious about how he might feel for himself. Thrilled on one level, she felt sure, because he was too generous and too human not to be, but on another she could already sense his fear of what it could mean for a baby to have a father with dementia. They would work it out though, she told herself, too happy for the moment to let any shadows darken her horizon. She was going to do everything in her power to make sure he got all the enjoyment he deserved from his new son or daughter, for as long as he could.

After going to check on her mother and finding her still sleeping off her jet lag, she ran back downstairs to carry on paging through her recipe books in search of something special for dinner tonight. It wasn't that she was planning to break her news with Roxy and her mother there, but she had to do something to celebrate, even if she was the only one who knew about it yet.

She was midway through jotting down her shopping list when the phone started to ring, and scooping it up she felt her heart swoop with joy as she heard the long-distance echo before Amy cried tipsily, 'Hi, how's everyone over there? Is my daughter with you? I'm missing her like crazy.'

'She's here,' Lisa laughed, wondering if she could break it to Amy now without her spiralling off into unstoppable paroxysms of joy. 'What time is it with you? It must be the middle of the night.'

'Correct, but I'm missing you both, so I thought I'd call for a chat. How's she getting on? You said such lovely things about her in your email. I wish I was there to help out with it all.'

'Don't tell me you're feeling homesick,' Lisa teased, selfishly hoping it might prompt an early return. How wonderful it would be to have Amy back to help with the baby. Should she tell her now? She was practically bursting with the need to, but it wouldn't seem right not to tell David first. Then her euphoria dipped as she thought again of what a mixed blessing this was going to be for him.

'. . . but I love it here,' Amy was saying. 'It just feels a bit empty without my daughter filling up the place. What's she doing . . .'

'Hang on,' Lisa interrupted. 'I think I just heard her calling me . . .' Going to the door, she was about to shout for Roxy to come to the phone when Roxy screamed again.

'Lisa! *Lisa!*'

As panic surged through her Lisa dropped the phone and sped across the kitchen into the pool room, where she found Roxy kneeling over David at the top of the steps. 'What is it?' she cried, throwing herself down next to them. 'Did he fall? David, are you all right? *David!* Can you hear me?'

'He was getting out of the water,' Roxy gasped, 'and he just . . . like collapsed on his knees, then on to his side. I thought he was messing about, but then he . . .'

Too much blood was pounding through Lisa's head. She was shaking him, trying to make him hear her, but he wasn't responding.

'Call an ambulance,' she shouted. 'Quick! Do it now.'

As Roxy raced to the kitchen, Lisa clasped her hands round David's face. 'Are you breathing?' she urged. 'Can you hear me?'

Though his eyes were partially open there was still no response, and she was trying desperately to think what to do. Tilt his head back to open his airways. Listen for his breath. She did both, but could hear nothing over the thudding of her heart.

492

She started to panic again, but quickly fought it back. What was happening? It had to be a stroke, but obviously bigger than the mini-strokes he'd previously been having.

'David! Smile!' she shouted, remembering one of the commands to detect a stroke.

His eyes remained half closed. His mouth was slack and unmoving.

'Oh smile, please,' she begged. 'Or move your arms. Can you move your arms?'

Still nothing.

Barely aware that she was shaking all over, she listened for his breath again, then just in case it might help she began CPR, pressing the heel of her hand between his ribs and pumping hard, then stopping to blow into his mouth.

'The ambulance is on its way,' Roxy cried, dashing back to join her. 'They want to talk to you.'

Grabbing the phone Lisa said shrilly, 'I don't know if he's breathing. I can't tell.'

'Help's on its way,' a firm but soothing voice assured her. 'Just tell me, is he conscious?'

'I don't know. His eyes are partly open, but . . .'

'Does he appear to be in any pain?'

'I'm not sure. I think it might be a stroke.'

'All right, this is what I want you to do. Ask him to smile.'

'I already have. I don't think he can hear me. Oh God, David, please . . . please . . .'

'I'm sure everything's going to be fine,' the operator told her. 'The ambulance is almost there.'

The next few minutes felt endless as Lisa held David in her arms, stroking his hair and willing him to respond, while Roxy opened the gates and ran out to the lane ready to show the ambulance where they were.

The instant it arrived both paramedics raced inside, and as one eased Lisa away from David the other began a rapid inspection of the vital signs. Then he opened his case, and clasping a mask over David's mouth he quickly attached it to an oxygen cylinder, saying, 'OK, let's go.'

'Oh my God,' Lisa sobbed, as they began lifting David on to a stretcher. 'Where are you taking him?'

'We'll check who can take him when we've got him on board. Are you his wife? Then you might want to come with us.'

'What shall I do?' Roxy cried, as Lisa dashed to grab her coat.

'Go upstairs and wake Granny,' Lisa told her. 'I'll call as soon as I have some news.'

Rosalind was in the garden with Lawrence, who was supposed to be helping her clear up after some high winds during the night. However, as usual he'd sneaked off to his tree house and was being his dreadful stubborn self about coming out again, and all because Lucy was at the vet's having her teeth cleaned.

The cold was biting, and it was still quite blowy, but at least the rain was holding off, and Ben had promised to come over later to take them all to the pub. Experiencing a pleasing lilt in her heart, which was happening quite often when she thought about Ben these days, she dumped an armful of branches into a wheelbarrow ready to transport to the end of the garden, and pushed the hair back from her face.

Her father had agreed to sit with Lawrence tomorrow night while she and Ben went to watch a ballet at the Hippodrome, which was lovely for Lawrence, because she knew he'd rather be at home with David than at Dee's. She just hoped her father didn't forget again, the way he had the first time she and Ben had gone out on a date. She'd had to call on Dee last minute in a panic. This time she'd be sure to text her father at least two reminders before he was due to leave. The fact that he needed those reminders inevitably brought a turmoil of black clouds to her heart, but she wasn't going to let them drag her down today. He'd been fine over Christmas, before going down with the flu, and the few times she'd seen him since then he'd been back on his feet, so if there really was anything wrong with him, it was all for the future and by then . . .

No, she wouldn't go there, because all she wanted to think about today was Ben, and how the time she spent with him seemed to be doing her the world of good. She wasn't getting quite so wound up about things these days, or needing to go into defensive mode, the way she usually did. Thankfully, the history they shared wasn't complicated by lies and betrayal, or anything at all that could make her feel insecure or unworthy. On the contrary, they went back over several years with an excellent business relationship, and in his eyes she was a capable and successful woman, who also happened to be quite pretty. He never put it like that, of course, what he said was, you're a damned intelligent and attractive woman, Rosalind Kirby, and she liked him more for using her maiden name than she did for the compliment.

The best thing of all was that he wasn't in the least bit awkward with Lawrence, and Lawrence never seemed particularly bothered when Ben sat next to him at the computer to watch the game he was playing. Only two days ago, when Ben had asked Lawrence about what he was learning at school, it had been hard to make Lawrence stop reciting all his lessons. Though it saddened her to know that he'd never been as responsive to Jerry, she couldn't deny that a spiteful part of her wouldn't have minded rubbing it in Jerry's face. Not that Jerry wouldn't deserve it for how seldom he rang to speak to his son.

Taking hold of the wheelbarrow, she was about to start the downhill trundle when she heard the muffled jingle of her mobile. Peeling off her gloves, she dug into her pocket, already starting to smile at the butterflies inside as she wondered if it was Ben. However, she was almost as pleased to see it was her father.

'Hi,' she said warmly, 'I was going to call you later . . .'

'Rosalind, I'm sorry,' Lisa broke in gently. 'I'm at the Infirmary with your dad.'

Rosalind reeled. 'What's happened?' she cried.

'I'm not sure yet, but it seems to be a stroke.'

Gasping for air Rosalind spluttered, 'I'm on my way,' and clicking off the line she dashed towards the house so fast that she tripped over the rake and hit the ground. 'Oh God, oh God,' she sobbed, as she tried to get up and slipped again. 'Lawrence! Come on, we have to go. David's in hospital.'

Appearing at the door of his tree house, Lawrence said, 'Can Lucy come too?'

'Yes. No. No!' and after grabbing her keys and handbag from the house, she dragged Lawrence across the garden and pushed him into the car.

'I know,' Lawrence said, picking up his mother's mobile as they sped down the drive, 'I'll send David a text to let him know we're on our way.'

Hello David, it's Lawrence. We are coming to see you. Lucy is at the vet's.

Lisa's heart ached as she read the message. Having picked up David's iPhone by mistake on leaving the house, she now didn't have hers with all the numbers she needed, but it didn't matter. Rosalind's was the most important, and Rosalind was on her way.

Someone had brought her here a while ago, to the intensive-care waiting room – or was it intensive treatment? What did it matter what they called it these days? They'd said David had been taken for an emergency CT scan, but that seemed like hours ago, so where was he now? Still there? On his way here? In surgery and someone had forgotten to tell her? If so, that would be fine, because they didn't need to tell her anything until they were ready to smile and say, 'Everything's fine. Would you like to see him now?'

'*David, Oh God, David,*' she cried silently. '*Why didn't I insist on going to Dr Knoyle this morning? She might have been able to prevent this.*'

Closing her eyes, she let her head fall back

against the wall. The bleeps and hisses of life-support machines in the unit next door were coming to her in muted gasps. The occasional squeal of a rubber sole, the distant bell of a lift, the ghostly thudding of her heart. How much longer were they going to keep her waiting like this? She needed to know what was happening to him.

She stood up, walked across the room and back again. There was a TV in one corner, piles of magazines stacked on a table, a box of toys stuffed under two of the chairs, a fridge . . . She tried to think about the other people who'd been here, the families and loved ones who'd paced as she was pacing now, but the momentary distraction offered no comfort at all.

The door opened, and she went rigid with dread as a nurse came in.

'I'm Kathy,' the nurse smiled, 'and I guess you must be Lisa?'

How did she know that? Maybe David had told her. Hope sprang eternal. 'Yes, yes I am,' she said. 'Where's David? Is he all right? Can I see him?'

'They're bringing him up now,' Kathy told her. 'Was it . . . Is it a stroke?'

'The doctor will explain everything. Is there anything I can get you?'

Lisa shook her head. She was waiting for Kathy to say it would be all right, or that there was no need to worry, but she was going to the fridge where she took out a packet of tea bags and a jar of coffee. 'There's milk and sugar,' she said, 'so feel free to help yourself.'

When she'd gone Lisa stood staring at the Nescaff.

They were bringing him up, Kathy had said, so he was still . . . She took a gulp of air. He was on his way here. She'd be able to tell him her news after all.

Hearing voices outside, she went to open the door. The grim, hypnotic rhythm of the machines grew louder. Two nurses were speaking quietly together, neither of them Kathy. They turned around, but not to her, to the lift where a trolley cluttered with tubes and bags all connected to a prone body was being carefully manoeuvred on to the floor.

Lisa's heart leapt to her throat. Was it him? 'David,' she gasped, as they wheeled him past.

His eyes were closed; his skin looked waxen and old. He was attached to a ventilator and some kind of monitor that might have been for his heart, but what did she know?

'You can have a few minutes with him before we put in the lines,' Kathy came to tell her.

Lisa looked at her blankly. 'Lines?' she repeated.

Kathy only smiled, as though knowing that even if she answered Lisa wouldn't be able to take it in.

David was being moved carefully on to a narrow bed. Behind it was a bank of monitors, and other equipment, but Lisa couldn't take her eyes off him.

'Can he hear me?' she asked as Kathy raised the cot sides.

'He's been sedated,' Kathy replied. 'Professor Cross is on his way.'

Lisa moved closer to the bed and put her hand on David's. She only realised then how badly she was shaking. 'It's all right,' she whispered, barely hearing herself above the hiss and puff of the venti-lator, 'they're taking care of you, and I'll be right here. Rosalind's on her way. She should be here any minute.'

The only movement was his chest rising and falling as the machine puffed and sucked air in and out of him. There was nothing to say he knew she was there, but she felt certain that on some level he must.

She was aware of people moving behind her, and wanted to shield him from them, even though they were probably there to help.

'Lisa?' She turned round, and seeing her mother's stricken face she gave a frightened sob.

'There, there, it's going to be all right,' Matilda soothed, taking Lisa in her arms.

Roxy hugged them both with her cheek pressed against Lisa's. 'I called Mum,' she said. 'She's ready to get on the next plane if you want her to.'

Lisa turned back to David. 'He won't be here for long,' she said determinedly.

'Mrs Kirby? Lisa?'

They looked round to find a thickset man with weathered cheeks and rimless glasses at the foot of the bed. 'Joseph Cross,' he told her. 'I'm the neurospecialist in charge of your husband's case.'

Lisa's heart skipped a beat. For a moment she didn't know what to say, then decided she should introduce her mother and Roxy.

Cross smiled politely in their direction. Then holding out an arm, directing them away from the bed, he said, 'They need to insert the lines now. We can talk over here.'

With a deadening sense of dread weighting her movements, Lisa forced herself to follow.

'The radiographer's provisional report is showing that your husband has suffered . . .' He broke off at the sound of the lift doors opening and someone running towards them.

'Where is he?' Rosalind cried, pulling Lawrence behind her. 'Can I see him? Please! Please. He's my dad.' She was so pale and distraught that Lisa almost couldn't bear to look at her.

'This is Rosalind Sewell, my husband's daughter,' Lisa told the doctor.

Rosalind's eyes were fixed on his face. 'Is he all right? He's going to be fine, isn't he?'

'The doctor was about to tell us what happened,' Lisa said gently.

Professor Cross smiled down at Lawrence, who stared glumly back. Then to Lisa and Rosalind he said, 'David has suffered a massive haemorrhage in one of the vessels in his head. We've managed to stabilise him, so the bleeding has stopped now, but I'm afraid the damage is substantial.'

Rosalind looked panicked. 'What does that mean? What damage? I don't understand what you're saying.'

His voice was very kind as he said, 'Your father has had a massive stroke, from which I'm afraid he's unlikely to recover.'

Rosalind turned deathly white. Then she started to shout. 'No! No, no! You don't understand . . .'

Lisa tried to go to her, but Rosalind slapped her away. 'This is your fault!' she yelled. 'If it weren't for you this . . .'

'Please,' Cross interrupted, 'this isn't anyone's

fault. We're going to do everything we can, naturally, but in cases like this we usually advise loved
ones to prepare for the worst.'

'No! No!' Rosalind wailed, almost collapsing to
her knees.

Roxy went to catch her, but Rosalind pushed
her away. 'Where is he? Please let me see him,'
she implored. 'He'll listen to me, I know he will.'

'The nurse is connecting him to a life-support
system,' Cross told her. 'As soon as that's done,
you can approach the bed.' He looked at Lisa. 'I'm
sorry,' he said quietly.

His words sounded so final that Lisa wanted
to pull him back and make him change them. She
wasn't ready for this, nor was David. It was all
too soon.

'What are those things?' Rosalind was asking
the nurse. 'What are you doing?'

'This is David's daughter,' Lisa explained, when
Kathy turned round.

Kathy's face instantly softened. 'I'm just making
sure he's comfortable,' she told her, 'and getting
everything he needs.'

She turned as another doctor approached, then
seeming to understand what he wanted she said,
'I'm afraid we can only allow two at a time around
the bed.'

Lisa looked at Rosalind, whose eyes were fixed
on her father. Lawrence was gazing in fascination
at the machinery, seeming to track each lead and
tube from one end to the other. She knew David
would want to hear them, if he could, so she sent
him a silent message to let him know that she
wouldn't be far away, and said to Rosalind, 'I'll

502

be in the waiting room,' but if Rosalind heard she gave no sign of it.

Going close to the bed, Rosalind touched her fingers to her father's cheek as she said, 'Hello, Daddy, it's me. Lawrence is here too. We came as soon as we heard . . . Oh Daddy, please wake up. We need you so much and we love you so, so much. Can you hear me? I think you can. You're there, really, aren't you? You always are. Oh, Daddy, I don't know what to do. Please tell me what I have to do.'

Becoming aware of Lawrence standing next to her, she turned to him and tried to smile through her tears. 'Why don't you talk to him?' she said.

Lawrence's eyes grew round. 'Lucy's having her teeth cleaned,' he said. Then after baring his own, 'Can you wake up now? Please?'

Rosalind turned back to her father and had to stifle a sob. He seemed so diminished by the equipment he was attached to, so dependent and unlike the capable man she'd always known.

In the waiting room Lisa sat quietly with her mother and Roxy. There wasn't much to be said. All they could do was wait and pray to a god Lisa wasn't even sure she believed in that David wasn't suffering any more than he already had.

'Are you all right?' her mother asked after a while. 'You look all in.'

Lisa glanced at her and gave a small shake of her head.

'She shouldn't have blamed you,' Matilda said.

Sensing where this was heading, Lisa said, 'Leave it, Mum.'

503

'But how can it have been your fault?'

'Mum, please. This is difficult enough. He's her father, remember?'

'And he's your husband. Doesn't she know how much he means to you?'

'She doesn't want to know, and now isn't the time to try telling her, so please, let it go.'

With a sigh, Matilda clasped Roxy's hand more tightly in her own. 'What are you going to do,' she asked after a while, 'if he doesn't . . .'

Getting to her feet, Lisa said, 'Mum, I'm sorry, I can't deal with your questions now.'

As she left the room, Matilda said shakily to Roxy, 'This is very hard on her. They've only been married a few months and what she's had to put up with in that time . . . Dear, oh dear . . . He was such a lovely man . . .'

'Gran,' Roxy whispered, 'he's still with us.'

Matilda blinked. 'Yes, yes of course,' she said, colouring. 'I just can't help wondering, you know, if this mightn't be a blessing in disguise.'

Roxy cast her a glance. 'Whatever you do,' she told her, 'please don't let Lisa hear you say that.'

Chapter Twenty-Four

At ten o'clock that night when ICU visiting hours were over, they were all sent gently on their way, being assured that if anything happened before two the following afternoon they would be contacted right away. However, neither the specialist, nor the intensivist on duty, anticipated any change at this stage.

Dee and Miles had arrived by now, and each had taken a turn to sit with Rosalind next to her father, while Lawrence joined Lisa and the others in the waiting room. Sensing his frustration and boredom, Roxy had taken him up to the cafeteria a couple of times, and once for a walk round the block, but the weather was so foul outside, with sleeting rain and wind, that they didn't venture out again until it was time to go home.

Having spent no time with David herself was quietly breaking Lisa's heart, but the last thing she wanted was for some kind of showdown to erupt between her and Rosalind next to his bed.

'I'll make sure it happens tomorrow,' she told her mother as they rode home in a taxi.

'I should think so,' Matilda responded, squeezing

her hand. 'It's not right, the way she's treating you. Anyone would think . . .'

'No more, Mum,' Lisa interrupted. 'We're all tired now, and very emotional.'

When they got to the house Matilda went to put the kettle on, while Roxy checked the answerphone and Lisa wandered through to the pool to stare at the spot where he'd fallen. The trauma of those terrible minutes had left no physical mark, and she couldn't think why she'd expected one. It was almost as though nothing had happened there, and yet somewhere deep inside her she could still hear the echoes of herself shouting, and see the helpless slump of his body as she held him. She found herself remembering other times they'd swum here, and felt drawn into the resonance of their voices, and the imagined splash of the water. Their dreams were the other side of the windows now, slowly fading into the dark, misty night. In spite of knowing how desperately he'd wanted to avoid his fate, she still couldn't believe he was ready to leave them so soon. She certainly knew she wasn't ready to let go, and putting a hand over her abdomen she fought back the tears as she realised she might now never be able to tell him that he was going to be a father again.

'I thought you might want this,' Roxy said, coming in behind her.

Seeing her iPhone, Lisa took it, and blinking back the tears she whispered goodnight to David in her mind and turned out the lights.

'There are loads of messages,' Roxy told her as she came into the kitchen. 'It's been on the news apparently.'

Lisa nodded vaguely and took the tea her mother was passing her. Then her phone rang and seeing it was Tony she clicked on.

'I've been trying to get you,' he told her. 'As soon as I heard . . . How is he?'

'They say he's stable, but . . .' She swallowed and had to wait a moment before she could push any more words past the ache in her heart. 'I don't really know what's going to happen,' she said hoarsely.

His voice was gentle as he said, 'Is there anything I can do? Would you like me to come over?'

'Not tonight, thanks. Mum and Roxy are here and we're all shattered.'

'I'm sure,' he said sympathetically. 'I met him, you know. Did he ever tell you?'

Too tired to feel much surprise, she said, 'No. When?'

'Just after Christmas. I'll save it for another time, but I left understanding that he was the better man. He's someone I'd like to get to know.'

Realising how unlikely it was that would ever happen now, she felt herself falling apart again. 'I have to go,' she told him brokenly. 'I'll call when there's some news.'

Unable to face sleeping in their bed without David, she said goodnight to her mother and Roxy and took the phone to one of the guest rooms. She spent the next two hours talking to Amy about David and the baby, and how perverse fate could be.

By the time the call ended Theo had booked himself and Amy on to the next flight home.

* * *

Lisa arrived at the hospital just before two the following day, hoping to get some time with David before Rosalind arrived, but Rosalind and Lawrence were already there. She stood quietly at the end of the bed, looking at David. In spite of knowing that he was heavily sedated she was willing him to open his eyes, or to move a hand beneath Rosalind's, or to make a small attempt to react to Lawrence. There was no movement though, only the monotonous rasp of the ventilator accompanied by the tuneless rhythm of machines.

'Hello,' Kathy the nurse said, coming to join her. 'How are you today? Did you manage to sleep?'

'A little,' Lisa replied. 'How's David?'

'The same. Professor Cross saw him this morning. He'll be back to talk to you later.'

'Lucy's at home,' Lawrence suddenly told her. 'She's unable to come to the hospital because dogs are forbidden.'

Lisa smiled at him, and hoped with all her heart that David knew he was there. 'I'll wait next door,' she said to Kathy. Then, so Rosalind could hear, 'Perhaps I can sit with him in a while.'

Rosalind didn't respond, simply kept her back turned, so after receiving a sympathetic smile from Kathy, Lisa took herself upstairs to the cafeteria where Tony had stationed himself with Roxy and Matilda in case he was needed.

By the time an hour had passed Dee and Miles had joined them, along with Dee's son and his girlfriend.

'I think I'll go back to the waiting room,' Lisa told them. 'I need to feel closer than this.'

'I'll come with you,' Roxy offered.

As they walked away Lisa heard her mother saying, 'I'm sorry if I'm speaking out of turn, Dee, but your niece isn't allowing my daughter any time with David . . .'

Lisa started to turn back, but Roxy kept hold of her arm and pushed her on. 'It needs to be said,' she whispered, 'and Dee might be able to make Rosalind behave more reasonably.'

On reaching the ICU they found Rosalind where Lisa had left her, but Lawrence was in the waiting room watching TV.

'Why don't you go and sit next to her?' Roxy suggested.

Lisa was hesitant, knowing Rosalind wouldn't welcome it. Then, realising that she didn't want to share her time with David either, she shook her head. Rosalind would have to leave him at some point, if only to use the bathroom. She'd take her moment then.

As they turned away, Roxy was just opening the door to the waiting room when Professor Cross came out of the lift. 'Ah, Mrs Kirby,' he said, seeing Lisa. 'I was hoping to find you here. I'd like to have a word. Shall we?' he said, directing her on into the waiting room.

Finding Lawrence engrossed in a cartoon, the professor led Lisa into a corner and sat down with her, while Roxy went to sit with Lawrence.

Cross's eyes were fixed intently on Lisa's as he said, 'I believe your husband has vascular dementia.'

She felt her mouth turn dry as she nodded.

'So it's possible he's made a living will?'

Understanding where this was heading, she desperately wanted to deny it, but how could she? The law was the law, and she had no right to go against David's wishes. 'If you're asking . . .' She took a breath. 'If you're asking if he wants to be resuscitated in the event of something happening, then the answer is no, he doesn't.'

The professor nodded sadly, and his expression was regretful as he said, 'I'm sorry to tell you, Mrs Kirby, that there is no possibility of your husband recovering from this stroke to a degree that will give him any quality of life.'

Lisa's hands went to her head as she started to cry. 'I'm sorry,' she choked helplessly. 'It's just . . . I never thought when he made the will that anything like this . . .' She couldn't go on. It was all too awful.

In the end, the doctor said, 'It'll be kinder and the right thing to do if we let him go.'

Lisa's eyes came desperately to his. *No! No! No!* 'I understand what you're saying,' she gasped, 'but . . . Oh my God . . .' *I can't do this. I don't have it in me to let him go.*

'Take your time,' he said kindly. 'Nothing has to be done right away. Would you like me to speak to his daughter?'

Lisa's heart turned over. How the hell was Rosalind going to take this? She'd never let it happen, *never*. Yet she too would be bound by David's will. They really didn't have a choice. 'If you wouldn't mind,' she said in a whisper.

A few minutes later, after being summoned by a nurse, Rosalind came into the waiting room looking as though she might fall to pieces if anyone as much as touched her. When her eyes went briefly to Lisa, Lisa detected no malice or hostility, only fear and the telltale shadows of a sleepless night. Her freckles, Lisa thought, seemed oddly larger, which made her appear even more vulnerable than she was obviously feeling.

As the professor started to repeat his advice Lisa hid her face, unable to bear the hunted look that was coming over Rosalind's. He didn't get far before Rosalind shouted, '*No!* It's not going to happen. I'm not even going to talk about it. He's my father, and I'm telling you he will recover.'

'Rosalind . . .' Lisa began.

'Don't speak to me!' Rosalind seethed. 'Don't utter one single word. She wants him dead,' she shouted at the professor, 'and if you're going to side with her I swear I'll sue you and this hospital out of existence.'

Apparently unruffled, he said, 'I believe your father has made . . .'

'I'm not listening,' she cried, grabbing Lawrence. 'Come on, we're going to sit with David. We have to make sure these people don't get near him.'

After the door closed behind her Lisa said, 'I'm sorry. I . . . She's very close to him . . .'

'It's all right, I know these decisions are difficult. Does she know about his living will?'

'I'm not sure. If she does, she obviously doesn't want to.'

'Perhaps you can try talking to her again later.'

Lisa shook her head. 'She'll never listen to me. She thinks . . . Well, you heard what she said.'

His eyes were sympathetic. 'You realise that as his wife, his next of kin, you can act without her agreement?'

Feeling certain she never would, Lisa said, 'We don't have to make a decision today, do we?'

'No, of course not. I'll see if I can have another chat with her once she's had some time to try and get used to the situation.'

Much later in the day Dee and Miles returned from the ICU to find Lisa with Tony, her mother and Roxy in the cafeteria. 'If you go down now,' Dee said, 'you should be able to sit with him.'

Heaving a sigh of relief, Lisa said, 'Have you spoken to her? Where is she?'

'She's in the waiting room, asleep. She's exhausted, poor lamb.'

Having no doubt of it, Lisa got up from the table and made her way to the door. There was so much she wanted to say to David, the words crowding in so fast that she could barely contain them. She needed him to understand how happy she was to have married him, and how much she loved him and always would. She wanted him to know that she would treasure their memories, their dreams and every single minute they'd spent together. She was going to carry on the work he'd started to help people with dementia, she would devote all her time to it, and call it the David Kirby Trust. She was even considering donating the house as a place for those with early onset to see out their days, because she knew already that she couldn't live there without him.

Most of all though, she wanted to tell him about the baby.

When she reached the unit she found the nurses at their station and Lawrence sitting alone next to

David's bed. Realising he was speaking she hung back, not wishing to interrupt. At first she couldn't make out what he was saying, but as his words became clearer, she felt her emotions starting to tighten her throat. He was obviously listing creatures they'd seen together at the zoo, or maybe around the lake.

'. . . and then there was the natterer's bat, the whiskered bat and the barbastelle bat. Mum didn't like them, but Granny thought they were cute. She liked the birds too. The pied flycatcher, the redstart, the siskin, and you saw a short-eared owl . . .' As he mimicked the raspy cry of the bird, Lisa pressed a hand to her mouth to stifle a sob. With all her heart she hoped David could hear this peculiar little recital. 'Shall I tell you what we saw at the museum next?' Lawrence asked, his curly head tilting from side to side as his legs swung back and forth over the floor. 'Alfred the gorilla, a thylacine, a kakapo . . .' As his list grew longer Lisa went to stand quietly behind him, her heart breaking to see how sunken and frail David appeared, attached to so many wires and tubes like a lifeless puppet. She felt suddenly panicked, because he didn't seem to be there any more, and she hadn't had a chance to say goodbye. She needed to be alone with him, but Lawrence was still in full flow and she didn't have the heart to send him away. It wouldn't have been what David wanted, she felt sure of it, so in the end she went over to Kathy the nurse to ask if Professor Cross had managed to speak to Rosalind again.

'He came back about fifteen minutes ago,' Kathy told her, 'but she was asleep so we didn't wake her.'

Feeling helpless and bereft, Lisa turned away, intending to return to David's side, but the waiting-room door opened and seeing Rosalind, tousled and weary, she stayed where she was, unsure what to say or do.

Spotting Lisa, Rosalind blanched. Then her eyes shot to her father, as though making sure he was still there. 'I told you,' she said to Kathy, 'you mustn't let her near him. She wants to kill him . . .'

'Ssh, ssh,' Kathy soothed, going to her. 'Please keep your voice down, there are other patients . . .'

'I'm sorry,' Rosalind mumbled, 'but I'm afraid of what she might do.'

'Rosalind, for heaven's sake,' Lisa said, 'I'd never do anything to hurt him, or to hurt you.'

'Then why is he lying there? Why is the doctor trying to tell me he can't pull through? I know you're behind it . . .'

Interrupting before Lisa could, Kathy said, 'You have to go back into the waiting room if you want to continue this.'

'I don't need to speak to her. I know what she's going to say . . .'

'Rosalind, please,' Lisa implored. 'Whether you like it or not, we have to talk.'

Kathy said firmly, 'You have to sort things out in a way that's best for your dad.'

Clasping her hands to her head, Rosalind cried, 'You don't understand, any of you. I can't let him go. He means everything to me . . .'

'I know that,' Lisa told her, 'and you do to him. God knows, I don't want to lose him either,' she said, starting to cry, 'but we can't think about ourselves now.'

'You can, because that's the only person you ever think about,' Rosalind shouted, as Kathy eased her into the waiting room.

'I swear to you, Rosalind, if I didn't know what he'd put in his living will I wouldn't . . .'

'He only put it because you made him,' Rosalind choked hysterically. 'He's a fighter. He wouldn't want to give up without trying.'

'But what would he be fighting for? To live out his days with dementia? He's already been to Switzerland to try to set up that way out . . .'

'No!' Rosalind yelled, covering her ears. 'He would never do that without telling me.'

'He didn't tell you because he knew how much it would upset you.'

Rosalind was shaking her head, shaking and shaking.

'This has been very hard for him,' Lisa told her. 'The last thing he ever wanted was to let you and Lawrence down, but there's no cure for what he has, and he was afraid of becoming a burden to us.'

'He'd never be that for me. I'll take care of him . . .'

'It's not what he wants. The indignity, the suffering, the years he would take from your life . . . He would hate it, Rosalind, and in your heart I know you know it.'

'Stop!' Rosalind cried. 'Don't tell me what I know when you don't have the first idea about anything. Why don't you just go? Go on, get out of here. You've done enough damage to our lives, we don't need any more.'

Coming back into the room Kathy said, 'Rosalind,

I have to ask you again to keep your voice down.'

'Then make her go,' Rosalind shouted. 'She's only here to try and convince everyone she cares, when all she really wants is to switch off his life support so she can get on with her own life. Well, I'm not going to let her.'

Seeing Lisa's distress, Kathy said, 'Rosalind, please calm down. You're not helping yourself, or anyone else, least of all your father, being like this.'

'I know, I know,' Rosalind sobbed helplessly, 'but I can't do it. I can't let him go.' Her eyes came desperately to Lisa's. 'Please don't make me,' she begged. 'Please. I love him so much, and I know what you're saying is right, but I can't do it. I just can't.'

With tears streaming down her own cheeks, Lisa wrapped her arms around Rosalind and held her tight. 'I know, I understand,' she said, 'and we don't have to do anything now. We can talk about it, and decide when we think the time is right.'

Rosalind nodded. 'Yes, yes, let's do that. Please tell me that you love him.'

'Of course I love him. You know him, how could I not?'

'He's very special.'

'I know.'

'Oh God, please help me!'

Lisa tightened her embrace, and through her own despair she felt relieved to the very depths of her heart that Rosalind wasn't trying to push her away. They needed to come together for this, or getting through it would prove almost impossible – and it was only now that she realised the final word had to be Rosalind's, because she herself hadn't known David long enough for it to be hers.

On returning to her station, Kathy glanced over to David's bed and noticed that Lawrence was no longer there. Then confusion hit like a hammer, turning rapidly to disbelief as she realised the machines behind David's bed had fallen silent. It wasn't possible. An alarm sounded if anything went wrong, but as she rushed over to check what was happening she could see already that none of the equipment was working. Then she spotted Lawrence under the bed with his legs crossed and his head clamped in his hands. If the power was disconnected, how could an alarm ring?

'Oh my God,' Kathy murmured. 'Lawrence, what have you done?'

She didn't wait for an answer. She raced back to her station to call for backup, then returned swiftly to the bed. Lawrence was still under it, rocking back and forth and humming, while David lay above him, still attached to all his lifelines and breathing softly. He could so easily be sleeping, but she knew even if he were to wake up, which wasn't likely, he'd have no normal brain function at all.

Without giving herself any more time to think, she returned to the waiting room and said to Rosalind and Lisa, 'I need to tell you that Lawrence has disconnected the power to David's machines.'

Rosalind gave a cry of shock, but as she started forward, Kathy put up a hand. 'There's still time to reconnect him,' she said, 'help is on its way,

517

but this could . . . You might not want to make the decision this quickly, but there is . . .'

Letting the sentence hang, she went back into the unit just as the emergency backup team arrived.

Rosalind looked at Lisa, whose face had turned ashen. She was saying something, but Lisa wasn't quite hearing it. Then it reached her. 'If it has to be done,' Rosalind was whispering raggedly, 'then maybe . . . Oh Dad!' she cried. 'Am I doing the right thing?' She gulped for air. 'Maybe we should let it be now,' she said to Lisa.

No, no, no, Lisa was crying inside. *I've had no time with him. I need to tell him about the baby and that I love him and I'm going to miss him so much I just can't bear it.* Her stricken eyes went to Rosalind, and what she said was, 'I think we should say goodbye together.'

Seeing them come out of the waiting room, Kathy murmured to the backup team to stop. She eased them away from the bed as Rosalind and Lisa came to stand beside David.

Knowing that she didn't have to be concerned about the tubes any more, Lisa lifted David's hand and held it against her, as she said in a voice that was shredded with grief, 'I'm here, my darling, with Rosalind. I know it will make you happy to think of us together. We understand why you've chosen to leave now rather than come back to us, but I'm going to miss you so much.' Sensing Rosalind turning away, she leaned in closer and whispered, 'You've given me so much, David, but the most precious gift of all . . .' She broke off, her words blocked by tears. 'We're going to have a baby,' she finally managed in a voice that was barely audible. 'Isn't that wonderful? Thank you so much, my darling.' She took another breath as more emotion engulfed her. 'I want you to know that I'll love it and take care of it,' she whispered shakily, 'and I'll make sure it always knows you're its dad and how special you are. Oh David, I love you with all my heart. You've made me a better and a stronger person. I just wish we'd had more time . . .' She couldn't say any more, her heart was too full and her throat too tight.

She turned to find Rosalind at the nurse's station with her face buried in Kathy's shoulder. Whether she'd overheard anything was doubtful, since she was too far away.

Realising she could speak to her father now, Rosalind stepped forward and tried but failed to keep her voice steady as she took his hand and said, 'Daddy, I know this is what you want, but please forgive me for not wanting it too. I can't imagine my life without you and Mummy, but I'm going to do my best to be strong for Lawrence. He's here, under the bed, listening to us. He's far braver than I am, because he found the courage to do what you wanted. You've always been his very special friend, the one who understood him the best, and now I think perhaps he understood you too.' As her emotions threatened to choke her, she struggled for control. 'Daddy, I love you so much,' she gasped. 'Thank you for giving me such a wonderful life and I'm sorry for all the heartache I've caused you. God bless you, my darling. You'll always mean the whole world to me,' and as she stooped over him sobbing, Lisa held her and cried too, neither of them aware of Professor Cross coming into the unit behind them until he whispered gently, 'He's gone.'

Chapter Twenty-Five

Three days later Rosalind was walking along the lake shore, wrapped warmly in the dusky pink coat her father had always liked, and a black woollen scarf that sparkled in the winter sun. The sky was a pristine blue, while underfoot the ground was crisped by a glistening white frost. This was a trail she'd trodden often with her parents, and it seemed fitting to follow it today, winding through winter-bare copses and crossing the marshy inlets via old wooden bridges.

Her mobile began to ring for the third time in as many minutes, but she'd already decided that the only person she wanted to speak to this morning was here, walking with her.

'Maybe you should check to see who it is,' Lisa suggested, as they came out into a meadow. 'I'm sure everyone's worried about you, and if you didn't tell them where you were going . . .'

Accepting that she was probably right, Rosalind took out her phone and seeing it was Jerry she felt tempted to go on ignoring it. However, to continue avoiding him would serve no purpose, and feeling unexpectedly more confident with Lisa beside her she clicked on with a brief 'Hello?'

'At last,' he sighed in relief. 'I've been trying to get hold of you. Why didn't you return my calls?'

She didn't answer, because he'd surely have known why without having to be told.

'Rosalind, I'm so sorry,' he said earnestly. 'When I heard . . . It was such a shock. How are you? Is there anything I can do?'

'You already have, thank you,' she told him. He probably wouldn't fully understand that, but it didn't matter, she did, which was all that counted now. 'It's good of you to offer your condolences,' she said.

'But of course I would. He meant a great deal to me, I'm sure you know that. And I'd like to come to the funeral . . . I mean, if it's all right with you.'

Was it all right with her? Did she want him around as a reminder of the past when they'd been happy, all of them, with no idea of what the future held? Desertion, dementia, death. Did all bad things begin with D? 'I'll make sure someone lets you know when and where it is once it's all finalised,' she heard herself saying. 'I hope you're not thinking of bringing . . .'

'Oh no, no, no,' he assured her. 'That wouldn't be appropriate at all.'

'Exactly.' Then, because she thought he ought to know, 'Ben Fortune will be there as my partner.'

There was a pause before he said, 'Is this someone . . . Do I know him?'

'I've no idea, Jerry.' Did it matter? Did she care? 'Thank you for your call. I won't forget to let you know when we have a date and time.'

As she rang off she felt Lisa glance at her, but

kept her eyes straight ahead, squinting against the sun as she said, 'Thank you again for letting me organise the funeral. It means a great deal to me.'

Having felt certain it would, and knowing it was very probably what David would have wanted, Lisa said, 'You know I'll do anything I can to help.'

'Thank you,' Rosalind said again, sounding stiffer than she'd have liked, but holding in so much grief wasn't easy. This was a world without her father in it, a life that would be empty without him. She looked around and saw a field where only his ghost would wander now, a valley where the memory of him would linger for a while and eventually fade. She couldn't bear it. Everything felt wrong. She couldn't lift her eyes to the sky, but she was aware of it, dazzling and clear, and she prayed that he was up there somewhere with her mother, otherwise there would seem no point to anything any more. And yet this woman walking beside her, his new wife, would that be what she wanted? Surely not.

'How's Lawrence?' Lisa asked.

Feeling her heart jolt as her thoughts moved to her son, Rosalind said, 'He hasn't mentioned Dad since . . . I've tried to talk to him about it, but he just shakes his head and starts to get angry. Dr Knoyle is going to refer us to a specialist counsellor.'

'That's good,' Lisa said softly.

Rosalind nodded abstractedly. Her mind was already moving back to the reasons she'd asked Lisa to meet her today, and as they stole like dark shadows over her courage she cast her a quick glance, trying to gauge what she might be thinking. So far she'd betrayed no hostility or resentment for the way she'd been treated, but that wasn't to say she didn't feel it. Was she angry, or vengeful? Her offer to hand over the funeral arrangements didn't suggest it, but perhaps she was just glad not to have to deal with them herself.

Sensing Rosalind's need to say something, Lisa was searching for a way to try and put her at her ease. She longed to tell her about the baby, to let her know that they hadn't lost David altogether, but it wasn't something she could just blurt out and she had no way of knowing how Rosalind would respond, anyway. She made herself sound warm and friendly as she said, 'I promise I'm not here to make your life any more difficult than it already is. It wouldn't help either of us to do that, so whatever you have to say, please, just say it.'

Taking a breath, Rosalind struggled to summon the carefully chosen words she'd rehearsed in her mind a dozen times overnight, but when they came they were hesitant and fractured by the fear of what she could be about to provoke. 'I know,' she began, 'that I probably don't have the right to ask . . . I mean, it's not really my business, but I wondered . . . Were you and Dad . . . Were you seeing one another while Mum was ill? You see, she thought you were and so did I and if you were . . .'

'Sssh,' Lisa said gently. 'Actually, I saw him once, that's all.'

Rosalind's breath locked in her chest, causing it to burn with dread. She didn't want to go on hating this woman, but if her worst fears were true . . .

'It wasn't planned,' Lisa went on. 'We ran into one another at a party in Paris, and then we had coffee together the next day.' She paused in case Rosalind wanted to say something, but she was keeping her head down as they trudged slowly on through the grass. 'I didn't know at the time that your mother was sick – I think she might have been in remission, I'm not sure, because we didn't . . . Well, there was no reason . . .'

'Did you realise you were still in love with one another then?' Rosalind interrupted.

'No, because I'm not sure we were. You have to remember that over twenty years had passed since we'd last seen one another, and though I won't deny we probably felt some of the old attraction . . . Well, we didn't discuss our feelings. It was just good to see one another again.'

'So you . . . You didn't have an affair?' Rosalind said shakily.

'No, we didn't. You must know that your father would never have cheated on your mother.'

Rosalind swallowed and gave an almost imperceptible shrug. It was what she wanted to believe, and now perhaps she could.

'He wasn't cut out for disloyalty or deception,' Lisa continued, knowing that no amount of reassurance would be too much for Rosalind right now, 'and I'd like to think that I'm not either. Anyway, I was in a bit of a mess at the time, breaking up with someone who I'd been with for many years . . .' Realising that had no relevance right now, she dismissed it with a wry, 'Broken relationships can be very tricky at times.'

Thinking of Jerry and admiring the understatement, Rosalind managed a fleeting smile. 'You know what's the most difficult?' she said. 'It's that I'm not sure she ever truly believed Dad loved her.'

Melting with pity as she realised how heartbreaking that would have been for her, Lisa said, 'Then that's a shame, because he did, very much. I know that with all my heart, and I think it's important for you to know it too. There's no doubt in my mind that your mother was the big love of his life.' The fact that he was the big love of hers wasn't something she could think about now; it was all too painful, and she was missing him so much.

Having to bite her lip to stop herself from crying, Rosalind somehow whispered a tremulous thank you.

Understanding that she needed some time now to get past the enormous swell of emotions in her heart, Lisa walked on quietly beside her, trying to keep her own grief from spilling over. It had no place here today, it was for the privacy of her home and to be shared with her family, not to be loaded on to Rosalind, who was already carrying too much. Yet at the same time a voice inside her was crying out for David so insistently that she could hardly bear it. She was feeling a need for him that was so much stronger than she'd recognised while he was alive. Everything was out of kilter without him. The house was a shell. The future was an empty road, but thank God there was the baby. The mere thought of this very special gift he'd left her with, so precious and so wanted, sent a wonderful warmth spreading through her.

Thank you, my darling, she whispered silently, *thank you, thank you for giving us this tiny little life that I'm going to hope and pray will bring Rosalind and me together in a way that we never managed ourselves.*

'I was wondering,' Rosalind said finally, 'would you mind . . . ? How would you feel if I buried him with Mum?'

As a surge of denial rose up from Lisa's heart, not because she didn't want him to be with Catrina, but because she didn't want him to be dead at all, she gave herself a moment before she said, 'I think it's the right thing for you and for them.' Which, of course, it was. They were a family, and she'd been a part of his life for such a very short time.

As Rosalind's emotions engulfed her again, she pressed a hand to her mouth and waited for them to subside. There would be time later to let go, and she'd promised herself she wouldn't today. 'I'm sorry,' she whispered brokenly.

'Please don't apologise . . .'

'No, I mean, I'm sorry for the way I've treated you . . .' She took a deep breath. 'I don't deserve your kindness. I know now that I got it wrong about you, and I wish I knew how to make up for it.'

'You don't have to. There are many more important things you have to face now.' She wanted to offer to be there for her, to try and help her through them, but maybe it was too soon for that too.

Starting to notice where they were, Rosalind stopped walking and looked up at the magnificent house on Carlisle Court Lane. Her cheeks were red with the cold, and her brilliant blue eyes sparkled with tears. 'It's always been the most spectacular house in the area,' she said. 'Are you sure about donating it to the new trust?'

Lisa gazed up at it too, and felt her dreams crushing her heart. So much love and hope, a beautiful wedding, a fleeting look at how life could have been . . . 'I think so,' she replied. Then, making herself sound more definite, 'Yes, I am. I don't want to live there without him, and I know how much it mattered to him to help people with the same condition.'

'So where will you go?' Rosalind asked.

Lisa inhaled deeply.

'I'm sorry, it's none of my business.'

'No, no, you have a right to ask.' She didn't add, I'm your stepmother, after all, because that was a relationship, a tie that neither one of them had yet come close to acknowledging. 'I just wish I could be more specific with my answer,' she said. 'I still have my flat in London, of course, but I also have temporary custody of my niece, in that she's at uni and will need somewhere to come home to for the occasional weekend. Maybe I'll try to buy somewhere small for the two of us, not too far from Oxford.'

Rosalind said, 'Is money an issue? I mean, if giving up the house is going to leave you . . .'

'No, it's not,' Lisa assured her. She was well taken care of financially, David had seen to that, and she wouldn't mention now that Tony was insisting that she and Roxy should think of his Cotswold home as theirs. She hadn't told him about the baby yet either, but she probably would after the funeral was over. She felt sure he wouldn't withdraw his offer, that wouldn't be Tony at all. As for what the future might hold for them as a couple, she had no idea and wasn't even ready to think about it yet. 'What matters now,' she said, 'is where you go from here. Is it serious between you and Ben?'

Giving a shaky laugh, Rosalind turned her face to the sky. 'I'm not sure,' she said, 'but I think, maybe it could be.' Then, surprising even herself as the confidence came tumbling out, she said, 'Looking back over this last year, which has definitely been my worst so far, the best thing – and I really mean best thing – that happened to me was Jerry leaving. I can't explain why, exactly, but after the initial shock, it started to feel as though all the confusion and insecurity and madness had gone with him.' She shook her head, as though amazed that she was only just realising the truth of her words. 'Trust is such a big thing, isn't it?'

Lisa nodded. 'The biggest,' she agreed. 'If I'd had it with my ex when we were together, well I suppose we'd still be together now.'

Thinking of Ben, and remembering how he too had found out the hard way what it meant to be betrayed, Rosalind put it away to consider again at another time. It wasn't necessarily the basis for a relationship, but it must surely help when it came to building understanding. Turning her thoughts back to Lisa, and who might be waiting for her in the house on the hill, she said, 'Your sister's here, isn't she?'

'Yes, she is,' Lisa answered.

The words were out before Rosalind could stop them. 'I wish I'd had a brother or sister.'

Understanding more than ever how lonely she

must be, Lisa said, 'Amy would like to meet you before she goes back. I mean, not just at the funeral . . .'

Rosalind turned to look at her. 'Thank you,' she said softly.

Lisa smiled. 'It would be . . .'

'No, not for saying that about Amy,' Rosalind said. 'Well yes, for that too, but thank you for showing me how foolish and ridiculous and destructive it is to judge someone without even knowing them.'

Having been there so many times herself, Lisa wanted to hug her, but held back just in case Rosalind didn't welcome it.

'And thank you for coming to meet me today,' Rosalind continued. 'It was long overdue, which is my fault, of course, but I hope you'll be able to forgive me. No, no, you don't have to answer. I know it is, and I'm sorry.' Embarrassed now, she glanced at her watch. 'It's probably time I was getting back,' she said. 'There's a lot to do.'

Suspecting she probably couldn't cope with any more for the moment, Lisa felt sad to be letting her go so soon, but simply said, 'Don't forget, if you need anything, I mean anything at all, you only have to pick up the phone.'

Rosalind nodded and gave a quick smile. 'Bye then,' she said awkwardly. Should she shake her hand, kiss her, what should she do?

'Bye,' Lisa whispered.

Since they were now going in opposite directions, they both started to turn away.

'Actually, there is something,' Rosalind suddenly said.

Surprised, and pleased, Lisa turned back.

Giving a self-conscious shrug, Rosalind said, 'If you're free on Saturday, I'd love to go out somewhere for lunch.'

With a laugh that spilled over with tears, Lisa didn't hold back again, she simply gathered Rosalind up in her arms and held her close as she said, 'It'll be my pleasure, and my treat.'

That was when she would tell her the news.

Acknowledgements

A huge thank you to Dan Norris MP who treated me to a fascinating inside glimpse of Westminster; and to the Right Hon David Miliband the then Secretary of State for Foreign Affairs for taking some time out of his hectic schedule to chat about his world.

Thank you enormously to Tim Parry of The Alzheimer's Research Trust, and to Vivienne Hill for sharing her experiences with her mother who is tragically suffering from this disease. I am deeply indebted to Sarah Cullum, Consultant in Old Age Psychiatry, and Dr Judy Haworth, Psychiatrist specialising in memory care, for guiding me through the process of detecting and diagnosing early onset dementia. Also to Professor Tony Bailey of Oxford University for his help with Asperger's Syndrome.

Further thanks to Robin Johnson for helping with the character of Jerry Sewell. Also to my good friends Ursula Gantenbein and Jorge Wengle for their invaluable help with the Zurich sequence. And to Hans Muralt of Exit for talking me through the process of assisted suicide. Another very big thank you to my hero, Carl Gadd, for help with the emergency response. And a huge thank you to Sarah Smith for sharing her invaluable knowledge of intensive care.

Much love and thanks to my dearest friend Denise Hastie for acquainting me with the Chew Valley which is where, loosely, the book is set.

If you have enjoyed *Forgotten*, why not try Susan Lewis' compelling new novel *Stolen*?

Lucy Winters' parents have always been there for her. Loving, gentle and kind they have given her everything she could have wished for. Now, estranged from her husband, she has moved to the country to take over their thriving auction business. The moment she begins to prepare for her first sale she knows she's made the right decision. And she dares to hope that at last she is living the life she has always dreamed of.

But then, quite suddenly, her world is thrown into turmoil. She discovers a shocking truth, one that forces her to question everything she has ever known. And it becomes frighteningly possible that the very people who should have protected her are the ones who have betrayed her in the most devastating of ways. Can she ever forgive them? Can they ever forgive themselves...?

Turn over to read the first chapter

Stolen will be available in paperback from September 2010

For more information about Susan Lewis and her forthcoming titles, visit her at www.susanlewis.com or become a fan on Facebook

Chapter One

Now everything was going her way, Lucy Winters wasn't at all sure this was what she actually wanted. Except it was, of course it was, she just couldn't help worrying about being careful of what she wished for, and all that . . . This wasn't going to backfire on her, was it?

Since it really didn't seem likely, she resolved to hold firm and hang on to the courage of her convictions, while Joe, damn him, didn't seem to be in the least bit fazed by what he was doing. If anything, he seemed to be rather enjoying himself, which might have been annoying if she hadn't known it was a front.

Joe was good at those – when he wanted to be.

As she stood in the bedroom doorway watching him, Lucy's deep brown eyes kept flicking to the mirror that was propped up against the opposite wall. They'd had this mirror for nine years now and Joe still hadn't got round to putting it up, so good job Lucy hadn't been holding her breath. Without her in it, the mirror would show a busy landscape of wild-flower wallpaper, a faux-leather head-board, one nightstand with a recycled Tiffany lamp and a pile of sports mags (on Joe's side), while hers had a matching lamp and various books about running a business and understanding antiques. With her in it, the mirror became a kind of portrait frame around a tall, gangly woman of thirty-seven with long, shiny dark hair that flopped loosely around her shoulders and a delicate heart-shaped face that became radiant when she smiled.

Not much radiance going on at the moment.

In fact, Lucy was wondering how she was managing to show no emotion at all when she was watching the start of

1

her life as she knew it coming to an end. There was plenty going on inside, a whole party of dread, excitement, hope, anticipation, romance (of the strictly non-sexual variety), and *sooo* much she wanted to say that she simply couldn't understand how she was managing to stay zipped up.

Probably because what she was feeling hadn't yet formed itself into words that she felt safe enough to speak.

Hearing a door slam downstairs, she tensed and listened. It was either Ben, their son, returning from his friend's who lived over the newsagent's at the end of the road, or Hanna, their daughter, leaving home. She hoped it was Ben, not only because of how much steadier she felt when both children were in the house – as if each of their forays into the outside world was going to end in disaster, and plenty did around their neck of the woods, but don't let her get started on that – but because Ben, at eighteen, was so much better at handling his fifteen-going-on-twenty-five-year-old sister these days than Lucy was.

So, they were either both downstairs now, or no one was. Given the silence she had to accept it was the latter, which meant that Hanna had stormed off. This caused a mixture of relief and worry to start battling for territory in Lucy's conscience, and she knew already that the latter would win.

Joe had always been great with their daughter, or that was what he liked to think, and it was true, they were close, but parenting skills had never really been his forte. However, should the need arise, Lucy was willing to believe that he'd dash into a burning building to rescue one of his offspring, as her own father had once done for her. This would be out of love, of course, and because Joe liked to consider himself a hero. She used to think of him as such during the first years of their marriage, but a lot had changed since then. For a start Hanna had grown up, and, in Lucy's opinion, it was because Joe had never yet grasped the concept of saying no to his darling daughter that they were now having such problems with her. Since she'd been old enough to understand, or manipulate, Hanna had always turned to her father for whatever she wanted, which made Joe, in her eyes, God, Santa Claus and Merlin the Magician all rolled into one. He could make any wish come true, or so it seemed to Hanna, and Joe was nothing if not gifted at glossing the myth. This meant that over the years most of the discipline had been left to the snarling old dragon called Mummy, who, Hanna had lately come to realise, needed to get over herself and get a life.

Well, Hanna was right about that.

According to Hanna everything that was happening now was Lucy's fault, and in this instance Lucy had to admit that Hanna had a case, since it had most definitely been Lucy's decision to get out of the rut they were in. Actually rut was far too mild a description as far as Lucy was concerned, because to her it felt like their very own pothole with endless passageways and no exit, and for someone who'd never have dreamed of taking up such a bizarre hobby she'd long ago reached a point where she needed to get out. Unfortunately Joe, youngest of the infamous East End Winters brothers, didn't think they were in a rut at all.

To Joe, this hallowed turf (his words, not hers) was the only place he'd ever wanted to live, or ever would, and his chosen career was the only one he intended to pursue, or ever would. In the case of his brothers a career meant either flogging from the back of a lorry at market (Charlie), or driving a taxi (Vince). In Joe's case it meant acting, mainly because once, way back when, he'd been cast in a soap opera that had run for several years and turned him into a household name. However, these days even the lowliest walk-on parts were proving almost impossible to come by, since reality TV had jammed a finger in the dyke of drama (Joe's choice of phrase, not hers). So, now, in between auditions and the odd commercial or voice-over, he was most often to be found in one of 'the lanes' (Petticoat, Brick, Leather), working the markets with Charlie; or driving Vince's minicab when Vince was too hung-over to crawl out of bed. The rest of the time he pumped iron at a gym owned by one of his uncles, or just as often he might be found at the Feathers catching up with a couple of his fellow thesps who, like him, weren't only role-less, but ageing and agentless.

Coming from such a different world herself – the only child of a modest and somewhat nomadic couple, thanks to her father's job setting up new offices for a multinational

3

insurance company – when Lucy had first met Joe she'd been totally captivated by his fame and family and the whole nine yards of what it meant to belong to the same community for generations, dubious though some of the connections might be. It was everything she'd ever dreamed of: being part of a neighbourhood where everyone knew each other, the children played together, the men all supported West Ham, and the women exchanged recipes and beauty tips. To quote Joe, their part of London was as tight as a boxer's fist, and don't let anyone try to mess with them or they'd be sorry.

They'd met when Lucy was only seventeen and Joe was twenty-eight and starring in the soap as an East End bad boy. The nation had loved him back then, and so had she from the minute she'd started her work experience as a runner on the set of his show. She'd been in her first year of sixth-form college at the time, but once they'd realised how they felt about each other – or, perhaps more accurately, once they'd found out she was pregnant – all thoughts of further education and dazzling careers were banished from her mind. Joe Winters was so madly in love with her that he wanted to marry her and have at least five kids with her. She was going to be *the wife of Joe Winters*, who half the nation's women were swooning over! It was no wonder it turned her teenage head, especially after all the years she'd spent on the outside, always the new girl in class, the one who was teased and ostracised and made to feel worthless and ashamed. How she'd longed to see the faces of her tormentors when her photograph appeared in the papers with Joe Winters! And her dear, gentle parents, poked fun at by everyone for being so old, had been as won over by the roguish Billy Crowther, aka Joe Winters, as she was, so had simply shared her joy and barely even mentioned her age, or lost opportunities.

What a curse a little bit of fame could be, she often thought now. Had Joe simply been the bloke next door, with dodgy prospects and an equally dodgy reputation, would her parents have been so lenient, or welcoming, then? Come to think of it, would she have been as smitten? The answer was probably yes, because he'd been so heart-stoppingly good-looking and full of charm that it was hard to imagine how any starry-eyed girl of her age could have managed to resist him, fame or not.

It wasn't so hard now she was in her mid-thirties, and the sense of belonging she'd always craved had dwindled in the first few years. It was odd how having two children of her own, two brothers- and sisters-in-law, four nieces, three nephews, a father-in-law and dozens of extended family still hadn't managed to make her feel as though she fitted in. She wished she could understand what was wrong with her, why nothing, apart from her children, ever seemed to feel right, but the only answer either she, or her mother, could come up with was that she'd never got over being an only child with no aunts or uncles or cousins to help fill her world, since her parents had been only children too. The sense of isolation, and of feeling so apart from everyone else, particularly when she'd changed schools so often, must be so deeply imbedded in her that maybe it would never go away.

Perversely, she could only be glad now that she did still feel like an outsider, because leaving would have been so much harder if she were trying to disentangle emotional ties. Not that it was going to be easy saying goodbye to all the tradespeople she'd come to know and respect, and it wasn't as if she didn't care for Joe's family at all, because she did. However, she had to move Hanna away from here before things got any worse than they already were.

'You're a bloody snob, that's what you are,' Hanna had raged when Lucy had first told her they were leaving. 'Everyone says it about you. You think you're better, just because you speak with a stupid stuck-up accent and you started up an effing book club. But you only do the same job as Auntie Sandra down the call centre, and at the end of the day your shit smells too.'

Recalling the coarseness, Lucy winced. Hanna might be extremely pretty, with Joe's blond hair and blue eyes, and she might have a TDF – to die for – figure, but being lovely on the outside was no guarantee of being the same within. OK, she was a teenager so being headstrong and challenging was only to be expected, but the way Hanna was carrying on went far beyond what Lucy was prepared to tolerate. Just thank God she hadn't fallen pregnant yet, but two of

5

her friends were already mothers and at least three had had terminations. Thankfully, Hanna had asked to go on the pill when she was fourteen, but even so Lucy detested the idea that she was having sex so young, especially with the kind of boys to whom she seemed attracted. Even Joe, who usually let Hanna get away with just about anything, had started to take a dim view of the crowd she was hanging out with. Not that he'd spoken to her about it, he didn't see that as his role, but he was prepared to agree with Lucy that Hanna needed a firmer hand. He especially didn't like to think of her rolling around drunk with her friends, mouthing off at the police and staggering into gutters, where her brother had found her on one memorable occasion. Thank God Ben had brought her home before anything worse could happen, and while Joe had dutifully sat next to her bed to make sure she didn't choke on her own vomit Ben had talked seriously to his mother.

'You've got to do something about it,' he'd told her. 'She's putting herself in real danger getting smashed like that.'

'I know, and I am doing something,' Lucy had assured him. 'I haven't told her yet, but when she breaks up for the summer we're leaving this house and we won't be coming back.'

The way Ben's sleepy blue eyes widened with interest had made her heart sing with love. Unlike Hanna, nothing ever seemed to faze him.

'You know how Granny and Grandpa have always wanted me to take over the business one day?' she'd continued. 'Well, I've had a long chat with them and it's going to happen sooner rather than later.'

Ben was clearly impressed. 'Cool,' he responded. 'Are you pleased? Sure you are, you've been dying to do it.'

Lucy wanted to hug him. He was the only person in her world who seemed to understand her need to make more of her life, and moreover he never took it personally, or tried to make it about him, the way Joe and Hanna did. 'I'd always intended to wait till Hanna went to uni,' she reminded him, 'but with the way things are I'm not even sure uni's still on her agenda. If I could see her doing what you did at her age, working to save up for a gap year,

6

studying for your exams, I wouldn't dream of making her change schools now. I went through that too often myself to want to inflict it on her, but there's no doubt in my mind that I have to get her out of where she is.'

'You're doing the right thing,' Ben assured her. 'They're a real waste of space, the kids she's hooked up with. A couple of them even carry knives.'

Though Lucy had guessed this, hearing Ben confirm it had made her more anxious than ever to get the move under way.

'So what's going to happen? Will you live with Granny and Grandpa?' he asked.

'Only when we first get there. Once we're settled they're going to move to the cottage on Exmoor. Grandpa's not getting any younger, and Granny's quite keen for him to retire, so the summer holidays seemed like the perfect time for them to hand over to me. That way Hanna will have a few weeks to acclimatise before she starts her new school – and you'll already be off on your travels so I won't have to worry about you.'

Ben's grin was mischievous.

'All right,' Lucy conceded, 'of course I'll worry, we both know that, but at least I won't be interrupting your education or taking you away from a home you don't want to leave.'

Seeming to approve of the logic, Ben said, 'So where does Dad fit into all this? Don't tell me he's going to give up living round here.'

'No, he isn't, but he accepts that it would be best for Hanna to continue her education at a private school near Granny and Grandpa's. We'll have the money to pay for it once they've signed everything over to me, which is happening even as we speak.'

'Wicked,' Ben murmured. 'So you're going to be rich?'

'Not exactly, but we'll have a house that belongs to us and a thriving business to help keep things going.'

'And Dad's going to do what?'

With a guilty sigh Lucy said, 'He's decided to move in with Uncle Charlie and Auntie Kell for the time being. Their house is much bigger than ours and we're not sure he can keep up the rent on this place on his own.' He wouldn't have been able to pay a mortgage either, if they had one, but since the dark days, back in the mid-nineties when they'd had their home repossessed, they'd never managed to get on the property ladder again. Of course her parents had offered to help, but having learned the hard way how unreliable, even irresponsible, Joe was when it came to money, Lucy had flatly refused to let them take the risk. 'But he'll be coming to see us at weekends,' she told Ben brightly, while not adding that she actually wished he wouldn't, because more than anything she'd have liked to make this a trial separation between them. However, Hanna was going to find it hard enough being uprooted as it was: if she thought she was hardly ever going to see her precious daddy, Lucy was afraid of what she might do.

'So when are you going to tell Hanna?'

Lucy swallowed. 'Soon, and I know it won't be pretty.'

How right she'd been about that, because it really hadn't been. In fact it was so ugly at first that even Joe had ended up raising his voice to the girl, which had the happy result of making her run away. For two days and two nights they searched the neighbourhood, interrogated her friends, enlisted the help of the school and eventually the police. When she'd finally turned up looking a total wreck and sobbing her heart out, the reek of booze and relief that she was safe had finally convinced Joe that his hallowed turf was no longer the right place for his little angel to be. Until then Lucy had been half afraid that when the time came Hanna would manage to cajole him into letting her stay with him in London, and faced with that she really wouldn't have known what to do.

Fortunately that was no longer an issue. There were plenty of others still to be dealt with, however, not least of which was how much she was hurting Joe by leaving.

'Personally, I think you're off your head letting him go,' Stephie, one of his cousins, had told her. Stephie had no idea what Joe was really like, because she wasn't married to him. In fact, she wasn't married to anyone, but would give almost anything to be a wife. 'You don't want to know what it's like out here,' she cried passionately. 'The chances of meeting anyone else, or anyone sane, with hair and teeth and a decent job are next to zero, especially at your age.' Since Stephie, who was thirty, was a serial dater thanks to Match.com and various other Internet sites, Lucy was willing to accept that she had superior knowledge when it came to the foreign land of Sad and Single.

However, Lucy didn't want to meet anyone else. That wasn't what this was about at all. Now she was standing here watching Joe sorting his belongings into one of the hold-alls they'd taken on honeymoon, so many happy memories were drifting in from forgotten lanes that she found herself wondering what he'd say if she told him she'd changed her mind. Not about going to Gloucestershire, it was far too late for that, and besides she could hardly wait to get there, but did she really want to view this as a trial separation? After all the agonised discussions, tears, fighting, persuading and even the occasional threat, would Joe be willing to carry on now as though she'd never even suggested such a thing? Knowing him as well as she did, she guessed he'd open his arms and smile in the way that always used to melt her heart, and tell her that all he ever wanted was to make her happy. He genuinely believed that was the truth, because he'd managed long ago to convince himself that she came first, when in actual fact no one ever mattered more to Joe than Joe himself. Which made him sound selfish and egotistical, inconsiderate and disrespectful, and he was indeed all of those things, but there was a lot more to him besides, such as his generosity and love of fun, willingness to help old people across the street and kindness to animals.

Why hadn't her marriage been a success, she wondered. Was it her fault? It couldn't have been all his, so what was wrong with her?

Why did nothing ever feel right? Even when things were going her way and she had every reason to be happy, all too often the shadows of unease and doubt would start looming in a way that made her feel out of kilter with her world and even sometimes estranged from those she loved. Well, perhaps not from her parents and children, but certainly from Joe, and the craziest part of it was that the longer they stayed together the more distanced from him she seemed to feel.

Why was that happening? Should she try to discuss it with him? She knew she should, yet at the same time she knew she wouldn't. All she did was continue watching him pack and wonder how far she would let him go before she suddenly blurted out something she'd very likely end up regretting.

'You keeping an eye on me in case I steal your jewels?' he teased, as he stuffed a pile of unpressed boxers into the holdall. She could have ironed them for him, she thought with a pang of guilt. She always used to. She'd forgotten now when she'd stopped. Had it been to punish him for being more like a child than a man, dependent, stubborn, always wanting his own way unless her needs happened to chime with his own, when he could put on such a convincing act of being the most big-hearted husband in town that even she was taken in?

She didn't have any jewels.

Remembering a time when they used to say what's mine is yours and had never even imagined dividing their assets, she said, 'We're doing the right thing.'

His arresting blue eyes came to hers in a way that made it hard for her to meet them. 'Yes, we are,' he agreed, 'so don't go upsetting yourself now. It's a brave decision you've taken and hard as it is now, for both of us, I don't have any doubts that everything will turn out for the best.'

This could only mean that he was happy for her to go, because if he weren't he'd be stomping about and throwing a Hanna-style tantrum, making her feel even worse about breaking up their home than she already did. And if he was happy for her to go it had to be because he already had something, or someone else, waiting to take her place. 'What do you think is the best?' she asked hoarsely. 'That we get back together, or end up going our separate ways for good?'

Coming to stand in front of her, he cupped a hand round her face and gazed into her eyes. 'What's best,' he said, 'is that you do whatever needs to be done to become the woman you think you might have been, if I hadn't turned you into a wife and mother when you were still not much more than a baby yourself.'

Her laugh was mangled by a sob. 'I was a willing party,' she reminded him, 'and I wouldn't change a thing.'

The irony that tilted his smile crushed her with yet more guilt, because they both knew that given half a chance she'd probably change everything.

'I know I made you a lot of promises that I haven't been able to keep,' he said, going back to his packing, 'so I'm hoping this will turn out to be a good opportunity for me to try and sort myself out too.'

Why was she feeling so bad about not asking him to come, when she knew very well that he wouldn't even if she did? He'd always been adamant about that, and she definitely didn't want him ruining her plans, which he almost certainly would given his enthusiasm for bending and stretching laws, plus his complete aversion to paying taxes or bills if he could get away with it. They'd have been in trouble by the end of the year and possibly in prison by the end of the next. His reckless generosity with other people's money, including hers, was why they still didn't own a house, or a car that could manage more than a dozen journeys without breaking down, or many of the trappings that most average families could boast these days.

Glancing at his mobile as it started to ring, she left him to answer the call and went off to the bathroom to start sorting his shaving gear and toothbrush into a spare toiletry bag. When she picked up his cologne the smell seemed to wrap around her like an embrace. She reached for the towel he'd used that morning and held it to her face. It was as though he'd already gone and she was trying to conjure him out of the essences he'd left behind.

By this time next week they'd all be gone. This shabby terraced house where they'd lived for the past sixteen years, a stone's throw from the high street, would be a partly furnished shell with no voices or music, or love, or laughter bringing it to life. It would stand silently waiting for the next tenants to come and revive it with a whole new set of characters and a story that Lucy guessed she'd probably never know. Whoever they were, she hoped they'd be as happy here as she had often been, and didn't suffer anything like the same heartaches and frustrations.

'No one's life is perfect,' Joe had reminded her on more

occasions than she cared to recall. 'It's only you who seems to think it's possible.'

But it wasn't perfection she was after, it was something else that she couldn't quite define, but it had to do with stability and feeling as though everything was worthwhile, and for some reason she hadn't been able to find it here. Maybe in Gloucestershire, with a home and business of her own, she would finally feel settled and stop this restless searching for she knew not what.

In the bedroom Joe was finishing his call. '. . . sure, yeah. No rush, whenever you can get here.'

Guessing it was Carlos, one of his actor chums, who'd offered to come and help him move over to Charlie's while Charlie and Kell were in Tenerife, Lucy continued the dispiriting task of removing her husband's toiletries from the forest of those left behind. It was kind of Carlos to help out, but since he only had a car because Joe had sold him their old one for less than half its worth, as that was all Carlos could afford, in Lucy's opinion Carlos jolly well should be chauffeuring his mate around.

They had another car now, a twelve-year-old Peugeot Estate which they'd have entered into the scrappage scheme had they been able to afford to change it, but they hadn't. Lucy was keeping it for the time being to get herself, Hanna and their belongings to Gloucestershire, then she might be in a position to buy something newer and more reliable.

Would that cheer Hanna up, to go shopping for a new car? It would take a lot more than that, but please God the country air and new friends would start to free her gentle and loving daughter from the shell of aggression and hostility that currently imprisoned her.

'Carlos'll be here in ten minutes,' Joe told her as she returned to the bedroom.

Tucking the toiletry bag into a front pocket of the holdall, she said, 'I'd have given you a lift.'

He flashed her one of his disarmingly ironic smiles that seemed to say 'I know, but I've decided to go my way, thanks.'

Though she was annoyed, she wasn't going to allow herself to start rowing with him now, or her guilt would no doubt force her into saying plenty she'd end up regretting.

Besides, it had all been said before, and though she really did detest herself for calling him a loser, as she had on more than one occasion, the fact that he went on so few auditions these days and was so rarely cast never seemed to suggest to him that it was time to start rethinking his career. He just kept plugging away at it, staying as upbeat as if his phone never stopped ringing, talking up his fifteen minutes a storm to anyone who'd listen, while suffering more let-downs and rejections than even a thick-skinned Jehovah's Witness could surely have borne.

Joe never seemed to mind about being broke, probably, Lucy realised, because he could always come to her for what he needed, and scrape up the odd few days of work with his brothers. This was how he financed his club and gym memberships, shelled out for more than his fair share of rounds at the pub and took her somewhere for dinner a couple of times a month. Everything else was left to her, such as claiming their tax credits and child allowance – which had promptly halved on Ben's sixteenth birthday – putting food on the table, clothes on their backs, paying bills, handing out pocket money . . . It never seemed to bother him that she was the main provider, and maybe it wouldn't bother her so much if her job had allowed her the time to pick up a few qualifications along the way. As it was, in order to make ends meet, she had to grab as many hours as she could at the call centre where she'd been promoted to shift supervisor about eighteen months ago. Hardly the career dreams were made of, at least not hers, but the money wasn't bad and someone had to keep a regular income flowing their way or they'd starve.

She'd worked her notice now and had sunk a few glasses with the girls last Friday night to celebrate her 'great escape', and the start of a brand-new life running her parents' small auction house in Gloucestershire. Everyone had promised to stay in touch and even to be her best customers, but she knew it wouldn't happen. Still, the sentiment and encouragement had been uplifting at the time, and she was definitely going to miss the female camaraderie that had sustained her through many a crisis during the years she'd been with them.

Hearing her mobile ringing in the kitchen, she left Joe to his packing and ran downstairs. By the time she got there the call had already bumped through to voicemail, so allowing a few minutes for Stephie to leave her message, she opened the back door to let in some air. Not quite the heady elixir that would soon be wafting her way from the countryside around Cromstone Edge, but the tantalising aroma of Indian cooking drifting down from the Taj Palace wasn't entirely displeasing. In fact, she was probably going to miss it.

With a sigh she surveyed the mess in the backyard: old bikes, a broken lawnmower (and they didn't even have a lawn), terracotta pots too chipped or cracked to bother taking with her, a rotary washing line with sagging wires and various other items of junk that needed to be dumped. Deciding to tackle it tomorrow, she turned back to the cluttered galley of a kitchen where, unsurprisingly, Hanna had failed to wash up as requested before leaving, and a pile of dirty laundry was slumped in front of the washing machine as though it had struggled to make it this far and now needed help over the finishing line. Since most of it was Ben's she couldn't blame Hanna, which had been her first inclination, but nor would she pick it up the way she usually did. It was high time both children learned that she wasn't their skivvy, and Hanna at least was soon going to find out that when they arrived in their new home she intended to run a very different ship.

Good luck with that, she was thinking to herself as she reached for her phone, and not bothering to listen to Stephie's message, she clicked to return the call and got straight through.

'Hey,' Stephie said warmly. 'Can you talk? How's it going?'

Glancing down the hall to where piles of shoes and bags were bunched up under the overloaded coat rack, Lucy said, 'He's still upstairs packing.'

'You're kidding! He's actually going?'

'He doesn't have a choice, we've given our notice on this place.'

'Oh my God. How are you feeling?'

'Strange. Like I'm not really myself.'

14

'I bet he's feeling pretty weird too. I don't know how you can do it, but at the same time I suppose I get where you're coming from. Have you told your parents yet that he's not coming with you?'

'I spoke to Mum last night. She sounded a bit distracted, so I'm not sure she really took it in. Anyway, you know what she's like, she usually finds a way to support my decisions rather than get into a fight, even if it means her darling son-in-law is being cut out of the loop.'

With a smile in her voice Stephie said, 'She's such a sweetie, your ma. I always hated having older parents myself, they were so stuck in the mud and out of touch with everything. By comparison yours are a dream.'

'Believe me, you wouldn't think so if you'd had to suffer growing up with them. It used to drive me nuts never being able to have a good row. Still, I suppose I'm making up for it now with Hanna.' And Joe, she didn't add.

'Is she there?'

'No, but hers could be the key I can hear, so brace yourself.'

Stephie chuckled as Lucy watched the front door open. Seeing the sour expression on her daughter's young face, transforming her in one scowl from beauty to beast, she felt her insides contract with a mix of guilt and annoyance. 'Are you OK?' she said. 'Where have you been?'

Throwing a viciously daggered look her mother's way, Hanna tossed her hair extensions over one shoulder and flounced off up the stairs, no doubt to go and sympathise with her father – or to try again to persuade him to rescue her from the wicked witch who was threatening to turn her into 'an ugly little country bumpkin'. Hanna was nothing if not melodramatic.

With a sigh Lucy returned to her call. 'If only she was still the sweet little thing we used to know and love, she might be looking forward to this as much as I am. It could be a great adventure for us if she'd just enter into the spirit of it.'

'She'll be all right once you get there – or at least once she's made some new friends.'

Trying not to wince at Hanna's probable opinion of that, Lucy said, 'I wonder what's keeping Ben. He said he'd be

15

back by four thirty and it's almost a quarter to six. Maybe I ought to give him a call.'

'Teenage boys are notoriously bad timekeepers which you know very well, having one of the worst culprits living under your roof. Where did he go?'

'To Ali's to sort out some last-minute travel plans. Ah, this must be him,' and with a quick unravelling of relief she watched her handsome young son lope in through the door, all mussy dark hair and his father's deep blue eyes.

'Hey Mum,' he called down the hall. 'Where's Dad? Is he still here?'

'He's upstairs,' Lucy answered.

After propping his guitar against the wall, he took the stairs two at a time, shouting to let his father know that the rock god was coming his way.

Smiling and feeling terrible, Lucy said to Stephie, 'I suppose I ought to go and join them. Are you doing anything later?'

'Would you believe, the security guard called again, so I'm seeing him tonight. I know I should have played harder to get, but hey, life's short and I'm desperate, so why waste time with games? They never work anyway, or not for me.'

'I thought you said he was boring and smelled of must.'

'It's a Saturday night and the sun's shining,' Stephie wailed, 'anything's better than staying at home on my own. You know, I've been thinking about getting a sperm donor, but we can discuss that another time. Maybe when I come to stay for a weekend. I'll call later, or tomorrow to find out how everything went. Good luck, and I still say you're mad, but hey, what do I know?'

Aware how unlikely it was that Stephie would ever visit for a weekend, Lucy tried to stop herself feeling bad for not minding too much, and gathered up a linen basket full of clean sheets. As she started to climb the stairs she was wondering if she should embark on the next family scene by asking Ben to bring the last two suitcases down from the attic. Or should she try to avoid it altogether and go and lock herself in the shed?